A DEAD MAN IN DEPTFORD

A DEAD MAN IN DEPTFORD

Anthony Burgess

Carroll & Graf Publishers, Inc.
New York

First Published by Random House Ltd

First Carroll & Graf edition 1995

Carroll & Graf Publishers, Inc.
260 Fifth Avenue
New York, NY 10001

Library of Congress Cataloging-in-Publication Data

Burgess, Anthony, 1917–
    A dead man in Deptford / Anthony Burgess. — 1st Carroll & Graf
ed.
       p.   cm.
    ISBN 0-7867-0192-7 (cloth)
    1. Marlowe, Christopher, 1564–1593—Fiction. I. Title.
PR6052.U638D42   1995
823'.914—dc20
                                                          95-10410
                                                              CIP

Manufactured in the United States of America

To Sam Wanamaker (and family) as a
tribute to his courage in bringing back
from the dead a playhouse that
Marlowe never knew

A DEAD MAN IN DEPTFORD

PART ONE

OU must and will suppose (fair or foul reader, but where's the difference?) that I suppose a heap of happenings that I had no eye to eye knowledge of or concerning. What though a man supposes is oft (often if you will) of the right and very substance of his seeing. There was a philosopher who spoke of the cat that mews to be let out and then mews to be let in again. In the interim, does it exist? There is in us all the solipsist tendency which is a simulacrum of the sustentive power of the Almighty, namely what we hold in the eye exists, remove the eye or let it be removed therefrom and there is disintegration total if temporary. But of the time of the cat's absence a man may also rightly suppose that it is fully and corporeally in the world down to its last whisker. And so let it be with my cat or Kit. I must suppose that what I suppose of his doings behind the back of my viewings is of the nature of a stout link in the chain of his being, lost to my seeing, not palpable but of necessity existent. I know little. I was but a small actor and smaller play-botcher who observed him intermittently though indeed knew him in a very palpable sense (the Holy Bible speaks or speaketh of such unlawful knowing), that is to say on the margent of his life, though time is proving that dim eyes and dimmer wits confounded the periphery with the centre.

I see, reading the above above the rim of my raised alemug, that I am in danger of falling into the dangerous orbit of the playman Jack Marston and being betrayed into use of the most reprehensible inkhornisms. It may well be that plain English cannot encompass a life so various, tortured and contradictory. And yet it was Marston who in his innocence called him Kind Kit. He did not know him. Words were moreover to him more than human reality. It was surely wrong of him to emend the verse about shallow rivers to whose falls melodious birds sing madrigals to his gallimaufry of Cantant avians do vie with mellous

3

fluminosity. And not in jest neither. There is a limit to all things.

Cat or Kit I said, and indeed about Kit there was something of the cat. He blinked his green eyes much and evaded, as cats will, the straight gaze either from fear of fearful aggression or of some shame of one order or another. Even in the carnal act the eyes were not engaged, at least not often, and it may well be that the sodomitical seek to avoid ocular discourse as speaking too much of the (albeit temporary) union of hearts. Of Kit's heart I must be unsure and can but suppose, or so I suppose. Of his feline face I may add that the nose was wide of nostril and chill and moist. The underlip however was burning and thrustful. On the overlip, which was long and Kentish, it was a matter more of whiskers than of true mustachio, the beard scant also, and it may be said that he never grew to hirsute manhood. The hair of his head was an abundant harvest, though not of corn. Let me speak rather of hayricks burning. In dry weather that augured thunder it would grow horrent. Of his bared body I observed but little hair, the mane thin above the fairsized thursday. The flesh was smooth, the shape fair, the belly flat. It is, as I can personally avouch, untrue that he bore a supernumerary nipple.

He ate little but drank much and vomited proportionally. He was given, when Sir Walter Stink, the Lord of Uppawaoc, brought the herb into fashion, to the rank tobacco of Barbados and filthy pipes that whistled and bubbled with brown juice. Sometimes, when he was pipeless, he smoked the cured leaves wrapped in a great outer leaf, but this opened and flowered and flared and he would cast it floorwards cursing. At first as at last he was a fair curser and ingenious in his blasphemies, as for example (God and the reader forgive me and the licensers of print, if this should attain print, avert their eyes in Kit's own manner; after all I do but report as to posterity's own Privy Council, this is not my mouth but his) by the stinking urine of John the Baptist, by the sour scant milk of God's putative mother the Jewish whore, by St Joseph's absent left ballock, by the sore buggered arses of the twelve apostles, by the abundant spending of the stiff prick of Christ crucified, and the like. I omit to mention his height, which was no more than five

4

foot five inches. This is not to be considered pertinent to the cursing.

Well then, let us have him at Cambridge, an undergraduate of the college of Corpus Christi, in his drab trunks, patched doublet, hose blobbed with darning, humilous scholar's gown, committed, by the nature of his Parker scholarship, to the tedious study of theology and the eventual taking of orders. His companions in the room for study he shares are all parsons' sons and so mindlessly devout that they invite such blasphemy as I above instance. So that Mr Theo Fawkes of the wry neck says: I cannot. I know I will fail. But how will you have your dialogues, reader? I will follow the foreign fashion and indent and lineate. So Mr Theo Fawkes of the wry neck and for good measure pustular says:

— I cannot. I know I will fail. So Kit replies:

— That is the sin of despair, one of the two against the Holy Ghost, hence unforgivable. And young Mr Fawkes:

— Well, perhaps God will grant one so ready for his holy work the benison of a pass, however meagre. And Kit:

— That is the sin of presumption, the other against his or her or its ghostliness and equally unforgivable. Mr Jno Battersby looks on Kit with wide eyes, though the left one does not keep exact direction with its fellow, saying:

— I protest at your invoking pure papist sins since we have done with them. And Kit:

— Yes, we found our faith upon protest. We protest against, not in holy fervour cry out for. Against the Pope in Rome and auricular confession and the sacred cannibalism of the mass. I protest against protest.

— That means you must veer back to what is proscribed, says Mr Robert Whewell, son of a rural dean, scratching an armpit. Have a care. Kit says:

— I am what Harry Eight, may devils ceaselessly prod his gross belly, I am what he and his mumbling ministers, may their fiery farts be bottled and uncorked on Unholy Shatterday, I am what we have been made. And all for a black-haired whore he had put in pod.

— It is not of great pertinence, says Whewell. What is of import is that we have the Holy Word restored to us direct, not to be filtered through the addled brains of the foul tribe of priests.

— And what is this Holy Word? sneers Kit. Addled prophecies and a God that loves the smell of roast meat and even, in its lack, of the raw blood of massacres. He makes light first and then the sun after. This sun is made to stand still by Joshua when, as all know, it was standing still already. And young Fawkes says:

— For all I care you may blaspheme against the Old that the New supersedeth. Blaspheme against the New and we will have you.

— Oh, the New is good in that it has wiped out the vindictive God of the Jews, though he is vindictive enough on Good Friday. But there are things that be unholy enough if we douse our protestant hypocrisy. Thus, the Archangel Gabriel is no more than a bawd for the lustful Holy Ghost. And Christ used his beloved disciple John in the manner of Sodom and Gomorrah. Will you now have me burned? It will relieve the tedium of your studies.

— Mr Kett shall be told.

— Mr Kett is not here to be told. Mr Kett was gently delivered into the arms of his parents, who came up from Exeter for the purpose. This was yesterday.

— No.

— Ah yes.

Ah yes in truth. Francis Kett, Kit's tutor in theology, had been sequestered for some weeks and his cats had been let loose on the streets. Of these he had had many, but twelve in particular that he called his Apostles and named for them. Kit had now the stink of those cats in his nostrils still. He had sat often enough in Mr Kett's study, the cats playing ambushes with musty folios all over the filthy floor. And Kett, the last time, smiling in a manner of manic eagerness, had said:

— All that is written may be subjected to the anatomising knife of the sincere enquirer. Holy Writ included. We need no book to tell us of God's existence nor convince us of the necessity of his taking on mortal flesh for our sins.

6

A cat on Kett's knee had purred at him as in approbation. Kett had said:

— Not that Christ is God as yet. No, not God but God *in potentia*, a mere good man that must suffer not once but many times for the world's iniquities. He will have his ultimate resurrection and then he will be God.

— Have you delivered this heresy at high table?

— Ah no. We must observe discretion. Machiavelli says that we must conform and show the world what we are not.

— That is for men of power only.

— What is great men's power to God's power? And Kett had inclined closer, the frowstiness of cat on his clothing bidding Kit close his nose holes. God has placed Jesus Christ in Judaea, together with his disciples, it is the gathering of his Church. We must all go in good time to Jerusalem to be fed on angel's food.

He frowned at a black cat that boldly relieved itself on a Jerome Bible on the floor in a corner. He pointed a shaking finger at it and said:

— That one, see, is Judas. Yes yes, we must go. Costly but needful. How much money do you have?

— None. A poor scholar and a cobbler's son.

— Well, I will go help prepare the way. I will walk thither and I will beg. Kneel with me now among these creatures made by God on the tenth day of Creation and let us pray for the realm's purgation, lustration, salvation. Kneel.

— I am not here to kneel.

— You are not? Kett spoke mildly with mild interest, his face thrusting into Kit's. You are not here to kneel?

— There is a time and place for kneeling.

Kett of a sudden boiled and cried aloud:

— Kneel kneel kneel damn you kneel. You are to be blasted, sir. I know of your sins. And he trembled, a struggling cat in his arms.

Did he know of his sins? Was that a sin that the Greeks approved, that was practised by holy Socrates? Kit said now to his fellow students:

— Clearly out of his wits. No longer as he had been, intermittently in his senses. Religion can do this to a man, nay to a
whole nation can it. See, look, there is sport outside.

And indeed through their bottle-glass window they could see
a sort of riot beginning to proceed outside the tavern opposite,
the Eagle. Undergraduates, their gowns aswing, were kicking a
man into the mud. There was much mud after long summer rain.
Wonder of wonders, the Vice-Chancellor of the University stood
afar looking, ordering no quelling of the riot.

— We'll join, Kit said. It has happened at last.

— What has?

— You're deaf to all except God's doubtful Word. This has
been coming. Walter Raleigh got the farm of wines. That means
the right to license whatever vintners he chooses and collect one
pound a year from each one in the country. The Queen gave him
this right, but the Queen's writ does not run here. That is why
there is no interference. The fists of the students are doing the
Vice-Chancellor's work.

— It is not godly to stick a man's face in the mud.

— Ah come.

Down there in the street the man enmudded was permitted
to rise from his cursing misery only to be thudded down again.
His wife at the tavern door howled. A man called from an upper
window of the tavern:

— Sir Walter shall know of this. I am Sir Walter's agent.
You hear? There shall be writs. This is rampant breaking of
the law.

Kit saw flushed glee on raw student faces. They had done
with the tavern-keeper, they would now have at his wife. But she
slammed the door, giving her dripping dirty husband no chance
to enter. He ran dripping down the street. He would turn at its
end and make his way in by a rear door. It was all over, save for
the crying of the man at the window. An official call of Arrest
him from afar was translated into student stone-throwing. The
man withdrew and fastened the casement. A gentleman by Kit,
finely dressed and in a red cloak, whined:

— See, there is mud over me. This is filth.

8

— You take your chance, sir, Kit said. But the mud will scrape off. Though it must dry first.

— I cannot ride on to Newmarket like this.

— You had done better not to dismount, sir.

— It is on my face too. I must wash. Where can I wash? As for my horse, it is at the farrier's, a matter of a loose shoe.

— If you would deign to honour the humble lodging of a student, I can bring water in a bowl and find a tough brush for the brushing.

— I must be in Newmarket by nightfall.

— Night falls late this season. This way.

The bedchamber Kit shared with young Ridley, at that time lovesick and gathering flowers by the Cam, was very bare. His visitor, cloakless now and displaying a slit doublet, black velvet over, gold silk under, also a collar of cobweb lawn, nodded at what he saw, saying:

— Very bare. It was the same at Bologna. I took my degree there. I.V.

— Ivy?

— I.V. *Iuris Vtriumque*. Proficient in either law, civil, canon. Thomas Watsonus I.V. studiosus. And you?

— Christopher. The other name is unsure. Marlin, Merlin, Marley, Morley. Marlowe will do. Wait. Thomas Watson. They were showing around Sophocles done into Latin. The *Antigone*. Are you the same Thomas Watson?

— My *Antigone* was a mere boast. I prefer to be known for my *Passionate Century of Love*.

— An honour, Kit said, though he did not know the work. I would send out for wine if I had money. A poor student of divinity, no more.

Watson dug a shilling from his purse. Kit yelled for Tom. Watson started. But Tom was no uncommon name. The Tom that entered was a boy, tousled and with an incisor missing, bare feet filthy, in cast-off trunks and jerkin too large. Kit told him to bring sherris and be quick. Watson took from Kit's table a scrawled sheet. He read aloud:

9

What armes and shoulders did I touch and see,
How apt her breasts were to be prest by me?
How smooth a belly vnder her wast saw I?
How large a legge, and what a lustie thigh?
To leaue the rest, all lik'd me passing well,
I cling'd her naked body, downe she fell.
Iudge you the rest: being tirde she bad me kisse,
Ioue send me more such after-noones as this.

Ovid, he said. Fifth Elegy of Book One.

— Correct. And not fitting for a divinity student.

— I like the *breasts prest*. A rhyme confirming that there are two of them. You are a lover of breasts?

— The swinging udders I was nursed at? I am given otherwise but here I am but the English voice of Ovid.

— Otherwise? I see. The slim flanks of a boy. The choristers of the King's Chapel are known, I believe, for their delectability and amenability. Ability, in a word, to arouse.

— I am of Canterbury. I was briefly in the cathedral choir. I learned early what men could do with boys.

— Here you have your own ragged catamite?

— Not young Tom. Young Tom is sacred. I take it you are not that way inclined.

— I follow nature up to the point where nature says *breed*. There is something absurd about grown men rubbing their beards together and untrussing. Something pathetic but appealing about the traffic of man and boy. There is much of it in the theatre. This line of yours, where is it, yes – *Ioue send me more such after-noones as this* – it seems to me for some reason to be a theatre line. I hear it on the stage. You know plays?

— In Canterbury we had visits from the Queen's Men. Dick Tarleton and his *Seven Deadly Sins*. The Earl of Surrey's troupe came to regale us here. We were not impressed.

— And you propose for yourself life in a country vicarage?

Kit looked at him. Watson was some ten years older than himself, fixed, he could see, in a world where country vicarages were a shuddering nightmare, sole end of men from the

10

universities whose talents lay not in advancement in the secular fields. They must all come to it unless.

— Unless, Kit said, fortune my foe becomes my friend. What is there? My ambition, you may have guessed, lies in poetry, but no man can live on it. Patrons are hard to find. The stage? I have not thought of the stage.

— It diverts both the washed and unwashed. I shrug but I work at play-botching. They talk of Tom Watson's jests. In balductum plays. You know the word?

— Trashy, tawdry. Groundling stuff.

— You know of groundlings, then. Shillings slide into my purse and shillings, by mean alchemy, turn to gold. But my *Passionate Century* sold well. You must come to London.

— To do what?

Young Tom brought, panting, the sherris from the buttery in a crock. He dealt copper change. Watson lordily bade him keep it. Kit unhooked two battered college tankards from the wall. He poured. They drank, toasting what they did not know.

— To prepare your advancement. But you must first dissemble your distaste at your prospects. You have a father in orders who sent you here to sustain a family line of comfortable clerisy?

— My father makes shoes. I came on a scholarship from the King's School, holy orders being the one end in view. Your lips twitch at the shoe-making.

They were meaty lips under a Turkish nose. The black eyes caught the summer afternoon light and dealt it at Kit more in compassion than merriment.

— Who would laugh at shoes? We shall go on needing shoes until our feet are permitted to tread the golden street or dance on hot bricks. The trade is noble enough. Dissemble and take your degree. Be a master of arts, without that you are nothing. But you have the long vacation coming. You propose returning to Canterbury? Come to London. Stay at my house. In the Liberty of Norton Folgate.

— Liberty?

— It is in London and yet not in it. Outside the jurisdiction of the City officers. I am at the corner of Bishopsgate Street and Hog Lane. Close to the Theatre in the Liberty of Holywell. You shall see the Theatre. Also the Curtain. More important, you shall see Sir Francis Walsingham.

— Walsingham. A holy name. And what is he?

— Universities forbid universal knowledge. You are cut off. You know nothing of the Service?

— Tell me. See, the mud is dried. It will soon come away.

— I will tell you of Sir Francis, Frank as I call him. We met in Paris. I was seventeen, studying if it could be called that. He was England's ambassador. He was kind without condescension. He corrected my Latin verses, listened to the songs I wrote. It was perhaps a relief for him in the midst of such troublesome business St Bartholomew was preparing. You know surely of the massacre? The mob screaming for the blood of the Huguenots. Two thousand Huguenot corpses on the Paris streets.

— We all know of this. See, it is as if there had never been mud. I will pour more.

— Listen. The Queen has never been willing to see how the faith of the Huguenots is England's faith, or near to it. She sent a baptismal font, all gold, worth all of a hundred thousand, when the French king's daughter was born. She stood as godmother, imagine. The font was taken by Huguenot pirates in the Channel. Friendly with a France that murders Protestants. She calls it diplomacy.

— Which means double-dealing. Go on.

— Sir Francis is no double man. Perhaps it is easier for a woman to deal double, in state affairs as in the amorous life. They are all Eve's daughters, treacherous by nature. However, Sir Francis runs his service mostly from his own purse. This is love of country at its most shining and laudable. He knows the Catholic threat.

— And not the Puritan one?

— Pooh, that is nothing. There is no Puritan candidate for the throne. But there is a Catholic one, and she is the daughter-in-law of the Medici bitch who has all the French power. I weary you.

— No, you do not. But I must consider myself unworthy to receive confidences about affairs of high state import.

— Pish, all the world knows them. Sir Francis needs spies. There is money in spying. There, that is something new for you.

— You wish to turn me into a spy?

— I wish nothing. I tell you only a way of advancement. I shall be in London during the summer. You know where I am.

— I shall note it on the verso of this Englished Ovid. There, you may dress again, as immaculate as before you were maculated.

— Do not try your pretty word-play with Frank Walsingham. He is a plain man. Well then, we shall meet. I thank you for your hospitality.

— It was all yours. The wine, I mean. A cup for the stirrup.

He poured. They drank, and Watson spat the lees from his lips: pt pt. He took Kit by the shoulders and seemed about to lift him to tell his weight.

— To my mother in Newmarket, then. Master – what is it – Merlin? Marlin?

— Marlowe will do. Or Marley. Marl is clay and lime, my name's lowly constant. I will be in London.

Kit had copied from the manuscript of Sir Philip Sidney's *Defence of Poesie*, then in circulation in Cambridge, these words: Nature never set forth the earth in so rich a tapestry as divers poets have done. Her world is brazen; the poets only deliver a golden. Kit thought: I am a poet, I must not be lowly. London must not terrify me. If I see London. As he stood with his eyes beyond the world (brazen), his roomfellow young Barnabas Ridley came in, a different dream in his own eyes. He said:

— Ah, she is cream and strawberries. Such a straight leg.

— Which you saw entire?

— Handled. In the hay of the barn I covered her with flowers.

— Enough. There is a party of us going swimming in the river. You will come?

— That is forbidden. Nakedness. A whipping in the college hall by the Proctor. I beg you not to.

— Grantchester. There we shall not be seen. Cleanse from your body the sweat of the fornicator. I can smell it from here.

— I do not fornicate. I am in love.

As the summer moon came up Kit splashed and swam with George Taplow, Jack Fothergill, Abraham Curlew and small nameless boys of the village who loved the water games but ran home to their mothers when the play took a different turn. There. Now. Have at thee. Ease of the body, turn and turn about. Under the elms by the water's margent. Naked. Altogether too animal, save that animals did not. The work of breeding too urgent and life too short. Love? Mind and mind? It did not apply.

So, then, I suppose it to have been. I saw Kit for the first time in London at Burbage's theatre, named aptly the Theatre, when I played Bel-Imperia in *The Spanish Tragedy*. He was on a stage stool, next to Watson, much taken by Ned Alleyn, younger than he by a year but altogether the quavering ancient as Hieronimo, Marshal of Spain:

> *What outcries plucke me from my naked bed*
> *And chille my throbbing heart with trembling feare,*
> *Which neuer daunger yet could daunt before?*
> *But stay what murdrous spectacle is this?*
> *A manne hang'd up and all the murdrers gone!*
> *And in my boure to laye the guilt on me!*
> *This place was made for pleasure not for death.*
> *These garments that he weares I oft haue seene.*
> *Alas it is Horatio my sweete son,*
> *O no but he that whilom was my son.*

— He would not say that, said Kit. This was after, in the tiring room. I was unwigging myself, wiping off the white from

14

my chubby boy's face, easing myself out of bodice and fardingale. Kit saw me an instant in a boy's nakedness and seemed to glow. The tiring room the afternoon sun had baked was a cram of players, Dawson, Hawkes, Crampson, Digges, Birkin, Timmes, the rest, transformed now from Portugal and Spain their notabilities into men and boys of the street, cursing at their thirst, thumping each other over tripped entrances, slowness on cues, a stutter, a finger-snapping momentary forgetting of a phrase put right by Haddock the bookholder. Tom Kyd, whose play it was, was there, a timid little man with bowed legs though not timid in defence of his work. He said:

— The distracted brain can oft turn to a kind of logic which we see as mad, absurd also, but the absurd can be a face of the tragic. This Seneca knew. This I know. You are one of these university puppies that think they know better.

— Cambridge has taught me Seneca. Puppy I may be, but I am right to whimper at that *whilom*.

— *Whilom* is very good, Ned Alleyn said. It is old-fangled but so is the speaker. There is nothing wrong with *whilom*.

— I defer, Kit said. I was moved. My back hairs bristled. I sweated. It was hardly to be believed.

And Ned Alleyn, removing from his young and blank face the paint of lined age, smirked, a creature of null person as of null features, the condition of his art, the empty vessel to be filled with what the poet brewed, what there was of him so to say with the buskins off was a nullity that nonetheless gave off a manner of heat. He said in a voice as of song, wiping:

— The skill is long to learn. Meaning he had been at it some five or six years, starting like myself as a bound prentice to his company. Long, yes, it seemed long. And then: We will go drink. Then Smigg the door-gatherer came in swinging his leather bag, so Alleyn asked what was the take.

— Two pounds thirteen and some odd bad coins.

— Ruination, said James Burbage, who owned the Theatre and the Curtain and whose son Richard had his own ambitions, the chief of which was not to be an arm-swinging actor like Alleyn. Dick Burbage, who had carried a pike, said:

15

— The ruination will not come from low takings. We shall be closed. An officer I know to be of the Lord Mayor was looking in for another prentice riot.

— They were quiet today. Besides, we are in Middlesex, not London. The Mayor's men may keep their long noses out.

— London prentices, London laws. And Dick Burbage shook his head. It is all a shaky business.

The Unicorn on Bishopsgate Street had as landlord Ned Alleyn's elder brother Jack. Kit and Watson, Alleyn, Kyd and I trod the slimy cobbles thither. I was young but, motherless and fatherless, was under Ned Alleyn's protection, lived with him; he was as yet unmarried, but that was to change. In the street we saw Philip Henslowe, who said Well met, I would have a word. Alleyn nodded. It was Henslowe's stepdaughter Joan Woodward, no more than a girl, little older than I, in whom Alleyn was said to have an interest.

The main room of the Unicorn was a cram of drinkers who had come from the Theatre, and some greeted Alleyn as ever with What outcries pluck me, which had become a catchline of the time. He waved his arm, smiled as from aloft, and led us to a back or private room. Jack Alleyn, as to make up for his brother, was of a face not easy to forget, with a black jutty beard, jutty eyebrows that were fierce, a fierce eye, one only, the other walled and sightless, and the flame cheeks of one that knew his own potions. He himself brought in my small beer, beer not so small for the others, save for Watson who had a pewter mug of sherris. Henslowe laid money on the bumped and scarred table, saying:

— Earned on the flat of their backs.

He was a coarse man, and he alluded to one of his brothels. He had other interests and of one he now spoke, saying:

— The situation is known well enough. James Burbage is spent out. Said ruination, did he, well, no wonder. Too much of Jack Brayne's money in it. His groceries do well but his soap-works in Whitechapel dissolves into suds, it will soon be no more. You know the strength of his investment. He says the playhouse is rightfully his. Now, as you know, Brayne is

Burbage's wife's brother, so we shall see what we may call a family feud. There is no future there. I see you pull your beard in some dismay, Mr Watson. A matter of the lawyer who acts for Burbage, am I not right, Hugh Swift, and you to marry his sister, have I got it? You will be forced into the taking of sides, which you will not like, for the salt and sauce of your paid quips are spread over the whole players' commonalty and you would be neuter.

— Neutral, Watson said. You know too much, Henslowe.

— That is my trade. I have a new one, and that is to build a theatre. Give me three months and it will fly its flag ready for autumn and the opening of parliament. The Burbage houses are wrongly placed. Bare fields like open country though full of dogmerds and dead cats. It will not do. The future of the business lies on the Bankside, among the other bringers of joy and diversion. The bullring and the bearpit and you know what.

— So, Alleyn said, we play against roars and screams and the rapture of dying. He meant, as I knew, the spending of Henslowe's brothel clients.

— Well, it is life, it is joy. I have bought a share in the bearpit and, a hundred yards off, a very pretty rose garden. In that garden I am ready to build what I shall call the Rose, which is an apt name. And you, Ned, shall help with the planning and the design of it.

— So we are to leave poor Burbage and set up over the river. What will become of poor Burbage?

— To each man his own misery. Drain those and we will refill. We shall need plays, Mr Kyd. Who is this one here (beetling at Kit), in the fine velvet cap with a pheasant feather? It was true that Kit was dressed not like a poor scholar but like a London gentleman, and I guessed that he was wearing some of Watson's discardments. Kit said:

— How much is there in the writing of a play? Henslowe said:

— Work you mean, or money? Kyd said:

— Too much work and too little money. What have you done

then? He spoke jealously. Alleyn took sheets much blotted from
his bosom and said:

— Listen.

> *Yong infants swimming in their parents bloud,*
> *Headles carkasses piled up in heapes,*
> *Virgins half dead dragged by their golden haire,*
> *And with maine force flung on a ring of pikes,*
> *Old men with swords thrust through their aged sides,*
> *Kneeling for mercie to a Greekish lad,*
> *Who with steele pol-axes dasht out their braines.*

He then went hm hm and spoke of a grammatic fault: one
Greekish lad with all these poleaxes?

— Licence, Kit said. Kyd said, more jealously:

— Fantastical. Infants swimming, who taught them to swim,
they are not fishes. And what is all this wantonness of cruelty?
I would never go so far.

— The Trojan war, Kit said. It is a play of Dido and
Aeneas. Aeneas speaks.

— Not the whole of the Trojan wars would have spilt enough
blood for a fishpond.

— You think in terms too literal. What you cannot show
you will not have.

— But that is how I have improved on Seneca. Seneca
but reports, and that is bad play-making. Our groundlings
have read no Seneca, they come to see as well as hear.

— So you would have Oedipus tear out his eyes in full view?

— So I would. They pay to see horrors not hear of them. I
see you go shudder shudder. The fine Cambridge man pedantical
about his classical authors.

— We will save up money to send you to Cambridge, Tom,
Watson said. Or to the other shop if you would wish it.

— My Latin is as good as any's, Kyd cried. I had Mulcaster at
Merchant Taylor's. I acted Seneca on the school stage, and they
came from far and wide to hear. Then I saw that they must also
see. So behold me, Cambridge or not.

— This will not do, Alleyn said, his head swinging in a slow shake. This business of Jupiter and Ganymede. It is sodomitical.

— Ah, both Kyd and Henslowe went. And Kyd: You cannot bugger on the stage. Though in his eyes it seemed he cherished the notion though not as an act of twofold pleasure: he relished the fancied scream as the punitive rod of flesh struck home.

— Oh, it is only in prospect, Alleyn said. It is all words. There are good words here, he added, but alas they are not for me. I am not Aeneas. Though Jack here (meaning myself) would be a fetching Dido. Ah well, you must try again. And he handed back the bundle to Kit, who took it, somewhat abashed. Kyd squinted and said:

— A very foul copy.

— He has not been trained as a noverint, Watson said.

— Noverint? Kit said in puzzlement.

— *Noverint universi per praesentes*. Let all men know by these presents. Tom Kyd was a scrivener. He scrivens very handsomely.

— So, Kyd growled. Is this to be accounted a curse to me?

There were sounds of soothing about the table. Henslowe drained his pot and said he must go. A little trouble with one of his newly indentured harlots, it was supposed. A girl named Deborah, a good Bible name, who drank illicitly and flailed with her fists. This would not please all customers, though, if made more formal with whip and nailed club, it might pleasure a few. I take it, Henslowe said, that my proposition goes down as well as my ale treat. We will talk further. He went to the door, opened, peered out, returned, frowning. The bravoes are in there, he said. They have cleared all out with their brawling. Your brother Jack looks to be paying out protection money, as they call it.

— Who?

— Bradley, Orwell and Simkin.

— I've told Jack, Alleyn said, that he must not. Give a groat and it will expand to a noble. They tried this at the Theatre. We were too many for them and they were surprised to find muscle under our gaudy onstage raiment. Armed?

— Their usual short daggers. You have nothing save niefs.

— Niefs not knifes, I said. Must we be prisoners in here till they be gone?

— Oh, we will go, Alleyn said. We will take supper at the Triple Tun. So we drained, rose, and followed Henslowe out to the main room, which was indeed empty save for the three ruffians at a table in the corner by the door that led streetwards. Jack Alleyn was saying:

— You have drunk enough. This penny should take you safely to the spewing stage. His brother said, as we neared the scene:

— Keep up with these disbursements, Jack, and you do no more than feed their greed.

— You may be right, and Jack Alleyn picked up the brown coin and pocketed it. Will Bradley was an unwashed rogue, burly enough, with tangled wires of black all over his lousy scalp. On his finger-ends were black demilunes. He said:

— We know well enough what you and your fellow sellers of the well-watered are at. You send bullies with clubs around to my poor old father to have him hold his son out of the tattery taverns where the filthy players do booze. Well, here you see a free man with his companions as free who will go where they choose and slice any that say not.

— You had best choose to booze at your dear dad's foul den, Jack Alleyn said. He meant the Bishop's Head at the corner of Holborn and Gray's Inn Road. So go.

Bradley's companions sat behind the table and, much at their ease, tilted their chairs on two legs and leaned back to make dirty the roughcast wall with their greasy jerkins. Orwell, a deformed braggart, humped and with a skew-mended broken left arm, leered at me, twittering:

— Untruss, sweetheart, that I may embrown my piggot. And how doth filthy Neddy?

— Why then I'll firk you, Simkin mocked. It was Kit who said:

— These players seem clean enough. I would say that you three gallows-fodder have the monopoly of dirt here. *Ah no*, went Watson under his breath, his hand on Kit's arm. Orwell said:

— Big words. A Latin and Greek boy. Monopoliology. Thou also piggesnie might do well in a back-butting. And he smiled foolishly and smacked kisses at the air in Kit's direction. Kit then. He should not have but he did.

Kit then with two swift hands rammed the table edge so that the whole sizeable hunk of elmwood was down on Orwell and Simkin so that they were on the floor heavily. Then he seized Bradley by the back hair and wound it tight what time he thrust two fingers ugh and ugh up his filthy nostrils as he would reach his very pia mater, and Bradley's blind fingers sought his dagger. But Kit by his distasteful nose hole-boring, the distaste in his face much evident, had borne Bradley over and now had him on the splintery floor planks where he danced briefly upon him, on the watch for recovering Orwell and Simkin. Bradley's dagger had escaped from his belt and Kit now joyously seized it, making for Orwell and Simkin who were staggering to their feet though firmly drawing. As Bradley was rising cursing, Kit dealt him a kick on the chin which thrust him temporarily out of combat. He then slashed Orwell's daggering wrist, making Orwell howl and seek to drink the blood to stem its flow. Simkin crying no no he then ripped in the trunks so that his shame would be exposed to the world. This was enough for those two, though Bradley on his feet with panting oaths and arms flailing made to encircle Kit's neck, which, as Kit wore a newly clean ruff to be prized, Kit would by no means have. So he buffeted Bradley to the wall by the serving hatch, took a quart pewter mug that rested there, and battered his lousy head till it lolled. All this time we others watched and gaped. Kit then panted that he would have water to wash his hands that were so defiled that he was like to vomit, and Simkin, hearing that word, began to take it as an injunction to do so, which he did in green and yellow copiosity. Jack Alleyn's two potboys pumped up water from the well in the yard that backed the inn and brought it in three buckets. Kit washed and washed and washed as he would never cease washing, then all three loads were flooded on to Simkin and his puke. He left howling and soaked and tottering and the others followed with breathy threats. Kit bestowed a kick in valediction on Bradley and thus

the Unicorn was restored to a kind of cleanliness proper to that
emblem of virginity. But Jack Alleyn shook his head, saying:

— They will have you. They will slit your throat. His brother
said:

— Where did you learn?

Kit, who panted less and drank thirstily of a near-quart,
sat and said:

— It was in Canterbury. Fighting the Huguenots. The Huguenots can be very filthy fighters.

— God's big body, Henslowe said piously. Are they not
our religious brothers?

— I have no love for the Huguenots.

— Come, Ned Alleyn said, to supper. You, Jack?

— I stay. There is a barrel to be broached. He nodded direly
at Kit. So we left. Henslowe made for the Bankside but Tom
Kyd, penniless but hungry, kept close to us, though Watson,
who said he would pay, had not meant that he be included in
the supping company.

— Vomit, Kit said to him. I said the word and that ruffian
did it. It is somewhat like Seneca and Thomas Kyd Esquire,
would you not say?

— I am no esquire, Kyd muttered. Your meaning?

— For the one the word suffices, the other is lost without
the action.

— I do not follow you.

— No matter, Kit said as we walked, oft slithering, the
cobbles were slimy and rats peered from the kennel as the sun
westered and would break the heart of the man who yearned
above our filthy lot with its vision of heaven in trumpet colours.
Masterless dogs scavenged and cats with staring coats darted or
limped. And so we came to the Triple Tun, with its trinity of
barrels on the sign that creaked in the sunset wind. Within,
the lamps were already swinging from the rafters, the flames
of candles danced, and fat was in the fire of the kitchen open to
the view at the far end. So we sat and were greeted by Shilliber
himself who, with his wife, bade the ordinary thrive with its
coffined meats, browned fowls, flummeries, tarts and syllabubs.

Good red wine, he announced, had come the long journey from Bergerac. Jolly eaters waved or nodded at Ned Alleyn, and some gave him the fanfare of What outcries. So we asked for the great veal pie with its minced dates and a mingling of cream in the peppery gravy, also wine in a crock drawn bubbling from the cask. And Kit, in exhilaration of his dousing the bravoes, grew talkative. He spoke of Machiavelli and his *Prince* and of Simon Patricke's Englishing of Gentillet's *Contre-Machiavel* which had been his bed-book at Corpus Christi. He said:

— I have lines for him. The man himself, old Nick, on the stage in black, croaking:

> *Though some speak openly against my books,*
> *Yet they will read me and thereby attain*
> *To Peter's chair; and when they cast me off*
> *Are poisoned by my climbing followers.*
> *I count religion but a childish toy*
> *And hold there is no sin but ignorance.*

I forget the rest, but it is all writ down.

— You spoke that too loud about the childish toy, Kyd said. See, there is one looking and one taking it down on his tablets. There are spies all over.

— Not my thought though my words, Kit said. But I see the danger. A man can be identified with his creation. Create a villain and you become a villain.

— Those devilish verses would be in the manner of a prologue, Alleyn mused. But the prologue of what piece?

— Machiavel is no Satan, Kit said. It is his honesty that astounds. We have seen in our time men sent to the flames or the hangman's hands on the grounds of their rejecting the holy word of God as our prelates interpret it. These prelates have lifted up their eyes as they were swooning with joy at the salvation of the sinner through deeply regretted agony inflicted. But they were and are hypocritical. They love the pain of others for in it their own power is made manifest. It is the one thing men want. Not knowledge, not virtue, but power. This Machiavel knew, this he has taught us. And so the show of holiness is in the service of the love of power. But our prelates would be shocked to be told it is but a show. They do not gaze deep into themselves. Machiavel counsels this and sees virtue in dissimulation if it be exercised in the pursuit of power. You yourselves look shocked so I will say no more.

By this time the coffined veal had been placed steaming on the board by Shilliber's younger daughter Kate, whose hoisted bosom was well on show. Ned Alleyn took the great ladle and dug in and the spiced aroma rose. We proffered our dishes and he unladled with a clash of metal on metal. Kyd's watering was visible to the depth of his chin: saliva played in his reddish beard. He ate greedily and Tom Watson gently disengaged his hand from his horn spoon that grace might be said. I, at Henslowe's nod, said it:

— May the good Lord bless our victuals. As our bellies fill with thankfulness may our souls fill with grace. Amen.

— Well, Kit said, but toying with his sauced veal, it is a good grace. Meaning that there is no harm in it. But God's grace is no special condiment. And it is more of a bestowal for the abstinent than for the gorger.

Kyd gorged. Tom Watson ate with delicacy. Kit drank deep and praised the Bergerac red. Watson said, delicately munching:

— I see some great giant striding the stage in the pursuit of power. There are such giants out there in Europe but topicality is dangerous. Machiavel, they say, is the Bible of the French queen mother. Put her on the stage and that would put you in jail.

— The topical, Kyd said indistinctly, veal sauce colouring his beard, must ever be inserted as it were on the side. My tragedy is of Spain and Portugal but on the side. To bring in King Philip would be indiscreet, however we know him to be the enemy. Young sir, you must learn of discretion. London will teach it if Cambridge not. And he fell to again.

Kit smacked his lips over a fresh potation, saying: By God this wine is good, call for more. And then: Discretion is a great killer of God's truth or the devil's. We must not wound, we must not discharge a nauseous stink in the nostrils of the hypocritical.

— Talk not of stinks, Ned Alleyn said, when we are eating.

— Yes, I see that and say pardon. Discretion is a matter of good table manners. But it is not more.

— You must learn, Kyd said, dish held out like an alms bowl for a second serving. Discretion at the last will save your neck. You will regret indiscretion when your dying eyes see in an instant the cutting out of your beating heart and the tumbling into the air of your bloody bowels.

— I beg you, Ned Alleyn cried in pain.

— Well, he must learn, Kyd said. But I cry you regret. He impelled me to it.

— To turn your belly to a wineskin, Watson warned, is the royal way to a quelling of discretion. And tomorrow early you must be of clear eye and brain. I will not call for more.

— More, more, cried Kit. In youth is pleasure. Then, grinning like a fool, he stroked my unfeeding hand, which was to his right. Is it not so, you luscious Bel-Imperia that was, nay, you are better as you are, women are but machines for breeding, boys are perfection. To be young and of lucent skin and luminous eye, the flesh not yet disfigured with the gross hairiness of what is termed maturity, to be of youth's sweet breath and unpustular and unblemished by fatty comedones –

— What is that word? I asked, reaching for a bread manchet with my left hand.

— It is Greek. It means sebaceous eruptions.

— Please, said Ned Alleyn in agony.

— You are wrong, Kyd said. It is Latin.

— I will wager you it is Greek.

— It is Latin. A *comedo* is a glutton.

— Then you, sir, are a *comedo*. But I still say it is Greek.

— You try to be too much the Greek, said Kyd. This is not Plato's Symposium. Learn discretion. Take your hand away.

— Discretion discretion, Kit cried to the whole ordinary, so that many, chewing, looked. And he opened out the four syllables with a verberant gong stroke on the *on*. Then he sang to a tune of his own devising words of his own devising:

> *So breathe then of the dusty floor,*
> *Thou pallet I may lie upon,*
> *And I shall thrust till both are sore*
> *But ever with dis-cret-i-on.*

Shilliber came up to us, chewing his nether lip, and made eye-gestures of plain meaning though not to Kit. Tom Watson sighing said:

— Well, I had a mind to eat your hayberry flawn, but I have a duty to my guest.

— That is another fine word, cried Kit, and he sang *duty duty duty* like some loud bird. Then he became suffused with a kind of green sickness. Ah well, he murmured in some sobriety, we are but the guests of life, we begin aghast and end a ghost. And he raised himself abruptly so that his chair fell and suffered himself to be led away by Tom Watson. But outside in the street on their way to Hog Lane corner he could be heard singing with force but tunelessly:

> *Grant us the duty to believe*
> *What reason saith is dead and gone*
> *And let us curse our mother Eve*
> *But ever with dis-cret-i-on.*

Tom Kyd shook sadly his head as his horn spoon dug into a dish of flummery and, in a mood of prophecy, said he gave him but few years.

I MUST suppose, I suppose, that Kit was giddy with his crapula when he stood before Mr Secretary of State at eight the following summer morning, the enfeebling sun in his eyes. Mr but a knight, this being Sir Francis Walsingham, lord of the Service as it was called. He was a frail dark man that the Queen, who liked him little, called the Moor. This was royal ingratitude, since on her behoof, and partly from his own pockets that were not bottomless, he maintained fifty-three sniffing agents between Calais and Constantinople. These he called his eyes. He said, and it was a strange echo, as if he himself had eyes that could pierce a man's breast:

— Duty with discretion. Sign your name here. And he pushed forward abruptly on his paper-loaded table a particular paper, neatly scrivened, which, so Kit with his painful crapulous sight descried painfully, said something of an oath of secrecy and lifelong fealty and much more of a binding nature. Kit felt as if two men, each holding an end of rope that was coiled about his neck, pulled and pulled opposedly. He said:

— Wait. I cannot be so committed. I am still a student with years of study to go. Mr Watson here has doubtless told you of my situation.

— One that is committed to the taking of holy orders but is also a poet of sorts and is wavering in his allegiances. This signing is by way of fixing the ultimate allegiance which is above both. We will have no wavering in this respect. (And he fixed on Kit stern eyes black as hell's hobs.) The Queen, the Queen, and her holy Church. A man who will not put his name to such a testimony of allegiance may well call himself a traitor.

— I am no traitor but I am dubious about signing.

— Dubiety is in itself a sort of treachery. Sign.

So Kit dubiously signed with a swan feather and ink black as the gaze of him who was to be his master. Sir Francis frowned at the scrawl arsiversy, saying: I see the first name is Christopher and a good name, one who bears Christ on his back, but what is this other?

— The beginning is sure, being Marl or Merl or sometimes Morl, but we are not clear in the family whether it be Marley or Morley or Marlowe. I have in my time been called Merlin, the magician's name. This I write is, I think, Marlowe. May I now sit?

— You would do better to brace yourself to attention in soldier fashion, for you are now a soldier of the cause.

At this, Tom Watson, who lolled in a fine Spanish chair all

knobs and curlicues which should have been wooden heresy to
Walsingham but displayed his ironic temper, smiled and smiled
and Walsingham sourly released a smile as if he must dearly pay
for it, saying: Eh, eh, Thomas?

This study in Walsingham's mansion was small and stuffy
and, as it were, penitential, the window shut tight to the summer
air of noisy London as though the very motes were charged with
enemy poison. There were bulky papers bound in tapes, some
near-tumbling from their shelves, and there was a drawn map
of Europe with red-headed pins to mark the loci of spies for
England, not all of them English. Walsingham said:

— You will have to meet Poley, for Poley will be your
help and guide and master under myself, but at the present
Poley is in the Fleet prison, only for a supposed and fictitious
crime, for he is there to nose out priests. He will be out soon.
You will meet him at Dover, for he must be your cicerone into
a Europe black as hell.

— So. I am to go into Europe. Kit could not hold back
a shiver of pride, that he was to go into Europe.

— Yes, and soon. You are to visit the city of Rheims.
Tell me something of Rheims.

— It is in France. I know little more.

— Our Catholic traitors pondered their coming onslaught on
our realm and its lawful monarch in the town of Douai. They
had been sluiced out of the Lowlands by William of Orange
and rightly. Philip of Spain, the inferno is being stoked for
him, founded the university of Douai because he feared the
protestantism of his Dutch subjects, and what they call the
English College was set up there. Set up for the training of
filthy priests to come to our land disguised as dancing masters
to mutter the mass in priest-holes and dare the risk of capture
and drawing and quartering. It is a kind of courage but as much
may be said of the kitticat cast in the tub for drowning that swims
and swims. The Pope in Rome, the devilish pincers are waiting to
drag out his nails everlastingly, puts a hundred gold crowns each
month into this venture. It has left Douai and is now established
at Rheims, a nobler town where kings are crowned. So Rheims

goes with Rome and Spain and hell itself as loci of diabolism that menace our Queen and must be prayed against. And, here you come in, acted against.

— Then what must I do in Rheims?

— Watch, watch and learn. Learn what is intended, listen for talk of assassination and rebellion, find out names of traitors who propose treachery. You speak French?

— I learned French of the streets from the Huguenot children. I went to lessons given free by a Huguenot teacher. Canterbury is my town and it is infested with Huguenots.

— Infested, you say infested? They are our brethren in arms, they are of the reformed faith. You do not know of the Bartholomew butchering? You will use another word.

— Indiscreet, I apologise. But it is only honesty to say that the Huguenots are not liked in Canterbury. They were moved inland from the coast to check their buccaneering. The city is full of them. They have taken possession of the river for water for their weaving. They bring no trade, they have their own bakers and butchers.

— Also, Tom Watson interposed, shoemakers, I take it.

— Those too. They are their own world and speak their own language. Nay, they pray in it. Part of the cathedral is reserved for them and it resounds with French.

— Would you, Walsingham browed at him, rather have a Catholic Englishman than a French protestant?

— You try to trick me. But it is true to say that some men of Canterbury are driven back to the secret practice of the old faith because they do not like these Huguenots with their French prayer-books. That is in the nature of how humanity behaves. Blood is thicker than belief.

Tom Watson howled like a hound at that, though in a manner of comedy, and Walsingham, hands clasped behind, sharply looked out of the window, seeing mostly carts. Then he turned and sternly said:

— Faith is the one binding force. The Musulmans of many colours attest this. When I was ambassador in Paris our doors were opened to protestants of all races fearful of the Catholic knives and bludgeons. Her Majesty, God save her, argued hotly against the cost of such hospitality, but I reminded her that it was her own faith that was under attack. We were not there as cold English bystanders of the Paris massacres. Our enemy was the Catholic enemy and our friends were the protestant persecuted. And yet she prates, argues I would say, of the good policy of keeping France a friend against Spain. Have you thought of this? Have you your own thoughts about France?

— Sir Philip Sidney calls France a sweet enemy.

— Ah, Sir Pip. A good son-in-law, the flower of the chivalry of the Reform, no man braver, no greater hater of papistry. Walsingham waved him away as he had waved away Poley, whoever he was, though as though he were a more substantial cobweb. But he is a poet, and poets are given to the half-lie, Plato would say the whole one. He meant the sweetness of their women and wine and comfits. But mark the word enemy. Enemy he means. You are to enter the territory of the enemy. You have things to ask?

— Money, expenses I would say. The time of going. This is the long vacation but it does not go on for ever.

— Ah, sweet Jesus, it is always money. July the sixth you must be in Dover, there is an inn called, let me see, yes, the Luce, whether fish or flower is not certain. There Robert Poley will meet you and tell you all and disburse. You are not in this for profit.

— The profit of the realm, Kit said, standing to greater though factitious attention. God save it and her. Walsingham looked for the ironic but did not find it. He nodded and said:

— Well, then. It is fortunate that Canterbury is near Dover. You will in any event be making a family visit so need not claim from the Service for your costs of travelling thither. Thenceforward it may be different. God save the Queen.

— This could be taken as a dismissal, but before Kit could bow and leave, the door was thrust open and one entered. Walsingham frowningly said:

— This is mannerless, sir. Here be grave matters proceeding and you blunder in as it were a common tavern. Pray leave and come when you are called for.

The entrant mooed like a calf but in insolence looked about him. He saw Kit. Kit saw him. Nay, it was more than pure seeing. It was Jove's bolt. It was, to borrow from the papists, the bell of the consecration. It was the revelation of the possibility nay the certainty of the probability or somewhat of the kind of the. It was the sharp knife of a sort of truth in the disguise of danger. Both went out together, and it was as if they were entering, rather than leaving, the corridor outside with its sour and burly servant languidly asweep with his broom, the major-domo in livery hovering, transformed to a sweet bower of assignation, though neither knew the other save in a covenant familiar through experience unrecorded and unrecordable whose terms were not of time and to which space was a child's puzzle. He was a young man of Kit's own age it seemed, lank locks of auburn parted and flowing, long face above a long body, so that Kit must needs look up at wide blue eyes and wide doubtfully smiling mouth, the white collar open at the girlish throat, hose wrinkled and points carelessly tied, a light dew on him as though he had come from tennis or fives. From him rose a faint odour of sweat and rose water. He said:

— Grave matters, was it?

— Not so grave and over anyway. Kit was aware of his voice grown phlegmy. He cleared his throat. Are you too in what he calls the Service?

— He uses me at times, not often. He is my cousin and pounds at me like an uncle. He is grave but not to be taken gravely. I think we must have met before.

— You and I? I think not. You are not a Cambridge man?

— I am not anything save the most discardable of the Walsinghams. A younger son who does not inherit. Thomas, whose name taught him to doubt. Let us get out of here. It smells of stratagems and death.

— But you wished to see your cousin?

— There is no haste. I am thirsty after my bout. The Crown is round the corner.

— You were at the foils?

— I call myself a sort of swordsman. And, when the major-domo had opened the door for them, he breathed in London air, which was not sweet, as it were all country blossom and birdsong. Better, he said. I like not the town, all horse dung and hawking. I shall ride back to Scadbury tomorrow.

— Which is where?

— An easy canter by way of Chislehurst. You do not sound like a London man. Who are you, by the way?

— Marlowe or Marley or Morley. You have a choice. The first name does not equivocate. Christopher.

— Which is Kit, so you are Kit, come, Kit, Kit, Kit. A university youngster on the make, and why not. You have spying ambitions?

— Rather poetic. And perhaps in the playhouse.

They had reached the Crown, which held a brace of drinking draymen. These took in indifferently a gentleman indifferently dressed and another in exquisite and mostly borrowed raiment, apt for the grave matters of the court or the airy concerns of city leisure. Thomas Walsingham shrugged with a smile at his lack of a purse, but here they would slate his order; Kit eagerly paid out pennies for ale.

— A poet. I have no skill, but I have been the object or recipient of verses. Not often good verses.

— It does not surprise me.

— That the verse should not be good?

— That, yes, the age smells of bad poetry, but chiefly the other.

— That I should be what I said? Well, sometimes through compliments to me fools think they may reach my high-placed cousin. You came another way.

— Through Tom Watson. A chance meeting, a common concern with poetic trafficking. I am lodging with him. To revert to what you said earlier. You seemed to think that we had already met. I had the same feeling though I knew it was not

32

possible in the way the world calls meeting. But this sometimes happens. Plato or some of his followers might posit the prior or prenatal collocation of souls.

— Does he not also tell some legend of a unity capriciously split by the gods, so that half goes wandering in search of half? But that is a pretty doctrine of male soul and female soul conjoined if they are lucky, which is rare, after an eternity of seeking.

— Male and female are grossly conjoined following nature's wish that they breed. There is an airier or more spiritual mode of conjunction.

They drank and drinking looked each other in the eye or eyes. Thomas Walsingham said:

— More spiritual? Angels holding hands?

— Holding hands, yes. Effecting more intimate joining. We have bodies, we are not all soul. There is a higher order than what crass nature dictates. Nature does not want poetry, nor music, nor the eyes of the seeker looking upward from the dungy earth. Nature does not want the love that she would call sterility but we could designate otherwise.

— Well, we have known each other some ten minutes and you are already anatomising unnatural love.

Kit blushed. He said hurriedly:

— Unnatural love is a bad phrase. What is against nature is sin, so the religions say. But what makes man what he is is unnatural if we raise him as we must above eating, dunging, begetting, dying.

— Well, these be high or deep matters for a morning cup and a first meeting. In youth is pleasure. (Kit started: someone, perhaps he himself, had said that that previous day or night that seemed now much in the past.) I mean that thought is the enemy of doing. My grave cousin is always saying that thought both makes and undoes life's fabric. If, he says, he thinks too much on racks and thumbscrews and what he calls the apparatus of the finding of truth then he grows sick. And yet, he says, what is the big conflict but a grinding of thought against thought. Some think that bread can be God and some that bread is bread and God but a hovering thought over it.

33

And some that the Pope is the devil. It was different a hundred years back. Thoughts change and become perilous. What, then, are the things that do not change? In youth is pleasure.

He pledged that in a draining of his tankard. Kit did not drain his. He said:

— I beg pardon for bringing in the high or deep matters. *Altus* in Latin is both deep and high. I was seeking some answer to the question how a man can have a conviction that he is drinking with an old friend –

— You feel that? That we are old friends?

— I feel at ease and yet not at ease. And you will know why not at ease.

Thomas Walsingham looked away at that. He looked at the street outside the open door. An old nag, much galled on its flanks, was pulling a cart of country produce; the wheel had jolted against a hitching post and the horse was being blamed. Then he turned and said:

— I know not why not. You may be at ease, he said in a parody of a captain's tone. Wholly at ease. And then: There is the boy in this thing of Plato's. A slave boy without learning. Yet Socrates shows that the boy knows Euclid and Pythagoras. So the soul lives before birth.

— You have done some reading.

— A little. I leave reading to my man Frizer.

— Frazer?

— He calls himself Frizer. Ingram is his other name. He is often called Mr Ingram. It's no matter. Very devoted. He has more money than I and yet he is my man. He has ambitions for me. He thinks of buying an inn in Basingstoke, the Angel, he thinks the name apt for some reason, and I shall be the landlord and he a mere tapster. Oh yes, highly or deeply devoted.

— He loves you, then. I see.

— You do not see, and the tone was sharp. If you mean the love you spoke of, no. Frizer is a dog and a good dog. He likes being a dog. He is never happier than when fawning and cringing. There are some men born to be dogs. And yet he reads and tells me what he reads. He would serve me in all

34

ways. Lackey and groom and schoolmaster. He licks my hand, but there the licking ends.

— And you live together at – I have forgot the name of the place.

— Scadbury near the caves of Chislehurst. My brother Edmund is Lord of the Manor. But he is so little at the manor house that he grants me the run of it. Sir Thomas our father left him all and me little. So Edmund takes pity on me and says Behold this is yours. In a manner, the manor in a manner. He knows what he is. He knows he is a whoremaster and thinks it no shame. He has become here in London the thing of Lady – I will not speak her name. Enough for Mr Edmund. Well, Cat, Kit I would say, you are no dog –

— You rhymed. Shame name.

— If you are a poet you may put together rhymes for me properly considered, not dealt by chance like two aces. What have you now in stock?

— This.

> *It lies not in our power to love, or hate,*
> *For will in us is overruled by fate.*

And then some more I have on paper but not in mind. And then:

> *Where both deliberate, the love is slight.*

I am too bashful to give you the matching line, but you may guess it. It ends with *at first sight*.

— Hm, hm, hm. Well, we shall meet at some other place. I must go see if my cousin has yet called for me. We shall meet, though, make no mistake of that.

It was this first encounter, I believe, that put Kit in a fever that had to be allayed. We were not playing at the Theatre that afternoon, and he sought me out at Ned Alleyn's lodging. Alleyn was with Henslowe and Peter Street the master builder, sniffing roses and stringing measuring lines on earth cruelly stripped of its bushes. And so he found me alone, conning the part of the Queen in *Hamlet Revenge*, a half-finished play of Tom Kyd's (all these Toms, a world of toms like a night roof top). His eyes closed, muttering strange words and also groaning, he had me stripped and himself stripped and was soon at work that seemed strangely loveless. Then his cat's eyes blinked in shame as he wiped the sweat from us both. It could not be animality, for animals are directed by the gods of increase, and animals have no shame. He kept crying God God God as in some form of repentance but there was nothing to repent except the spending of seed in barren places, the fault, if it be fault, of fortuity, as in Christ's parable of the sower that went forth to sow.

So let us have him riding to Canterbury. The horse was his own, his father's gift when, but recently, he had been monied enough to stand as a marriage bondsman. This was Brown Peter, fat and a little slow, well tended in the Cambridge stables, a sort of yeaing and naying friend to whom Kit sang or tried out verses as he clopped through Dartford, Gravesend, Chatham, Sittingbourne in the fine summer weather. And there he was – Pound Lane, his own old school by the City Wall, Burgate, the great cathedral. A single solemn bell mourned a death. Here the faith had been brought from Rome so that a king of many wives might reject it, here a witness to the Church of Rome against the power of another king had been slaughtered, his holy shrine made most rich and then despoiled. There was perhaps a curse on the realm. Certainly there was a curse on his father, whose new house in St Mary's parish he had to seek by asking. John Marley or Morley the shoemaker? By there, or near. He had moved from St Andrew's for non-payment of rent and was installed now in premises, Kit knew, not commodious. Down in the world, the fault of the Strangers.

— Let us look at you, his father said, intermitting his hammering, spitting nails from his mouth. The two apprentices too ceased their hammering to gaze. Velvet blue and gold, a cobweb collar. I like the cloak, his father said, his arms about him, and you smell sweet and Londonish. God knows why you seem up in the world. Let me see those shoes, they could be better. I will give them new soles before you go back.

— I go on. To Dover and then take ship for France.

— God help us, you are indeed up. That sounds like state business.

— War on the papists.

— For God's sake leave at least the English papishes alone, they have suffered enough. There is enough trouble here with the frogs and frogesses. The little froglings would grow up into proper Kent citizens if they were permitted to speak our tongue. Here comes your mother from marketing.

His mother, plump but not country rosy, came near-running down the street with her basket. She was of Dover and liked to believe the sea salt stayed in her skin, a sea girl. She kissed and embraced and admired. Quite the gentleman.

— And the girls?

— Joan has a great belly, Meg scolds her tailor for dithering about the day, Anne is well and that leaves poor Dorothy.

— Poor Dorothy.

— She sits with her wooden doll. The French are not all bad, a French carpenter made it for her. Of course, this is all strange to you. You do not know the house.

— Small, Kit said, as they both led him in, hands on him, their only son.

— We were better off near Bull Stake, his father said. Get the girls off our hands and there will be room enough. Your mother and I and poor Dorothy.

The apprentices went back to their hammering and through the smell of leather that was his boyhood and unchangeable, unlike thought and faith, Kit was led to the main room, as he took it to be, with its sad pledges of a dead prosperity – betrothal chest, rocky table, chairs that were wooden emblems of family degree, from infant to father, though not in themselves a family of chairs. Young Dorothy sat on the brown-stained boards and drooled over a little wooden lady in a wooden skirt. She was twelve years old and an idiot. She sat in a pool of wet. Her mother ran to her, lifted her, finding her smock wet and warm, so she had just done it. She cried for Meg and Anne, who should not have left their sister alone so, and then their feet, unshod from the sound, could be heard on stairs and the door opened and they entered. Margaret was twenty and her betrothal to the tailor had gone on too long. Anne was fourteen and marriageable too, had not Joan two years back married when she was thirteen? And now she was fifteen and carrying. All ready to breed, even poor Dorothy who, if they let her loose in the fields, would be served by some farm lout as readily as mare and stallion, save that season for humanity was sempiternally there, like faith and thought. But he, Kit, would deceive nature, ever and never in season, a paragon of the cheating of the true end of what was called love. Now he was kissed and kissed, women with bosoms eager to give milk. Poor Dorothy, being wiped and changed while the wet floor was mopped, looked at him without recognition, doll clutched to her own growing bosom, a finger in her mouth.

What was there to tell them? Triv and quad but nothing yet about his defection from orders. Girls? He had met no girls. Nay, wait, and he resexed, as in one of his own poems, Mr Walsingham into a lady of luscious hair, fine carriage, great prospects, but he must mind his books, get ready for the cloth, find a parish, then and then only think of a holy family. His mother and the girls, Dorothy drooling at the tail, clutching her doll, went to the kitchen to get supper. The kitchen was small, the flagged floor uneven, but the pots and pans shone with their old refulgence. Kit stood at the door, watching, talking, listening. The girls, save Dorothy, had much to say. John Moore, their father's once chief apprentice, had his own shop by the East Gate, not far from the abbey, St Augustine's, that the Queen's father had pillaged and then turned to a palace. Joan, his wife, though but fifteen, was disdainful of her spinster sisters. And she now carried a great belly before her in pregnant pride. They were to have for supper beef boiled with carrots. The bread, today's, was fresh. Kit mumbled a torn crust. There was a firkin of Kent ale. Kit could have wept.

Wept? Why? At the comfortable cycle of life that smelt of bread and beef seething, round and round for ever if the preachers and governors would allow it, and he himself a tangent to the cycle. Wept at a future that, he knew, must be perilous. Wept because they, his womenfolk and his hammering father, would weep. Weep when? That he did not know. He could hear weeping on the wind.

— Brown Peter, his father said, as they sat about the table, is well looked after. He knew not his old stable at first but then he knew it and whinnied. You have been a good boy with him. A man and his horse are one in the big world of affairs. Here I do not need to ride. I am nailed to my soles and heels.

— I shall walk to Dover, Kit said. Twenty miles, it will be good for me.

— I shall give you new soles tomorrow.

— Kitticat, Meg said, the Reverend Kitticat, mender of men's souls.

— It will be a year or so. I must become a Master of Arts, you know that. And till then a Walsingham man.

— Walsingham? Anne said. That was a holy town, and the Milky Way in the sky showed the way to it.

Kit explained who Walsingham was. They listened, all except poor Dorothy, who fed a sop vainly to her wooden doll. Kit looked in pity and anger at her idiocy. He said:

— It is sometimes hard to give praise to God. Dorothy is always the same, we thought it was a prolonged childishness, but she is almost a woman and she wets the floor still and says nothing.

— She says a word or so, his mother said. She has learned some words since you left. She knows the names of her sisters but she uses them turn and turn about. *Sky* she knows, and *sun*, also *rain*.

— And, his father said as he cored a pippin, she knows that God is in the sky. But she thinks that God is the sun.

— So did we, so did the Emperor Constantine, Kit said out of his learning. Sunday is the Sabbath. The theological question is whether she has a soul to be saved. If yes, then she shall burn for the heresy of saying God is the sun. If no, she's dissolved into elements when she dies, like any beast of the field.

— This is terrible, Meg said. Is this what they teach you at Cambridge?

— Oh, we're taught a lot about the soul and who is saved and who damned. It seems everyone is damned who does not belong to the English Church, and there are times I grow sick of it.

— Sick of your studies? his father said. Studies are for raising you, this you know.

— That and that only perhaps. In themselves nothing. They are a bunch of keys for opening doors. Feet are for walking but they need shoes. That is a useful art, the making and mending of shoes. I am being apprenticed to the useless.

All about that table save poor Dorothy looked at him in disquiet. His mother at length said:

— And yet they employ you on high business, young as you are.

— The high business of searching for enemies of the realm. So they can be apprehended and brought home and hanged. It is the hanging and drawing and quartering that is important. A bloody show meant for a warning to the people, but the people take it as diversion. Well, I mean to give them diversion, but the blood will be pig's blood.

They did not understand him. Poor Dorothy had been long in the situation they seemed only to have arrived at, but she tried to tear the head of her doll and cried what sounded like *Gog*.

— There, you hear, her mother said. Clever girl, she crooned at her. Say God. Say sky.

— *Koy*.

— She has said her prayers, Kit said in weariness. I will say mine and sleep. The sun is down and I will join the crows and starlings, black-suited choristers that crark. I have not had much sleep of late. Where do I sleep?

When a son must ask this in his own home, then perhaps he is past thinking of it as his home.

He walked, as he said he would, to Dover. His shoes were freshly soled; he carried on his back the flat leathern sack which held two newly washed shirts and three pairs of hose. A good mother. Oh, they were all good, the kind embracing round to which he must be the tangent. He walked the round earth that looked tangential. Kind clouds were propelled above him by a kind wind. The summer weather held. He walked over fields and along paths, seeing sheep and shepherds. These did not pipe. They were as leathern as his sack. If they sang they sang coarse ancient songs with *swive* in them. *Pastores.* The good shepherd. But this raising of shepherds predated Christ searching for lost lambs, he who became a lamb to be slaughtered. Theocritus and Virgil. Why this need to purify them into Damon and Lycidas? No fleece oil on their hands, their smocks white. Clean Mr Thomas Walsingham sat on a knoll, piping. Swive in deep grass while the sheep cropped and occasionally went baaaaa.

He ate his bread and drank spring water at Shepherdswell or Shepherdswold, the name was uncertain. Lydden, Temple Ewell, Buckland, another ruined abbey. Then the castle was ahead and the salt was on his lips. A jumble of dwellings whose dwellers preyed on the sea and its travellers. He found the inn named the Luce (fish or flower?) on a sidestreet sheltered from the strong Channel wind. He asked a roundly chewing dirty-aproned sweeper who swept ill, for Mr Robert Poley. The two London gentlemen? Two? One of them appeared, clattering down the stairs. He was not Mr Robert Poley. He called himself Nick Skeres.

There was a room where they were to take supper. Skeres opened the door to it with a kind of blind familiarity, his black eyes on Kit. From the white of Theocritan shepherds to the black of the dirty world. Skeres was dirty to match that world. It seemed not the casual dirt of the careless, rather as applied as Alleyn had applied white and lines to his young face to render it ancient. I will be a dirty man for all to wonder at. Skeres wore with pride long dirty hair, and the hairs in his skewed nose had trapped scraps of dry mucus. The teeth conceded to a lighter colour, but not white. His slops were dirty but he had a clean-bladed dagger which he had taken from its sheath at his belt. He juggled with this in his long dirty fingers.

41

— Well, we will sit, he said, and wait for bonny sweet Robin. He is a clean man (and he tapped the *clean* as to emphasise his own dirt) and washes himself from toes to scalp in clean cold water. It is the way he is. And you?

The accent was, Kit thought, from the south-west. He had heard from Alleyn what he called the Sir Water Devonian. Skeres burred and rasped.

— Am I clean, you mean? Some would say we were bent on a dirty business. I do not say it, but some would say it.

— You're a young beginner. You know nothing of it. But you will keep at the business and learn. A dirty business for keeping clean the realm, so they say. It is a trade like any other. But once in the trade you will not be out of it. Clean Robin will shrug but not everybody will shrug.

— Shrug at what?

— At a man's coming and going and following his own desires, as they call them. But he will tell you more of that.

Clean Robin appeared, a marvellous proper man, as they would say. Of Corpus? I am of Clare. He shook hands with vigour. Straw beard well trimmed, spotless cambric, silk under the slashes of the trunks, doublet well tailored, well pressed. The face cheerful, guileless even, as if he had shunted guile on to Skeres. The eyes even merry, the white smile welcoming. He asked if the fish had been ordered. Skeres nodded direly, as if this were a code for a killing. Poley said:

— Fresh Dover fish, flat and overhanging the dish at either end. It is worth coming to Dover for the fish. So, Marley or Morley, we are to go over together on the morning tide, Skeres and I then ride to Paris, you not.

— Not by way of Paris? I had a mind to see Paris.

— Another time. You marvel at Nick here, I can see it in your eyes. They fear Nick, but they do not fear me. They fancy that he is all malevolence. And so he is, so he is.

He spoke cheerfully and even laid a clean affectionate hand on dirty Skeres. When the fish came in, brought by a shy maid at whom Skeres, as if taught to do so in some stage comedy, leered, the dirty fingers were delicate about dissecting it, the bones were

42

spat out near silently. He drank his Dover ale with little finger finickingly spread. At the end of the meal he begged pardon for his belch.

— *Eructat cor meum*, Poley said cheerfully. Skeres cheerfully responded:

— *Et cum spiritu tuo.* Then he nodded direly and left. Poley said now they could talk. He poured wine and said:

— You know of me? Sir Francis spoke of me?

— He said you were in jail to trap priests.

— They talk in their distress, many secrets are divulged in a prison. But I am glad to be out and breathing sea air. Still, they will talk to me for I speak their language. I was born in the year that Mary, bloody as they call her, married Philip of Spain. So I was brought up in the old faith and some believe I practise it. So I will, I will go through the form, take the bread that is God but know now that it is only flour and water. Some know me for what I am, the more so as Sir Francis put me into the service of Philip Sidney while he was readying himself to be governor of Flushing. For there is no greater pope-hater than Sir Philip. Take some more of this wine, have Skeres's share. Oh, I have money for you, a little, I will give it you tomorrow. And I have your orders. You are to enrol at the College, saying you are studying for the Church but you have doubts about it. They welcome waverers.

— I am not to pretend to the old faith?

— You would not deceive them as I can. Be a waverer in sincerity and humility. You seek the light. But in truth you seek those who are to come over to be devilish plotters. They are plotting already. The pope has excommunicated the Queen, who, for good measure, is said to be illegitimate, which, if we reject divorce, she is. The Queen may in all Catholic holiness be driven off the throne and another queen installed there. Which queen you know.

— You mean plots to kill the Queen?

— That sounds coarse, worthy of Skeres. Some talk of removing and sequestering, granting the sad berth at Fotheringay which will then be vacated. Some raise holy eyes to heaven in shock at talk of killing a queen, but it is all show. They will assassinate if they can, and they think they can. The bad times are coming. France and Spain lick their lips in prospect of restoring England to the fold. You have a holy work in hand.

— What can I do?

— Listen. Take names. We will be waiting at this end. If you had Skeres with you there would be quick dispatching in tavern brawls. Skeres is good at brawls, as you may imagine. He is probably into one now, but that will have nothing to do with our business. He goes with me to Paris, chiefly as my protector. In Paris I need protection. It is a filthy city. But no more of that. Leave Paris to me. You will like Rheims. It is a gentle town where they gently talk of gently killing queens. Would you wish tonight to share a bed with Skeres? No, I can see not. Well, you shall have your own rough pallet.

— Skeres said something about shrugging. Shrugging things away. What does he mean?

— It is the two stages of leaving the Service. Shrugging is the first, the second is not shrugging. But you are young, ambitious, a Cambridge man, and you will not leave the Service. To protect the realm is a life's work. A man does not in flippancy abandon it. But enough of that. You have more questions?

— How long must I be in Rheims?

— You may stay as long as a month without charge. They are welcoming because they think they have great gentle power of gentle persuasion. You tell them what you told Sir Francis, that you are a student of divinity but the studies have engendered grave doubts. These you wish resolved. They will try to resolve them. (Here he chuckled.) After a brief time go to mass, even to confession. In confessionals a lot can be heard. And in the taverns and the dormitories. I do not doubt you will pick up some names. With luck we sail at dawn. I spoke to the captain of the *Great Eliza*, a pretentious name for a Channel packet. He speaks of calm waters but I do not believe him. To bed.

*

44

H E was in Rheims, which the English had once held but Jehane la Pucelle recovered by witchcraft. He was in Rheims, very weary and still queasy in his stomach after a rolling voyage of which he recalled best the vomiting of the passengers and Skeres's jeers at his own crying of Jesus Jesus Jesus as he gave bread and fish and wine to the tigerish waters. Yet the poeticising mind rode high above his body's distress and he saw drunken marble as if Rome had melted. Poley remained below but Skeres stood by him at the taffrail, relishing his agony. But it was Skeres who brought a hot posset, saying it would give comfort. It did not.

At Calais there was French and English chaffering about horses – a deposit greater than the worth of the raw nags offered, charges for hire exorbitant. As Kit mounted he voiced a wonder he had had in his mind, namely was he to be alone and trusted on this mission, he a young beginner, as Skeres had called him. Poley, who had asked to be called Robin, was rosy and smiling and unscathed by the voyage. He said:

— Fear not. There will be somebody along. You shall not be alone. We are not fools in this business.

So he had ridden the long way to Rheims, jolting on ill-made roads, seeing the French farms not much different from the English, drinking warm milk fresh from the udder and the day's new bread. He was not at his best when he sat before Father Crawley in his study. On the wall Christ writhed on his cross, and there was an Italian painting of the Madonna and child. The Madonna, Mother of God, was not much seen in England now. The priest's desk was massive and Spanish. There was a smell in the room that seemed to Kit Catholic and alien – incense on the skin brought in from the chapel perhaps. Something close and frowsty, and from Father Crawley a faint odour as of bad teeth or an ailing stomach. Yet the glance from his lined face was shrewd. He asked:

— Are you a Walsingham man?

— The shrine, you mean? There is no longer a shrine.

— I think you must know my drift. Have you been sent?

— Sent by my own doubts.

— You must not think us innocent here. We are open to

all comers but we remain watchful. What is it you wish?

— To meditate a week or so. Talk and be talked to. Attend lectures, services, anything.

— You're welcome to such hospitality as we can give. A bed and spare diet. Tell me, what is your view of the Seven Sacraments?

— That there are seven and not fewer.

— So our late king believed and wrote. His treatise earned him the title of *Fidei Defensor*. He retained it when he no longer believed. And so for the Queen and her successors. This is hypocrisy. I recommend that you meditate on the Seven Sacraments. Above all the Holy Eucharist. What are you taught of the Holy Eucharist?

— At Cambridge we learn that the bread and wine are commemorative. That there is no transubstantiation.

— This is in spite of Christ's own words. *Hoc est corpus meum.*

— It is taken to be a manner of metaphor. It is said the unreformed faith is one of cannibals.

— Well, you will learn.

He seemed to grow weary, matching Kit's own state. He tolled a small bell as in exorcism of the heresy that clung to Kit's travelling cloak. A fat young priest beamed in. Father Hart, said Father Crawley. Father Hart led Kit to a wing of the College where beds were ranged in, so to say, the symmetry of triv and quad propositions. He might take this one at the end. He might rest. He rested. Those who were to be his fellow sleepers were awake and out and at work. The building reeked of fresh size. The faith was renewing itself for battle.

Awake on his third day, having eaten soup meagre and munched bread among rowdy puppies who were to be priests, he homed to the cathedral. Homed because he was cathedral-bred, ever in hearing of bells, ever aware of strong and authoritative stone, a pretended solidity in Canterbury, where it had been one thing and was now, stripped and scrubbed, another. Here though, in the sumptuous God's house of Rheims, the grudging hammers of reform had not struck at saints' statues, nor stained glass, nor the images of the Virgin Mother recognised, through

46

the cold sharp eyes of the north, as an incarnation of the foul goddess Ashtaroth. Kit looked up to his neck's limit, at the groins of heaven, about him at the chapel-suburbs of the immense stone city. Jewels and gold unfilched illumined the grey; sunrays pierced like God's swords the high windows whose tints refracted pure light into the sevenfold covenant of his bow. Old women in black knelt about. Kit stood. The winking light of the reserved sacrament was coy with him. Three students in black entered, crossed themselves with water, genuflected, nodded at him. He had been near to them at supper; they had asked his name and purpose in coming hither. They too knelt. He, playing his part, knelt also, playing at praying.

I cannot pray to you because you do not exist. *A small matter. I contain both existence and its opposite.* You cancel out yourself. You condone too many murders in your name. *I condone nothing. I am above such things. My name is not myself. When men use my name this means they do not know me.* What shall I do? *What you are driven to do.* And if I refuse to believe in you? *My existence does not depend on your belief.* You are then detached from men. What then is meant by God's love? *The passionate acceptance of myself as my own highest achievement, manifested to senses live and yet unborn in the universe as my palpable garment. Men are a strand in that garment.* Why did you have to come down to earth as a man? *I do what I will. Men must be taught. The loving community of men must figure the perfection of the divine order.* Men have learnt nothing. Does not this argue a flaw in the divine substance? *When men have destroyed themselves utterly there will be left one man who has learnt. That will be enough. And I can wait.* This is not you who speak. It is only a voice among the many voices that dart like wind about the crevices of my brain. *Did you expect it to be otherwise?*

He rose angry from the paving on which he had, sorely and stiff-kneed, knelt, and, leaving, cooled his face with the water that was called holy. He went out into the cathedral square and God howled down at him from the sun. Poor Dorothy was right. There was God. And out of the sun he entered a small tavern and said *Du vin.* It was gloomy and there was a smell of garlic which struck him as most heartening. It was devil's bane. It was health. Dull gold gloomed at him. It was a garment. Thomas Walsingham was sitting there, not alone. Well, he was foolish not to have expected this.

— Come then, Kit Kit Kit, you see I have remembered the name. My grave cousin was mumbling of Morley and Marley and Merlin, but Tom Watson said Kit was enough. And this is my man Frizer.

Frizer sat a table's distance away from his master, sat as though it were not decent to sit in his master's presence, but this was after all a foreign country. He seemed well pleased to stand and bow and then remain standing.

— You were quick after me, Kit said, sitting with his wine. It must have been the next packet from Dover.

— Ah no, I was in Paris. We were in Paris, were we not, Frizer, and Frizer did not like Paris. We were waiting to spy on Poley, but Poley seemed to be there to start spying on us. And there was this dirty man with him, a cutthroat, what was his name, Frizer?

— Nicholas Skeres.

— An old acquaintance of Frizer's, it seems, but I do not enquire further. Well, you are here and I am ready to start spying on you. Or shall I say keeping you from trouble? Tom Watson said you were a pretty sort of fighter in taverns. That will not do in this holy city.

— You too are enrolling in the College?

— No, we are removed from that business, we are in an inn, are we not, Frizer? Frizer sleeps on straw and does not like it.

— I like what it is my duty to do, Frizer said. It was a Thames voice whose sounds were made all in the middle of the mouth and whose tones were the tones of a whine. A Thames rat, then, sleeked up for a servant's office, the devotion a kind of chronic sickness. He said: I will leave you gentlemen together, you are gentlemen together. He did not add: I know my place. He bowed leaving and limped as he left, donning an old velvet cap Kit knew must be greasy.

— And so, Thomas Walsingham said. He has his duties to

perform, bed-making and ordering dinner. And Kit and Tom can be free. I tell you, you will find nothing here, all are too cautious.

— Poley talks of conspiracy centred in the College. I have the impression of somebody coming that all await who will nod at the beginning of something.

— It is all very simple, Kit Kit Kit. The Queen of Scots is to be put on the throne, then the Spanish and French will be invited in to restore us to Rome's rule. But all that is needed is the evidence of conspiracy, and then Sir Francis will do the rest. You know of the Act? No, well, the Act that has been passed says that if there be conspiracy proved, even if the Queen of Scots knows nothing of it, then she is as guilty as if she instigated it and may lawfully be executed. You did not know that?

— It's not the kind of logic they teach at Cambridge. It seems not merely illogical but monstrous.

— It is what they call statecraft. Tom Watson said you were shouting about the greatness of Machiavel in some eating house or other. Well, here you see Machiavel in action. What is imported from Italy is not all saints and madonnas. Shall we go?

— Go where?

— Oh Kit Kit Kit, you know where. To my inn and my room, whether the bed be made or not, with the door locked and our linen off for the heat. There are no spying eyes of London here. I could see in your gaze that day what you wanted, all hidden under your fine talk of Plato and Petronius.

— I never mentioned Petronius.

— No? It must have been somebody else and other.

He carelessly threw coins on the table and rose. There was fever in Kit, he had lost voice and was panting. They walked together past the great brooding monster of the cathedral where kings had been crowned, round the corner to the rue des Boulangers or some such name, and at the end was an inn with no signboard but flowers of the season in pots on its sills. And they mounted to find Frizer bed-making. Walsingham said he might leave that, there were urgencies between Mr Kit here and himself, let him take a cool glass of something somewhere and brood on the infamy of false religion, here are foreign coins which are here not foreign.

Well, it is not my purpose to describe the acts performed, since they are enough known. *Oscula, oscula,* engagement of light beards and *oscula oscula* elsewhere, *amplexus, complexus,* and also *sugere* of this and that, and then *interjectus* and also *insertio* and great *clamores gaudii, laetitiae, voluptatis.* Two young and naked men, the unchanging under faith and thought, yet not of the cycle, threshing, making the bed shake, dislodging with a thrust ecstatic foot a pot with flowers of the season from its stand, so that dancing soles became wet and empetalled. Walsingham wrenched the lower sheet from its moorings that they might wipe off the sweat they had not lapped. They lay on the palliasse breathing like achieved runners, and Kit looked up at the ceiling to see if God's head would poke through. But God lay indifferent in his shrine, converted to bread. Walsingham, now merely a Tom, another to clog our narrative, was spread on his bed snoring. Kit *testiculis basia dedit* and dressed. He had said he would attend a lecture.

A poet, he knew the difficulties of that word *love,* which meant too many things for any man's comfort, but it was the one word that sprang from the heaven of release and he must regard it with the care he had given to the abstruse terms of the schoolmen. *Love* was the lyric cry of desire and then release and gratitude for release; should it not rather be the expression in frigid sobriety of the awareness of mingling of souls, and yet what of soul did Tom Walsingham possess? True, being human he had a soul that theology would say was there for divine salvation or damnation, but that was a formal attribute of the same manner as pure being. But what of soul with extension and properties? Was there substance deserving of a lover's homage? He thought not. Had this wholly blissful encounter of singing nerves been but of the order of the blind thrusting on the bank of the Cam or in the dusty London dark of the haunts of prostitute boys? Was it trussing up and then the fingers to the lips in goodbye, we shall lie so in pleasure again (not most like)? Did he now possess a friend or lover who would give and take eternal avowals (eternity invoked with lying lips, since eternity was God's province)? Kit felt as it were steel hoops of self-committal in compress of his ribs. Did the term fidelity apply? It was not of the covenant of man and woman who must hold the nest of their progeny together. Infidelity, he had heard of in such instances, was the knife-sharpener. He, Kit, carried no knife, but he sensed that there could be knives here too. He had heard of one in London who had carried the knife to his faithless boy paramour. The morality, if there was morality, was encased in the narrow world that two built. Of exterior morality there was none save what Church, reformed or unreformed, delivered. He had an itch of merely scholarly import to learn of the nature of and punishment allotted to such love, if love it was.

The lecture he attended, already begun, was (he twitched sourly amused lips at it) of God's love and the reconciliation of that with God's punishment. There were thirty or so black-clad students in the College hall, with, like a random scattering of flowers, visitors in gaudier dress. The lecturer was a Father Pryor, a lined and croaking man from Lancashire, where the old faith had held out longest. Love, so he said, was graced with the limitless power of forgiveness, but there came in God's eternal time the moment when justice supervened thereon. How is it possible that forgiveness without limit, he asked, can be so reconciled with punishment that seems to our frail sublunary sense of a truly monstrous order? No earthly judge or ruler could conceive of pains as severe as those of hell for acts of a limited evil, since man is not the devil. And yet God, who loves his creation, is ready to cast sinning fragments of it into eternal fire. A mystery, brethren, that may be resolved by taking thought that love has no categorical substance, that it is itself a facet of justice. It is just that we love the lovable, and it is unjust that we love what is not to be loved. Must we love the devil, contrive a forgiveness for evil whereof God himself has no capability? One of our fathers once heard a child pray that Satan might be made good and happy, but the child was in the dreadful state of innocence and the notion was at once whipped away. Our first parents too, you will say, were innocent and were blessed because of it, but theirs was a primordial innocence untouched by knowledge of evil until the fatal fruit was devoured. God may not love sin, though he may love the sinner in the expectation of his becoming cognisant of the sin and ready for lustration and repentance. If there be, to the all-knowing, no hint of such future cognisance, then the sinner has already joined the ranks of the damned. I call, at this point, for questions.

Well, Kit thought, it is better here than at Cambridge, where hunks of doctrine are imposed like deadweights and the crushed hearer granted no breath. It was one of the gaudily clad who now asked:

— Must we descry a distinction between the doer of evil in all conscience and whosoever is drawn into evil through ignorance?

— Properly, the old priest responded, we must regard ignorance as sinful when the light is shown but disregarded. The souls of the Indians of America are ignorant but not damned. Granted the light and wilfully blind to it, the privilege of damnation follows.

Some quietly laughed. In old man's anger the priest shook and said:

— Yes, yes, I say that word. For damnation and salvation alike are the signs of God's holy care of his highest creation. In this chiefly are we raised above the beasts of the field.

— Must we love Queen Elizabeth? asked a student in the rough tones of the priest's own county.

— She is not Queen Elizabeth, despite her crown and orb and sceptre and the other trappings of royalty. She is illegitimate in the eyes of God's Church.

— And therefore to be deposed? It was the man dressed brightly who had been the first asker.

— This is to be assumed. This must come in its time. But he who asked of sin must be answered. We must love our enemies as we love our friends, but we must not love their sin.

Kit left, unnoticed. It was leafy outside, a sycamore cast kind shade over the forecourt. Blessed tree and blessed birds, that were to be neither saved nor damned. Blessedly the birds flew over the screams of the charred heretics or the traitors who saw briefly and in disbelief their intestines cast into boiling water. All beasts are happy. They thrust in their season and know nothing of love. Kit sat on what was said to be a thunderstone, a bolt from the heavens, and watched emerge the priest's auditors. He had seen the back only of the gentleman who had asked about the deposition of the Queen; he saw now his bulk and ruddiness, a soldierly man with a sword, who was telling laughingly two younger men, one of them in black, the other in russet and violet, of the need for tolerance within limits.

— It is the nature of the limits that promotes argument, he was saying. Our preacher, lecturer I would say, was drawn into the forbidden when I put my question. God and Caesar – did not Jesus Christ speak wisely of the division of authority, though some would say that God being above Caesar there is no division. The Zealots were in their way logical. But no matter – we must cling to our limits of action. I keep to my narrow way.

They were away around the corner and Kit heard no more. What he noted in the speech of the speaker was a property that was not of the language of London, though otherwise the soldierly gentleman spoke that language in due conformity to what was known as the Queen's usage. Our language is rich in what our orthopeists term the rhotic (I know these things; I was brought up an actor), that is to say our dog sound is a firm roll in words containing the letter r. But this gentleman was weak in it and spoke *argument* and *preacher* and *Caesar* with but a limp tap. It seemed at the moment nothing – a mere way of walking or of agitating of the hands, or the outlandish cut of a doublet or the tilt of a feather in the hat. And so Kit forgot it, or so he thought, stood and wondered whether he should go back to Tom's inn and propose resumption of what they had done or else supper, or else hand-holding and talk of Plato. But his shyness overcame him. It would be a shy moment to face him again in all sobriety and perhaps be impelled into utterance of the word *love*. They stood or lay equal, man and man, and who must say it first? And Tom had spoken darkly of another meeting he had in the evening. At remembrance of that Kit sweated a moment in jealousy. He would think of the work for which he was paid and slink slyly into a student tavern, there to listen.

And so he did. Les Trois Couronnes, which three crowns were meant was uncertain, was near the meat market, so that the scent of blood was on the street before one entered. Here French Catholics of the lower orders – draymen, ostlers, butchers and the like – were taunting English Catholics, of moneyed families though in exile, with their impotence to restore their faith, a deformed faith since these were English, to their island of mist and snow and no vineyards, without the aid of French arms and money. And, said they, *votre roi avait douze femmes et préférait que son peuple fût damné s'il pouvait inserer son bâton dans une treizième*, adding too that their present queen *la vierge était en réalité une grande putain*, and much more of the same. With this, despite exaggeration, they would have been disposed to agree, except that some nerve of patriotism was set ajangle, and a young and burly aspirant to Catholic orders clanked his winemug on the sleek head of a lawyer's underclerk and set a minor riot afoot. In this Kit would not have joined had these French truculants let him alone, but as he was standing not sitting he was easy to trip and went over in his clean garments on a filthy floor to the partially toothless derision of the strawy ostler whose large tripping muddy boot he at once grasped and so upped the leg and had him down. The fighting was brief, for the tavern-keeper was of notable muscle, as was his wife, and Kit was chosen for the attention of the latter, whose bare arms were like thighs. So, with bruised head and blood on his jerkin, he departed with some of the Catholic English to another quieter tavern, where there was song and pedantic theology enough. He would, when he had both money and his mastership, buy himself a sword.

By midnight he had vomited thrice under the moon, not in pain since it was the mere mechanical voiding of a surfeit, and one more cup of wine settled his stomach but set his drunkenness newly awork. He tottered towards the inn where Tom Walsingham was, battering the locked door and crying *Courrier*

important de la reine d'Angleterre pour le milord Walsingham. He
was doubtfully admitted and clattered up the stairs to the known
room, finding it unlocked and, in strong moonlight, Tom awake
and startled in his shirt. Kit called *Mon amour, me voici* and
ripped off the shirt as well as his own bloodied raiment. What
he then did was more brutal than before, making Tom howl.
The news from *la reine d'Angleterre* must, so the wide-awake
keepers of the inn must now assume, be of appalling gravity.

The next day Kit woke alone in the *dortoir,* his sleepfellows
long out and at their lectures. He found Tom Walsingham's
man, Ingram Frizer, standing over him, chewing a straw. So it
was he who had been part of a dream of being newly pummelled.
Frizer was ready to pound again but desisted on seeing bruised
Kit blink in the painful light. He spat out his straw and spoke,
saying:

— I will not have this, master.

— Not what?

— Blood upon him and he sorely battered. My office is to
protect him I serve and I will not have you nor any other do
him harm by slyly getting under what is my guard. So you are
warned and told.

— What are you, fellow, that presume so? Kit asked with
scorn under an aching sconce.

— You know what I am, fellow yourself, what are you in
spite of your fine bloodied clothes and your graces and airs? A
boy student and no more, that had better mind his book than
meddle with my master that is brother to the Lord of the Manor
and will inherit. So keep away from him or it will be the worse.
Here he bunched a mottled fist in threat.

— Learn manners, mannerless lout. Raise your fist at me
and you will be beaten black. By God, I will leave my bed
now to do it.

— Aye, aye, and Frizer retreated though bunching still, you
are good at beating, we all know of you. Well, you are warned.
You are no more than a drunken booby and foul bugger. And I
do not speak of myself, for I can put men on to you that strike
to the very liver.

— Aye aye yourself, and Kit sat on the edge of his bed
in some queasiness. Off, off.

— I saved him from drowning, know that and keep it in
your black heart. And I can outbook you in learning if I wish.
I know the Greek word *tupto* and can act on it.

So saying he left, and Kit straightened his wrinkled hose,
blindly attached his bloodied trunks thereto, and put on his
dirty shirt. He was in need of a hot posset. This he got in
the College kitchen, where he instructed an undercook in the
curdling of hot milk with wine and the adding of cinnamon and
cloves. Then he went to the College chapel and sat in its cool
dark in a manner of self-disgust. There were confession boxes
here and, the hour being eleven, some students were lining up
on their knees at one of them. Auricular, as it was called, from
the Latin ear, but auric meant gold. Golden confession, a trinket
of the old faith reformed out of being. Now one confessed, if at
all, to God direct, but God rendered no absolution. He creaked
over, his headache still at him, to join the end of the line, asking
in a whisper:

— What is the formula?

— How?

— What do I say?

— I see, your first time. Say: Bless me father for I have
sinned exceedingly in thought word and deed through my most
grievous fault. And then peel your sins off one at a time, *seriatim*
if you prefer.

When his turn came he found himself in a dark cell with
a *prie-dieu* under a curtain of black lawn through which, by
grace of light beyond, he dimly saw an outlined seated figure.
A sacramental seal, a double anonymity. He said:

— I have committed fornication.

— So have many, my son. With women married or unmarried?

— Never. With boys and with men. (Married. Unmarried.
The rhotic weakness tried to strike a nerve, but the nerves
would not stay still for the striking.)

— So. That is a foul sin since it is against nature. We
have not merely the condemnation of Holy Mother Church

56

herself, which ordains burning as Sodom was burned, but the prohibition of reason, since the male seed is for purposes of generation.

— Is all waste of the male seed equally heinous? Is mastrupation as evil a sin?

— Less so since it does not win others to sin, but souls resident in man's seed *in potentia* that might at the last people God's kingdom are thwarted, nay murdered by an unnatural act. And sodomy is most unnatural, iniquitous and beastly. I beg you to give up that sin.

— I cannot, save by vowing celibacy. I am drawn to my own sex, not to the other. I was born so.

— No man is born so. Male and female created he them. You have been perverted at some point in your life recoverable to memory.

— Not so. I am as I am. I can no more repent than I can change my skin or grow another finger.

— You say cannot, I say will not.

— If I say I repent, I lie. If I undertake to turn my face from it, this as I am told being a condition of forgiveness, then the undertaking is a lie.

— Well, my son, you must needs be damned.

— And if I say that damnation itself is a lie?

— Then you commit yourself to atheism and what sins you will. But make no mistake about damnation. When you die you go to hell and stay in hell for ever. This is no matter of supposition. Holy Mother Church is built on the rock of Christ's ordination. Turn your back on truth if that is your will, since all men have free will, but be prepared (prepared, prepared, arhotic) for the ultimate fiery embrace of the Father of Lies.

— I say that my condition is condoned by Christ's own love of the beloved disciple.

— That is foul blasphemy and sulphurous ignorance and shows lamentable perversion in confusing *eros* and *agape*. You seem to be a lost soul.

— Amen.

He left black in mood and ready to fist Frizer to jelly, though his headache was cured. He sat in the refectory with students on whom no sanctity seemed yet to have descended, for they threw bread pith at one another and lifted their arses from the bench the louder to rap forth. They were quiet though when one of their number stood at the lectern to read of the sorrowful but triumphant end of a chosen Catholic martyr, one Thomas Braintree who saw Christ in his glory as the flames ate first his skin, then his flesh, then his bones. It was not a savoury accompaniment to a meal of charred mutton and unsalted turnips. And what of the martyrs under bloody Mary? Kit cursed as he belched and burnt flesh and bland turnip met in his mouth in ghost taste, tenuously bowing one to the other. By the supernumerary testicle of St Anselm and the withered prick of Origen, he would be away from here. By the renneted milk of St Monica, he could stand no more of it. After the meal he went to stand near the inn with its flowers of the season in pots, but Tom Walsingham did not appear, nor dare he enter after last night's fury of love or whatever it was to be called. He went to sleep on his pallet in the dormitory where one sick student only moaned and called on his recusant mother. At sunset, a great drama of flaming armies, he sought a new tavern, ready if need be for fight, and found there the soldierly questioner of yesterday, much at his ease and ordering wine for a student circle around him. Kit asked of the tapster:

— *Qui est ce gentilhomme?*

— *C'est le capitaine Foscue.*

— *Bien connu ici évidemment.*

— *Assez bien connu.*

The captain was quick to hear the enquiry and said in good humour:

— It is their version of Fortescue. Do not sit alone. You seem sad. Here is good belly cheer. Join the company.

— Fotescue? (The r was weak.) I am Marlowe or Morley or Marley.

— Fortescue. Sit. Unsure of your family name, is it? A name is what we hear ill and, alas, write ill. For long we did

without these additions. It was enough to be named as in the
Holy Bible. Enough to be a John, like my friend Savage here,
or a Gilbert, like young Gifford here, though a Gilbert is not in
the Bible and comes from where? And you are what?

— Christopher.

— Not in the Bible either, but who would not be a bearer
of Our Lord Jesus on his back? Well, Christopher, drink. And
to what do we drink? To a Scots queen or a carroty Tudor? To
faith old or new-fangled? Well, for dear Gilbert we know what
the answer is, but Jack Savage is chronically unsure. This makes
him savage.

Kit took in the trinity – Captain Fortescue in silver-buttoned
doublet, cape gold-laced, black-bearded, black of eye, at ease
with himself, easily pleased; Gilbert Gifford (was it?) in a student's black that made the more intense an extreme pallor as of
bloodlessness; Savage rufous, in rutilant taffetas threadbare but
defiant. Savage said:

— It is all a struggle. And the taking of sides may as well
be on the roll of the dice. Let us for God's sake go back to
our fighting, for, fighting, a man is freed of the bondage of
thought.

— He fought well, Fortescue assured Kit, and will fight well
again. That was in the Low Countries whence we come. In a day
or so we take ship for England to raise a new company. We will
do for the Don.

— My brethren in the faith, Gifford said, but to hell with my
brethren. When England was Catholic we could have Catholic
enemies. I hate the French as I hate the Spanish and I have had
to live among them. Too few see the true injustice of the Reform,
that it makes false alliances between peoples opposed in blood.
What did my family do wrong? We were in Staffordshire back in
the mists, serving the God that was good enough for Harry Seven
and his son till the black eyes of the whore Bullen seduced him.
We stay, we do nothing, we become traitors. Then Gifford drank
bitterly. Fortescue's eyes were, it seemed to Kit, very catholic in
their sympathy. Kit said:

— Here in Rheims we seem to be in a limbo where the

blood of opposition is drained away. I mean protestant and
Catholic may meet without rancour over wine. I study divinity
at Cambridge –

— I am an old Caius man, Fortescue said. You?

— Corpus. Divinity, as I say, and am drawn here to resolve
doubts. Doubts dissolve in knowledge that religious change has
never been truly religious. Faith is corrupted by matters of state.
Christians should be Christians, that and no more.

— There has to be work for curious theologians, Fortescue
said. They thrive on division. Leave it to them and go your own
way. The bread of the altar is what you think it is. Forget religion
and think on justice. It is unjust that slobbering Spaniards bring
their racks and thumbscrews *en el nombre de Dios* to oppress the
honest Dutch. The Hollanders are men of trade who would be
left alone. I fight Philip of Spain in the spirit of one who hates
empire.

— And, Gifford says, in the extending of his empire he may
put a Catholic monarch on the English throne. The Giffords
may be restored to the ancestral seat in Staffordshire. By grace
of Spain. What am I to think?

— Do not think, Fortescue said. Drink. Sing.

> *If we'd but eat and drink*
> *And swink and so to sleep*
> *There'd be no time to think*
> *And hence no time to weep.*

His voice was high and pleasing. The words and tune were
his, he said, but he had gotten no further. Could Christopher,
whom he would call Kit with his permission, add aught, he had
the look of a poet. Kit tried:

> *We'd be content with play*
> *And have no souls to save*
> *And follow the year with profitable*
> *Labour to the grave.*

— You lack a rhyme, but no matter. (Weak the r in *rhyme*
and *matter* but what Kit thought might be so was not possible.

There was a limit to contradictions.) Now Jack here will sing of shepherds. It is deep in the race, this longing to be at rest on a grassy knoll, piping to sheep. And see what happens. Christ rightly calls himself the good shepherd, but the bishops carry metal croziers that would never disentangle a baaing prisoner of a thorn bush. So by metaphor all things be in time made false. Sing, Jack.

So Savage sang:

> *Come shepherdess and be my wife*
> *And we will live a goodly life*
> *Eating the fruits that days deliver*
> *And drinking of the crystal river.*

It was now that Tom Walsingham entered, alone and smiling. He knew Gifford, the others not. Fortescue said:

— Of the tribe of Walsingham that is the Argus of the Queen, God bless her?

— Argus as faithful watchdog, Argus of the hundred eyes. Not so many. Yes, his cousin but not in his service, Heaven forfend.

— And you do what here?

— I am here with my friend. (He stroked Kit lovingly.) To help ease the torment of decision.

— Where is your man? Kit asked.

— Beaten soundly for presumption and went whinging to bed. Is it song we are having?

Savage said he could not remember the rest. Kit said they might try this:

> *And we will sit upon the rocks*
> *Seeing the shepherds feed their flocks,*
> *As loving friend to loving friend.*
> *That Jove should part us Jove forfend.*

— Pretty, Fortescue said, but the pastoral note is lost. Are we (in change of tone) all for High Mass tomorrow? I suppose if we seek the solace of singing voices we shall find that best in the heavenly choristers of the cathedral. And the candles and the

colours of the vestments and the divine and intoxicating smoke
of the incense. (He widened his nostrils and inhaled deeply as
if it were already being wafted through the tavern.) What I say
is this, friends, that what the soul craves at times is the majesty
of high ceremony. The deeper meaning skills not, the lifting of
the spirit to strange regions is fulfilled as much by the mass as
by the purple tragedy of Sophocles. It is the elevating that is all.

— So, said Kit, feeling the hand of Tom Walsingham begin
to caress his sitting buttocks, it is not all eating and drinking
and swinking and snoring, as in your song?

— No, if we come down to it, the shepherd's life is not
enough. The senses need more than the stink of wool and
sheep dung. But I speak of the senses. I do not speak of
thought. Thought has killed millions and will yet kill more.
Let us drown thought in another jug.

IT was in a field on the hot Sabbath under an elm whose
leaves were a tumult in the wind that promised a change of
weather that Kit and Tom consummated, in all gentleness, the
love that could be spoken aloud not in the disguise of French or
of Latin. They lay naked, and on Kit's back the sparse flue was,
as in the cooling of pottage by the lips pursed, agitated lovingly
by the breeze. God was safely locked away in his cathedral. God
was obliterated by love. This is then for ever? One cannot say so,
but perhaps there is an eternity untouched by God's covenant that
meaneth no more than the feigning dead of time, and that is there
ever to be sought in the mingling of limbs. And what shall the
future hold? While time feigns death there is no future. I mean,
England, whither, in a day or so, the ship will bear me though
not you for you speak of Paris business. It shall be Scadbury,
the caves of Chislehurst, never London, for London is all talk.
There must be a measure of patience, and if patience will not
hold then there is the communion over distance, communion
most holy, through imagination and the five-fingered playing on

an instrument. Faces medallions in our minds. Scents sewn into skin, sounds held in ears as the sea in seashells. We must have what we can. Fidelity? That is between essence and essence. *Fidei defensores.* We monarchs to each other will hold the faith better than monarchs.

So to it again – *femures, recta, ventra, ala.* Cows ambled up munching roundly to watch, and one left an ample pat in tribute near to their thrown clothes. It steamed to the sun and its wholesome odour was borne in to them on the veering wind. There were enough birds above and about them, flying low since they had received messages of weather change, to make it seem that whirring wings of Adam's paradise and a jangle of song withal were there to bless them. The scriptures had a lone Adam before that unhandy work with his rib, but what man could doubt that there had been a nameless companion for him expunged by God's hunger for multiplicitous children to be tormented or saved according to his caprice, hence the machine or miraculous contrivance of procreation, which pretended love, love being there but a trick? And so as the wind freshened they colled in the finality of their naked coupling among the insects, then dressed, then hand in hand walked to the town, though, reaching it, not hand in hand.

Tom rode off to Paris the next morning, Frizer on a nag fitting his lowliness behind. Kit was not there to bid farewell, the streaks of dawn at his back. He slept late, sometimes tossing in dream knowledge of many troubles ahead, sometimes still and soothed by a new assurance of the surety of what seemed sure. The following day, having taken courteous leave of his brief mentors, armed, as he thought, with a kind of intelligence, he steered his hired horse towards Calais, sleeping two nights in barns. The weather had cooled but the sky but dribbled. On the quay at Calais the clouds opened and the sea churned. He slept, since the packet would not yet set forth, in a foul inn where fleas and bugs bit his flesh and the landlord his purse. Then he embarked and was very sick. At Dover he stayed a night with the Arthur family, these being his mother's people. That the house reeked of fish ensured no quietening of his stomach. The slow

walk in windy weather to Canterbury was by way of a cure. He
heard Tom's voice and once turned as he really heard it, but it
was the wind sawing at a broken branch. He was impeded on
the city's outskirt by a march of geese that held the road and
snapped honking at his ankles, while the goosemaster with his
gnarled stick laughed. And so he was home, very weary, sleeping
much of a day away while poor Dorothy clambered over him, still
not knowing who he was. Brown Peter, well groomed, whinnied
at seeing him, and Kit welshcombed his mane and clapped his
flanks. Then, in warming weather, he was waved off to London.

In Tom Watson's house, at the corner of Bishopsgate and
Hog Lane, Kit found the poet at work. Kit was now troubled,
as I must myself be, by the fact of three Toms in his London life,
for Kyd was like to be a kind of rivalrous friend, and one Tom
of them most especial, nay crowned and golden. Tom Watson
said:

— Well, you are back and looking none the better for your
French jaunt. Of it I will ask nothing. You will see what I am
doing here. It is the making of a rosary of poems, not all mine.
Blount asks for it. Sit, sit. Lie down on the floor with a pillow.
Very weary, I can see, and thinner. What verses did your brain
churn out on your long rides? I need your verses, it will be a
beginning for you.

— You shall have something. First I must report to Robin
Poley.

— Not to Poley, Poley is in Paris with his cutthroat. Mr
Secretary himself asked after you, were you returned.

— So. I see Mr Secretary.

Mr Secretary, in the musty small room that was a mockery
of the rest of the spacious mansion on Seething Lane, bade Kit
sit on a manner of creepystool and levelled on him the black
gimlet eyes of the interrogator. Had he been tempted, seduced
he would say, by the discardable knacks and tawdries of a foul
faith, who and what had he seen, what suspected?

— There was a Captain Fortescue. He spoke of coming
to England to raise troops for the Low Countries.

— What of him?

— I think he was a priest.

— Why think you that?

— A matter of his voice. I heard that voice in both the tavern and the confessional.

— Pursued it from one to the other, did you?

— In a sense. There was the weakness of a sound of speech. He was disguised as a soldier but his voice he lacks the skill to disguise. That skill must be left to the players. Like Mr Alleyn.

— Well, this is no discovery. We know Captain Foscue, as the French call him. A certain Father John Ballard. This you could not know, but your guessing may be accounted a kind of intelligencer's success. He had tavern companions?

— I noted their names. Gilbert Gifford. A Catholic and bitter in enforced exile. And there was a John Savage, a soldier but else I know not what.

— These too we know. So. They are coming.

— In August.

— No no no, I mean more. Many are coming. It is the conspiracy.

— There will be arrests?

— No arrests. Ballard could long ago have been on the scaffold. No more. It is a waiting matter. We shall see.

— Now what must I do?

— I said it was a waiting matter. Go back to your studies. You may go to Phelips and tell him delta grade. He is three doors away.

— Phelips?

— Or Philips. It is all one. He spells his name Phelips. That is his humour.

Kit found this man in a chamber greatly larger than Walsingham's own. He was at a high desk and was flanked by two clerks as they seemed to be from their quills, which squeaked busily. As Kit entered and delivered his message, Phelips-Philips descended from his lofty stool by means of two rungs, holding out a hand in courtesy and welcome. He wore spectacles. He was small and thin, was yellow in hair and beard, and his face, which leered, was much pocked.

— A young beginner, the name? The name I now have, the grade is as he said. Well, it is here.

He unhooked a great key from his girdle and opened with a rasp a trunk of iron that sat squat on a table else unencumbered. From it he took with his thin hand a tiny leathern bag and, with a giggle, threw it at Kit who caught it.

— We play at ball, eh? The great game, and the balls are the souls of men. We shall win, have no doubt of it. And so off with you.

In his bedchamber in Watson's house Kit untied the bag and emptied money on the coverlet. Nobles, marks, groats. He counted. It was near five pounds. Half of England's parishes had stipends of less than ten a year, a third under the five. So the Archbishop himself had complained. Elation made his member swell, visibly in his codpiece, and he was thus led to the composing of a poem of love.

DROUGHT year, drought year, so they called it. A parched Michaelmas, and a Michaelmas the more parched for the aridity of studies that oppressed one who had smelt of the kitchen of great affairs, drunk French wine on French soil, more, most, had gorged on what was to be termed love. And so in the schools he was insolent in the exercises, seated on his tripod, delivering his logic.

— Should Aristotle have placed a wife among the goods of a philosopher?

— Goods are possessions that are deemed good, that is useful. In the sense that what is good conduces to the higher moral life, such goods are not of necessity good. Possessions may be inanimate, as plate, houses, land, also animate as slaves, cattle, horses. Hence a wife, being animate, may be accounted a possession. But in that a wife, being a woman and hence a human being and hence endowed with freedom of will, may contradict all other possessions in a capacity for choice, she may not be accounted so. Thus, Xantippe chose to feed her husband Socrates on little but boiled lentils and, in her wrath at his absence from the house in colloquies with the youth of Athens, emptied a pisspot on his head. So I argue that a wife, being a free soul, cannot be accounted a possession.

— Why is it decorous that undergraduates of a university should be clothed humbly?

— I argue *contra*. Study is a noble activity and through the acquisition of learning a man, however young, glorifies the whole race of man. This glory may be made manifest in outward show, fine dress enhancing the body but, in a figure that may be termed sacramental, emblemising the shining quiddity of what animates the whole being. The students here should all be clothed in silk.

— Wrong, wrong and again wrong. This use of the term *sacramental* is blasphemous. You will put off your finery instanter and revert to the subfusc as is proper.

For Kit was dressed in purple and primrose and a shirt with cobweb collar. His buttery accounts had grown and he was quite the gentleman. So attired, he was easy to find when Nicholas Faunt came looking for him. Kit was at study in the library on a foul day of late November. Faunt came up and peered at books that had nothing to do with divinity, saying:

— So this is your study, Tamerlaine and Techelles and what is this, yes, Usumcasane, and Bazajeth and Alcidamus. In my day here at Corpus we kept our noses close to our Latin and Greek. Faunt is the name. I am one of Sir Francis's secretaries, as he terms them. Come away and we will talk in the back room at the Eagle.

— Is it Service business we are to talk of?

— Call it that, call it that. Do not speak so loud. See, that boy intent on his Jerome looked up. Come your ways.

They sat then, having crossed the street where the blustering wind made ripple the plentiful puddles, in that back room over ale which Faunt called for. Faunt said:

— I take pride in being the one Cambridge man among his

regulars. I come looking at Corpus for recruits and yet you I missed. You went in another way.

— I would not say I was *in*. I have other ambitions.

— Like in the direction of the history of Persia?

— I propose a play.

— Whose theme is?

— Power. Pitiless, merciless, absolute.

— So power appeals to you, young as you are? How young?

— I am of age. Power, yes, power cut up and anatomised. I want the power of chronicling power. I have read my Machiavelli.

— Doubtless, all young men read it. Well, you think yourself not to be in the outer lanes of the labyrinth of power, but you are, you are. You wear Sir Francis's money on your back. You have been in Rheims, yes? Yes. In Rheims you met Gifford and Savage, yes? Yes. Tell me about them.

— Gifford is an exiled Catholic most bitter in his exile. Savage is hard to fathom, but he fought in the Low Countries. This argues his hatred of what Gifford stands for. But what can I say when I was told that his captain is a priest?

— It is all a wilderness. Gifford is in the Service, you must know. He has persuaded Savage that his duty is to murder the Queen.

— Which queen?

— There is only one. The other lives in a secluded state of abdication. Her time will come when Gifford is brought over. The proposal that a true queen be murdered is of Sir Francis's engineering, but only that a false queen may in all legality be beheaded. Does this make sense?

— A wilderness. I am bewildered. What have I to do with this?

— Poley is short of couriers. You must take ship and find Gifford. Savage we have, though he does not know it. He is learning law at Barnard's Inn. Gifford we need in London. Our informers say that he leaves Rheims on the twenty-fifth to stay with Thomas Morgan in Paris. He must be given a letter. You will be given that letter, cunningly sealed so that you may not in youth's curiosity tamper and pry.

— Why myself?

PART ONE

— Walsingham speaks well of you. Both Walsinghams.

Kit shuddered at that and took a draught of cold ale to quell a certain mounting heat in his veins. He said:

— It is still term time.

— It is near over. Your absence will do no harm. Remember that great power boils and thunders behind you. Hardly, hardly. There is no noise and must be no noise ever. Let me say something of Thomas Morgan in Paris. He is secretary to the Queen of Scots and most dearly and deeply trusted. She has ever been a trusting woman. Morgan is Gifford's passport to the lady. She is a most beautiful lady and she heats the blood of our Catholics, especially when they are drunk. She is the Jezebel whom Knox execrates and she is also the Virgin Mary *rediviva*. Women are terrible creatures. I think we may ride to London together.

And so they did, Nick, as he was to be called, proving, des pite the rain and wind into which they rode, a man cheerful and, though moral scruple in the higher affairs affected him little, tender towards snotnosed starvelings in villages and even towards a dead pied dog that lay with swollen belly ripe to burst on the road. He gave a reasonable rendering of Catullus's *irrumabo*, approving pedication as a punishment though not as a pleasure, and listened to Kit's half-remembered versions of Ovid with an approving ear. He was dark of eye and skin and beard like Walsingham his master, and Kit thought on the utility of such colouring when centres of Spanish intrigue must be broached. He spoke of Machiavelli and the need to understand the ferocity of certain acts of policy, as for instance Sir Walter Raleigh's massacre of the Irish five years, was it, back, women and children on their knees begging for their lives ruthlessly slaughtered and all justified by the need to wage war fast and then forgotten. Did Kit know Sir Walter? Kit did not. Strange, for their two names had come together in a pretty posy of poesy a month or so back printed by Ed Blount, was it. No, Kit did not know, he had not been told, he had received no copy, he felt aggrieved. Well, if the time should come when Sir Walter's strange doings with mathematicians and atheists had needs be probed by the Service, then Kit, might he call him Kit, had his

69

entrée. Yes, he knew some French. It was known he knew, and that was a recommendation.

In London, where a high wind clattered down the bricks of chimneys and women were skirted and men shod in mud, Kit went at once to Tom Watson's house. Tom's servant, the humpbacked Ralph, let him in and said he might proceed at once to his master's bedchamber, as from tomorrow though no longer his master, and Kit, entering, saw at once the vindictiveness of a servant dismissed, for Tom was frotting away in full nakedness with a wench or woman or lady, naked too, the covers of the bed all fallen, clothes hastily doffed mingled with the rushes of the floor. Kit excused himself and felt sick. On a table in what Tom called his study he found four, five, six copies of a thin book with the title *Gaza*. Samson and his blindness? No, *gaza* was the name of the treasure house of a Persian king, hence of any foreign prince. In it, his fingers atremble, he found his poem:

> *A gown made of the finest wool*
> *Which from our prettie lambes we pull,*
> *Fair-lined slippers from the colde*
> *With buckles of the purest golde . . .*

And he found also a reply:

> *Thy gowns, thy shoes, thy beds of roses,*
> *Thy cap, thy kirtle and thy posies,*
> *Soon breake, soon wither, soon forgotten,*
> *In folly ripe, in reason rotten . . .*

No. He read all through, his poem entire, the other, called a reply, entire, then quatrain answered by quatrain. Then the names – his and that of the great bejewelled courtier whom the Queen called Water and he himself, in grandiose magnification, Ocean. Kit, the very sound of dripping, kit kit kit, faced the roar and swell. Up in the world sang a far hautboy. Tom Watson entered girdling his nightgown about him, his face thunderous. Kit excused himself anew, blame Ralph. Tom said he had already buffeted him out. The lady? My lady wife. No. Yes. My lady. We are two months wed. Your lady. My heartiest, my most cordial, it

70

is a surprise. It was sudden. Yes, you were not told of your poem in print, Raleigh, well there was the wedding and the ways mire and the carriers slack. My heartiest. It will do no harm, this dour response to pastoral prettiness. Much happiness. It will help sell the printing, already four hundred odd on sale in Paul's yard. Why are you here? An eternity of. My thanks. Why here?

Kit saw Robin Poley the next morning. Poley was all smiles and amiable strokings. Here is the letter sealed and here a pouch to enpouch it. You must be armed, you know that? On the Queen's service in a perilous city. You have no sword but here is one I loan, my father's, God rest him, and precious. The scabbard worn and the belt frayed but no matter. It is foul weather for riding and expect a rough Channel which they call the Sleeve or *Manche*.

I must guess and suppose as ever, but that Kit was in Canterbury that November is attested by his name in good black ink in the form Marley. The last will and testament of a certain Mrs Benchkyn bears it as fourth witness. I spoke to one who had seen it, but this is of no moment. I see Kit as queasier than before on the bouncing packet over seven or more tumultuous leagues of churning bile answering his own, hiring his horse at Calais with money but adequate that Philips or Phelips had rung out, and proceeding to Paris in the foul weather that lashed and enshivered northern France as much as southern England. Paris put fear into him, a city of monstrous size to which London was but a market town. Its ambages of streets bewildered. He had been told he must seek the lodgings assigned to Service agents great and small between the rue de Champ Fleury and the rue du Coq near to the Louvre. Here were stinks and ordure enough, beggars and pimps, cutpurses and cutthroats, whores with pocked bosoms open to the wind and rain. It was termed a safe house, the one to which he rode. Its street door was open. Kit dared not yet enter for fear that a Paris prigger of prancers would steal his mount under pretence of holding, but an ostler that was English, though of rascally appearance, doubtless fled France to escape English justice, appeared to lead the horse to a stable. Then Kit found Berdon, or Beard, a name for one place and another for another, Walsingham's Paris agent in chief, a man who appeared with a bone in his fist, chewing and weighing up the visitor. He said:

— Well, you must shift as you can, we are crowded out. We keep a deal of straw for our odd helpers to doss on. Do not be made afraid by such as you meet, few are fine gentlemen. We must use what we can. You are a philosopher? You have studied of how old absolutes must yield to new relatives? There is but one crime for us now and you will know what it is. A man may be a thief or murderer and yet shine in the great virtue of loyalty. Who are you after?

— Mr Gifford.

— Aye, dear wayward Gilbert that goes his own way and is hard to track. Here he is called Monsieur Coleredin. He will be here for his London post though none knows when. You talk of urgency. There is nothing that is not urgent, so London says. But there are relative urgencies. You may come and eat.

A sort of dinner was proceeding in a room fairly furnished in the French manner, a couple of silent men in black dipping each a half of an avian carcase of some kind in a brown sauce and finickingly though drippingly biting off what flesh was left. Berdon or Beard made no introductions but offered Kit bread, a highly stinking cheese, and a decanter maculated by greasy fingers. Then he said:

— There are troubles coming here. St Bartholomew will be nothing to it. They talk of the war of the *trois Henris*, you know enough French, good. That is the Henry that is the Third, him of Navarre and him of Guise. And behind the King is Medical Kate as we call her, bitch and woman devil. Him of Navarre is out of the succession because the Pope has damned him to hell for ever, and Guise, who is a duke, is going to kill all the Huguenots. He is to get the crown, they say, and help put Scottish Mary, who is another French bitch and harlot, on the Catholic throne of England. He is a cousin or some such thing. So you see what we are in the midst of. Beware of the streets. Eh, friends, eh?

That was to the two carcase-chewers. They chewed and nodded. Kit asked to hear more of Guise.

— Guise? They call him already King of Paris. You know the rue St Honoré? No, not yet, you will not. There is what they call the Hôtel de Guise and when he emerges in his finery they all bow down to him and beg to kiss his arse and the women to lick his poxed prick and there he is waving his hat of many feathers and crying to kill the Huguenots, rob their shops, knock out their teeth with crowbars and much the same, rape the women and roast the babies on spits. And then off the blackguardly rogues go to do as they are bid, it is all great sport for them, eh, bullies, eh?

Kit left the straw-filled garret that danced with fleas early the next morning. He had half-slept with his fist round the pommel of the borrowed sword. Rogues snored or lay awake or sat awake, sucking their teeth and scratching, looking at him. At dawn he saw an act of buggery proceeding, a double act, turn and turn about with the straw flying and a sneeze timed with a final thrust, *irrumabo*. The look of the act of what could be love or lust did not please him. The beauty was all within, behind the locked doors of the eyes. He had, back in Cambridge, taken one of Jem Follett's boys for a penny, an envisioned Tom Walsingham in his head like a god and the motion towards irrumation like a prayer. He rubbed his face and hands with rose water, a mother's gift, before seeking a shop where hot possets might be sold. But they did not know of hot possets in the tavern where workmen downed harsh red as a breakfast, eyes on him the sworded stranger. He drank a mug. He was given the morning's bread.

— *Anglais?*

— *Anglais. Et bon catholique comme vous. Exilé.*

They spat before leaving. A French flea jumped from his hand to his shoulder. And with this weight I'll counterpoise a crown or with seditions weary all the world. Words often came to him thus, they were dealt by a ghost called the Muse. Since all cards are within your hands to shuffle or to cut. A clinching rhyme needed. Surest thing. Deal yourself a king. Fill in the lines. He went out into a street enlemoned by a weak sun. The wind had dropped to sleep. He caught and crushed another flea, or perhaps the same, on the sleeve of his doublet. I'll either rend it with my nails to naught or something something. How high could a flea leap? Scale the high pyramides. It was a long walk to the rue St Honoré. In a tavern where he took a second cup he heard men talking in French he could barely follow. Come from Châlons-sur-Marne where the League was (what league?) to meet *les seize*. The *arrondissements* were planning their final *coup* under him. *Vive le duc*. He thought he understood. He did not wish to see the duke at his street *levée*. He could fashion a better duke in his brain. He saw this duke enstaged, ranting in rhythm. Heroes were in a sense lining up for his inspection. All of the age, however set far back in the mists. Was then that a mission, to give the times their images of pure power, an alembication of Machiavelli (himself no mean playmaker), pure in that the heart with its allegiances and meltings would not pollute it? He could hear now as he sat near the mean spitting fire of this tavern a noise some streets off, that of a crowd howling, belike for blood. *Le duc*, an old man nodded.

He left, leaving small English silver, it was all one, and walked away from the noise. Where could he go, where could he wait, for it was all waiting? November Paris was plaguily cold. He entered the first church he came to and warmed himself at a bank of candles. A low mass proceeded with few worshippers kneeling on the stone paving. *Hoc est corpus meum.* He kept his eyes coldly on the raised host. A Huguenot gesture so he bowed. Tavern, church, tavern, a host in each. He left and walked aimlessly but briskly. His feet, one two, one two, were a faint drum to the recorder of his verses:

> *From jigging veins of rhyming mother-wits*
> *And such conceits as clownage best befits*
> *We'll lead you to the stately tent of war*
> *Where over-reaching Tamburlaine doth roar*
> *Threatening the world with high astounding word*
> *And scourging kingdoms with his conquering sword.*

The point was, he thought, that a poet, cast into jail or forced to the walking of chill streets, needed rhyme to affix verses to his memory. But in the playhouse the verse must be blank, why blank? The Earl of Surrey had seen it as an indignity to Virgil to render a rhymeless Roman into rhyme, so he had cut out rhyme from language that cried to have its nakedness clothed in a vestment that had bells sewn to it. So lo we have verse close to speech and most proper for the playhouse which is all speech when it is not blood. But could it be poetry?

> *Unhappy Persia, that in former age*
> *Hast been the seat of mighty conquerors,*
> *That in their prowess and their policies*
> *Have triumphed over Afric and the bounds*
> *Of Europe where the sun dares scarce appear*
> *For freezing meteors and congealed cold.*

Congealed cold indeed. Where could the poetry lie? Perhaps the line only could grant it, not the couplet, not more, which stabbed or bludgeoned the ear.

> *Won on the fifty-headed Volga's waves.*

That, whatever it was, was not prose. And there was another thing, and this his walking feet steadily beating told him. The five to the line was not natural. There were no fives in nature save in cinquefoil flowers. No, wait, five fingers, but the thumb was of a different make and purpose. He meant that the rhythm of two or four was in nature, for it was the heart beating and the walking legs. So then the line pentametric was unnatural unless its fifth beat was taken to be starting a new suppositious four. To ride in triumph through Persepolis. There was a pause, sure, after that, and a long one, either in the air or in the head. There was a justification for end-stopping and the line as a bludgeon. Moreover.

He was shaken out of his prosodic brooding by disorder on the mean street of shops whereon he walked. There was a stall that sold eggs and the corpses of chickens that had a day or so before laid them, and there were rough men smashing the eggs and stealing the chickens and seeking to smash the woman that

75

sold them along with a boy that seemed to be her son. A man, a cobbler like his own father, peered out of his shop to see, then, spitting nails and wielding a hammer, ran to the woman's rescue. *Huguenot, Huguenot.* And the woman with open mouth and bad teeth cried that she was not nor her son and made over and over the sign of the cross in proof she was not. Those that did not smash the eggs and steal the birds cracked eggs open to drink of the yolk and slime. But two men more lecherous sought to strip the woman to her shame while the small boy beat at them with fists most ineffectual. The cobbler gave a fair hammer blow to the sconce of one who turned in time and so reeled without falling, so that most now turned on this man, whose two prentices ran out now with their own hammers. Kit felt blood rise then brim in him and then remembered that he was now acting the gentleman, for did he not bear a sword? A sword though could slay and here he was, strange in a strange city. It would be enough to brandish, so he did. He ran across brandishing, smelling the putridity of some smashed eggs that had not been laid that morning, nor even yesterday, and cried *Salauds salauds* (taken back to the Canterbury streets an instant). Then he was sliding and slipping on egg-mess on the cobbles. His sword-point pierced a fat buttock and would have gone deeper if the howl of the ruffian so struck had not been so loud. He withdrew and then was hit from behind by something hard. A stone, he saw, turning, staggering. The ragged grinner who held it cracked him on the brow and he went down and entered a vague world where Tamburlaine swore he would crack the egg of the universe.

He re-entered the day to find himself in his father's shop, safe in the smell of leather. No, it was not his father. *Mon père aussi*, he was saying. *Comme mon père qui fabrique les souliers. En Angleterre.* It seemed the fracas was over, though this cobbler was bruised. Kit's head beat like a heart, the ache was not to be described. He lodged where? He remembered what that woman had been selling, old hens and perhaps cocks. *Rue du Coq.* The prentices would escort him thither. It was not far.

So he nodded them off, he had no small coins for them, at

the open door of the house called safe and limped in, seeming to knock at the door on the left with the bruise on his brow. Ready to fall again. The door was ajar and his body opened it fully. A bright fire. A table that was a warped plank set on builder's trestles. Iron boxes, somewhat rusty, upon it. He took the first chair he found with his right hand and sat, looking at the two men who stood wondering. Beard or Berdon in a robe with a collar of mangy fur, hatted like a rabbi, the young man he had met in Rheims, very fair, quite bloodless.

— So what is it?

— A street fight. Sons of the Church and the Huguenots. I interfered.

— No warning, Gifford said to the other. Newcomers must be warned, Beard. They must not interfere. It is all their own business.

— Walsingham would see that as heroic.

— But it is foolishness. Are you the man that brought the letter? Stay, we met at Rheims. I see you have an egg on your brow. Ready to hatch from its swelling.

— It was an egg woman. It is here in my breast.

— So, opening the pouch, breaking the seal, reading. I am ordered back. Contacts, contacts, doors swung open, a queen's French perfume, words, words, then acts. At once, he says, no delay. A night ride and Calais at dawn. You, what's your name, can be with me. It will be to your credit.

— Marlowe or Marley.

— Real name?

— I am what I am what I am what I. Forgive. They hit with a stone, a rock, my brain rocks.

— Go lie down on Beard's bed. We leave at dusk.

— You are, Kit said, noting Gifford's finery and collar of cobweb lawn, no longer a student.

— I never was, not of Rheims. Some day soon we shall all be done with disguises. Go sleep.

On the dawn packet, the sea unseasonably smooth under a cold sun and little cloud, Kit's ache abated and his brow, soothed with rose water, bade the swelling recede. He was still little coherent either in speech or thought, nor did he understand the wheels that drove the brain of Gifford.

— Truly a Catholic?

— Not truly anything. Are you truly anything? No, a lump of pain with an egg on its brow. Truly an Englishman who hates the French and the Spanish and the Italians and puts England before all. Catholic England if it were possible but it is not. So England at peace enough under protestant rule. My father thinks differently but he no more than I would have the old faith restored by grace of Spain or France. He pays his recusancy fines cheerfully. He thinks change will come about in good time.

— He knows what you do?

— To know would kill him.

— But he *will* know if all goes as you plan it.

— *Que sera sera.* Is your evident queasiness the egg on your head? The sea keeps calm.

— The prospect of killing the innocent.

— Can you call her innocent? She is called Queen of Scots but she is pure French. She will have the French in and the Spaniards. She shall be tricked into treason. And my father will be tricked, small things yielding to great. Our estate is near Chartley where she is under lock and key. I shall be there. It will be a matter of getting something from her in black ink. Then there will be an end to it. See, there are the white cliffs. And the gulls scream us in with the shrillness of welcoming trumpets.

— You are something of a poet.

— Something of nothing.

IT was the lump on the brow incurred in a good if minor fighting cause as well as the prompt bringing home of Gifford that conveyed to Mr Secretary a sense of the utility of employing Kit in these small matters of courier service. The contusion was visible evidence of a young man's seriousness in the cause. But he was let go back to Cambridge with two crowns in his purse, and the Walsingham plan proceeded without him. He would be brought in later.

It is to me somewhat of a relief to sum what happened between Christmas and Whitsun without occasion to besmirch Kit with the dirt of it, for I loved and yet love his genius and if I sometimes hated the man it was not because of craft and deviousness, rather because of a candour of word and act that, being a fruit of innocence, would at length stick in his throat and choke him. So I will speak of Gifford, traitor to his faith, and what he did. He, after his reporting to Mr Secretary, lodged with Philips or Phelips in Leadenhall Market for a time, from there visiting the French ambassador with letters from Morgan, the Queen of Scots her Paris secretary and most treacherous to her, that testified to his devotion to the Queen and the faith they shared. And it was made clear to the ambassador, who at first had his doubts, that Gifford was seeking a way whereby Her Abdicate Majesty should be made aware of what proceeded in the outer world through the contrivance of a secret post that he, Gifford, was most eager in his loyalty to set working. So when he had confirmed with Savage, then at his studies at Barnard's Inn, that the killing of the lawful Queen should, despite Savage's qualms and wish to delay, be assigned to that summer and no later, and when he had caroused with Father Ballard, seemingly firm in the regicidal resolve, who, as Captain Fortescue, was a flame in the London taverns and closely watched yet most free, he proceeded to his father's estate in Staffordshire, lodged with the steward, one Newport (Gifford's father at that time being in jail for some remark he had made detrimental to the peace of the realm though truly not grave), then spoke in simple words to a Burton brewer who delivered beer each Friday to the Queen of Scots her household, saying that he was to deliver also messages rolled in a tube and hid in the bunghole of the cask that should be chalked with a cross as a sign of its presence. And when he collected the cask empty he was to look for a tube and at once hand it to Gifford or one that deputed for him.

There was an agreed cipher that Morgan had imparted to
Gifford, and the unravelling of this when fingered out of the out-
going barrels was a yawning sleepy work for Philips or Phelips,
most expert in it, who passed all on to Walsingham in clear
English. The letters, then resealed by one Arthur Gregory, who
was proud of that skill, none could ever detect his interference,
were then taken by Gifford to the French Embassy, and thence
they went their ways under the cloak of diplomacy to whoever
was to receive them. This business started soon after Christmas,
yet by Easter there was nothing found incriminate, which soured
Walsingham much. There should have been an acquiescence in
the killing of the Queen regnant, often urged in Gifford's letters,
but Queen Mary, though she had been foolish in love, was not
so foolish in statecraft. There could, of course, be an acceptable
forging of treasonous intent by Philips or Phelips, but this was
thought to be somehow a manner of cheating, and games in
which cheating is permitted are but halt and blind games. So
then Mr Secretary cast about for a new strategy and was at
length apprised of the name of Anthony Babington, who, in
some manner yet to be sifted and brought to the light, might
prime the engrossing of an intent that would lead many to the
scaffold but one above all.

This Babington was of Derbyshire, his country seat being
near Matlock, and, though a Catholic and a true one, he had had
luck in being able to cling to property by no means small. At one
time the Earl of Shrewsbury had been jailer to the Queen of Scots,
and the boy Babington had been his page. He had conceived a
childish devotion and love to the Queen, who was indeed state-
ly tall and most beautiful and with a voice that enthralled, and,
during that period of her mostly kindly and loose incarceration,
before her grimmer transferral to prison at Chartley, he had,
through a Paris visit, found ways of conveying letters through
Morgan to Mary by way of the Shrewsbury household, but now
all that was over. He served now the cause of the priests, with
money and places of refuge, but that was most perilous, being
not merely treasonous but highly treasonous, that is to say High
Treason. He was but twenty-five and much loved, though not to

the point where his High Treason might be condoned. But some shut eyes to his actions.

I do not know for sure that Kit became embroiled in these matters at the time of the entry of young Babington, all innocent and unknowing, into Walsingham's great plan. But he said that he did, at the time of his first playhouse triumph when he became drunken and talked purple untruths in the manner of the poet he was. The manner of it was, he said, this. He had been summoned from Cambridge, again by Nick Faunt who was on a recruiting visit, to see Robin Poley. Poley had met him with: Dear Kit, dear helper in the cause and most helpful a helper, now is the time for you to endue the great mask of simulation. I am born Catholic and am believed to practise the faith, for me there is nothing hard in false smiling and fraternal embracing, but it is what you must learn. Faunt said something of your writing plays, so simulation and falseness you will know something of. We go to meet Captain Foscue, as the French call him, and one other in a tavern, a back room I need not say, there to talk privy matters. You are to be a good Catholic.

— Foscue or Fortescue I know. He saw me at a time when I spoke of my Jacob wrestling with the agonies of faith.

— Agonies resolved, you are converted. But if you move wrong through inattention or worse – I need not say more.

— A threat? I hear a threat?

— You hear a *pignus* of your committal. No more.

Kit did not well understand, though he shivered on that chill spring day. They went together to the Plough by Temple Bar, and in an inner room they met Father Ballard the carousing soldier and the delicate Babington. Ballard or Fortescue remembered faintly the Rheims meeting. Christopher, a noble name cattified to Kit. Aye aye, it all comes back. Well, let us drink as friends and, I take it, all of the faith. Kit said:

— I may now call you reverend father.

— Call me nothing. Poley said:

— I fear suspicion of me grows. I have been bound by two sureties whereby I must present myself each twenty days.

— Before the magistrates?

— That. I had thought of escaping, though not from Dover where there are watches set. But it is a matter of getting money.

— I will gladly advance fifty pound, Babington said. That for a beginning and more later.

— God and his holy mother bless you for that. But I have here my young friend to protect that is restored to the faith and has been too loud in his joyous professions. He has to learn discretion. In protecting him I am in some danger, but no matter. There is the other business that bids us all stay.

— The Holy Trinity shower blessing on it, Kit said. It was extravagant, but extravagance might be forgiven a convert. The others even murmured Amen. The reverend father in his gaudy soldier's extravagance said:

— The rising must all depend on the help of Guise and King Philip. The attack is in preparation. But Babington said:

— Drag us by the heels at Tyburn before that the stranger enter our gates. The State here is well settled, and with the Queen alive though excommunicate nothing may be done.

— The means, the means, Ballard said. It is made. There is one that took the oath.

— God bless his valiant heart, Poley said. He will leave his musty law books and strike.

— God forbid, it is a terrible thing, said shocked Babington. The removal of her is a different matter and toleration and the freeing of our lady Mary to be made a condition of her release. But I know not truly what is to be done.

— Yet we know what you have, Poley said. We are in this together and may be shown. And he put out his hand with a kind of reverence.

— It is almost a holy thing, Babington said, fumbling with buttons at his breast.

— Heaven forbid it be a holy relic.

— Amen. And Babington drew out a letter with a broken seal. Kit leaned across to read it, for it was now in Poley's hands. It was to Babington and not in cipher. Here was the royal hand: *I pray you therefore from henceforth to write unto me as often as you can of all occurrences which you may judge in any wise important to the good of my affairs.*

Poley nodded, with greater reverence, and said that Babington had been writing to Nau that was the Queen of Scots her French secretary. Whereupon Babington flushed deeply and asked how he knew. I know, I know, I must know things, a man must protect himself.

— I asked, Babington said, if you were to be trusted. With so great matters afoot it was in order.

— And so it was, so it was, you were right. And you received assurances that I was and am?

— Indeed so.

— And what can you now offer?

— In the matter of what I said? Though still I do not properly know. There are gentleman enough of stout courage. Gentlemen pensioners who would seize and hold her against our sovereign lady's release.

— The time is not yet, as you know. You must continue your writing to her and holding to her replies as they were precious gold.

— Amen. I talk of the usurping competitor.

— That is a discreet phrase. You talk to whom?

— I have drafted a letter to her not yet delivered for Gifford's sending. I write of doing her one good day's service. I ask that she direct us by her princely authority and so forth.

— You have this draft upon you?

— It is at home.

— Have a care, have a care, in the name of God have a. There be thieves enough about. Well, shall we sing a bawdy catch and tipple more? Or shall we be about our business that is termed lawful? Even so. And close our meeting with the *signum crucis*. Which they made, Kit too.

— You lodge with Tom Watson? Poley asked, out in the wind of Temple Bar.

— No longer. He said he would not marry but he has married. The sister of this lawyer Swift. I ride tonight to stay with Tom Walsingham. But I shall be early in tomorrow, as you request.

— From Tom to Tom. Well, you see how things went. It will still be a slow business. And shaking his head he led the way to his house on Bishopsgate that was called the Garden, where Kit's horse was stabled. Then Kit rode north to Scadbury with the wind against him.

THERE was a cottage on the estate where Kit had lodged before. He was never desirous of entering the great manor house where Ingram Frizer stalked. He feared Frizer's mad devotion, which he could not well understand. It was so unlike his own, bearing in itself no epicene love nor even simple friendship, rather the desire to be abased and yet not abasement of a true lowly servant, for Frizer had money and much of this money slid into Tom's lean purse. How he got or had in the past gotten this money was never clear. As for meeting Tom behind the back of Frizer, this could sometimes though rarely be a matter of a dated tryst, a letter left with Poley to be delivered when Tom was at his cousin's, or, lurking among bushes, Kit whistling near a known and lighted casement of the manor house, which was absurd. The tune he whistled was Wilbye's setting of his own shepherd poem, already well enough known about the town.

Anyway, this night they lay together in a cottage which had been that of an estate woodman long dismissed. It was, as it were, an abode pared down to love, for there was little in it but a bed with straw-filled mattress and blankets of stitched motley pieces, the work of the woodman's wife. There was a fire fed by the ample branches and logs with which a leaning shed was well stocked, but, for fear that prowling Frizer might wonder even at nighttime smoke under the moon, it was seldom flinted to life, there being warmth enough in their conjoined and amorous naked bodies. So, beneath the blankets in the spring dark, hearing the wind in the chimney and a far dogfox or a mousing owl, they kissed and colled and rolled and panted and were disengorged of their urgencies.

Then they lay and wiped the sweat the one off the other and talked.

— They will talk at Corpus of your absences.

— Your cousin swears that all will be taken care of. The Queen's service comes first.

— This is the Queen's service?

— This is one of the rewards of it.

— Very prettily said. And then, later: I think this will all soon be mine. I shall be Lord of the Manor.

— Who says that?

— Frizer says that my brother is very sick. Nothing stays in him, it is all vomit vomit.

— How does Frizer know?

— Frizer is a great peerer and pryer. Frizer will be glad when it happens. His young master will be fulfilled and there will be a major-domo's chain of office dangling from the Frizer neck.

— In Naples did I learn to poison flowers.

— What is that to do with anything?

— A line that came to me. Such lines often come. Then they must be joined to other lines that come, all complete and stopped at the end. Blank verse must not melt into prose. Yet as it came I seemed to see Frizer saying it and bowing deep. I take it he has not been in Naples.

— He says sometimes a rich grandfather sent him round the world, but it is all lies. He has a parish in radius all of twenty miles.

— And villainy enough in it.

— He is no villain, he is all devotion, though the devotion irks.

— He knows that your brother is dying. In devotion is he helping him towards his *quietus* or *nunc dimittis*?

— I should think my brother has the French pox. And Tom yawned in the dark. Then he encircled Kit with his arms and they fell to more kissing. At the end of a sore dawn coupling Kit heard his horse champing grass. Tom said:

— Give me a verse. Said not sung.

— This.

The shepherd swains shall dance and sing
For thy delight each May morning.
If these delights thy mind may move
Then live with me and be my love.

And Watery Walter's reply:

But could youth last and love still breed,
Had joys no date, nor age no need,
Then these delights my mind might move
To live with thee and be thy love.

— Raleigh, they say, must be watched.

— There is altogether too much watching. Frizer will be on his patrol shortly, seeing that none have stolen twigs from the trees. He will wonder at a horse chewing his master's grass. Best go.

IT was true perhaps that Raleigh must be watched, for, so it was known in the Service, he had been engaged with Mendoza, who was Spain's ambassador in Paris, in negotiation over a Spanish pension, since the Queen's favour, so he said, could not last. And there was one of his circle, whose godless speculations would, when the time came, invite examination, one named Anthony Tuichenor, who had put himself forward to Gifford as one who would convey the captured true Queen, provided no harm came to her, to a place of safety that Sir Walter himself would contrive. But all this was but a small concern at the time of the letter that Babington, guided by Poley and Gifford, sent to the Queen of Scots by the established beery channel, saying that *Forasmuch as delay is extremely dangerous, may it please your most excellent Majesty by your wisdom to direct us and by your princely authority to enable such as may to advance the affair.* And it was all laid out: the invaders were coming, this confirmed by Gifford, now in Paris and not to be seen in England more (he was to die in a brothel), the deliverance of the Queen of Scots and the dispatch of, as it was put, the Usurping Competitor. And he, Babington, would with six gentlemen and a hundred followers release her Catholic Majesty. Yet there was no invasion coming, nor a hundred men, and he would be hard put to find six gentlemen even. What Mary's reply was we know not, but that there was a reply we know, sent, in her words, by *une petite boîte ou sac de cuir*.

Also we do know that, by order of her Protestant Majesty, *Fidei Defensor*, Philips or Phelips breathed on his spectacles and polished them to forge a postscript that affirmed the Queen of Scots her complicity, for in it she is represented as enquiring of the names of the six gentlemen that were to release her and convey her to the throne. For it had never seemed to her Protestant Majesty, our late lady Elizabeth, Occidental Star, that the Act which condemned her innocent cousin for the guilt of others would prevail greatly in Europe. But here in Philippine good black ink was proof of conspiracy enough, and that would serve. Philips or Phelips, in forger's triumph, could not resist the sketching, in three broad lines, of a gallows on the outer cover of the letter. Perhaps, seeing this, Babington, who was no fool, began to have his doubts of the whole procedure. And the arrests began with the taking of Father Ballard, soon stripped of the swaggering Foscue disguise and reduced to a shivering priestling ripe for the rack of Mr Topcliffe.

It was Robin Poley who reported this to Babington while the latter lay slugabed one morning after a night of little sleep. Then Poley betook himself to hide in Richmond where Mr Secretary had followed the court, granting Babington the benison of an address so that he might clinch the affair with a palpitant culpatory missive. And indeed Babington wrote, saying *Est exilium inter malos vivere*, it is truly exile to dwell among the wicked, and Farewell, sweet Robin, if, as I take thee, true to me. If not, Adieu, *omnium bipedum nequissimus*, of all that walk on two feet the wickedest (and that alternative was just and to be Poley's best epitaph). He then concluded: The furnace is prepared wherein our faith must be tried. Farewell till we meet, when God knows well. Thine, how far thou knowest, A.B.

The date is well attested of the taking of Father John Ballard. It was on August 4, in the year of grace or something 1586. He strode aswagger, much the captain, into Poley's house, or rather the garden of the Garden, full of flowers dry in the heat, where he was to meet with Babington, and Mr Secretary's men were all about.

— And where is good Robin?

— If that means Mr Poley, he is already taken. This was Mr Secretary's man Francis Milles, who then ordered the arrest to be made by a Mr Casty that was a deputy alderman of Aldgate. It was not true that Poley had been taken, but there was to be a semblance of taking in good time, Poley in the Tower, having freely walked thither, there in his spidery script to write his long report and, ever piously mindful of the papist peril, to incriminate such as he found, priests starved and past dissembling and the like. It was said by the equivocator Southwell that Poley poisoned the Bishop of Armagh that is in Ireland who had been haled out of his diocese with a piece of cheese but this may not be true. Yet many-tongued rumour babbled over the years and the Catholics were at the last to know their enemy.

Babington and others fled north to the wilderness of St John's Wood, where, unprotected by either the Precursor or the Beloved Disciple, they wandered, sought shelter, ate sour apples, wore rags and stained their faces with juice of nuts. Savage that was to have borne the knife lumbered south, a large man and slow. All were caught with but little trouble, and there were among the final criminal band names that mean nothing now, these being attached to helpers and shelterers, pitiers when not believers, ploughmen and woodcutters and farmers' wives.

Kit said, truly in his cups after *Tamburlaine Two* but most plausibly and perhaps not weaving a play out of it, that, on Mr Secretary's order, he was made attend the trial on September 13, the Michaelmas term not yet begun, at Westminster before a commission of Oyer and Terminer, with Sir Christopher Hatton, the Queen's dancing man, as chief prosecutor. There could be no defence and so for the defence there was no counsel. The trial in the great hall under its high vaults, dusty sunlight shafting in, full of murmurers and growlers quietened by beadles and bailiffs, with howlers in the streets held back with pikes, was by way of being a play without plot or exercise in what the Senecans term stichomythia. Father John Ballard, with wrenched beard, torn hair and scarred cheeks, as well as a shoulder freshly deformed, was carried in in a chair.

— Rise. To sit is insolence to the court.

— I would rise if I could. My broken legs are somewhat of a hindrance.

— Do you acknowledge yourself to be a foul traitor and villain?

— If you seek villainy look elsewhere. Look to your chief torturer Mr Topcliffe, who while busy with the screws and stretchers did regale me with tales of feeling the breasts and belly of your lady the Queen under her kirtle. There is decorum in all things, even in the breaking of a man.

— We will not have this.

— It skills little what you will or not have. I am too weary and broken for your game. If you seek guilt you must probe among yourselves that threw away the true faith on a king's whim.

— You then admit your treason?

— To Christ our Lord never, to the true Church he founded never, to my sacred office that with all diligence I pursued never and again never.

— So you acknowledge yourself to be a villain.

— If in your tortured logic to be Christ's priest is to be a villain, then amen. Let me to my crucifixion and my reward.

— You are also a blasphemer. You shall have your crucifixion and worse.

— To that too amen. May this realm struggle out of its darkness towards the light.

When Savage, ragged and wild of eye and not belying his name, was thrust into the court, he was called at once an assassin.

— To assassinate is to kill. I have not killed. Ergo I am no assassin.

— We speak of your avowed intention.

— The intention was the fiction of one Gifford who is now
proved a double-dealer and author of a plot that should entrap
many, not least the Queen of Scots. I ever opposed it.

— We have letters of proof.

— Letters of forgery.

— You attaint the Queen's counsellors with villainy?

— The Queen's counsellors are doubtless best able to judge
of the morality of their acts.

— You are a foul villain and a treacherous assassin.

— How long must this wheel turn?

It was all a wearisome business, and by September 16 fourteen had been found guilty and condemned. Four days later
came the first of the two bloody public shows, the weather
continuing dry but not sunny, and Kit again much against his
will was constrained to attend at St Giles's Fields the hanging
and butchering of the chief conspirators, Ballard, Babington,
Savage, others, including the Tilney that, in his scaffold speech,
was challenged by a Dr White, that was learned in the reformed
versions of theology, and to him replied that he came hither to
die, not to argue.

Kit had no special post of spectation. He noted that the
chambers that Babington had used in Holborn, from whose
casements something of a view was afforded, seemed to have
been usurped by Philips or Phelips, Berdon or Beard, Faunt and,
he did not wish to believe his eyes on this, Tom as a Walsingham
presence. But he stood at the rear of the crowd of the ill-washed
but staunchly protestant, children even on fathers' shoulders,
gossiping matrons, even pie-sellers, taking in the stink as at least
the stink of life. The show began with the trugging of the sleds
through the streets, the crowd's groans and japes (they be given
free passage and no labour of limbs), then the untrussing of the
victims and the thrusting of them to the ladders. The hangman,
masked but known to be Jack Flood from his gapped grin and the
width of his shoulders, had two assistants, young boys already in
blood well steeped, and it was they that did the thrusting up to
the gallows with their knifepoints. Ballard was first and, at the
ladder's foot, gave with such dignity as a broken man might his

hope of England's seeing its folly and bathing at the last in truth's recovered light and much else. He signed the air crosswise, glad at least, he said, to be permitted at last to do this in the open, and voices called on him to repent. He smiled sadly, shaking his head, then was hauled up, firmly noosed, then kicked from the ladder. Here was skill shown. The single garment ripped down, the prick and ballocks exposed then sliced away, the first blood healthily flowing, then the cross-cut along the belly so that the bowels gushed out and, here was the skill of it, the victim saw before his eyes turned up. Then was the whole body cut down and chopped by the hangman and his two (never eat flesh more, vomited a girl that pushed her way away from it), the hacking most vigorous so that sweat showed on the bare chests of the hackers. The quarters were heft up as at Smithfield and thrown into the boiling tub, there would be a fair stew soon, it lacked but carrots and onions and the coils of entrails pulled by the two lads as to unwind a rope for the hangman's skipping. All this Babington saw, he was next, and swooned to be revived with a slash across the chaps with Ballard's own bowels (unfair that his eyes be shut, he must see all, that is the rule of it), noosed as he screamed no no, kicked off, lost what were termed his privities, saw, saw, saw in disbelief the door of his belly widely opened and his inner self gush out. His heart was held up, but the hangman cursed, as one failed in his craft, that he who was now heartless was eke sightless, there was no justice in the manner raw nature did ever seek to foil arts hardly learned, and then it was the turn of Savage (he is a rogue of bulk, there will be a fairsized knockmedown upon him, thou wilt see else). But Savage in his heaviness broke the warped rope and fell unhanged (there will be questions on this, old rope is for tethering your jennyass), so that he saw in living awareness the slicing off of his manhood and the bloodgush (fairsized, did I not say) and the uncurtaining of his entrails. So here was one that observed somewhat of his anatomy, his beatless heart included, before yielding the ghost and turning to fresh butcher's meat.

Of this Kit could stomach no more, so he shoved his way out (there is more to come, cully, you miss half the show), seeing himself in an overwhelming measure as the hangman by proxy, riding from Tom Walsingham's bed to sign that he had witnessed conspiracy and here were the names, he had taken bloody money before blood was spilt and converted it to bloodhued satin for his back. A kind arm upheld him as he tottered and a kind voice said it was all enough, let us breathe fresher air at the rear of St Giles's church. Kit looked up into the black eyes of he had forgot the name but soon he knew it, Skeres.

— Nick Skeres. We are a long way from Dover where we took ship that time. All for the cause, the cause.

They sat on a grassy tump behind the solid hulk that proclaimed God's protestant truth, and Skeres kindly watched while Kit voided his breakfast.

— Let us come away from there, you have made your offering or oblation or whatever a man is to call it. You need drink now to settle the inner being.

Kit retched and retched but stringy spittle only came up. He lurched on Skeres's arm to sit under the ancient oak. The sun had clouted away its cloudy obstruents and gushed heat like blood; here was shade. Skeres, Kit now saw, was in decent black as for mourning and was no more the dirty rogue of the feast of Dover fish. His nails were trimmed and a clean hand played with a clean dagger.

— It is all over now, the crowd is departing, pleased at a fine spectacle and no money charged. See them go, pleased and chattering. It is filth, filth and again filth.

— And we were both part of it.

— I do not see myself as such. The bodyguard of Robin Poley and now his daily messenger while he is in the Tower. He is well provided for, with his wine and victuals brought in and his work of writing it all down and a mistress when he has done his day's work. A happy man, you would say. And happy that he was not there to witness the outcome of his dealings and double-dealings. Squeamish, you could call him. It is all Plato with him, ideas skirling in the empyrean.

— You sound more scholarly than I would have thought should fit your office.

— Oh, I am no scholar. A picker up only. I cite bonny Robin. Well, the labours are not quite done. There will be the matter of rousing the people with fears and tremors before the head of the second bloody Mary can be struck off. That is a great and grave matter and it will not be at Tyburn or in St Giles's Fields. This striking off of heads and loosing by the knife of what is best kept hidden is no more to my taste than to yours. A strike to the heart should be enough, one thrust and all over and little blood. My hands feel sticky with it, I feel it will flow crying to heaven all over the fields and end here at our feet.

He feigned with his dagger to strike Kit to the heart, smiling rather than grinning.

— I go my ways and you yours, he then said. Get some ale in, it will wash the blood away. And he rose and helped Kit up. His gait was swift, he seemed to vanish in the flowing crowd that enjoyed the sun as much if no more than all it had seen. A small boy clinging to his father's hand, an honest tradesman by his look, looked up at his father saying And and and, hand firmly locked. Kit, a little bloody money in his purse, made his way to the Unicorn on Bishopsgate. Here was the realm of the playhouse, where only pig's blood gushed from bladders hidden, where swords of lath struck and axes were of pulped paper moulded. It was safer, all was pretence. But the tavern was crammed with onlookers at the show now seeking refreshment, the tables filled and many standing about, swilling, calling for more. Alleyn's brother, presiding, did not seem to remember Kit. Nor did, who was it, yes, Bradley nor Orwell, yes that name, who both sat in the corner covertly comparing cutpurse gains at the hanging. Kit found room at a table of honest tradesmen who discussed, disagreed, compared points of the executioner's art – that right arm is grown slow, Gosport that is dead was better at it, they say it all goes to Greenwich to feed the Queen's hounds, nay there are some that hunger for man's flesh but it is unlawful. Kit called for a whole quart. True, it settled him, washed the blood away but, as a mischievous spirit, rose to his head and bade him curse.

— Curse all who permit it, this butchery, and all for what?

A man should follow what faith he will, God grins at all this, but mayhap there is no God, a true God would not stomach it, Christ in heaven if there is a heaven and if Christ be in it must look down and cry drag them all to hell if there be a hell.

He cursed only to the table and the honest burghers about it. One said: Have a care, and the others looked for watchers, officers of the law, ragged informers. But at the neighbour table a bald man with a long grey beard, much lined, his habit decent and his drink but a small chalice of sherris, nodded and said:

— Aye aye, it is the way all must feel that have a spoonful of the compassion that our Saviour taught. And even the Queen, that has most cause to be vehement against her enemies, even she feels it, for has she not decreed that tomorrow the agony shall be lessened? The hanged shall be properly hanged and dead before that the cutting up commences.

— How, how? called some. Where did you hear this?

— Flood himself told me. He is by way of being my grandson in law.

Some would then touch the old man as if he were holy, one that was a link through the flesh of his granddaughter to a great one of the day. Kit called for a new quart, drank deep and belched on the yeasty froth, standing staggering to cry to the tavern so that all were stilled to listen:

— If religion does this to men's bodies, then let us have no more religion. We shall all be happier without God and his black crows of ministers. I do not forget what was done under bloody Mary and know it will happen again if the Spanish take us over. It is all one, true reformed or true papish. It is religion itself that is our enemy. Who is there that needs it save those that relish the blood it lets or grow fat on benefices and advowsons and tithes and Peter's pence? Cast down God like a wooden puppet. He and his angels and saints are fit only for oaths. By the six ballocks of the Trinity and the cheese of the milk of the Magdalen and the hundred prepuces of circumcised Jesus I cry out on it.

A black-bearded bravo came towards him with clutching hands to cry:

94

— You shall be in the Clink for this, bastard. I will not hear God and his Church and she that is head of it put down.

There were many growls of those that agreed.

— Hypocrites all. You know nothing of God or anything. And Kit, who knew he had drunk enough, threw his near-quart into the black beard, clattered with his tankard on the head one who would bar his leaving and, staggering still, left. God's air, God's sun. No, they were not God's. Nature's, that framed us of four elements. He had now to head to Poley's Garden, defiled, defiled, to free Brown Peter, that he had left enstabled with ample oats, and then ride to Cambridge. He would not stay another hour in this befouled city, where the bells still rang jubilantly and death's celebrators staggered in drink and sang their dirty songs. Well, he too was a staggerer, and, as Brown Peter whinnied him a greeting, he found support against the warm flank, put his arms about the sturdy neck for comfort, sobbed a minute or so, then drew him out and clumsily mounted. He would travel back to a citadel of pure mind and essence in the company of a beast that was pure muscle and instinct. What did Brown Peter know of Aristotle? And yet to live and die in Aristotle's works seemed at the moment of steering out of crammed London the summit of all aspiration. It was the all too human passions between planes that, all too disjunct, were yet akin in sanity that were from now to be avoided.

He had not thought to ride to Scadbury. To ride to Scadbury was to plunge to the heart of the human passions. Tom had said that he would be there and that Frizer would be in Basingstoke. He had London business (Kit now knew what) but would be back in early afternoon. Jove send me more such afternoons as this. No, not now if not no more ever. The genitals were for slicing off that blood not seed might gush. The passion of the butcher's knife was the passion of coupling. There was a foul amity between the acts of the bed and the acts of the scaffold. Let the brain ride aloof: these warm animal flanks supported the regrettable apparatus that supported it. A man could not get away from his body. He would eat no more meat, he would divorce from his munching of bread and sipping of wine the memory long ingrained of Christ taking these for his body and blood. He would prepare for the Michaelmas term in the conduct of a kind of Lent. Yet what was it that he was writing but a celebration of human passion? This was another matter, this was words, it was an Aristotelian purging of the real through the fanciful. The poet was chained to his passions, true, but only that he might discharge them in the splendour of language. The lips spoke and the shackles fell. So let it be.

WHAT happened in London could not but have its rever-berations in the scholarly fastnesses of Cambridge. In October there was the matter of a trial in secret at Fotheringay whereby Mary Queen of Scots received her death sentence, though the passing of this was not made known to the people till December. Cambridge mimicked London with the clanging of its church bells and the lighting of fires round which the students danced. Fire is for warmth, Kit told himself as, chilled by writing in his freezing chamber, he stood by a fire on the banks of the frozen Cam. Let us cling to the elemental and not think. For to think was to be shamed at the knowledge that it could be no true trial, since the Queen of Scots was not subject to the foreign power that was England, and that her condemnation was supported by but a doubtful parliamentary act and a certain forgery. News had come through that the death warrant had not been signed, the Queen of England had become squeamish in the face of the prospect of her vilification by her peers of Europe. Assassination? There might well be an assassination.

Snow lay heavy over Europe that winter. Snow encased Cambridge and kept Kit, to his small regret, bound in. He gathered wood and sat by his chamber fire and, on the day

of the feast of the birth of the child he could no longer see
as his Saviour, he was busy at his play. In January the thaw
came briefly and passed. On an icy road Nick Faunt's horse
slithered and recovered and slithered again as he returned to
London from northern business, pausing awhile at Cambridge.
He came to Kit's chamber burring with the chill, bowing to the
fire like a son of Zoroaster.

— You have been out of things. Skeres told me of your
heaving and spewing. You are become the good student again,
I note your ragged black. But this that you are writing is not
student stuff. I recall your Techelles and Bajazeth. Now you
have kings of Argier and Fez and Morocco. In your fancy you
travel wide. Yet you hug yourself to yourself.

— Are you come with orders from Walsingham? I am done
with it all.

— You will never be done, as you know. Hoops of steel
and the like. But you talk of Walsingham, and you would
pity the man if you saw him. You know of Sidney's death at
Zutphen?

— We had sermons till we were sick with them. Thy need
is greater than mine. The Protestant Knight.

— And Walsingham's son in law. He has to see to the
creditors he has left behind. That will delay the state funeral,
he says. It would be unjust and shameful to bring out the black
plumes while poor creditors scream for payment. Sir Francis is
a great man for justice.

— Aye, a great man. Has he found means of killing a
queen in the full odour of justice?

— There has to be a new plot afoot. It was thought you
might wish to be part of it. Something to do with the French
ambassador putting gunpowder under Queen Elizabeth's bed.
Forgeries, of course. That will put him under house arrest and
stop his crying to his king for pleas for Scotch Mary's release.
And there must be rumours of Mary's escape and Spaniards
flooding into Kent and Sussex, then marching to set London
afire. You could help spread the rumours.

— I will have nothing to do with it. You may tell Sir Francis

I am returned to the state you see, a poor scholar that works for his master's hood and is bound to his books.

— Sir Francis will weep bitterly. And Poley still in the Tower will weep yet more.

— There it is. Poley was by way of being my tutor and keeper. And Poley is done and so I am done.

— And yet, Faunt said, taking up a sheet from Kit's table, you dislike not the great world of power.

> *A god is not so glorious as a kynge*
> *I thinke the pleasure they enjoie in heauen*
> *Cannot compare with kinglie joies on earth.*

And all this of riding in triumph through Persepolis. You are on fire with the great world.

— Reduced to a poet's perspective. Enlarged through his fancy.

— Shall we eat at the Angel? We can ride the ice without the motion of a leg muscle.

— Mr Secretary will pay and bind me to him again?

— Ah no, this is money from another source. A man must have many sources.

The death warrant was signed on February 1. Queen Elizabeth feigned reluctance, it was but a matter of the need of the nation with the Spaniards already landed in Wales and the capital guarded of necessity by armed levies. As for Mr Secretary, sick in his chamber, *the grief thereof*, she said, *will go near to kill him outright.* And one week later the Queen of Scots, given but a day's warning, was beheaded in a late sunrise of winter, and her little dogs trotted out from under her skirts to lap her blood. So all were happy, with the London mob lighting a great fire outside the French Embassy and knocking on the door to beg wood for it. The fires and dancing and bells and songs would have gone on like an endless carnival had not the imposed Ash Wednesday, though it was truly a Thursday, of Sir Philip Sidney's funeral shut the toothed mouth of rejoicing. Many of the fellows and students of Cambridge rode down, some even walked, that they might witness the obsequies. Kit stayed where he was. Tom Lewgar came back bubbling with a piece of poetastry he had writ:

The broken launce, the battle axe reversed
Came far before the corse of him inhearsed,
Portcullis bore the spurs, Blue Mantle next
The gauntlets, Rouge Dragon then elects
The plumed helmet for his charge. See yet
The tabard in the arms of Somerset,
Richmond the shield, Clarencieux King at Arms
Beareth a banner torn by war's alarums,
Then fourteen yeomen, aye I counted all,
Bore the black coffin with its velvet pall.

— A good torchecul or arsewipe, Kit said. Bad rhymes, foul
metre. You dishonour one that was a poet before he was a
soldier.

— Can you do better, eh, can you do better? Little Lewgar
frothed and danced in his little rage.

— *Better* does not come into it. Is a lion better than a
flea? But here we have a flea that is lame and blemished and
cannot jump. Go back to your study of ballockless Origen and
leave verse to them that have ears and counting fingers.

— I know of your atheism too.

— I descry no pertinence there. *Next* and *elects*, though.
That could be accounted worse than atheism. Go away.

IT was a few weeks before the beginning of the long vacation
that Tom Walsingham came, unaccompanied by Ingram Frizer.
Kit found him in his room, reading sheets of the play that was
coming to its close. Barnabas Ridley, still Kit's chamberfellow,
sat at the same table conning lecture notes. Ridley was one of an
ancient breed that could not internalise the words he read: he was
mumbling about the heresy of Sabellius. Tom, not mumbling,
said:

— Good bloody stuff here.

Thy streetes strowed with disseuered iointes of men,
And wounded bodies gasping yet for life.

And I like this of the sun-bright troop of heavenly virgins on
horsemen's lances to be hoisted up. So this is why we have not
seen you. Immured with heavenly poesy or some such thing.

— Barnabas, Kit said kindly, is it not time for your amorous
visit?

— Oh, I have done with her. I decided it was not meet
and fitting.

— We can go out into the sun, Tom said. Leave your
friend to his holy studies.

— But Sabellius was not holy, he was a heresiarch.

— Very well, Kit said. So they went out and walked.

— A long time, Tom said, kicking a dead cat out of his
path. From summer to summer, near. I would have come earlier
but there were things to be done. My Machiavellian cousin had
employment for me in one place and another.

— I should have thought there was no employment left
after Sir Francis Machiavel had killed a queen.

— Oh, there is rage in France about that killing, and the
Spanish are whetting their knives and caulking their bumboats.
There have been things to do and still are. That is why you must
ride back to London with me.

— Must must must?

— You are still in the Service, so they tell me.

— But this is the sole cause of your visit?

— There are sunderings and there are reconciliations. But
was there a sundering? I cannot recall our shaking hands on
a parting with it is better so dear friend.

— We shared something though at a distance one from the
other. A Walsingham, so I took it, had to be there. What we
might have shared is a shame and a revulsion at what can be
done with a man's body.

— Ah ah. Strowed with dissevered somethings of something. Streets, yes. But it was green grass, brown really with
the drought, that drank blood and was the better for it. Well,

100

you know that had to be done. And we, in our several ways, worked for it.

— You can smile? Yes, that I cannot argues my innocence.

— Innocent, you innocent? You were never so innocent. In Rheims, remember? You knew all about tearing men's bodies and making blood flow where no hangman would have looked for it.

— Trickle, not flow. There remains the great mystery.

— Jesus, we are now on to mysteries. He thrust aside with some force a sycamore twig that would have pierced his eye. They walked on into sun that leaves did not allay.

— I mean the body and the soul, whatever the soul is. Oh, I know what the soul is. Plato's butterfly. Love and so on. Mingling of entities.

— Here is a true butterfly on my hand, Tom said. Cream and vermilion or some such colour. Away to whatever butterflies do. And he puffed breath at it. Yet it flapped off in its own good time.

— Yet, Kit said, and he picked up a fallen branch and switched his leg with it, we are ensnared in a manner. You talk of reconciliation. How do we reconcile the throbbing of the nerves with that essence that some call – Oh, no matter, never mind.

— There goes the schoolman. You think too much. Is it not enough to enlace bare bodies and do what was done, and no guilt. Life, as we see, is papilian. Is that the word? Frizer picked it up somewhere, a great picker up. You must come back and brave Frizer. When you have done what has to be done. And we can pass a night at an inn on the way. Where? At Bishop's Stortford? I think that a bishop's stort must be a great fleshly weapon, but that is my fancy only. Or at Harlow that is nearly your name.

— My rhymesake. Well, we will ride.

Riding, he tried out to the fields, the wind, and his companion:

> . . . this fair face and heavenly hue
> Must grace his bed that conquers Asia
> And means to be a terror to the world.

Brave words, and some of their lilt and superbity were in his voice on Seething Lane when he stood before Walsingham and said he would not go. Mr Secretary looked very weary.

— You are committed. I have your name somewhere on a document. But it is not inky blots that matter. It is words like country and danger and loyalty and the truths that lie within those words. So sir, we will not have this frowardness and you will do your duty as you did it before, not that it was much of a duty.

— It got men hanged and disembowelled and the head of a lawful queen lopped off.

— Lawful? You say she was lawful? She that would have flung this realm into a riot and lopped off heads uncountable of true protestant believers?

— I will not be party to more shedding of blood.

— You will be what I say, sir. And you may look to your standing at the university, whichever it is, for there is more to the conferring of degrees than passing in your attendances and your disputations.

— You mean you could block my mastership?

— Block, block, aye, a good word block. You shall be blocked and be bleak and black in your future if you do not what I say.

— So I am threatened.

— We are all threatened, damn you. The Spanish threaten us.

— I have heard this before about the Spaniards in Kent and Sussex. It was a cause of laughter in Canterbury and all a great lie.

— Do not you talk to me of lies. They will be coming in their great ships and the thumbscrews of their inquisitors ready if the war party has not its way.

— What is this war party?

— Sit, sit (for Kit still stood), you know nothing, a boy at his books. I am a tired man, see, and age etches deep and I am not in myself well. And there is much to carry and little thanks. And poor Poley dare not leave the Tower yet so I am not rich in good men. It was Poley who said you might do it.

— Do what?

— As I say, there is the war party. There is also the peace party. This will make peace with the Duke of Parma in the Low Countries. The Queen is for this, for she hateth war. But the war party would have Drake, you know of Drake, no you do not, why should you, have him I say raiding the Spanish coast and so instigating war. I am for war.

— For blood. That I understand.

— You understand nothing, puppy. Have the Spanish come and so make an end to it. Drown Antichrist in English waters, let it come and be damned to them all. Then that will be the end of the Catholic menace. Then we may breathe easy a while and gird our loins for the other enemy.

— Which is, who is?

— Ignorant of all but the staleness and dust of libraries. I know you, fool. The Brownists, the republicans, the purifiers as they call themselves. They will be purified, I can tell you, fool. They will be as a puff of the wind that blows from their bowels to their lousy text-chopping chaps.

— Disembowelled, of course. And their manhood scissored off.

— Enough, you make me more weary than I am. My dear son in law, despite his damnable debts, he was the best of men. He was of the war party and there was a great flow of letters from Flushing.

— Where?

— Flushing that the Dutch call Vlissingen for some good reason they hold to their fleshy bosoms. Because Sir Philip, rest his broken bones, was governor there, it is a town of ours, and his younger brother Sir Robert is not half the man, nay not a quarter.

— Quartering is also in your mind.

— I will not have this insolence, do you hear me, I will not have a half-bearded chit jibing when there is a full-grown beard to be singed. Well, you are to take ship at Deptford and proceed to Flushing and no argument.

— There what to do?

— To get news from a man named Wychgerde, Witchguard, some such name, I cannot say but here it is writ. His first name is Jan which I take to be John. He sells butter and fish and wheat of the Baltic to the Spanish armies. He sells English cloth on the Rhine. It is to him trade, a matter of indifference, but he leans most to us being of the true faith and hates the Spanish for their cruelty. But he is close to the Duke of Parma. And what is his lousy grace of Parma at at this moment? Why, he is besieging Ostend which has an English garrison but with no large force or conviction. So what is this? Is it because he wishes to negotiate peace or is it to cover a true and bloody attack elsewhere in the Low Countries? Wychgerde will know. If it is for peace then Drake may raid and instigate war. Do you follow me? I see your eyelids droop.

— I think I follow. So if it seems there is to be peace you will start a war. And this is the message I bring back and the Spanish will capture me riding a lonely road and be forewarned?

— There will be no written message. Yes for war and no for the other thing.

— A little word to set spinning a war. How do I meet this Dutch butterseller?

— Through Baines. You will know Baines, he was at Rheims the time of your assignment.

— I know no Baines.

— Well, he knew you. He watched you at your carousal with foul Foscue and the others. When you see his face you will know his face. A young grave man that yet frequents taverns and walks the waterfront. He awaits English ships, he will find you. Go now to Philips or Phelips and draw passage money. You are a bold young man (here he softened) and your speaking out offers little offence. It signifies that you know your friends.

Kit did not well understand this. He went to the room where the pocked and bespectacled one wove his villainies, nay he must not say or think that. But when he found him mole-blind and trying to grow eyes on his finger-ends he could not resist saying:

— A holiday then from forgery.

— Eh, eh? Who are you? They are broke. They fell and this fool or that fool, both deny it, planted a heavy hoof and they shattered. A grinding of new takes long. So he says of money for passage. You, filthy Howell, get the box and here is the key and I can finger out what is needful.

And so the boat from London Bridge to Deptford, where the *Golden Hind* stood to be chipped of its timber by those that came to admire, where too the shipyards rang loud with hammering. On glass unflawed the *Peppercorn* took the Thames tide and put to sea to reach the mouth of the Dutch river Schelde, and Kit felt no qualm, felt rather he might yet prove a sailor. And here at Flushing he heard hardly one word of the neighing Dutch tongue, it was all Englishmen, many soldiers, some wounded awaiting shipment, others formed up in their squadrons to march inland against the Spaniards. And on the quay indeed there was Baines, Dick Baines, with a horny hand to greet but no welcome in the face that was thin and too watchful. A bell tolled, and it was of the English church of St Nicholas. That, said Baines, is the Gevangentoren, it is their town prison, and my lodging is behind, and there you may lie the night or two that is needful. See, how those Dutch boys spit at us, they are all ungrateful bastards. Come to that tavern there and wash the salt from your mouth.

They sat and drank Dutch beer from ceramical mugs, they were chipped and fragile, not good English pewter.

— Pewter? Baines said. Aye, you may well talk of pewter. Pewter is become my life, it is why I am here. I will get them yet, you will see.

— Murky, like this beer. This is noisy. And Kit blinked through the near-dark at swilling and bragging soldiers. Who and what?

— The coiners. There is no money for the English that fight for Spain. They are cut off from what money they have in England, and the Spanish are slow and bad payers when they pay at all. So there has to be coining, and the metal is pewter with a wash of silver over it.

The beer was indeed murky but it had an airy quality that rose easily to the head. Kit said, after thinking: If it passes and purchases and keeps passing it will serve as true money.

— And so royal heads may be stamped with no royal mandate? Is not this cheating and treason? Baines looked very sternly on Kit.

— Who is doing this?

— Gilbert that is a goldsmith and reputed a good man in metals, though he is a villain. And others here and elsewhere. Gilbert should be haled home and sent to trial but Sidney the governor is slow to issue a warrant. There is a part of his head that cannot see the crime. What passes for money, he says, must be accounted money. This is rank heresy.

— Have you any of these?

Baines took with a hard look the purse at his waist and shook a few ill-shaped pieces shilling-sized out so that they clanked dismally on the table. A drinking soldier peered, hearing the dull ring, and took one without permission to try with his teeth. He threw it down with a loud mouth-fart. Kit peered too. It had an ill-wrought Queen of England on its face. Baines said:

— That man there, see, knew it for bad goods.

— But with a right stamp and worthless metal any man could do it?

— There are many taught by Gilbert how to do it. I will kick him into the hold of the ship that takes him to the gallows. It is a foul crime and a heresy.

— I am not altogether sure of the foul crime but I am ready to be taught. *Heresy* is not the right word.

— I say heresy because my faith is in good money. All other faith is nothing to that, since the work of the world comes first, a man's bread and milk for his infants, and for the rest it is a matter of what governments decree. I follow the true Church but do not argue. I would not go to the gallows for faith of the spirit. My god is Gresham, and the State would agree.

— I do not know Gresham.

— No matter. All that matters is that the Spanish do not invade. Are you for peace or war?

— You mean the declaring of war? Let us have more of this murky beer. I am not for anything, a man must be passive and wait on his masters. But I am to see a Dutch butterman. Witchguard or some such name. He will say whether there is to be war or no.

— Wychgerde you mean. There will be an unlading of cloth on the *Peppercorn*. It will go into his warehouse and he will be there tomorrow or next day. Here is more of the murk.

They dined later in a Dutch ordinary on fish of the Schelde that tasted of mud, though the mud was well overlaid by a salty sauce. They had a beer that was clear and not murky. Baines had but two rooms over a baker's shop. The hot breath of its ovens, which rose through cracks in the floor, was heartening. Baines would not give up his narrow bed: Kit must sleep with his nose to the fumes, covered with a threadbare blanket, his head on his leathern bag. But before bed Baines took down from a shelf that held a pot and a comb and a spare boot his Greek New Testament.

— Do you read this?

— I have studied it at Cambridge. I do not read it for pleasure. It is filthily written.

— You dare to say that?

— The truth or untruth of it is not thereby affected.

— You speak of untruth, is that possible?

— There is one truth I will admit, and that is religion was founded to keep men in awe. You seem shocked.

— I am not so. I submit to believing what I am bid to believe, but I hold as a true protestant that a man is free to enquire of the meaning of what he reads.

— Amen to that. It is the Old Testament I most quarrel with. There be authors of great antiquity, some of them of India, some of antiquity some sixteen thousand years agone, and yet Adam is proved to have lived within six thousand years. And I have no great opinion of Moses, an Egyptian juggler that used tricks to keep the Jews in awe. As for his forty years in the wilderness, that journey could be accomplished in less than a year, and he kept circling round that those privy to his subtleties might die and a new generation be born to an everlasting superstition.

— You say all this openly?

— I am ready to do so in open disputation, but I am snapped off before I may begin.

— You are one after my heart. But you must learn of the primacy of money and of the foul sin of coining.

— You have then what might be termed a theology of money?

— Morality you might say, God does not come into it. Oh, he may, he may damn the coiners, it is something to be thought on. For to coin is to lie, and does not God hate a liar? It is to say that what is nothing in itself is much, for money is but a token of things made or done. And so this lie and nothingness escapes on dark nights from here to them that fight for the Spaniards, and Sidney the governor will do nothing. *Pecunia* is from *pecus* which is cattle, and cattle are a solidity. But this coined money is but air. Aye, God must come into it. Gifford Gilbert must be burned as a sinner and scream as he burns.

— Gilbert Gifford?

— You have it arsiversy. Aye, I know the other name and the man too, he was at Rheims. But it would not be possible to turn coat so fast.

— There is enough turning.

— Aye, enough. Baines had been so intent on his commination of coining that he had stripped himself entire unawares and so stood. Now he recovered and masked blushing his bare privities with his hands. With this masking reduced to one hand he masked his bare body by getting into his bed and then masked himself totally and his guest too by dousing his one candle. Kit smiled at this as he lay with his nose to the gush of baking. From the dark Baines said:

— We have forgot our prayers.

— Take them as said.

— Aye. Jesus Christ in a manner offended against good money by beating the bankers in the Temple. Have you thought on this?

— Never.

— I think much on Christ.

— As a man should.

— I think on him and the beloved disciple John and ask why he must like better one than the eleven others.

— A man may have a particular friend, it is in nature.

— Did they then lie together?

— Christ was a man. A man may perform the act of Sodom. Ergo Christ may have done this and thought it no shame.

— But that would offend the Godhead in him. Would it be so offended if he lay with Mary the Magdalen?

— This is no time for speculation of Holy Writ. I have had a long voyage. That fish does not sit well.

— Aye, a fish. They turned Christ into a fish. It is a kind of false coining.

Kit feigned sleep but Baines muttered. Before sleep came to either there was a noise on the cobbles without and below: it was of troops being marshalled for a night march inland, and the cries of ancient or sergeant were loud. The setting off was ragged and there was swearing in the ranks. The shogging feet distanced, and Baines through the dark spoke, saying:

— The Holy Ghost filled Mary the mother of Christ while that she was yet unmarried. Does that render her dishonest?

— Some say so. Why do you raise these matters?

— There is none to whom I may speak here. Your coming is to me by way of being a chance of the opening up of minds. It is the primacy of money that sets up my doubts. For bishops and others that feed us with the faith are paid but produce nothing. They are not as brewers and bakers and shoemakers. They eat the substance of them that work and themselves do none. This is dangerous talk, that I know.

— With me you are in no danger.

— That too I know. And in such security I sleep.

This meant little. Kit tossed while the baking fumes came up and Baines breathed deep and steady. Baines was up at dawn and Kit would fain have slept longer, but there was the matter of meeting this Dutch butterman. They went, Kit tottering somewhat, to the tavern of yesterday, and there Baines was nice in the ordering of right English lamb's wool, though it was no cold morning. The beer hot and roasted apples pounded in, then ginger, nutmeg, cinnamon, cloves, then there were your apple shreds floating in beer as shorn wool flew in a windstorm. Kit got the reward his nose of the night claimed in fresh bread and Dutch butter. The butterman, he at length said.

They walked to the warehouses that lined the quay, and Baines spoke Dutch, Flemish rather, and got shaken heads from warehousemen. He is not here, he said unnecessarily. They say he is at Zeebrugge or else Knocke. You must go thither.

— Are they not very close to Ostend? Will there not be Spaniards about? Is it safe for an Englishman?

— Not safe. We had best go back to our discussion.

— When does the *Peppercorn* sail?

— On the evening tide, they say. You are eager to go home? You cannot be blamed. Perhaps my talk wearies you.

— No no no no. Would it be a manner of false coining if I took home the supposed words of a Dutchman I have no strong desire to meet? Mr Secretary wants war, well, let him have it.

— It will begin with robbery, Baines said. Spanish gold pouring in in ships of English pirates. And fools will think that an augmentation of wealth whereas it will be the opposite. Let us sit there under that elm and shake heads at the folly of the world. Look at those fishermen there with their morning catches. They are base fellows neither of wit nor worth. And Christ's apostles were fishermen. What think you of that?

AND so, with no nod from Mynher Wychgerde, Kit sailed back to Deptford on the *Peppercorn*, took a boat to London Bridge, and made a false report to Mr Secretary. Then he found Tom Walsingham alone at Scadbury. Frizer was at some distant task, beneficent alike to master and servant, that entailed coney-catching. Kit took the whole house as an unravished bride. He lay with his love in every room that invited. Then, weary but elated, he rode back to Cambridge. He patted in his breast a sealed paper, given to him by Walsingham, that was marked *To Whom It Concerneth*. At Cambridge the man was swiftly demoted to schoolboy.

Thomas Norgate, Master of Corpus Christi, sat at a paper-loaded desk that yet found room for a human skull. This grinned without mirth at Kit. Norgate was a cold man and, even on this summer day, had his casement tight shut to enclose, like precious frankincense, the smell of himself and his frowsty learning. Coldly he said:

— What are you – Merlin or Marlin or Morley?

— Merlin is a magical name. Some call me by it.

— Well or ill bethought. You know one Thomas Fineux?

— A boy of Dover. A gentleman pensioner, so called, and but begun here. He was hanging about me and I thrust him off.

— I am told he has been going into the woods at midnight and praying, God help us, that the devil may appear. Is this your work? He says that it is.

— I told him to go to the devil more than once. He seems a literal-minded youth.

— This fits to a pattern. You have not yet gotten a title. It argues a rejection of orders. Why is this?

— I have not yet found a rector willing to accept me as a curate. I search and search but vainly.

— I put it to you that you search otherwhither and with false intention. I put it to you that you are joining the Catholics here.

— Never that. I have listed names of the papishly inclined and was minded to submit this roll of infamy but it is become lost among my papers.

— So what is this of your travelling to Rheims? Your absences have been noted. They are in excess of what is allowed.

— I paid one visit to Rheims, another to Paris, one final

one, from which I have returned, to the Low Countries. On business which I may not divulge on high instructions.

— You are but a student, sir, and may not speak so high-handed. I have information from Thomas Lewgar that you talk loosely of religion.

— This is the malice of one who thinks himself to be a poet but is no more than a deplorable rhymester.

— Well, after much consideration, and with an unanimity of opinion that may not be gainsaid, the decision is that your *Supplicat* is not to be entertained and you may not proceed to *Magister Artium*.

— This, if I may say so, is an outrage and an injustice. I have fulfilled all obligations for the degree.

— This may be so, but the unsoundness of your religion, your frequent absences, and the derogations of your fellows forbid the granting of it. Your baccalaureate is intact, your mastership denied. There is to be no argument. You may leave.

Kit did not leave. He drew from his breast a sealed paper.

— Master, be good enough to read this. It is not addressed specifically to you, but you it concerns.

— In my good time I will read it.

— I would that you read it now, and aloud. I know not its content but do know that I am in some measure its subject. In what measure I wish to know.

— You may not give me orders.

— I beseech you.

Norgate grumblingly broke the seal and spread the parchment. He read to himself first and then to Kit. He had a wart of some size on his left cheek. This, while he read, he irritably scratched.

— Whereas it was reported that Christopher Marlowe (so that is your name) was determined to have gone beyond the seas to Rheims there to remain, their Lordships think it good to certify that he had no such intention and that in all his actions he has behaved himself orderly and discreetly, whereby he has done Her Majesty good service and deserves to be rewarded for his faithful dealing. Their Lordships request that the rumour thereof shall be allayed by all possible means and that he shall be furthered in the degree he is to take this coming Commencement; because it is not Her Majesty's pleasure that anyone employed as he has been in matters touching the benefit of his country should be defamed by those who are ignorant in the affairs he went about.

— The Privy Council, Norgate then said in an aliger voice. What have we at Cambridge to do with the Privy Council? They must let us alone here, we govern ourselves, we are by way of being totally autonomous. (The plethora of t's there made his tongue titubate, yet it was a brave show.) We rejected that farm of wines, we will reject other things.

— The Queen's name is not there, Kit said, but perhaps that of the Archbishop of Canterbury is.

— Well, Norgate later said, some thirty seconds, it shall be considered.

Kit was not to forget that date, July 4, which was called Commencement but was truly a triumphal end, and yet in a manner it was a commencement for now, gowned and hooded as *magister*, mark that, *artium*, of arts a master, proceeding to music, M.A., he might begin a few years of achieve and mastery, bringing to the playhouse the firm ground or pinning of his learnedness matched to his own fire, yet but a few years, alas, a very few, alas alas, a very very few.

PART TWO

AM not, so I suppose I must suppose, yet done with supposing, though from now, which is the latter half of the year of grace or otherwise 1587, I have Kit much in my sight as a citizen of London. More than that, and indeed in especial, he has become one of us, the playmakers, the feeders with bloody or farcical fodder of the maws of the seekers of diversion. He came to live on the upper floor of a house, no more than a cottage, in Bishopsgate Street at the corner of Hog Lane, not far from Tom Watson's dwelling, though Watson was now a tutor to the son of William Cornwallis in their great house in the Bishopsgate region (spying too belike, since the Cornwallis family was Catholic, and with the smell of Spanish invasion all about, such had still to be watched). Here elms rustled, and the turning of the spars of the three windmills of Finsbury Fields made a soothing music for the eye. The Theatre and the Curtain were near, this was the playman's district, though the latter was near done for and the former yielding in trade to our new playhouse across the waters.

For, though later than he had foretold, Henslowe was now able to view with proprietorial pride the completed edifice of the Rose that had supplanted the roses long planted on the site. The Rose smelt of no roses, rather still of size and paint and the armpits of the groundlings added. It lay between the bearpit and the bullpit, which resounded with snarls and the tearing of collops of flesh of the baiting dogs that yelped their descant. Here blood spattered on to the dirty jerkins of them that paid to behold the entertainment of biting and rending, but that was a prized prize, see I have here and I will not wash it off blood from the veins of Sackerson or Harry Hunks and the hounds that have no name. And here too were Henslowe's brothels, where no blood was let save that of twelve-year-old virgins, very costly and only for the better sort. The blood let on the stage of the Rose

117

was in manner of a second letting, blood already let of pigs and enclosed in bladders themselves enclosed in the garments of our players who, in the comedy of killing, must gush out their lives to the mob's applause.

We who played there thought the Rose a fine structure. Its plan was much the plan of the innyards wherein our trade had its ignoble genesis. That is to say, there were upper and lower galleries all around though with no bedchambers behind, furnished with benches from which the shilling-payers could look down on the penny-payers. And the stage itself had its upper gallery, called the terrace or tarrass, and above that a tower with a flag that flared in the wind during the two hours of performance. The stage was a platform that thrust into the midst of the standing auditors, pillared so that the roof or heavens, zodiac-painted under, might be supported. There was a trap-door that opened on to the cellarage, which could be our Christian hell or else a cooler pagan underworld. At the rear of the stage was the space we termed the study, wherein players might be disclosed at study, talk, or murder, for it was curtained or uncurtained according to need, and the curtain was a fine embroidery of roses stitched on by Henslowe's whores in their not ample free time. Exit and entrance were by left and right doorways. None could ask better for our swift traffic of the afternoon: here were all the possibilities of speed and change, here is Scythia, here is Persia, or not, here is nowhere but the fire of words, and that fire could rain down on the groundlings who gaped up or flare on the highest payers, gentlemen of the Inns of Court, that had their chairs as frame to the action. And beyond our noise was the noise of dogs and bears and bulls and the imagined noise of them that came to their blissful dying in the trugging houses of Henslowe.

Well, here we had *Tamburlaine*, that Kit had been working on all that while while feigning his divinity studies or, not so feigning, snouting out the dissidents on Mr Secretary's instructions. It was a thunderstorm to our stage. Oh true, we had Tom Kyd's *Spanish Tragedy*, that pleased ever, but little else save ill-wrought clanking scrannelpipe confections, of which Tom Kyd's *Hamlet Revenge* was one. It could not hold, its mad prince was but Hieronimo writ small, its one memorable cry *Blood is a beggar* was a poor pennyworth, and if the script was lost to the future it would be no hardship. But with *Tamburlaine*, in which I played the divine Zenocrate, there were voices that spoke to a world greater than the playhouse, for they were voices that bade us better comprehend the times and question old assumptions. What was Tamburlaine? No more than a nothingness that rose to universal power through a thrust from within, not a favour bestowed from without. So here was Cosroe:

> *What means this diuelish shepheard to aspire*
> *With such a Giantly presumption,*
> *To cast vp hils against the face of heauen*
> *And dare the force of angrie Iupiter.*

And here was Ortygius:

> *What God or Feend, or spirit of the earth,*
> *Or Monster turned to a manly shape,*
> *Or of what mould or mettel he be made,*
> *What star or state soeuer gouerne him . . .*
> *Whether from earth, or hell, or heauen he grow.*

But there was Tamburlaine:

> *Nature that fram'd us of foure elements*
> *Warring within our breasts for regiment*
> *Doth teache vs all to haue aspyring mindes:*
> *Our soules, whose faculties can comprehend*
> *The wondrous architecture of the worlde*
> *And measure euerie wand'ring planetes course,*
> *Still climbing after knowledge infinite*
> *And alwaies mouing as the restlesse spheares*
> *Will vs to weare ourselues and neuer reste*
> *Until we reache the ripest fruite of all*
> *That perfect blisse and sole felicitie*
> *The sweet fruition of an earthly crowne.*

I cite the text I have, having forgotten what I once knew by heart. But in memory I hear still Ned Alleyn's thunder or, to me

119

as Zenocrate, the honey of wooing, and, from backstage, see his throat bared to the dust as to a dagger while he gulped what he termed his lubricant ale. Then back onstage to conquer Persia, Africa, Europe, Asia, India, ride in triumph through Persepolis, slaughter the Turks, the Tartars, the Babylonians and even yearn towards enchaining the meteors, the moon, Saturn, the sun. And always this lust not easily slaked, except when he turned to me, his divine Zenocrate, transformed to a manner of courtier no court could have taught.

I say lust and lust again. It was all Kit lusting, a male body augmented to a world his prey and no retribution. In a dream of lust all is permitted, tear his throat out, madden him that he batter his brains to a pulp, harness him like a horse, lay on the whip. Some thought the beastliness went too far, when Tamburlaine offered captive Bajazeth meat on his sword-point with Here, eat sir, take it or I'll thrust the blade to thy heart, and Bajazeth taking it only to stamp on it, and then Tamburlaine crying Take it up villain and eat it, or I will make thee slice the brawns of thy arms into carbonadoes and eat them. And Usumcasane mocked: Nay, 'twere better he killed his wife, and then she shall be sure not to be starved, and he provided for a month's victual before hand. And then Tamburlaine: Here is my dagger, dispatch her while she is fat, for if she live but a while longer she will fall into a consumption with fretting, and then she will not be worth the eating.

— A sniggering kind of brutality, Greene said in the Unicorn, unworthy. The anthropophagous is no subject even for tragedy, and here it is a kind of comedy.

— That, Kit said, was Tom Watson's contribution. He is always calling for the seasoning of laughter.

— It is the wrong laughter, it is the laughter of excess. All that could happen in the most fevered of nightmares is made to happen, and pathos is murdered by excess and the throat is tickled against its will to laughter. Have you not seen men being dragged to the scaffold laughing? Where there is laughter and no simple causative that is harmless and wholesome, well then you may suspect an excess of the brutal. It is unworthy.

120

Kit looked on Robert Greene. He had seen him at Cambridge often enough, another profane one, drunken often, swearing much, taking his mastership at Clare College in Kit's own fourth year at Corpus Christi. He would now be thirty and looked more. His fiery beard was pointed like a steeple spire in a lake's reflection; his hair, uncut, stared to all the points of a compass rose. His teeth showed their rotting waists, his nails, much chewed by them, harboured the grease he scratched from his lousiness. His stockings were silk but foully twisted and the cloak tied at his breast but thrust over his shoulders was of the pitiful green, much spotted, of a duck's turd. He said:

— And I utter this condemnation if you will take it, as you must, since you are my junior and backward in morality, that here is the atheist Tamburlaine and no hint of his wrong, no chorus warning of the downfall, no hovering Christian dove bespeaking judgement – You follow me? It is as though we are all to kneel before him and say yes yes, this is the crown of life to which we would all aspire an we were let. It is an immoral effusion.

— Are you so much for morality?

Greene looked suspiciously from his pig's eyes that were of a piss colour saying:

— I know what you think. Here is one living with a trull whose brother is a cutpurse and who has begot a brat –

— I approve the name Fortunatus. It could also be Faustus.

— Whatever you approve, here it is. Now you must consider that a man may embrace the divide between body and spirit.

— A divide is a nothing and cannot be embraced.

— Let that pass. I have done wrong, no man more, but I recognise the heavenly light of goodness the better for splashing in the mud. I call myself a moral man. Am I not a moral man? he asked his companion, his minder and mistress's bully, also her brother.

— If you will it be so, Cutting Ball said, a reeking ruffian in a black hat of exorbitant but drooping brim.

— He is one of the innocent, Greene said to Kit, who have never been oppressed with morality. He thinks a moral to be a mulberry. He would go as your Tamburlaine goes if he could, he altogether approves of the whipping and the killing.

— You too. You are there many afternoons.

— I thought to enter the game myself. Pamphlets are well enough but there is a pleasure in hearing one's fine lines mouthed.

— This you know without the testing?

— I have sung out some to the morning air. They promise well. I have a ten-year advantage over you. I have read more.

— He is, Cutting Ball said, a magistrate arses.

— *Magister artis, artium*, fool. So is he here, but his ink is hardly dry. I will out-Tamburlaine you, you will see else.

— I must go. And he went, somewhat flown, to dig pen in (hardly dry was right. Learning stood out sophomorically) and endite *Tamburlaine* the second part. Paul Ive's *The Treatise of Fortification*. Ortelius's *Theatrum Orbis Terrarum*. The lore of the physician:

> *I view'd your urine and the hypostasis*
> *Thicke and obscure doth make your daunger greate:*
> *Your veins are full of accidental heate*
> *Whereby the moisture of your bloud is dried;*
> *The humidum and calor which some hold*
> *Is not a parcel of the elements*
> *But of a substance more divine and pure*
> *Is almost clean extinguished and spent,*
> *Which being the cause of life imports your death.*

This is Tamburlaine dying not because of assassin's knife or blow in battle but from nature which framed him of four elements. And I died too, divine Zenocrate. But there was life enough, with Ned Alleyn in coat with copper lace and crimson velvet breeches drawn in his chariot by the Kings of Trebizon and Soria with bits in their mouths, lashing them and crying:

> *Holla, ye pamper'd jades of Asia,*
> *What, can ye draw but twenty miles a day?*

It was in the November, with breath steaming from the

122

groundlings, that true not pig's blood was drawn and, in a manner, the needful gory baptism, desired by all architects for their new erections but rarely fulfilled, was, in a rare fashion, fulfilled. The Governor of Babylon was tied to his turret post and was to be mock-killed with a caliver. Timmins, charged with this shooting, saw too late that the charge was live, and, in deflecting his piece, aimed at a child, a woman big with child, and a man near her. The woman was killed, as was the child *in utero* and the one *ex utero*, and the man hurt in his head very sore. The play, by consent of the majority of watchers, proceeded, as nothing would be served by feigned regret and mourning. This was the afternoon that there were viewers in the lord's box.

This lord's box was a contrivance of Philip Henslowe, being a room curtained, supplied with good chairs and a fire and what of drink its occupiers wished, placed between left and right upper galleries and costing for the afternoon's hire some ten shillings. The better sort did not cavil at this, as a whole noble family, from tiny prattler to chumbling great grandfather, could with ease be accommodated, but this day there were only the Earl of Northumberland and Sir Walter Raleigh. They had come in a private boat with liveried oarsmen, in finery but masked, so none knew who they were until the play's end and the dispersal of the brawling, base and popular. Then they appeared unmasked in the greenroom to much fawning and twittering. Henslowe was near on his knees with obsequious adulation: what will your lordship take, and you your worship Sir Walter, it is no trouble, it may be sent out for, dust those chairs boy, we are highly honoured (with much breath on the *honoured*, though none on the *highly*). So the two were seated, and the Earl, who was young but reputed learned, indeed called the Wizard Earl for his skill in necromantics, enquired pleasantly if there was a true slaughter at every performance, and Henslowe replied in his fluster Alas no. It was as though, if his lordship wished, another could be contrived at their next visit with ease. And Sir Walter in his thick Devonian that appeared to encrust his utterance with sea salt said:

123

— Well, it was done so in the plays of Nero's time. Were not condemned criminals made unwilling actors in the action, beheaded in bloody truth on the stage and not in histrionic fancy? Perhaps some link or marriage might be made between our hanging magistrates and your company, Mr Mr I know not your name.

— Henslowe, Philip, Sir Walter, Henslowe, some say Hounslow.

— Hounds low more than hens, no matter. And who is your Tamburlaine? Ah, I see him. A burden to the voice, your part, sir. Slake, slake, continue, you need it.

— And where is the poet? the Wizard Earl asked.

The poet was with myself in the rear of the tiring house. I had appeared for the final jig in my Zenocrate skirt and bodice to show I was resurrected from my death, and, now naked, Kit had seized me with loving congratulations on my performance. He seemed unfaithful to Tom Walsingham, or else, sundered, they had made some bargain about vicarious colling and thrusting unclear to any outside their covenant or compact. Now Kit heard himself called for, smacked a kiss on my lips heavy painted in ochre, then went to his summons.

— So, he said to Sir Walter, I meet my poetic rebuker.

— Oh that, oh that. The wisdom of age answered youth's hot avowals. Yet not hot either. A cool and sweet pastoral, very pretty. This that you gave us today was not so pretty. No rebuke, a balance rather.

— The dramatic opposes the lyrical. But here was something of the lyrical.

— To entertain divine Zenocrate, aye aye. Sitting's as cheap as standing, sit.

— In his lordship's presence? Never.

— There are kings and emperors and sultans enow about, his lordship said, seeing players not yet uncostumed. The beauty of your craft is the showing that rank is but show and no reality. Your true hierarchy is not decreed by birth's accidents. You have made some study of the colliding faiths, I see. Mohammedans and Christians embattled and neither better than the other. You

124

have had your sharp eyes about the court. What was the line,
Sir Walter?

— I'll ride in golden armour like the sun. There is only
one man I know of with golden armour.

— I had heard of it, sir, Kit said, from Mr Watson. He
heard it from others.

— Well, my ostentation as Captain of the Queen's Guard is
for the first time exalted. Like the sun, eh? And why not like
the sun? You have heard of the Priest of the Sun?

— You mean Bruno?

— So you know of him. He left us two years agone and
a loss to us despite his Italianate Latin. *Chaelum*, indeed.
Exchelsis, indeed. Your play opened doors, sir. I could smell
the dust dispersed by your broom. I must reward you with the
quintessence of newness. I had thought of a play to spread the
news of it. You know where I am?

— Indeed, sir. Durham House.

— That. Haunted by Durham's Catholic bishops, but they
are easily smoked out.

— Talking of that, his lordship said, rising and hatting.

— Yes, yes. The nymph beckons. And Sir Walter too rose,
his hat very ornate with shed feathers from a whole aviary.
Gentlemen, it was diverting, oh more. Very earnest. Keep your
powder dry.

This was the prologue to Kit's, it may so be termed with
little exaggeration, tragedy.

FIGHTING, sir? You look belaboured.

For Kit presented himself at Durham House with a bruised
cheek and a torn collar.

— Perhaps, he said, I should have gone home to change
or else cancelled my visit. But you will be habituated to frays
and the frayed in frays. A man in the street accused me of the
murder of his wife and unborn child. He said it was in the play

and I had writ the play. The watch had to be called. One of the rarer hazards of the poetic craft.

— I have somewhat to soothe. But perhaps not yet. You like my turret?

It had maps and a *mappamundi*, Florentine Raleigh said. Books, of course. And the wide window looked on the Thames that bristled with masts under boiling clouds of early winter. Raleigh was not in his costly finery whose intention was to amaze; Kit was not to be amazed. He wore a shabby black gown and was in old slippers; the bare legs were haired like a satyr's. A fine seacoal fire smoked, following the caprices of the wind. Read this, Raleigh said. Read it aloud. I think Hariot has an inner music even when he discourses practicalities. Kit took the open book and read:

— The leaves being dried and brought into powder, the inhabitants of Virginia take the smoke thereof by sucking it through pipes made of clay into their stomach and head from whence it purgeth superfluous phlegm and other gross humours, openeth all the pores and passages of the body and not only preserveth the body from obstructions but, if they have been of too long continuance, in short time breaketh them . . . So, Kit said, what is this panacea?

— Panacea is right, and Raleigh slapped his thigh. We need a play to disseminate the truth of it. This kneaded and daubed gallimaufry of Anthony Chute – you know the man? No, why should you – is meant for the stage, but none will have it.

Kit read the title from the ill-ordered manuscript Raleigh took from his ill-ordered table: *The Transformation of the King of Triniidado's two daughters, Madam Panacea and the Nymph Tobacco.* He said:

— This last name, which I do not know, seems not a feminine name.

— Well, she may at first strike you with a masculine buffet, but thereafter she is gentler than love. And all that Hariot says is true. You know Hariot? No, but you will. There are many that you are yet to know. Are you willing to yield to the nymph? You look doubtful. Well, I will demonstrate.

126

And Raleigh opened up a cabinet under his window. It held rows of long tubes, as he showed, curved gracefully and ending in a shallow bowl. Clay, he said, as in Virginia, but here I have one especially fashioned in silver. It glinted in the firelight. And here is the nymph. From a drawer of the cabinet he took a fair pinch of a herb, strands of yellow, brown, black, and stuffed this in the silver bowl. Smell, he said, proffering. Kit sniffed. Heady, outlandish, altogether new. And now, Raleigh said, her enlivening and curative spirit riseth in smoke. He took from a pot a spill and enflamed it at his fire. Then he inflamed the herb, the herb smouldered, he drew in smoke and, in a blue jet, emitted it. The aroma sidled towards Kit; Kit coughed gently. Aye, you will cough more when you kiss her. But the cough will be in the manner of a cleansing, a disgorgement of the grosser humours, you may even vomit them up. There is a bowl beneath that table. And then no more coughing, only the bliss of inhalation. Curse it, my talking has doused her. And he refired his spill and relighted. The blue jet bore his words: Will you try?

Kit tried. He held the warming clay bowl in his fist; the fumes crept up the narrow tube. He drank to his lungs. And then his whole body burst in the manic fit. Aye aye, Raleigh said, kicking the spew-bowl from under. Be not shamed by it. I too when I began. Cough cough, my boy, cough out the rottenness of the age. And then gently draw. Gently but gently.

The one draw was for the moment enough. His stomach settled, his lungs shrugged an acquiescence, but his head danced. His eyes took in a reeling room then bade a stiller image ensue. There sat Sir Walter, calm, drinking in his smoke, saying:

— There is a philosophy in this. As some say the love of boys is the higher refinement of coupling – I cannot agree, being by temperament given only to the enjoyment of women, nevertheless – they say this, I say, meaning that appetite is no longer chained to what nature wills, as with animals, so with tobacco eating and drinking are refined to an essence beyond the reach of gross nutriment. You follow me? I think you do. Hariot will give you a lecture on this at our next meeting, which to you will be the first. Now draw gently and say how you are to grow in love with the nymph. She enjoys the company of wine.

Raleigh rose, took from a corner table with sextants and astrolabes on it what seemed to be the new-born child of a ship's bell. He tolled and soon a man that seemed a salted mariner in livery entered and was told to bring Malmsey. Soon, smoking intermitted by both, Raleigh settled to a musing discourse, saying:

— Your *Tamburlaine* rang certain bells within me. It seemed that you were not at the business of easy diversion but pouring out a truth of the times. And the truth is that a man may rise from nothing, and it is the man that doth this that is most likely to gain the summit. For me, I was nothing, one of lowly Devon family that had not even joined in the ennobling pillage of the Reform. You know them, at least you know one, and that is Walsingham of what he terms the Service. There are others – Leicester, the Cecils, others. Now I grow old, I am in the middle of the road of the Italian poet Bruno was ever citing, yet I hold favour. This house was the Queen's when she was a princess, now it is mine, a royal bestowal. I have but the rank of a mean knighthood but that is at least a *signum* of things done. I have founded a colony in the name of her virginity, though the founding has been done by means of an unworthy remoteness, since she would not let me go, holding me to the court as her minion. But there you have the greatness of Hariot, no man like him, sailor, mathematician, skilled in the arts of navigation and all else needful, myself in spirit on the raging ocean. Ocean, Ocean, aye, I call myself but am by royal decree land-bound, beached. Take more of this Malmsey. Well, in your *Tamburlaine* you caught me, the passionate shepherd riding in triumph through where was it?

— Persepolis. You are unjust to yourself. Tamburlaine is all cruelty.

— And so am I, of necessity. Machiavelli has unveiled the truth of our natures. The slaughter in Ireland and my cold eyes looking on at the massacre of women. You have that in your play.

— So you saw the first part?

— I was told of it, but soon I will see it, it is ever being

revived. You too, eh, a passionate shepherd riding in triumph
through wherever it is. Bruno talked much of what he called
mezzi and *fini*, meaning means and ends. Some ends, he was
always saying, might not be justified because of the baseness
of the means. He was sometimes more in the past than the
present. The present, as indeed the future, tells us, tells us
that this is outmoded and rubbishy doctrine. The condemned
Babington sent me a thousand pound to speak up for him. I
did not so speak but I kept the thousand. I needed all I could
get for the Virginia venture. What is your view of the morality
of this?

— My breath goes. It will come back.

— A tobacco shock, call it. It is you and myself that are not
of the ancient nobility that have to be weaned out of the old way
of sorting among the means and rejecting, coughing out I would
say, it is apt, it is a response uncontrollable, spewing out the
mezzo that harms the innocent. And yet if the world could be
saved by the slaughter of one such innocent, a child say, would
we not do it?

— It was attempted, I believe, in Palestine some sixteen
hundred years agone.

— So you may say that God himself approves the cruel
means to attain the needful end. Even so, we must school
ourselves to the quietening of our stomachs, as with tobacco,
delicious nymph. There are some that need not be so schooled.
You have heard of the Earl of Essex?

— Heard and, I think, seen. There were two in one of the
galleries at the first *Tamburlaine*, common people, a merchant
and his young wife, or so it seemed. There was talk that it was
my lord Essex and my lord Southampton, but which was the
wife and which the husband was in doubt, the name Mistress
Risley I think it was was heard, and both peered from what are
called Venetian dominoes.

— Risley is Wriothesley, which is Southampton's family
name. Aye, it would be Essex at his tricks, taking his minion
to taverns and other places of common resort, surveying his
kingdom. A minion of a minion, a minion of the moon that

is Cynthia. A boy only, nineteen or twenty, but of an ancient family, we grant it. He boasts of going back to Edward III, his blood richer than the Queen's, who has that of the bitch Bullen in her. He speaks to her very familiarly and she shows her black pegs in complaisant laughter. Games of cards till the birds herald the morning. Well, I thought I had done for him. That whore of a sister of his, Dorothy. You start at the name.

— Another Dorothy. Pardon, continue.

— You know not the story? Well, she made a marriage against the Queen's express command, some rogue who shall be nameless, and they broke into a church with a holy clerk to conduct the ceremony before her family arrived on royal orders to stop it. She creeps back into the court, and there is Essex to plead pardon and reinstatement, but I scotched them both, saying she was in the back row as of your players, one obscured who will opportunely dart forward, and the Queen was angry and then Essex was angrier and he called me a knave and a wretch.

— You were present?

— I was not, but I heard of it. So the Queen pleads that we be friends and Essex says he will kill me first, and by God he means it. It should be swords out, but one my age learns prudence.

— You honour me with this confidence, but I must ask in humility where it leads.

— It means there is a great division in the world, and all who are Raleigh's friends are enemies of the other. Me he will not harm, not yet but the time will come, for now the Queen would not abide it with the war at sea approaching.

— A war? Of this I had not heard.

— I thought you were with Walsingham, no, they said you had left his employ. Well, there are enough captured documents to tell of the Spanish preparations. You will know in time. Meanwhile, my orders to see to the south-coast defences are delivered and under lock. More of that when the time comes. Mark my words of the division. We are not yet friends, but we will be. I have tasted of the quality of your mind. You are of us, who look to the future and are bent on disassembling the old way. You will see what I mean when you come to our next meeting, which will be on Friday at night. You shall be of our party and must expect danger. But a man who does not scorn danger is half of a man. And a great part of the danger will come from Essex. Here, take a pipe and a screw of tobacco. In the solitude of your chamber court the nymph.

He took Kit down the stairs and out of the front door, which may be accounted an honour. He shuddered at blustery November and, giving Kit his hand, a hard one as of a labourer in the fields of the world, said finally:

— The armour is, in fact, of silver. You caught my dream of its being gold. It may yet be gold, we shall see. What name do I call you?

IN the solitude of his chamber, with a fire going and a discarded page of the second *Tamburlaine* as a spill, Kit courted the nymph without delicacy. He drew her in coarsely to the very base of his lungs and caught hints of her beauty. But then she struck him like some ugly vindictive crone. He vomited into his jordan, not yet emptied from the morning's libation, and as he vomited he thought he had a vision of hell. He called, and as he called his cool brain all above the paroxysm noted with wonder the names he called, he called on Jesus and Mary and even St Joseph. They derived from a Catholic past before his begetting. Oh God God God, he also called in his retching. For, as we all may attest, no agony is worse than this wrenching and tearing of the inner self, the body assailed by demons or by the devil who rules them in all his filthy majesty. After the last strings of spittle joined the coloured mess mingled with *mingo mingere* in the jordan (the river of holy baptism) Kit lay on his floor spent and moaning and cursing the nymph that was in truth most diabolical. Then he must needs sit bare-arsed on his jordan, hand scooping sweat from his brow, and void much black nastiness. His torchecul was yet another

131

discarded page of his play. Heaving then from wretched odours of ordure that filled his little room, he opened the window to a raging November sunset. *Streams in the firmament* came to him and he grinned sadly at the division of brain and body, that proof of the independence of the soul, the making mind ignorant of the disintegration of corporeal elements. He tottered from his room, jordan in hands well held away from him, to empty his voidings on to the dunghill that festered at the corner of Hog Lane. This was to be cleared by the paid cleansers – the hovering kites did not find it to their taste, preferring the eyes of traitors' heads set above Temple Bar (eyeless Father Ballard had seen eternity there, the pecked skull long removed, Kit had passed it shuddering). Then, with emptied jordan rinsed in a raintub on which flowers of filth were afloat, he walked manlily back to his chamber and threw himself on his pallet. He slept long and awoke to the watchman's blessing (past four of the clock). Then hunger struck with no shame. On his table was part of a loaf not yet stale and a hunk of cheese whose redolence did not appal. First he took a draught of wine that was vinegary; in the jug, he saw now from his flinted candle, was the floating white mother that was charged with the ensouring. Then he sat on his bed and ate. His cleansed stomach rumbled reluctant thanks; it had not been well treated. And then, to large surprise, came another hunger, and that was for the nymph. The name, the poet noted, had no English rhyme, save for a street cry never to be heard: *What do ye lack O, here is fine tobacco.* A trade to come, an enshipped commodity from Virginia and where? Trinidad, trinity, the Indies of the West that were no Indies. His pipe contained some still, overlaid with its cinders; there was a wet bubbling in the stem. How was it to be cleaned? Sir Walter would know. A thrust wire perhaps. He scoured the bowl with the point of the cheese-knife and recharged. He took yet another *Tamburlaine* spill and bade her make smoke. He smoked, the word would come in though some would prefer *drinking*. But here was an organ summoned for a pleasure innutritive, the buggery of the lungs.

It was true pleasure, and he felt some guilt at it. If Christ had known it, would he have transmitted his substance in smoke? The eucharist in a pipe-bowl. He saw Christ an instant, smiling, bending no angry brows. Christ had been called on in that agony now past and not well remembered; the demons had not prevailed. The guilt lay in the pleasure that was not nature's trap and it was analogous, Raleigh was right, to that other pleasure. To rise above the cry of the maw that bread be turned to blood and bone, of the importunate gentleman of the loins that brats be begotten – was not that in a manner of the conquest of nature, vinegary mother that would pull us down? And to overcome nature was to exalt the soul? No matter, the drawing in of this divine smoke was an ecstasy and men would in time perceive it as a great benison to the world. Why did ignorant painted savages already know it? He drank out his pipe and filled another. Ecstasy to be renewed daily, a pleasure as necessary as feeding, there was the problem, with daily ravishing of the nymph no easy entrance to a Henslowe trugging house. The problem of supply and, brutal irony, the body begetting a need no baker or vintner could satisfy. Raleigh was for now the keeper of many keys.

— THERE is in the *Cena de le Ceneri*, the Wizard Earl said, the character named Prudenzio who is one of those that *voglion vivere e morire per Aristoteles* – live and die in Aristotle's works. The Nolan says we must purge away doubts and contradictions – *purga tutti i dubii e toglie via tutte le contradizioni* – by consigning Aristotle to the dust and consulting magic.

— Meaning no more, Thomas Hariot said, than philosophy and the mathematics. Magic smacks of the devil to the uninstructed.

The Earl of Northumberland, ninth Earl, Harry Percy who might, in this privacy, be called Harry, was of Kit's age, assured in his wealth and rank, no minion of the court, a corner of his mind smouldering with resentment at his father's death through holding to the old faith though himself no Catholic, no man of the Reform neither, free of thought (*thought is free*: there was even a round catch about it), eloquent though often hindered by a stammer which with grace he rode over, the Wizard Earl so called was of Kit's own age and handsomer. He was at pains to douse the magic, that other magic, of his rank in this assembly of the learned and enquiring.

They sat at their ease about Sir Walter's turret study, the black November night wrapping the Thames and its masts, though here and there a ship's lantern swayed afar – Hariot, the Earl, Walter Warner, their knightly host, Kit, all busily smoking, refiring, drawing, the chimney with its banked coals drinking up the blue fumes (smokers, they would say soon, make chimneys of themselves). The smoking was an outward sign of the inward grace of enquiry: it connoted the distant world whence it came and the ocean over which it had travelled. Kit rejoiced that in Raleigh's store-room was a bale not long arrived. Warner's tobacco had been dampened by a spilling of his Malmsey. He tore a page of the Acts of the Apostles to dry it, smiling, all smiled, there was nothing in a printed page to be revered, the word was one thing, the Word another. Warner did his drying awkwardly: he had but one hand, the other was a stump with five warts on it, a cuff like a pocket covering its shame. Sir Walter filled his pipe for him; Warner said:

— Giordano Bruno alone will not blow out the Aristotelian candle, not so long as the beast that Aquinas chained roams free and tamed in the synods and consistories. He was right, though, to say that we like candles better than the sun because of timorousness. We must smoke glass to look at our father in heaven.

— No perspective trunk, Hariot said, may be trained on him, but –

— *Tele*, afar, *skopein*, to see, Sir Walter puffed. The word is ready for you, *maestro*.

— I thank you. Our studies of the heavens lie elsewhere. Clearly there are stars that are not twinkling jewels set randomly to beautify the night but suns in themselves. These suns we may see, our own blesses or burns, an unmoving orb round which

we with the other planets turn. This we know, though some
still will not accept it. It diminishes man that he should not
be the centre round whom the sun gyrates. The heliocentric
– a shocking denial of Genesis. But in our occult law the sun,
and I thank Bruno for this, is a universal godhead that, if all
would accept, must burn out our sects and their dissensions.
Why must we take the Christian faith to the Indians I saw in
Virginia? God is enough, the sun his symbol, and it shames me
somewhat to think that this that I draw to my lungs is from a
place called Trinity. Shatter the trinity, proclaim unity. There
would be a word for it.

— Deusism, Deism, Theism, Kit suggested in diffidence.

— What you will, Warner said roughly. Michael Servetus
was burned in Geneva for saying the trinity was a three-headed
dog. He escaped the Romish and Lutheran burners to end up
in flames lighted by Jack Calvin. But I see his contention thus.
There is Aristotelian stasis in the trinity. It is not needed.

— You would say that Jesus Christ is not needed? Sir
Walter asked.

The Wizard Earl looked comically about the chamber, mapped
with strange regions and rivers, as though a spy of the Privy
Council might lurk disguised as an astrolabe. He said:

— In a sense for God to come to earth is a great poem. It
bewilders and yet reassures with the doctrine that spirit can be
made flesh.

— It denies the continuum, headshook Warner. Spirit becomes flesh by a miracle. We do not require miracles. Tom
Hariot here can perform more miracles than ever Moses did, if
we secularate or secularise a miracle into a new wonder that is
nevertheless explained by reason. By the continuum I mean the
flow of one thing into another. The contradictions that Bruno
wished to purge are either end of a linear continuity.

— Bruno, the Earl said, taught that opposites are reconciled
in heaven.

— He did not mean the Christian heaven, Hariot said,
he meant a mystical region that the enquiring brain may
yet encompass.

— Back to Servetus, Warner said in impatience. He encountered a world of stasis, with the blood of the body an unmoving cylinder. He saw the blood of the arteries and the blood of the veins, for he was a physician that observed and closely, and he saw how one became the other through the strange work of the capillaries. It seemed to him that, if there were a Holy Trinity as the churches taught, this must be unified through a manner of capillary action, Father merging into Son and both into Holy Ghost. So God is motile as the blood is. Bruno was right to turn our eyes towards the great burning circularity of the sun. I hear he is roaring out his Italianate Latin now in Wittenberg. That will shake the pigs of German Lutherans who still revile Copernicus. We here are shamed by his denouncings of our universities fed on costive Aristotle. You were at Oxford? he darted at Kit.

— At Cambridge. Alas, we never had him there to stir our blood.

— And all you learned at Cambridge was Aristotle?

— The Stagyrite as justifier of Christian doctrine, so long as that doctrine was Henry the Eighth's *donum morganaticum*.

All smiled; he seemed to be accepted. Hariot somewhat wearily said:

— I have been over the edge of the earth where once it was taught a man would fall into nothingness. The mathematics is the key to navigation. It enables us to charter the two worlds that are or were deemed opposed. I mean the infinitely large and the infinitely small. Contradiction or opposition again, you see, and the reconciliation effected through numbers. To add and to multiply one thing, to divide and subtract the same. Would my tables of logarithms be burned as of diabolic provenance? We are beleaguered.

— What are logarithms? Kit asked humbly.

— A logarithm, replied Raleigh, is the index of the power to which a number or base is to be raised to produce the number.

— I am no wiser.

— Nor I, said Sir Walter cheerfully puffing. Let us go back from logarithms to godarithms, pardon me, or God in his infinite rhythms and cross-rhythms and counter-rhythms. I propose that we accept as a needful proposition the existence of a God and ignore what the old schoolmen call the ontological. Ontological confronts hypothetical. Or may one happily live with atheism? Our new friend Merlin has pounded London ears with the atheistical ravings of his Tamburlaine. I am no dramaturge, but it would seem to me that what the creator aims to create is no more than himself through an optic.

— You know nothing of optics, Hariot said.

— I cry your mercy, master philosopher. Is Tamburlaine but the enlargement of Merlin?

— You are truly Merlin? the Earl smiled.

— Merlin or Marlin or Marley or Marlowe. The names of us common people, my lord, are subject to change in the process of onomastic circulation. They are fluid stuff. Nobler names are chiselled on stone or stamped on brass.

— I would as soon be Merlin as Percy. Have you not heard that an earth tremor at Glastonbury has disclosed a marble slab below the abbey's ruins? *Post mille exactos a partu virginis annos.* This is the warning of Merlin that the empire of Uther Pendragon, which our queen now rules, is due for ruin.

— Leave superstition, Hariot said. Are you not ashamed?

— Well, there will be the prospect of ruin, the Earl said, but I have no doubt that the ambitions of another empire will suffer. What was that about the necessity of atheism?

— Sir Walter is a fine poet, Kit said, but he will not have it that a stage poet differs much from your common striker of the lyre, not that his gift is common, may I be struck down if I say so –

— And who will strike you down? Raleigh smiled.

— I must create men and women and eke create voices for them, but they are not my voices.

— If you create them they must of necessity be yours.

— No, Sir Walter. There may be a directive will, Plato's charioteer, but there are many horses and they pull diverse ways. I may dream atheism and solidify that dream in *personae* that stalk the stage, but it follows not that I proclaim a damnable *non credo.*

— The soul is many rivers, nodded Warner.

— By whom or what damnable? the Earl asked.

— By the fools that exalt themselves by damning. My Tamburlaine has no argument. He puffs God out like his other enemies. In a sense he believes.

— And do you believe? Raleigh asked bluntly.

— Does belief or disbelief affect God's substance? I would put it this way, that there may be an unmoved mover. But this is not of necessity of intelligible make, no primary model of ourselves. What is termed God may well be a force as inhuman as the sun, and as indifferent whether to bless by warming or curse by burning. It may be a force progressing through change, whose faculty is built into its essence, and coming through the transformation of matter into spirit to a final realisation of what it is. At the end of time, so to say, there may be God realised, but God is till then no more than a *conceptus hominis*. We are in advance of God in possession of the concept. He or it must wait.

— Well, said Warner, nodding, you are on the right side. You deny stasis.

— Can you deny it wholly? the Wizard Earl asked Warner. You work in the chemistry that was called alchemy in search of solidities that by some miracle of sudden fusion turn into a new solidity. Things are not wholly continuous. And I would put it to Mr Merlin here that in denying a God with characteristics that seem human merely because we are made in his image, we are like him, he not like us, he denies also divine sanction or its opposite for human acts. There may be no great Day of Judgement, but all that would seem to matter is whether a man follows good or evil. I put it so, I am not of necessity one that subscribes to the belief that man is mere substance for moral adjudication, but must it be assigned solely to human government the business of defining the good, the evil, the right, the wrong?

— It is so assigned, Kit said. Our rulers decide, then call on God to justify. So God is dragged into presiding over the state's enactments, and God's eternal foe is conjured to inspire warlocks and witches, Jews and Jesuits and others of the heretical brood.

— And hath God an eternal foe? Sir Walter asked.

— If God exists he must have, Kit said. For the universe, though conceived as one thing as the name saith, yet is properly sustained through the action of opposites. That is, I think, good Brunonian doctrine. All change is the clash of opposites.

— And opposites, the Earl said, are not chemical or physical or whatever the term may be, they are moral, would you say that?

— Morality is to be kept out of it, said Hariot. Morality is made by men. The moral is the expedient, an empiric matter, no more.

— So there be two forces opposed and one may follow either?

— I see, Warner said, head shaking, that you require the pursuit of learning to be a matter of ecstatic spasms. The pursuit is not venery. I know what you are coming to. It is a matter of the imperfect balance of humours in you, I say this without intention of offending. You would be happy to conjure Merlin in Glastonbury or elsewhere and thus gain great knowledge without the agony of the long pursuit.

— Well, Bruno believes in the ecstasy of the magic of the sudden revelation. A truth flashes out from no place. By occult means one may invoke such flashes.

— You mean, Kit said, necromancy?

— Have a care, the Earl said. It is a perilous word and a perilous mode of enquiry, if indeed it be possible. To call on the dead is not in our province. And yet Holy Mother Church counsels praying to the dead. To enquire of the dead what shall be, to require of the dead a power not given to them that live – well, we all shake heads. Nonetheless, must not all roads be travelled? Some lead nowhere so, in no ill humour, smiling rather, though thinly, we must trudge back to engage yet another path. Is not this (to Warner) your agony of the long pursuit?

— When you and I have played at ruff or trump, Sir Walter began.

— And you have won invariably by some diabolic means.

139

— You have taken the cards and used them for conjuration. Nay, divination, a word that containeth holiness most unholily. Do you really believe they can foretell, or is it no more than a game to follow the other game?

— Cards, entrails, stars. Hariot here is a stargazer. *Surgentia sidera dicunt*, so Virgil prophesied. They talk to him.

— They are implacably silent, Hariot said gravely. I call myself an astronomer. Astrology is a noble term for an ignoble superstition. The stars tell us nothing except that they are there and very distant.

— But the Queen herself listens when the astrologers speak.

— The Queen is exalted by her blood not by her intellect. Oh, that is fair, her wit, she is a wise woman though no witch. Those books must be answered with scorn, this thing of Richard Harvey's of terrible threatenings and menaces in the stars. Harvey, and Hariot turned to Kit with brows abeetle, him you will know, he was at Cambridge.

— And his brother Gabriel. Asses, good for nothing. Asstrology is good for them both.

— The stars, the Earl said, rule us, so we are told. Stars reign at our nativity and allot us whatever it be they allot us.

— Ass, Warner said, trology. I see. That will do for the clown or vice in one of your plays. A joke, a jape, we must not be diverted by such in our graver dealings. So, my dear lord, I beg you, no talk of the stars or of conjurations or the like. Stern enquiry will, in a figure not a fact, lead us *ad astra*.

— I know, the Earl said, and I but play with the other conjectures. But there is a power in words. Can words work on matter? They can on spirit. Grinning, he mock-thundered: *Sint mihi dei Acherontis propitii; valeat numen triplex Jehovae; ignei, aerii, aquatici, terreni spiritus salvete!*

— *Avete,* Sir Walter corrected. There is better stuff to learn by heart. It is late, let us finish, you will need link boys. Merlin, throw open the door to let the fumes out. Good. Servants are never to be trusted, let my untrustworthy ones hear us fall to our knees and join in a prayer. For prayers, he roared to the departing blue smoke, are better than all these disputations.

Come, then. Our Father, which art in heaven –

POOR Kit's prancer had been prigged, cant of the moon
minions. Brown Peter, grazing near the Scadbury woods, had
got himself filched; some filthy thief had abducted him and he
was not to be seen again. It was the loss of a love, a whinnying
and nuzzling friend that, after munching of his oats, had loved
his treat of honeycake, who, as Kit had dreamed of other love
when mounted, had sometimes in the jogging brought him to
the blissful small death. So there was no more riding to the larger
bliss whereof that had been a comfit or kickshaws of parody, nor,
to tell truth, was the old love at all holding. Tom Walsingham
had laughed from the cottage bed when Kit had slunk back in
misery to announce he was bereft and must march the dusty
London road. And once, driven by remembered transports, he
had borrowed Ned Alleyn's pampered jade to visit, presenting
himself boldly at the manor house in Frizer's despite, there to
find Edmund the elder inheriting brother in full possession, Lord
of the, not dead of an imposthume nor poisoned by Frizer but
displaying all the outer *symptoma* of the French pox, nose two
great holes and such teeth as had not rotted out very black, cheeks
blotched, groaning with stiff joints, voice a muted corncrake call
with Who is the fellow? One that should not be here, master, for
he is a foul bugger. Kit had worn his sword, his own not Poley's
father's, but had made for Frizer with his fists. Then the great
door slammed, and was it Tom's far laughter he soon heard?
    Such love between men of age ripe for marriage could not with
ease be sustained, there being no nest to tend, no partitioning
of the labour proper to the bonding of the opposed and com-
plementary sexes God, perhaps in doubtful wisdom, had made,
he to work, she to the distaff. If there had been in Tom
Walsingham's brain a flame or even a flicker of response to
Kit's poetic ardency or the cunning of his learning, then there
would have been other linkings and knottings and the joy of

discourse in the cool of after love, but there was there a great idleness, a pouting for praise though nought to be praised, a too great leaning on Ingram Frizer who had him in a sort of fawning thrall that Kit could not for all of his taking thought comprehend.

I was at that time lodged with Tom Kyd, a man lonely and timid with boy and woman alike, moaning that his new play did not go well and yet seeking to instruct me in the right fashioning of what he called a decasyllabon. I had left Ned Alleyn because he was to marry and also because he had puffed himself up with fame and gave too many orders. Kit would sometimes come when Kyd was out to woo me to undressing with I love thee I love thee, but I was older and shaving once a week and conning the parts of young men, though this would be a sharp declension from the glory of Bel-Imperia and Zenocrate. I had come to hate the prying paws of the small gallants who came to the tiring room, by wine emboldened, saying What hast under here? – fardingale or stuffed bodice – and a moment only sweetheart, it is my need. So in something like gentleness I would thrust Kit away, and he would shrug and droop but bear small malice. One day I put it to him:

— Why boys, why men, why never girls nor women?

— There is a divine command, Lucretius calls on *Alma Venus*, delight of gods and men, and it may not be questioned. She commands me the way I must go and ever has, and nothing may be done.

— And why does she, what is the reason in nature?

— It is not in nature, *Alma Venus* rides all above her, one may say it is a rebuke to nature, we will go our own way nor follow the bestial law of breeding. And thus too we may escape from our mothers. To bed a woman, which I have never done, has a strong stench of incest.

— You like not your mother?

— I love her as a son should, but best from afar.

And he would cross the river to the Bankside, to visit the loud and bloody world where Henslowe ruled, where paid venery could not be free of the consort of bulls bellowing and bears

142

roaring for bass, dogs howling, yapping, screaming for alto and treble. And now and then there was a crying ape that rode a dog's back, and was rent, dog too, by the other dogs. In the Paris Garden house where Henslowe kept his geese there was a back room where gander goslings might be tupped for a tester. Kit's presence in a manner remained after his departure in the token of a tobacco reek, for he would pleasure his lungs with the nymph while he indulged the satyr in his loins. Some, though not often to his face, spoke of Mr TS, the tobacco sodomite.

It was in the April of the year 1588, for which the stars of their scryers made monstrous predictions, that Kit heard himself called in an alehouse, which was as good as a public place, by the name of atheist. This was grave, this was perilous, this was worse than an ascription of disbelief in God, for meaning denial of the authority of England's holy Church it meant also denial of the Queen her right to rule it and the realm over which it was an unsleeping paraclete. But the word was uttered by none in authority, merely by the ruffians William Bradley and George Orwell, who sat at their ease at a table in the corner by the door of the Unicorn.

— Mr Marlin the ace, he is.

— Pardon me?

— Atheist, he means, Bradley said. He has never seen the word writ down.

— He or you says say that I am atheist? You will recall some years back what I did to you and that other damned rogue. And Kit's right hand was on the sword handle. Have a care, filth.

— I am no filth. The damned rogue you speak of is in the Clink. A foolish rogue. And I do not say you are atheist, nor does he, it is what Ball the Cutter is shouting around.

— Cutting Ball is saying that I am an atheist? You know what the word means, scum?

— I am no scum. It is you that must have a care. George here, see, will have his dagger out. It meaneth one that says God must be spelt arsiversy.

Kit looked around. It was noontime, there were few drinkers.

None heard. Let it pass, these two were foolish. Ned Alleyn had said he would be here with his brother, there was business. Kit had for Ned a speech revised in his bosom. He went to the inner room and entered without a knock. The brothers looked up from bread and a cold roast fowl. There was a bottle and two glasses half-filled with red. Jack Alleyn raised his to Kit, saying:

— Well, we shall be brothers in the business, you may see at year's end if not before. The Unicorn shall go to another, and Jack Alleyn is to be with his brother Ned in the putting on of the plays you make. Commodities, playing apparels and the like. A cool head and no grasping in Henslowe's manner. Sit. Drink. Eat if you will. He called *Harry* loudly.

— I am glad, Kit said. Tavern-keeping is for lesser talents. But you will have money to put in?

— It will be slow work drubbing creditors. But yes, there is a little saved. Ah, here is a glass and a plate and a knife.

— Bradley and Orwell are there, Kit said. Bradley to me spoke the word *atheist*.

— Ah, Ned Alleyn said. That will be Robin Greene. He has it in print. *Atheist*. And for those that cannot read he has his bully Ball bawling it about. You must act about this. It does none of us good.

— He has writ a pamphlet about my atheism?

— A story of sorts. I have not seen it. It is on sale in Paul's yard. Beware of Ball though if you tax him with it. Cutting is a right name. He cuts more than purses.

— It is Greene I will see. Having stamped his unwashed bravo into the mud. I will not have this.

— Have a care with what you are doing, Kit, Ned said. I mean the play. It will be a fine play but the theme is perilous.

— Is everything perilous these days?

Ned Alleyn mused on that a space, then said:

— Aye, everything is. To act is and to put on plays is. They say we incite prentice riots, the killing of a woman with child is a small matter to that. And now you are to have calling up of the devil and the selling of a man's soul. It is a fine part though, do not mistake me. But you do not condemn.

144

— I have here, Kit said, withdrawing the sheet from his bosom, a speech that calls on God and is waterlogged with repentance. The play will be seen as manner of a stern warning to them that dabble in the forbidden.

— There be some that say, Jack Alleyn said, looking stern with his one dark eye, that you so dabble. Conspiracies of evil and the taking of tobacco in a hidden room.

— A small town this, Kit sighed, unlike Paris. Well, there it is, Ned, tell me later what you think. Now I will take a walk to Paul's and see me an atheist in print. Then I shall take Robin Greene by his steeple beard and topple him.

The yard of St Paul's was full of stalls with books for sale, all passed by the suspicious eyes of the State that the Queen's peace be not perturbed, nought subversive, heretical, republican, mild stuff all: *Let the Sad Sinner be Called to Breast Beating*; *Of the Manner of Life of the Virginian Heathens*; *Primulus and Hostilia*; *A Little Garland of Ditties of Love Unrequited*; *A Sweet and Most Easy Guide to the Rebeck*; *The Panacea that is Flowers of Sulphur and Much Else Thereto Appertaining*; *Perimedes the Blacksmith*. This last was by Robert Greene, Master of Arts. Kit paid his grumbling shilling and took it to the steps of the church to read in the mild April sun. He read that Greene had had it in derision

for that I could not make my verses jet upon the stage in tragicall buskins, everie worde fylling the mouth like the fa-burden of Bowe Belle, daring God out of heaven with that atheist Tamburlan, or blaspheming with the madde prieste of the Sunne. But let me rather pocket up the asse at Diogenes his hande than wantonly set out such impious instances of intolerable poetrie, such madde and scoffying poets that have prophetical spirites as bred of Merlin's race. If there be anie in England that sette the ende of scholarism in an Englysh blank verse, I thinke eyther it is the humor of a novice that tickels them with self-love or so much frequenting the hothouse.

So. He, Kit, was not termed atheist but the fabricator of one, but there he was as Merlin. Prophetical, how? Scoffing, how? And what did Greene know of the priest of the sun who was

Giordano Bruno? He flushed at that *hothouse*, which had more than one meaning but one most clear that saw Kit emerging smoking from.

He had the mean book open and near-splitting at the spine when he marched to Greene's hovel, truly in the ownership of Em Ball his *succuba* and that of many nameless beside, not far from his own dwelling that, now he thought on it, was little more than a hovel though cleanly cleanly. On the cobbles urchins waded barefoot through horse dung and sparse mud the sun engilded. One of these, though which one he knew not and it made little difference, would be the bastard brat Fortunatus that could also be Faustus, though Faust it was said was Alemanish for a fist. With book in fist he with the other fist fisted the door and Em Ball came to it chewing. Ah? She was slatternly but bright of eye and in no more than a stained gown. Ah? Kit strode in to find Greene at table eating and writing, needing a third hand to replenish with Rhenish a greasy glass. And there was another at the table, his gross belly forbidding a close encounter with it. Spice and aliger rode the bad air. Pickled herrings and mouldy bread. The other man, Kit saw with shock, was Dick Tarleton. Come low, God, how very low, Tarleton of the Queen's Men, the Queen's own unrebukable clown that had gone too far with his mock of the Earl of Leicester than whom no man with impunity might. Well, Dick Tarleton swollen and in decay, his belly a very *ascites* or wineskin, swilling deep of ale not of Rhenish. Cutting Ball was not to be seen, doubtless out at his cutting. Kit said, waving pages:

— I have read this. More, I have bought it.

— Every penny helps, Greene said, munching. Em Ball reseated herself with bold eyes on Kit, taking between her fingers the bony corpse of a herring soused to chew. Her teeth were whiter than seemed proper for a slattern. Tarleton sighed deeply after the deep draught and said: Here we have who?

— This is Merlin the Marlin that dared God out of heaven.

— The tambourine man that goes ding ding rattle to God's deep sackbuts. And he squinted comically.

— Not tambourine, Kit said. Though I like your quips

146

well enough. I was taken with your *Seven Deadly Sins*.

— You write for the Admiral? Well, he has lifted himself above the Queen, which is a foul fault. The Queen's Men, Tarleton sang waveringly, not beer and bread and beans men but fine men wine men music while we dine men. Let it go.

— You have some complaint? Greene asked.

— What do you know of what you term the blasphemy of Bruno?

— Caught that, did you? Sit, sit, eat if you will. There is not enough Rhenish to offer. It was discreet, what I wrote. I could have been less discreet. We all know what proceeds at Durham House.

— And what precisely proceeds?

— Talk, Godless talk I am told. Sit. Kit sat. He said:

— Charity compels pity. Your *Alphonsus* was poor stuff, rejected by all except the company at Stoke Newington, where it was howled off. Jealousy makes for poor writing. There is a sob of self-pity on every page. Poor Greene that lacks the gift. You stole too much from my *Tamburlaine*, a foul fault. More of this and I will act.

— How act?

— You know how. The stinking brother of your trull here will be thrown a corpse in Fleet Ditch first if he does not stop his foul chant that I hear of, then your beard for a beginning will be shorn and very roughly.

— You will not talk so, said eating Em Ball, though very mildly.

Greene leaned back comfortably, cursed his pen-point, then took a sharp knife to mend it. Mending it, he said to Tarleton:

— You see, Dick, what they are like. Scholarship mocked and loud words to conceal emptiness. Bow Bell clanging to call atheists to their devil worship. Look, he said fiercely, leaning forward, to Kit. What jealousy can there be in me? I wrote better than the stage deserves. I took your tone to make play with it, which pudding brains like yours could not see.

— You have much to learn, Kit said. If a play is not liked the play is bad. There can be no talk of too good for the

147

groundlings. You speak of scholarship and yet look at you. Living off holy mutton with a bare-arsed bastard. You may take offence if you will. I have taken it already. He tore the book and scattered it over the table. Now Tarleton spoke, his Socratic snub nose twitching:

— I will not have this of tibs and trulls and holy mutton. To me they have been kind and give hospitality where the better sort as they are called spit and spew at my presence. It would be unwise to have Dick Tarleton as your enemy.

— So, Kit said, you will have the Queen's Men making quips about Merlin the atheist?

— There is always the Privy Council to look in on you, Greene said. It is very perilous what you are doing. Ah, Cutting that hath done his butting and eke his rutting.

There was a shadow on Kit who sat with his back to the door. He rose with speed and turned. Ball, a black shape in the light. Kit said:

— You, what do you call me?

— What do I say, master?

— You say that you like not atheists.

— I like not atheists.

— And am I one?

— I know not this man, master.

— You know me well enough to shout scandal through the streets, Kit said hotly, cool hand on pommel. Say it to me now.

— I know not this one who threats me, master.

— Let it go, Greene said, tooth-picking with a clean quill. Let us digest our pickled herring in peace. This one is not worth the jabbing.

— You say jabbing, master?

Cutting Ball's fist was about his dagger, so Kit drew and his sword whistled as it dove to nick Ball's wrist. Ball saw blood, howled, and proceeded to drink of the red trickle. Enough. Kit turned to Greene, saying:

— You are a bad playman and you know it. I show compassion for your jealousy.

— Be on guard, pup. Blank verse for a blank brain. Five feet to an empty bombarding line and four bare legs in bed, a pitiful prick that shies at a woman making up the limping five. Go to your hothouse and be on guard.

OF the great events of that cold summer we knew nothing while they proceeded. Later Tom Kyd said he would make a play of them that would draw in all at the Rose, but others spoke of the danger of placing true personages on the stage, a danger Kit later engaged when he made his play of the Duke of Guise and Paris is worth a massacre. Kyd tried his hand, feeding his brain with many books and pamphlets, not many accurate as to the events, and I have some scattered pages of what was never seen on any stage:

KING OF SPAIN:
    The lighte of war, the father of his troopes,
    Hero of Lepanto, no seaman braver,
    Valiant and unconquer'd, now alas
    Hath met death's conquest. Therefore do we mourne.
    Our Marquis, aye, of Santa Cruz is gone,
    And he it was that put in preparation
    Our strike against the enemie. Therefore you,
    Our well-belov'd Duke of Medina Sidonia,
    Do we appoint to take our shippes in hande
    And name you our High Admiral.

DUKE:
    My lorde,
    Of sea and warre I nothing know. But wordes
    Are garboard strakes and calivers, no more.
    An admiral? Nay, a choice not admirable.
    I urge your grace to thinke againe and give
    The honour of sea lorde to one more fitting
    That will not this high honour so dishonour

149

As I, a lord of lande, am like to do.

KING OF SPAIN:

Pish, you speake greenlie, for the English fleete
Is mann'd by boies and drunken pirates who
Will put to sea unbless'd by our true faith.
Theyre barques are green wood, man, and all uncaulk'd,
And all the saintes in heaven will conspire
To dashe them on the rockes. So you, great duke,
Be of good hearte, vittle your ships, ensure
That to your store liste you do adde enow
Of what will make the beef-fedde Godlesse quake
With apprehension most deserv'd. I meane
Pincers and whips, gridirons, chaines and rackes,
Thumbscrewes and halters for their hanging, aye,
One whole shippe fill you with well-season'd faggots
To make fires for the burning of all them
That wille not bowe downe to our holy priestes
And make obeisance to a Lambe of God
Unsullied by the heathen's tarrie handes.

And then Kyd, turning the Rose stage into a ship, which
was a fair and ingenious fancy, with sailors ascurry from and
to below, which was the cellarage, and the Admiral looking out
to sea from the tarrass, had thunder and lightning and a storm
howling.

DUKE:

Well, we have now revitteled in Corunna
And may proceed. This weather likes me not.
What daie is this?

CAPTAIN:

My lord, Midsummer Eve,
When they saie witch and warlock do abounde
To do the Divil's bidding. In the heavens
Foule cloudes do gather and the churning sea
Seemes like to scatter us. There, see you not –
A ship torne from its mooring and a pinnace
That dragges its anchor – ah, *Dios*, it collides

With a proud galleon.

DUKE:

> Captain, we must sende
> A message to the King, how that the news
> Will reach the English and the Huguenots
> Whoss piracie at La Rochelle we know of.
> Are we thenne trulie scatter'd? Captaine, speake.

CAPTAIN:

> My hearte is heavie, good my lord, to see
> This curse upon us. Doth God turne his backe
> On this endeavour which in holinesse
> Of spirit and intente we did embark on?
> There is much sicknesse here among our men
> And well you know our putting back to port
> For refit, nay, and reinforcement too
> Yells in the winde as it were God's own worde.
> Let us seek peace on honourable termes.
> Such is my plea.

DUKE:

> Do that and we are lost.
> The King, may heaven protect him, obdurate
> And obstinate, aye, and of volition deafe
> To all but speedie victory, will not have it.
> I hear such stories of the English fleete,
> How the ships leap like greyhounds, how their guns
> Bristle about like hedgepig quilles, that know
> I am made sicke yet, sicke or not, obey
> A summons that will lead to more than sicknesse.
> Is Parma coming from the Netherland?
> Has there been news?

CAPTAIN:

> No news. The winds from north
> And east and west and south forbid it.

(That touch was Kit's, who loved to believe that *news* was made up of the cardinal compass points.)

151

DUKE:
> *Dios,*
> *Cristo, Maria,* see us tempest-tost.
> Grant us your aid or certes we are lost.

And then Tom Kyd moved his play to Devon, but briefly, that he might have dry land between two naval scenes, and here he had (this was most dangerous) Lord Howard of Effingham, our High Admiral and patron of our company, with Sir Francis Drake that was his deputy, awaiting the Spanish fleet that did not come.

HOWARD:
> How many troops has he?

DRAKE:
> My lord, they say
> Some fifteen thousand heading for Tor Bay,
> A most commodious harbour.

HOWARD:
> Tush, not so.
> Stubborn and ill-advised our Devon ports
> Where winds secluded are they do ignore,
> So saith this signal. Portland or the Solent
> Must be their aim. We followe.

DRAKE:
> Aye, my lord.

Kyd returned lovingly to his flagship scene and had the engagement fought out as from the Spanish view.

DUKE:
> Here safe in Calais roades, I am advis'd
> Our brother Parma who is lodg'd in Bruges
> Saith all is readie and the Narrow Seas
> Await with loving zephyrs our approach.

CAPTAIN:
> Your grace, you have but land-eyes, see you not
> The English fleete assembled?

152

DUKE:
  Where, where?

CAPTAIN:
  There.
  Mine eyes that temper'd are to the sea-gaze
  Spie England's shippe-force, less than a sea-mile,
  Galleons and merchantmen and men of warre.
  They seeke engagement.

DUKE:
  No, they cannot.

CAPTAIN:
  Yea,
  With most pernicious treacherie the windes
  Veer and the tyde is running to theyr wille.
  Fire, I smelle smoake, see flame, now what is this?

DUKE:
  They have sette some shippes aflame. 'Tis burning tarre
  Assails our noses. *Dios*, what be those
  That make like ambulant helles toward our fleete?
  They burne our pinnaces. Wilde, 'tis a wildernesse
  Of crashing woode and fire. Their cables cut,
  Our captaines lose all order.

CAPTAIN:
  Gales arising
  Speake something divilish. That is not Goddes winde.

DUKE:
  Theyr Godde, captain. All is done, our fleete
  All broken and a maze of fire, and they
  That with cut cables have escap'd its wrath
  Like to be now by Boreas' hideous breath
  Swift driven to the dragons of the north
  And shipwrack in the frozen Orcades.

It was too brief, there was not enough for the traffic of two
hours, and to have brought in, as Tom Kyd intended, triumphant
Gloriana striking a medal and granting the victory to the winds of

153

a protestant God that loved the English and hated the Church his own son founded would have met her scorn (I am no boy) and shut the Rose down for ever. True, she was no boy, she was all of fifty-five years and raddled and lacking teeth, and she did not show herself at the thanksgiving service at Paul's on September 8, that was the morrow of her birthday. There was a sermon delivered by a lawn-sleeved bishop at Paul's Cross and this spoke of the Queen's happiness, though in truth she was far from happy, for her great love was dead.

We may say that with no impugning of her virginity, though this has been seen as a virtuous lie, a raising of her to the rank of the Mother of God or the goddess Diana, or else a device of diplomatic dealing that rendered her a prize of alliances. That the Earl of Leicester, the Lieutenant and General of the Queen's Armies and Companies, was her one true love may not be gainsaid, but now he had died after the stiff work of raising troops to meet the invading Spaniard and was, some say, poisoned by the salty waters of the springs of Buxton that is in Derbyshire. Well, he was dead, and there was thus a great emptiness in the procession to Paul's, and it seemed that Sir Walter Raleigh, in his bravery, having done as good work as Leicester but greatly hissed, faced the dapper Earl of Essex as one gamecock faces another in enmity, but these, being men of ambition, yearned to fill that emptiness and by God one or other would soon do it.

It was Leicester that had picked out Dick Tarleton, a swine-herd on his estate, as a rustic witty clown to please her majesty, and he had risen to head of the company that bore her name. Now, one week before the rejoicing, he too was dead, lying on the lousy second bed in Em Ball's house in Holywell, a pace or so from Burbage's Theatre where he had played. The Queen's Men, despite their high name, were now nothing, and the Admiral's rose much, no little helped by the thrashing of the Spaniards by my lord Howard. The Admiral's banner waved high above the Rose from the turret, and it was Kit's play of the victorious early autumn that was itself a victory for the craft, for its like had not been seen before. He had read the life of the German necromancer John Faust, not yet in translation but extempore rendered by the Wizard Earl, and here he had him on the stage, calling up the devil and selling his soul for a few years of pleasure and knowledge. I would not play Helen of Troy, I was beyond it, and Ned Alleyn gave me though grudgingly the part of the servant Wagner, who is a sort of Faustus in a lesser figure.

— We will have a woman, Kit said. There be some of Henslowe's girl goslings that will for a shilling parade naked.

— We cannot, we cannot, Ned headshook, there has never yet been a woman on the stage. And to have a woman naked would close us down.

— Draped, not wholly bare of the arse and bubs. Walking across the tarrass first with no words. Then, with no words, below.

— And then I kiss her. Sweet Helen, make me immortal with a.

— You would prefer to kiss a woman than a boy, unlike some.

— Joan would not like it, even in play.

— A boy then, well-draped.

Now this *Doctor Faustus* had somewhat in it that was beyond itself and attached to Kit as it were a nimbus that was more than atheistic, being truly devilish or demonic. When Faustus stood in the dusky grove of what was in truth a bright afternoon, conjuring Mephistophilis, his words were:

> *Orientis princeps, Belzebub inferni ardentis monarcha, et Dema-gorgon, propitiamus vos, ut appareat, et surgat Mephistophilis. Quid tu moraris? Per Jehovam, Gehennam, et consecratam aquam quam nunc spargo, signumque crucis quod nunc facio, et per vota nostra, ipse nunc surgat nobis dicatus Mephistophilis.*

And this Latin, doubtless donated by the Earl of Northumberland, though understood only by the learned, had an effect of great devastation among the vulgar, who cried God's my life and Heaven save us, and one or two covertly made Faustus's *signum crucis*, though to a holier end. One woman in the lower gallery screamed and swooned when Rob Gratton appeared as a devil. And at one performance where I was not present, being plagued by a toothache and having handed my part to young Theo Hawkes, who did it not well, there were cries that there was another devil on the stage that was not in the company, and again there was screaming and swooning. It is to the point here, I believe, to say that there were more of these devils when we played out of London, during the closings for plague and fear of riot and the like, than in the city itself, for London the great capital was mostly above being afraid of devils. There is in Dulwich, which is a ride south from London, a great college called Alleyn's of God's Gift, which was founded in this wise. We were playing at Dulwich and the devil appeared grinning during my scene with the clown, and there was an outcry, we intermitted the play and, at Ned Alleyn's command, spent much of the night in praying and fasting. And Ned vowed some great monument of gratitude for our delivery from diabolic infection or the true Luciferian toils, so, when he had money enough, the foundation was set in hand and the College is there for all to see and for boys to be instructed under a master who shall, till time's end, be named Alleyn or Allen, and, as a kind of ironical aegis, both Christopher and Lucifer remain as its ever more shadowy presidents.

Christopher or Kit was known about the town, pointed at as one that could raise the devil with Latin, and with Greek call back Helen of Troy from the dead, and his frequent knocking at the door of Durham House was noted and speculation raised about what devils were to be conjured in the turret study whence black fumes floated. In truth and as ever the talk and disputation were on what undying truths could animate a new age unshackled from superstition and cleansed of blood and bigots, with men marching forward to reason's pure dawn.

— And yet, Thomas Hariot said, reason has its limitations. He stroked Kit's arm, for they were now friends, saying: Why should one line of poesy be better than another? Reason cannot hammer together a frame of adjudication. Why did the flue of my arms start up when Faustus cried that he saw Christ's blood stream in the firmament? I have hardly met this before.

I analyse and find in Christ's blood nothing to excite, and yet the poetic supposition that that blood is the dying light of the day, as also the force of that word *firmament*, make as it were a fusion of elements that finds its analogue in the constitution of chemical compounds. Something new is made and the outlawed term *miraculous* coyly intrudes.

— I have spoken before, the Earl of Northumberland said, of the occult power of words, and you would not accept it. Streams in the evening sky, it would not do. *Firmament* has occult strength beyond analysis.

— Leave this, Sir Walter said, and think of what you may prepare for the making of a book while I am away in Ireland. You see this damnable tome of a thousand pages and more extolling the truth of the Church of England – I do not have it here, I will not have it – and now the Brownists are peppering the bishops to, I may say, the Queen's secret delight though she may not say so. To arraign alleged truths unproved is in our office, meaning that the great book itself must, gently ever gently, submit to the probing of reason.

— It cannot be done, Warner said, it could not be published.

— Not in Antwerp, Basle, Geneva?

— Never Geneva.

— It is, I think, Hariot said, the divinity of Christ that must, gently in your word, ever gently, be questioned. His blood may stream in the firmament but it is the blood of a man. We are always coming back to Bruno and his one great sun flaring in that firmament.

— Denials of the divinity, Warner said, can be set forth and then ineptly countered. That is one way of the gentle inserting of the dagger. It has been done in the past. What was that book of Queen Mary's day? *A Blast Against the Arians*, some such thing.

— A Catholic book of course, Kit said, dark and depressed, of which I have a copy. The Arian heresies are clearly set forth only to be attacked. I studied it at Cambridge and have never been sure of its true intent. I can bring it. I remember it said something of the gospels showing Christ as a man subject to hunger, thirst, weariness, fear and the like, and these words

I had and have pat: To believe that a nature subject to these infirmities is God or any part of the Divine Essence is folly.

— And the objections are inept?

— Whether deliberately so I have never been sure. I can bring the book.

— Too much, Sir Walter said. Copy out the pages that are pertinent to our Brunonian thesis and bring those.

— I will. If I am low in spirits this day it is all *a proposito*. I received a gleeful letter from one that was a fellow student and is now curate of a parish. A foolish fellow and a bad poet. He witnessed the burning of one that had once been my tutor in divinity, a Mr Kett that held that Christ was not God yet but would be after his second resurrection. It was folly, yes, but held in sincerity. Well, he has been burnt alive at Ipswich, dressed in sackcloth, leaping with joy in the flames, clapping his hands and crying *Blessed be God*. I would join with the Puritans if I thought they were of a lesser vindictiveness than the bishops.

— So Kit mourns for Kett, Hariot said, stroking. All the martyrs will in time be vindicated, for whatever cause they were burnt. For us here assembled, and others of our kind in the cities of Europe, it is essential to avoid martyrdom.

— There is too much talk about, Kit said. There is leaking.

— If there is that, Raleigh said bluntly, it will be from one that cannot keep sealed under drink what has been said in sobriety.

— You mean?

— We are a sober company addicted only to tobacco.

— I see. I am not wanted.

— You are very much wanted, Hariot said, and he gripped Kit's arm. But you must learn discretion.

— Aye, I made a song about that once, and that was in drink. How would it go now?

> *Wrench feathers off the Holy Ghost,*
> *Deny that Christ was God's own son,*
> *Spew out the unconsecrated host,*
> *But ever with dis-cret-i-on.*

Now I must go. I settle to my trade, which is not dis-put-at-i-on. I have a play to make.

And the play he was making lacked discretion totally. The Duke of Guise that had driven the King from Paris had been on the King's orders, for now his gallic majesty was back, assassinated by thugs hired cheap. And the King had kicked the dead head of Guise over and over, complaining then of blood on his shoes. Here was Kit working on what he called *The Massacre at Paris*, which, if presented, would have the French ambassador raging at court and without doubt close the Rose for ever. But here he was with

> *Now Guise begins those deep ingendred thoughts*
> *To burst abroad.*

This was much like

> *Settle thy studies Faustus, and begin*

The same Machiavellian boastfulness was there:

> *That like I best that flyes beyond my reach.*
> *Set me to scale the high Peramides,*
> *And thereon set the Diadem of Fraunce,*
> *Ile either rend it with my nayles to naught,*
> *Or mount the top with my aspiring winges,*
> *Although my downfall be the deepest hell.*

He was much possessed by hell, he noted, relighting his pipe. When Jack Lyly and Tom Nashe came to call on him they waved the smoke away like preachers denouncing heresy. Kit greeted with:

— Lyly of the lilywhite boys. How go the squeaking thespians of Blackfriars? Ah, that is not too bad a blank-verse line. Sit, both. There is a kind of vinegar in that bottle. Find yourselves mugs.

They were both thin men like blades with bladelike noses. Nashe said:

— You have read the tracts?

— I read *Have you any work for the cooper?* I laughed. It

159

was right for Bishop Cooper whose wife empties pisspots on him. Married prelates are ridiculous. Celibacy is proper for priests.

— There is a smell of the old faith about your *Faustus*, Lyly said. He looked with disdain on Kit's poor lodgings, he that had become secretary to the Earl of Oxford, no less. Which means you must be against Martin Marprelate.

— I am against them all, bishops and black crows that preach through their noses. The bishops make me puke but Martin makes me laugh. Who is this Martin?

— A Brownist of course they think to be John Penry, Nashe said. He has what is called the Pilgrim Press because it is ever moving. Never in one place, and a heavy instrument to push around. Yes, he has the comic gift which, alas, the bishops have not. But there is episcopal money about. Did you see our plays?

— *Martin's Month's Mind* was at the Theatre. It lacked poor Dick Tarleton. That was of you both?

— Answer a fool with folly, Lyly said. A bishop's commission. It is a strange new world we are in, bishops asking for plays.

— And plays of some scurrility, Kit said. Martin poisoning Divinity to make her vomit. I do not think it decent.

— This stink is not decent, Nashe waved as Kit relighted. Call it the devil's incest, pardon, incense.

— It is by way of being a fumigant. There is a lot to fumigate – bishops paying for low comedy, believers in God being burnt. You prefer the stench of the burning of heretics? Catch this Martin and he will be burnt and doubtless there will be godly laughter.

— We come to you, Lyly said, with a view to collaboration. There was good comedy in *Faustus*, the clown and God forgive me he speaks Dutch fustian and the fireworks.

— The comedy was mostly Tom Watson's. If you want from me comedy about the Christian faith you will not get it. Faith is a grave matter.

— Strange words from one reputed to be atheistical, Lyly said primly.

— So Greene and his bravo are still at it? You believe me to be that?

— You may be what you wish, Nashe said, unnasally, since his handkerchief was at his hatchet nose. We are not here to exhort you to orthodoxy. We are merely at work on commissions. Your name would draw crowds and please their grades.

— Listen to me, Kit said, and he knew, saying it, that the me to which he referred was one of a parcel of many within, and he felt a manner of despair or at least desperateness in not knowing well which was to speak. It is easier to believe in this Church of King Henry's founding than not to. I believe, I believe, your worships, and the question of what is belief never arises. So, with this thin surcoat of belief, we may do our work and drink our drink and never be molested. To question faith is a grave matter, and here you are bringing your clowns in. An atheist at least has set working the engines of thought, and it is no easy matter to throw God out of his heaven. The truth is that there are no atheists, since who would be so witless as to assert what he cannot prove? Simply and in all candour we must shrug and say we know nothing. God's book is man's book, since God handles no quill. These bishops with their termagant wives throw the book at us and say believe because I demand belief and by God I will burn or hang and quarter you if you do not. By what authority is it affirmed that Martin and his Calvinists are wrong? How has the Church that Peter founded in Rome become so suddenly the Scarlet Woman?

— As I said, Lyly nodded, your *Faustus* is a work of the old faith. And by *atheist* we may mean you reject the Church of the Reform.

— Martin Marprelate is also a reformer, Kit said. Will not the Reform go on for ever?

— Come, Nashe said not unkindly. Your boldness is well taken. We did not visit you for all this. You are in a mood of protesting and this is not the occasion. All we came for was collaboration. To tell truth we are at our wit's end for new things the bishops will gladly pay for. If not comedy then some thunderous Tamburlaine lines on behalf of the God of the

161

Archbishop of Canterbury. Then the trapdoor opens and Martin is thrust into hell to scream his heart out. It would be in a manner a fine fusion of your two plays. A few scenes only.

— Hell in the cellerage, aye. Dust and beetles and a few squibs. Why this is hell nor am I out of it, that was the truth.

— You believe in hell? Lyly asked. Certainly you savour the smoke of it.

— Belief is not to the point. There are men around who do not believe in America nor in the existence of far constellations that reveal themselves through optic glasses. Hell may be there whether we believe or not. We are scurrying emmets or pismires with our sad little comedies. Religion is too great a thing for either the hen-pecked episcopacy or the followers of Robert Browne. Tell the Archbishop that. Belief makes nothing and unbelief strikes nothing out. Let me go back to my Paris massacre.

THAT was a summer in which Kit was hardly to be seen in London. He took, he told me later, almost daily a boat from London Bridge to Deptford, there to wander, drink, think not solely on his play of the Paris massacre but of poems, Ovid translations, a sort of chronicle of an England that was at war indeed for greed and conquest but not on behalf of a faith affirming that God had a special love and care for a remote and misty island. Also he saw, somewhat remotely and mistily, that his two plays already seen and acclaimed yearned towards a third, for in the first he had shown power through conquest, in the second power through knowledge, in the third there would be power through what? Money, he thought, though there could be no tragedy in it, money was no tragic theme. Meantime he was soothed by the noise of the waterside taverns, where there was much hard drinking by joiners and caulkers and hemp-dressers, for here were the navy yards where ships, merchantmen and men of war, were built of English oak and Russian spruce. The smell of fresh-cut wood mingled with that of fish not so fresh, tarry sailors, ale vomit. And Drake's *Golden Hind* that had made the three-year circumnavigation lay at anchor to be chipped in sacred relics by those that came to admire. A mile downriver the Privy Council would be meeting at Greenwich Palace, and Deptford was by way of being a suburb of the court, with musicians that made up the royal consort at their blasts and tunings, to which the royal hounds in their kennels howled a forlorn faux-bourdon.

In the tavern where he sat on a day sailors let loose after a long voyage regaled with stories not to be believed; it was the scurvies that did for them, aye, and the eating of rats for there was nought else but tallow and young blackamoors, and there be men that have one foot only so great that it serves them for shade in the heat, and there is fruit on the trees that does sing a catch, aye. The standing shadow in the doorway resolved on entrance into a known figure: a young man of grave face that hauled behind him his baggage, just landed.

— Just landed on the *Peppercorn*, you will remember. The name being Dick Baines. I will sit.

— And drink. English ale in a tankard of pewter.

— Talk not to me of pewter. The coining goes on but at last I am sent home for different work. Did they find out that you had not seen the butterman?

— No. But there was war just the same.

— Aye, and it goes on in the Low Countries. It was a great victory and they are building ships here, I see, in great haste for the Spaniards are not yet done with us. And what work are you on?

— No longer in the Service. I make plays for the play-house.

— No longer? You cannot speak so. Once in in always. I must report to Mr Secretary who is very sick. There will be a new master soon but who they know not yet. We hear much of the Earl of Essex.

— Here too. Well, I have done with it.

— And what be these plays?

— Plays that bring in money but not enough. You see that

great house there on the edge of the green? That is the Lord Admiral's. I write plays for his men.

— I do not see that clearly. Plays for sailors at sea?

— The companies of players must have a protector who shields them for being rogues and vagabonds. There are others than the Lord Admiral's. There is even the Queen's Men, but that is the worst of them.

— In Flushing there were no plays but ones in Latin done at the grammar school. But one that came visiting spoke of what he called Timber Lane with much swearing and cursing of God. Did you see that?

— It is mine. The title you have is not quite right.

— Ah, you are still at your old business of God and Christ and the beloved disciple?

— Not in *Tamburlaine*, no.

— I think much on Jesus Christ.

— As you once said. Where do you stay in London?

— I will lodge where I can. I will lodge with you.

— You cannot.

— You lodged with me in Flushing.

— That was different.

— You are not friendly.

— Mr Secretary or one of his secretaries will see to you. I am friendly enough.

— I do not wish to go at once to prison. I need a little time to see London that I have not seen for long years.

— To prison? What wrong have you done?

— No, to prison to smell out papish conspirators. There is still a plenty of those. Robert Poley in Flushing told me of his work in prison, he came out after the Armada. Now Poley is everywhere in Europe pretending to be a Catholic again. He is even in Denmark.

— I thought I was rid of Poley.

— Rid of? He is not one to be rid of. He is a marvellous operator of the Service. He spoke much of you. He said the time will come to use you again. So I may not lodge with you?

— Alas.

— That is not friendly.

AT the Rose that autumn there was rehearsal for a revival of
Tamburlaine, and I was no longer the divine Zenocrate but the
cringing younger son of the tyrant. Ned Alleyn, very hoarse,
awaited a quart of ale sent for at the Dansker's while he listened
in irritation to all Kit said. Kit waved his play about: it was full
of scratchings and carets and his hand was vile. For him *foul
copy* might well have been especially devised. Kit cried:
— Your objections of last year are not now in order, Ned.
What is here is the truth and truth red hot and fire new.
The French king murdered by a Dominican friar and Henry
of Navarre as king. It is the triumph of the protestant faith in
France and what can any here have against it?
Henslowe was there, fat of belly but gaunt of face, with his
account book and a worry that the French pox had stricken one
of his gentlemen clients. He said:
— You must not urge this on Ned or myself. It is not for us
to say aye or nay. All must now go through the Archbishop.
— That is matter of a formality, man. Yet what Henslowe
said was true. The Archbishop of Canterbury had been shocked
by the excesses of the plays against Martin, many of them very
filthy, and regretful that he had not merely approved but
instigated, and now all plays must be handed to a triumvirate,
most censorious, of one of the Archbishop's appointment, one
of the Lord Mayor's, and the Master of the Revels himself.
Yet this, surely, would go through, it was good protestant
meat.
— There are twelve murders and seventeen victims, Kit
said. It will cost a fortune in pig's blood.
— You give that fortune as a recommendation? Henslowe said.
— I do not see the arithmetic of the murders, Ned said,
though tempted.
— Will you or will you not?

— Let us have instead of this the usurious Jew you spoke of.

— That is not ready. Will you or not?

— Alas no, Ned said. Not now. Perhaps not ever. Take it to the Burbages at the crumbling Theatre and you will receive no different answer. Ah, thank God, here is my tankard. And Ned drank near all off in one breath, he had much of that. If we cannot have the Jew, he said, emerging panting, we must make do with this thing of Tom Kyd's. And there is Robin Greene coming up with the two friars and the comedy of devil-raising.

— Another theft from Greene? I will have Greene.

— Greene is not well.

— He will be less so when I have done with him. And Kit gripped his sword pommel so that his knuckles showed white.

— Well, then, there it is, we must continue the rehearsal.

— The usurious Jew, Henslowe said.

— Aye, and you shall play him. And Kit was off to the riverside where the boatmen cried Eastward Ho and Westward Ho, and he took a boat whose Charon had a roofless mouth and said hn hn.

Tom Watson was at work in Kit's own house, away from a wife's scolding and the drumming of Latin into an inattentive boy that nonetheless smelt sweet of cinnamon. He had taken time off to add comedy to *The Massacre at Paris* and, as Kit entered, at once said:

— I have this Murgeroun cutting off the ear of the cutpurse for cutting off Murgeroun's golden buttons, and the cutpurse cries O Lord, mine ear, and Murgeroun responds with Come sir, give me my buttons and here's your ear. That has the right laughter of cruelty.

— Good. We need money, Tom, and Henslowe and Alleyn will not take it.

— Try the Burbages. They are playing this afternoon. You can at least try. It is but a step. Take three sheets of it only, they will taste its quality.

— I will.

And he left, and there was William Bradley waiting for

him, very drunk, unbuttoned (no gold there) and waving a
sword about. He cried:

— I will have the bitch's bastard Tom Watson. Where is he?

— Whatever you call him, scum, he is not about.

— Scum yourself, atheist. Draw, I will have you first, swiver
of boys' arses, and then I will have that hogsdrop Watson. Come
on, thou.

— I am not *thou*, pig. *Now*.

And Kit drew and lunged. He was onstage, he had onlookers,
they were gathering at Hog Lane corner. Kit panted and Bradley
panted, drunk and on unsteady legs but eyes steady and right
arm skilled only in pot-lifting, swiping, this craft. Kit had been
offered practice in the foils by Tom Walsingham but had said
no, reserving arm for pen. Bradley parried with overmuch ease,
going *haw*. Real blood thou shalt have, not from bladders, and
it shall be thine own, thou pickest at the air like a lady at a child's
nits.

Kit, seeing blood, drew it. Bradley's wrist. Bradley dripped,
went *haw*, and took two hands to steady him for the piercing of
Kit's breast. Kit leapt, that he could do, and to relief saw Tom
Watson appear in his shirt, sword drawn. Bradley cried:

— Art thou now come, then I will have a bout with thee.
Out of it, frigger, I will have thee after like cheese after meat.

Bradley had now sword in right and dagger in left. He caught
Tom Watson most bitterly in the brow with dagger, there was a
wound like a mouth that spoke blood. Tom ran to the ditch which
was a border to the field where the windmills turned lazy and
indifferent, and there too were some gathering to watch; Tom saw
a drunken canvas-climber cry *Codardo*. Turn on him, *caramba,
madre de Dios*. Tom would leap the ditch. Bradley staggered on
its edge, recovered, Tom struck him on his beard so that blood
enlivened the thistlefield of it, then drew back and thrust once
forward into Bradley's chest that was bare being unbuttoned and
gauged by the thrust that he had pierced six inches. Bradley was
very surprised, took a palmful of his own blood to squint at, then
struck unhandily, then fell. *Muerto*, the drunken canvas-climber
cried. Kit came up to see. The blood issued in waves. He said:

— That is from the arteries. It circulates.

— Christ, panted Tom, I've killed him.

— Self-defence, all here saw it. See it pumping out.

Stephen Wyld, a decent small man that was constable of the precinct, had come with his two men with their bare bills for the quelling of riot. This was no riot. *Murder*, Wyld's lips framed silently as he looked up from the blood tide.

— Self-defence.

— A man dead. That is murder. Which of you?

— I hit first, Kit said. He came for me as I left the house, bravo-ing and with his sword drawn. Then Mr Watson.

— Arrested, both. My duty, no pleasure to me. You both I know. Him I know, knew. The blood still galloped.

— Where do we go?

— Sir Owen, Hopton that is, Lieutenant of the Tower. Our justice of the peace here. Norton Folgate, a brief walk.

— No resistance, Tom said. We come. There are witnesses enough of the self-defence. What do you do with the body?

— Sir Owen will see it. None will remove it. Leave it for the flies. The flies are quick, buzzing there. They love blood, it is honey to them.

Sir Owen Hopton was in his garden. It had been a dry summer, and he degged red Tudor roses. He was a stern man with a beard, apt for a gardener, cut spadewise. He must sign a warrant. They went into the house with him, and he kindly offered wine. With water, Tom said. They were both near dead of thirst. His forehead dripped, he begged pardon, his handkerchief was in the sleeve of the jerkin still in Mr Marlowe's house. Sir Owen said:

— Well, here we have it. On Suspicion of Murder. The coroner will sit tomorrow, you must abide the jury's finding. Alas, you must suffer committal to Newgate. Need they be manacled, Mr Wyld?

— It is what is done. But both are gentlemen.

— Why why? Kit asked Tom while they were walked to Newgate. Tom was counting what he had in his purse, his wound in the brow staunched, his jerkin on. Their swords had been taken from them.

— Something of a long tale. Jack Alleyn leaves the Unicorn to be with Ned at the Rose, Bradley owes him money he needs, bribes of protection construed as loans, he will not pay, Jack asks Hugh Swift who is the brother of my wife to threaten suit in the Court of Common Pleas, Swift calls on Bradley at the Bishop's Head his father's inn and is attacked by George Orwell who threatens a killing if the suit continues, Swift goes to the Queen's Bench for securities of peace against Orwell, Jack Alleyn and I, for Hugh drags me into this business as his sister's husband, we propose a like assault on Bradley to jolt him into paying what he owes, Bradley hears and gets securities of the peace against Jack, Hugh, myself, alleging himself to be in fear of death from us, you are into it as friend, associate, what you will. The rest you know.

— Here then ye be, masters. Here ye have the Limboes.

They were pushed, with some courtesy shown in the light or token nature of the push, through a hatch into unwindowed darkness where a candle set on a black stone showed walls of ill-hewn blocks, a floor uneven and slimy, what seemed to be initials of prisoners long gone carved on a wooden bench which was all there was for sitting, resting, sleeping.

— There is no air. We are below ground, Kit panted as he was manacled to Tom by the jailer, then both to the floor rings.

— Nay, ye be above the gateway. That black stone is the black dog of Newgate, but he will not bark till ye are in the way of dashing out your brains against him. Here then ye stay.

— Food, drink?

— We will see of that when your bellies do rumble for a breakfast. And he shuffled out in his filth and odour of ancient mutton fat. The thick door slammed, a key ground. Why, this is hell nor am I out of it. There were scufflings in the dark. Rats.

— We could catch one, Tom said, and eat it raw. Though rats are as they say inesculent. The learned word bounced hollowly.

— A man should not play with these things. Jails and privation and death. I sit comfortably with my pen penning men into pens of this kind. I did not think I could be so short of breath.

— Breathe deep. There is air enough. No, not enough. Husband what we have.

— We will be out tomorrow for the coroner?

— I think not. It is a verdict foreknown, Wyld said. He will be a witness himself, our proxy. There are witnesses enough, no question, self-defence. Acquittal without doubt. Then release.

— When?

— Alas, not till next Sessions. December, I believe. That makes two months.

— In this hole?

— Ah no, I know something of the procedure. This little hell is to break a man's spirit for the night. Then comes the larger purgatory. Though that is now a word banned by the theologians. What do we do this night, compose a play? No, we rhyme, it is proper for poets manacled. The beneficent chains of. Half a couplet each.

— I cannot. See those whiskers twitching, it smells us.

— Try. Country air, washed lambs, lilywhite shepherdesses. It is all a sham. The pastoral sham that denies the black holes and the foul stinks of true life, if that it can be called. Here we are with our precious learning in the anteroom of thieves and murderers and coiners. There was a time when we would have been Franciscans or Dominicans. Ah well. Beneath an oak the pouting Lycidas –

— I cannot. Wait. Saw not his flock that nibbled the green grass.

— Not good. His inner eye fair Phyllida beguiled.

— You cannot say that. Nominative Phyllis. In fancy not reality she smiled. I cannot. Let us cry to be let out.

— In the darkmans couch a hogshead. We must learn the cant. The inner world alone exists. The soul floats free.

At dawn, after fits of sleep from which Kit started yelping and while Tom awake and worried said *Calm, calm*, another jailer came to them, grinding the key and letting a cockcrow in, chewing bread most visibly, an unwashed Newgate veteran, in frayed leather and gaping boots through which black-nailed hooves peered. He said:

— The garnish.

— A tester? Tom knew the term, Kit not.

— You be gentry coves. A silver bit. Receiving the coin he bit it, stowed it, then set himself to loosing their shackles with a key that made rat-squeals. Now it is to be the Master's side, you be not common enough for the common. Middle Ward is crammed that you do use your chum's famble for scratching of a pock boil, Stone Hold is right aswim with the fever.

They followed him to a region where was grudging light and air, a sorry mockery of the true world without, with space and open cells with bedboards and men free of limb and shambling though groaning.

— And that is the boozing ken where a man may booze an he have the tink. You may pay the Master there.

The Master appeared masterly in a manner proper to a prison, in hose, doublet, ruff even much creased and greased and reechy, with face and hands proudly unwashed, with beard lousy and uncombed. He took from Kit what was almost his final shilling, biting it more in custom than suspicion, and lordlily showing that there was the boozing ken. It was a mere foul tavern under a groined vault. The cove of the ken was brother to the Master, and he served hard bread and pies, stewed prunes as this were a brothel, ale watered as he would, since none could go elsewhere. There were benches but most stood about. Here were upright men, rufflers, abram-men, high-pads, buff-knappers, rattling-mumpers, tat-mongers, wiper-drawers, kidlays and moon-cursers (I thank Greene and Nashe for the trade-names), as also gentlemen, like Kit and Tom, rendered unfortunate. Here strangely was a freedom not to be found in the free city without, since a man could curse Church and State without fear of arrest since he was already arrested. Kit cursed by the anus of Chrysostom and the pocked nose of St Anselm. Dick Baines heard him. He was ordering a lamb's wool to the tapster's grumbles and said:

— So the Jesuit-chasing grows hot. You two are my sup-
plements?

— Mr Watson and I are here as true malefactors.

— For true crime?

— We killed a man.

— God's my little life. You expect the rope? Perhaps it is
not discreet to ask. A life's but a span. I think much on its
brevity. There be great coiners here. I have met a Mr John
Pole or Poole, a papist and a most ambitious counterfeiter as it
is put. Coining and papistry go together, you know that, modes
of disruption and falsehood. He is a slugabed and late riser but
you will meet him.

There was generosity here, no man might go without for
lack of money, so by eleven o'clock of the morning Kit was
well on to sousing and could hardly see straight when Wyld,
in the mode of a friendly neighbour, came to tell them of the
coroner's verdict.

— It is as I said. The jury found Bradley killed in self-defence,
his body has been claimed by his father and is due for quick burial
because of this unseasonal heat. Mr Watson here may wait for
acquittal at the next Sessions.

— Why not now? glazed Kit asked.

— It is not within the coroner's authority. You, Mr Marlin,
are free to go now on surety of forty pound, since you struck
not the final blow, remissible when the Sessions clears you.

— Bail money? Where shall I find that?

— Raleigh, Tom said, no, Raleigh is in Ireland planting
outlandish tubers, the wizard Earl, no, not he, Alleyn, Henslowe,
no. Do, he said urgently to Wyld, tell all to my dear wife, she
will raise money to pay for my privilege of incarceration, she
will bring in pies and a roast and a flagon. Why do we labour
hard and lack money so much?

— Lack of money, aye, an old bent man of fifty or so said,
bowing but already bowed. I see two poets here, I am honoured,
Marlin, he said bowing to Tom, and the other one, bowing to Kit.
Mr Baines, he is beginning his day's work as informer, see, told
me of you and the interest you have in money. He is not good

as an informer, we inform him great lies and he is happy with them, my name is Pole or Poole as you please.

— God help me, it will have to be Walsingham, Kit said thickly with drink. Forty pound, oh no.

— I go, Wyld said, leaving you my copy of the report. I will do what you say, Mr Watson. And he left. Tom read: Instantly William Bradleigh maide assalte upon Th. Watson and then and there wounded strooke and illtreated him with sworde and dagere of iron and steele so that he despared of hys lyfe wherefore Thos Watson with his sworde of iron and steele of a valew of 3s 4d did defend himself and –

— Mr Baines, Pole or Poole said, has thought much on money but to little purpose. He will have it that money is nothing, a token of value and no more, whereas I have it that coin of gold and silver has a beauty of lustre. Heap it, I say. Coin it if you can, and to say it hath no value when a skilful coiner can take church plate and cut and face it to angels and the like is the veriest idiocy.

Kit felt he needed his head clear so took a draught of aliger from a jug that was seasoning a gentleman prisoner's oysters just brought in. He recited as best he could from memory;

> Bags of fiery opals, sapphires, amethysts,
> Jacinths, something, something diamonds,
> And seld-seen costly stones of so great price
> As one of them indifferently something
> And of a carat of this quantity
> May serve in peril of calamity
> To ransom great kings from captivity
> Something something something something something
> Infinite riches in a little room.

Pole or Poole attended avidly, a free bestowal from a poet, and said:

— That is fine, though there are too many somethings. And you put your finger on my meaning, which is that the wealth is in the thing and not in its most vulgar passing from hand to dirty hand, aye, gold comes first, but your fine stones follow. Amethysts, diamonds, aye aye aye. And fine plate in the churches and cathedrals stolen I may say here without fear by them that say that what was by good Catholics built is owned by good protestants. So the stealing back is by way of enforced restitution. Glastonbury, Canterbury, other edifices of the faith yield fine metals to be melted, cut and stamped. Mr Baines wished to know if I knew who had taken plate from Glastonbury and I gave him names of men non-existent and he wrote them down, he has this case with quill and knife and inkhorn. He writes much down.

— So, Kit said, we have as good a right to coin as the Queen her majesty?

— Aye. I like your line of a little room.

— Infinite riches in a. I must sleep.

Kit lay that afternoon on a bare board, sleeping little but transporting himself to the warm air of the Middle Sea, where his Jew named Barabas cheated Turks and Christians alike. Baines found him at dusk, saying:

— Well, now I may leave. I have crowned my stay, which thank God is over, with discovery of a Jesuit that was disguised as a trader of nags. He was heading his letter to a friend with AMDG, which as all know is *Ad Mariam Dei Genetricem*, foul idolatry, to pray to God's mother is forbidden.

— You have it wrong, Tom Watson said from the neighbour bed. It is *Ad Maiorem Dei Gloriam*. Has anyone come for me?

— Is that true? Well, it is all one, filthy jesuitry.

— You report to whom? Kit asked. Direct to Sir Francis?

— No, to Poley. Poley has been back in England these three weeks.

— Ask Poley to arrange for my bail. Wait. I will write him a note. And Kit took from his bosom his three pages of *The Massacre at Paris*. Lend me your pen and inkhorn.

— And, Baines said while Kit wrote, he was to end his letter with LDS, which I take to be a request for money, though he puts the pence before the *solidarii*.

— *Laus Deo Semper*, worried Tom corrected.

— Is that true? That makes it worse. You know much, he added in suspicion.

When Kit rose next morning but one after tortured sleep (here he was selling himself back to the Service, no longer even when freed from here a free man), he first pissed into the great sunken well of the Master's Hold. Then buttoning he passed blear-eyed into the boozing ken where boozing already proceeded. There he saw to little surprise Nicholas Skeres. Skeres greeted him familiarly with *Kit Merlin*. He was his first filthy self of the meeting at Dover that time and seemed much at his ease with whip-jacks, adam-tilers and clapperdogeons. He offered Kit ale and part of a cold pasty, asking him to ware of the fingernails therein. Then he said:

— There be two quick to act as Service sureties, Kitchen of Clifford's Inn and Humph Rowland the horner. Robin Poley was pleased to hear of your eagerness to be back at work after your playhouse diversions. There is much to do. Enemies everywhere, indeed from the extremities, Catholic and Puritan. You are to see him at Seething Lane. Sir Francis is very sick, all is in Robin Poley's hands.

— I am free to leave?

— Ah, here is Tom Watson. Ale for the swordsman.

— My wife? Has aught come?

— It will be a wearisome wait. Even the innocent are made to feel guilty. They say guilt is man's born condition, prisons are here to remind us of it. You must hope the Sessions jury is of the same mind as the coroner's. Aye, free to leave. Come.

KIT'S first act in his own dwelling, whose lintel he thankfully kissed, was to flint a candle and welcome the nymph into the very pits of his lungs. Then he washed with vigour and thoroughly and changed his shirt. Yet it seemed a prison dankness still clung to him and could be sniffed in the locks of his hair even when he had laved it. And when he confronted Poley at Seething Lane he felt the shame of a felon. Poley, fattened somewhat and very daintily dressed and with most clean fingernails, was inclined to smother him in love and welcome, my dear Kit, it has been so long, I have had a hard time, I know the hell of imprisonment, and I have had the rigours of much travel in the cause, thank God we are together again, call me Robin.

— Robin, Kit said doubtfully, well, sir, and so I call you Robin.

— You must listen with care to all I now say, dear Kit. You owe us, you know that.

— The forty pound will come back to you in December.

— There was cheating that time in Flushing, do not think we can with impunity be cheated, dear Kit, Baines told us everything, yet you could not be wholly blamed, Sir Francis's mind was made up, there was the Spanish danger about, I know, I know. Well, in effect you said Drake could attack Cadiz and we could proceed to war and the war was won and there is an end to it. But, and here he grew somewhat fierce and struck the table with the heel of his hand, there is no end to it. The war will be resumed. There will be no strike in the Channel, not ever again, ah no. So where will they strike now?

— I presume from another quarter.

— I like thy wit well i'faith, as the clowns say. I have seen plays, even yours of Faustus and the devil. I like *not* thy wit well at the moment. The answer is from the north, to wit Scotland. There be Calvinists in Scotland and Catholics in Scotland, so Scotland is a pretty parcel of enmity. And their king is in it, it is perhaps no wonder when we murdered his mother.

— So you admit to murder?

— Of course, murder, there was no other way. King James Sixth is a drunken fool and a known bugger and there be earls up there that have cajoled him into asking old Philip of Spain to send some of Parma's troops from the Low Countries to join with an army of Scots Catholics from the north to invade us. There, that is a surprise for you.

— It would fail.

176

— It must fail, true, but it will set the Catholic nobility here to thinking of ancient rights of succession. The Queen is old but still will not name a successor, you know that. You are a friend of one Catholic earl, he added in a kind of reproach.

— Hardly a friend. I cannot deny meeting with him if it is the Earl of Northumberland you mean. He is no Catholic.

— You are slow to lose your innocence. He remembers a father dead for the faith, old allegiances will rush back in if they are pricked by certain possibilities.

— What would you have me do? Robin, he added.

— Dear Kit, you must proceed to Edinburgh. It is a pleasant voyage from Deptford if this calm weather holds. You will resume your old guise as one converted to the old faith, that served you well that time you will not easily forget –

— Never never.

— It is a precept of Machiavelli that you must never see the bloodier consequences of your acts for those melt manhood. This you must have read.

— I do not think so. What must I do?

— Meet the Earl of Huntly. Young Fowler in Edinburgh also poses as a Catholic but he works for us. He has told Huntly, also Errol and Angus, that one hot for their cause will come from England to learn more of strategy and give the names of some below the border who will raise banners for the English side. You will have a travelling companion.

— Not Skeres?

— Ah no, not old Nick. It must be someone better able to assume high rank. You will see.

— When?

— Before their drunken sodomitical idiot of a king proceeds to Denmark for his wedding to their princess Anne. I shall be there. He will splutter out nonsense but it will not all be nonsense. There is somewhat required of their king.

— An undertaking not to invade?

— It will not come to that. In one week come to see me, do not forget you must hold to that as to an oath and no more spells in Newgate for brawling in the street. You have no sword, I see.

— Taken. Forbidden the use of a weapon *sine die* so that friends of the dead one may the more easily strike me down. But I shall keep myself safe and be here when you say. I am, he added grudgingly, beholden.

A CAULDRON for the Jew, Henslowe said, handling the sheets, that can be done.

— That is Tom Watson, Kit said. He has been beguiling his prison hours. You can say the play is near complete. Can you give me money?

Henslowe began to whine. Ned Alleyn said:

— I have a shilling or so. But things are not easy, what with talk of the censorship. The Queen's Men are snuffed out like a candle and the Admiral's are to take over the Theatre for half a year if we are permitted to act at all.

— Why leave the Rose?

— Money as always. Lord Strange's Men pay a fair rent for the Rose that they may become known. And they borrow me.

— I know nothing of this Lord Strange. Who is in the company?

— New men. Tooley, Ostler, Alex Cooke, Dicky Robinson. One newly up from the country trying his hand, Shogspaw or Shagspeer or some such name. There have been things proceeding behind your back.

— And who is Lord Strange?

— One that is more than the loaner of a protective name. He thinks highly of players, he had his own company up in the north where he keeps his estate. He thinks highly of Dick Burbage who is like to lead them. My lord Pembroke has, I think, put the notion in some heads. Truly his lady perhaps. Sir Philip Sidney's sister, it is in the blood.

— Sidney thought little of plays.

— She is in love with some Frenchman called Garnier. She

178

translates him. There is hope for us all on the lay side, the clerisy thinks us to be filth and disruption.

They were seated in a waterside inn named the Red Hat, whose sign was a devil clothed as a cardinal. Ned Alleyn had taken the pages of *The Rich Jew* from Henslowe. You cannot, he said, leave Machiavelli alone. And he recited to the inn:

> *Albeit the worlde thinke Machiavel is deade,*
> *Yet was hys soule but flown beyond the Alpes,*
> *And now the Guise is deade is come from Fraunce*
> *To viewe this lande and frolick with hys friendes.*

— And the tragedy of the Guise? Kit asked.

— In time, in time, Henslowe said. I tell you, it is a hard world.

— He means, Ned Alleyn said, that Sackerson the bear is to have a tooth drawn and the French pox is rampant. Fear not, Pip, all may yet be well.

— If life were but easier.

Kit found himself singing without much tune:

> *We'd be content with play*
> *And have no souls to save*
> *And follow the year with profitable*
> *Labour to the grave.*

It all came back to him, the evening with Captain Foscue in Rheims, the lie the doomed priest had sung about the deadliness of thinking. A mild-seeming man he did not know, fiddle-shaped brow and an auburn beard, nodded now at those lines. Kit rose. He must pack his three shirts and proceed to Deptford, a matter of catching the evening tide.

IT was with some surprise and no surprise, first one then the other, that he found Tom Walsingham was to be his fellow voyager. He was on the quay where the *Swiftsure* lay docked, his

man Ingram Frizer not with him, dressed exquisitely in pink with
gold beneath the doublet slashes, hair to his shoulders under a hat
with osprey feathers and a broad brim. His cloak was scarlet and
heavy. His bag was of new leather, perhaps Florence work. He
showed no surprise at Kit's coming; the disclosure of travelling
companion had been one-sided. He said:

— Dear Kit. After so long. She will not sail till dawn.
I have bespoken a night's lodging for us at Mistress Bull's.

— So. Over the smell of salt, distant offal in the slaughteryard,
fish not fresh, a remembered company of odours floated. It was
in odours that memory was entrapped. And where is Mistress
Bull's?

— A brief walk. Eleanor Bull is a hostess of some refinement,
she serves succulent fish dishes, her husband is a foul Puritan that
brings filthy Puritan print over from Middleburg. Robin Poley
that hates Puritans does not hate Rob Bull. There is a mystery
for you to ponder.

They walked together on the crackling dead leaves of the
garden of Eleanor Bull's house while she, a decent woman with
queen's hair and apple cheeks, dressed in the plain way of the
new reformists which Tom Walsingham in his discretion took to
be the plainness merely of her liking, oversaw the preparing of
their supper, a fish pie with dates and spices. Christ's blood, no,
not Christ's blood, streamed in the firmament, only the colours
of the autumn day bravely dying, a sweet sad swansong sung to
no ear. Tom said:

— We conquer mad fury, do we not?

— The fury of the flesh, so to put it?

— They impel me to winter before my time. A cousin dying
and a brother dying and myself last of the Walsinghams.

— Of your brother I knew nothing, of Sir Francis some
spoke of an improvement.

— To frighten his enemies and give hope to his creditors.
He is sick enough. Poley gives the orders. But there will be
no more orders for me when I play the part of Lord of the Manor.

— Your man Frizer has had his major-domo's chain ready
for some time.

180

— I hear the old bite. Frizer is beginning to think well of you. He once had ambitions as a stage player. He was, he says, overborne to an ecstasy of terror by your *Faustus*. He will not object to your becoming my resident laureate.

— Those are not for mere Lords of the Manor. You presume, or else you use some metaphor.

— The heat went out of us. We come to our autumns early.

— You must speak for yourself, Tom. I am still in my spring.

— Oh no. There was no spring in *Faustus*. We shall not share a bed here at Mistress Bull's.

— So you were in London for *Faustus* but had no thought of being there for its author?

— There were other things, he said vaguely. But I think that now we must be together.

— With Frizer blessing our chaste union?

— You must remember that Frizer saved my life. I was drowning. A swim in the lake and then a cramp came. You should be glad he was on the bank, watching, always watching.

— He saved your life, so I dutifully bless him.

— Let us go eat.

They ate, and after they slept in chambers somewhat removed one from the other. Kit woke from shallow sleep as the *noctis equi* plodded towards dawn. Well, to be self-serving, Scadbury Manor was altogether removed from the streets of killing rogues like Orwell. And there was the matter, truly perhaps a duty, of removing himself from playhouse business to serve – who? Erato? Calliope? He had not been in service to Melpomene, rather to her younger ugly sister Thalia. He had had in mind for some years rhyming the tale of the ephebe, hyacinthine-locked, drowned in the Hellespont with no salvatory Frizer plunging in. Of Tom's intentions he could understand little, he riddled overmuch. But Kit foresaw that Tom was foreseeing a kind of dutiful abandonment (duty, always duty) of the pleasure of entwined male limbs, the yielding to marriage, the continuance of the line. In that he would be following the nobility, Essex for one. Essex had, they said, arranged to marry Sir Philip Sidney's widow who was Sir Francis's daughter. The Walsingham red drowned in the Devereux blue. The Walsingham blood must not, like a summer river, dry. It must not be lost to history. Why then was Kit wanted (his own wing, Tom had said, sucking a fish skeleton)? A visible tangible temptation to resist or not resist? *My poet?*

They sailed downriver and began the long climb up England's eastern flank to the foreign country that was Scotland. There was ever the comfort to port of green land, ships at anchor, smoke from dwellings. The winds blew at their own caprice and there was brailing and loosing of canvas. They put in for the night at Grimsby and, inns being full, shared a bed as men often must. Naked, they touched. Tom said:

— Your body does not smell as it did. There is a rankness.

— Suffused with love of my nymph tobacco.

— Yes, you are one of Raleigh's tribe. Raleigh must be on guard.

— This he knows.

— You will be safe with me.

— Am I in danger?

— If Raleigh cannot easily be struck, others may be in manner of a warning. Come then.

They embraced, colled, clipped, roused nerves to breaking, joyfully died. And then on to Whitby. And later they touched Dunbar with rain squalls and flapping sails, Tom sick and Kit solicitous. At nightfall they nosed into the Firth and anchored at Leith. There was a brief journey on hired horses to an Edinburgh that smelt of peat fires. Their inn was on Spittle Street, south of the King's stables. Under a rainy moon Holyrood glowered. They lay, as before, in the one bed.

— Why are you here, Tom?

— For the delivering of a letter. Do not ask more. Here we become two not one. Sleep. And as to point their disunity he turned his back.

They awoke to the scent of an air diverse from London's. Still the peat smoke, now meeting them eyes and nose on from the smouldering fire in the room where they were to breakfast, the casement open, though soon at their bidding closed, to a tarter wind than any of the south. The goodwife who waited on them offered *parritch* and herrings. They must wait for milk from a cow or coo that lowed near by. Kit coughed over a noggin of *usquebaugh*. In the street after they must pause in their walk to avoid the brief deluge from an emptied jordan above, hearing the deformed French of *gardey loo* and knowing the territory to be foreign. Young Fowler they found in lodgings on Grassmarket. He made mock obeisances to his London visitors, bidding them sit, ready with a crock of Scotch ale. His English was of England though tainted with a Scotch rise that rendered each statement a question. Mr Walsingham might proceed at once to the palace where his majesty was at present and by luck residing. The two seals on Mr Walsingham's letter, that of the English monarchy, that of his grace of Canterbury, would ensure prompt ushering into the presence of some medallioned underling. As for Mr Marlin here, the Earl of Huntly was in Holyrood lodgings and would be told of the arrival of the London messenger, who must present himself at a dawn mass the morrow in St Mary's chapel, many thought this to be the dead queen already sanctified, the ignorance of the populace, there to take the consecrated bread as token of the sincerity of his faith and his office and after to deliver his package whose seal was not known to Fowler, nor to Kit, nor to Tom, but would doubtless be known to his lordship.

So Kit for a day had the freedom of this strange gaunt city, in whose taverns he heard the ancestor of his own tongue, though hardly to be understood. On Highriggs near sundown he saw one he thought he knew and who thought knew him. This man hailed him as Marlin, Merlin, Marley of Corpus Christi.

— Penry? Is it the same Penry?

— The same as what? I was at Peterhouse. Oh, you mean the Penry they search for. This sunset wind can be fierce. Let us eat.

They were given a small room in the back of a tavern named the Twa Corbies. The peat fire smoked. Penry coughed hard, showing good teeth. This scourge of the Church Established was no more than Kit's own age, red of beard and hair, fiery banners for one whose mission of fire was tempered with the

smoke of laughter, coughs and laughs being alike in that there
was no voluntary checking of them. Penry called for *usquebaugh*
and ale to quench it.

— We were both, I recall, under poor Francis Kett. You
heard of his fiery end? (This potion is fire enough.)

— With rage. And, answering your former question with
more than a cough, yes, I am both author and printer. I oft
wrote straight into type. You are eating herring with Martin
Marprelate.

— Where is the press?

— On a cart in a stable, I will not say where. I come
and go over the border. Here the Kirk protects me. But it
would be cowardly to cower in Scotland. They will get me yet,
I know.

— Not with assistance from me.

— I have to give you at least negative thanks. You did
not join in with the other play-botchers to attack poor Martin.

— I saw no cause to attack. Sir Walter Raleigh told me
the Queen herself took clandestine pleasure in the Marprelate
tracts. Her bishops are a wretched crew and she knows it.

— Oh, it is the whole damnable heretical nay heresiarchal
boiling that smells of hell. You knew me when I had to put
a cloak over my Catholicism. I have leapt over the casuistry
of the middle way to embrace the other extreme. But Christ
was always there, the same body whatever the garments. It was
Christ I hungered and hunger for, direct, untempered, naked,
body clasped to body. You smile. Why do you smile?

— Forgive me. You attacked your herring with such hunger.
I was thinking of Christ as *ichthyos*. And you must admit your
attachment to the Lord is expressed in highly physical terms.

— Ah well, it is the shortcomings of language. The saints
have bodies, else they would be angels. The smile, I must say,
is that of a cynic.

— Only among cynics will you find tolerance. I confess I
have been engaged with others in denying Christ's divinity. In
the honesty of free enquiry. Is that wrong? Free enquiry may
end up in inability to press the denial. Through the thornbushes

of thought thus to arrive at what the unthinking must take as a dogma.

— We must strip off all to arrive at his celestial presence which is also a fleshly presence. The miracle of God's becoming fallible humanity – the head reels more than with this *usquebaugh*.

— Surely not fallible?

— Flesh failing, flesh responding to pain, then the glory of the resurrection.

— This we find hard to accept. The physical Christ ascends to a physical heaven. Hariot the cartographer cannot map its whereabouts. When your people come to power will they burn me for this?

— We will think of burning others when we ourselves have gone through the fire. But he spoke with a smile that showed fishbones in tooth crevices. And, not now smiling, I will go through the fire when the time comes, for come it will.

— You accept martyrdom?

— As the final expression of love.

— Love of Christ which is not love of God.

— Christ *is* God, he is God tempered to our weakness. We may expunge from our view the fiery Jehovah of the Hebrews. Christ in glory is still Christ in rags. And then: Why are you here?

— I accompany one who delivers a message to the King of Scots.

— On what matter?

— This I am not permitted to know.

— It will be about a Catholic invasion of England. Nothing will come of it, I can tell you. There have been Spaniards here nodding in their beards aye aye and then sailing back to the Low Countries. All depends on King Jamie, and King Jamie dithers. He thinks he will come to the English throne in time and he may be right. He is learning to love bishops. Us he hates, but the Kirk is powerful. So you come here with a Catholic emissary.

— In a manner, keeping my own thoughts secret.

— You, Penry said, leaning over the broken herring earnestly, must put your house in order. You believe nothing.

— I believe in the power of words.

— Power on behoof of what?

— This I must learn.

— The time is short and groweth shorter. And, as though the eating of a herring were a frivolous expense of it, he said: I am glad to have met you again. I will pray for your soul. Christ will hear me.

Kit slept alone that night; Tom must have been granted a bed in the palace. When he came down to the smoky fire, the wind dashing rain against the panes, the dawn all tumbling clouds, he refused breakfast, first not knowing why and then knowing. The sacrament on an empty stomach. But it was no sacrament, it was but bread. And yet throughout all of the Christian time it had been Christ's body. Could the edict of mortal men, preening in fine robes, cancel Christ's own words? But Christ was but a mortal man. Or Christ never was.

— *Hoc est corpus meum. Haec est enim calix sanguinis* –

He retched on the round wafer. It would not be swallowed, it clung as flesh to flesh. The bulky man at the far end of the altar rail and the black-clad thin man at his side had marched before Kit down the short aisle, the bulky one limping, clad in the doublet and hose of the south, though very sober, but with a sort of blanket over his upper body, as for the cold, in what Kit took to be the colours of his clan. Now both looked toward the sound of retching, and he in black whispered to his companion after the ciborium had passed.

— *Ite, missa est.*

They met in the chapel porch, waiting till the scant worshippers, mostly poor old women, had gone out into the wind and rain before speech. The Earl of Huntly donned his bonnet. Kit could not comprehend his words. The other spoke the English of London, saying:

— I am Shelton that serves his lordship. You are come with a letter?

— And to collect one. Kit handed over his sealed package. The Earl tore open the outer wrapping with great and clumsy hands. Frae Pawley.

— From Mr Poley. Him perhaps you will know. He has been this way before.

— Know of. He has suffered prison and torture for the cause. Mr Shelton did not look innocent. He was brisk and with the discreet features of dissembled Jesuitry. None more trustworthy, he said.

— Amen. And Kit almost retched again. And for him?

— This. And he took from his breast a letter with a threefold seal. Kit stowed it.

— The Earl of Huntly surveyed Kit from sad grey eyes under eyebrows shaggily grey and licked chapped lips that showed red through a grey beard in need of barbering. He spoke.

— He says you must keep clear of the martyrisers. You have the look of one most vulnerable. He bids you pray to the mother of God for protection.

FREE, how free? he thought.

— Free, totally, Robin Poley pronounced. They were in the Garden, whose garden was all sleeping trees and bushes frost-crusted. Your discharge is confirmed and the bail money remitted. In another sense you are not free, this you know. You will never be free till England is free of the threat. Nor I, he added.

— The message is what you expected?

— Sir William Stanley is building his force in the Low Countries and paying his men with coined pewter. The invasion will not be yet. Time to sow fears, hates and so forth. And the Scotch king has declared against the Catholics, we have his own word for that in his own fist. He loves the Archbishop of Canterbury and adores our royal lady. So now they must seek an English claimant to the English throne and who will that be?

— How can I know?

— You are closer to him than you think. He has no mere nominal patronage of players. I mean Lord Strange. Stanley is his cousin. King James Sixth and Strange have blood in common, James from the elder sister of Harry Eighth, Strange from the younger on his mother's side. There is little to choose between them, but James hopes to succeed the easy way. He is a drunkard, a sodomite and a coward.

— Is there evidence that Lord Strange plots to succeed? He is no Catholic. He insists that his players pray before performance, and it is not Catholic prayers. And all must kneel to pray for the Queen at the end.

— Subterfuge, dissembling. He would have full-blooded popery back on us tomorrow if he could, and all the bishops Spanish. He must be watched. It dies hard with these northern earls, the old faith. The people have rejoiced in a lost armada and are ready to sleep again. They must be pricked awake to the danger. Fears and hates must be sown.

— As you said.

— As I said, and you look sour enough about it.

— I picture Christ on the Mount preaching fear and hate.

— This is hypocrisy, you know it to be so. Merlin the atheist.

— Slander.

— It may be slander but the imputation doth little harm. The true English Church makes atheists and Catholics sleep under one blanket. And how did you enjoy taking the Catholic eucharist?

— How do you know of this?

— My meetings with the Scotch earls always begin with a mass. I take it your encounter did too.

— It was not pleasant.

— Oh come, man, a morsel of bread, no more.

— To them, no. To us no for a thousand years and more. It was not decent. The host would not be digested.

— Superstition, man. I was brought up on eating to my own damnation, which you were not. It is flour and water. Well, enough. You need money for drink, your digestion will soon improve. Philips or Phelips will have some silver for you.

188

— Have I now paid my debts? Am I free of the Service?

— Kit Kit Kit, you will never be free. Or rather in that service to the Service lies your only freedom. Go now.

Kit went then. Whither and to what I do not know. But I know that on the vigil of the Nativity he was about in icy Eastcheap, wishing himself nor any others joy in the season. There were many in the dusk streets spewing into the kennel their devotion to the child of the birth that was approaching. No great star shone; the sky was murky. Kit took his early dinner at the Three Tuns, where, his past rowdiness forgiven or forgot, he was welcome enough as Mr Tom Berlaine or Dr Forster. He asked for a baked pigeon with a forcemeat of saffron and dried rosemary. He could eat little but was thirsty for ale. He sat alone at one end of the long table at whose other end was a laughing company of stuffers and swillers. Alone though not long. Soon Ingram Frizer came in with Nicholas Skeres, making with the draught of their entrance the candles dance and with Skeres's stumble a chair rock. They were drunk, though gently, and recognised Kit, sitting on either side of him without invitation, Skeres tearing a tiny leg off the pigeon that cooled untouched and tearing the flesh with finicking teeth. He was, doubtless for his Saviour's nativity, clean and cleanly dressed. Frizer was as always in sober black. Kit said:

— No major-domo's chain as yet?

— I have it but do not flaunt it. My master asked you to come to him but you have not obeyed. For this Yule, said he. There is to be a great fire tomorrow in the great hall and the tenants and servants are to be given drink and pasties. Holly and ivy are all about, aye.

— Mr Walsingham is doubtless Lord of the Manor at Scadbury but he is not my lord and you may not talk of obedience.

— I cry your mastership's mercy. He is, he told Skeres, to be the poet that resideth. A good poet, he admitted, I have some lines off.

> *Was this the face that launched a hundred ships*
> *And burned the topless towers of Iliad.*

— A thousand. Ilium.

189

— All one.

I'll be in Paris and for love of thee
Instead of Troy shall Winchester be sacked.

— You do not have it right. But it is good for you to have
me even if deformedly by heart. Do, Mr Skeres, devour all my
pigeon. I have no appetite.

— No? Is there roast pig? he asked young Kate Shilliber,
in whose bosom some ivy rested. We shall have roast pig. We
will, he told Kit, have roast pig, being entitled to it. We have
roasted our pig and at leisure we will crunch his crackling. No
more.

— I said Winchester, Frizer leered, because I was thinking
on Winchester geese. They are all across the river in the Bishop
thereof his jurisdiction. But they hiss not in my direction, I will
not have it. Cleanness of life, master poet, is the clench and the
out-about. So I attain where I am through cleanness. In buying
and eke selling. And if there be coneys to be catched –

— Enough enough, Skeres said, digging the stuffing out
of Kit's dove with a long clean finger.

— Aye, discretion. Take counsel from one that knoweth. My
master's brother that had been Lord was pecked most viciously
by the geese. A skellet with holes all agape. When he died, I
was there, the forcemeat burst out of him.

— No, no, Skeres protested, desisting from his finger-poking.
Be cleanly, we are in gentlefolk's company. Gentry coves they
call them in the place that shall have no name.

— So, Frizer said, each night after supper you will recite
what lines you have writ in the day and my master will nod or
shake according to whether they be good or no. I have a pretty
taste in such things I may say, I have read books to him.

— You are then raised above major-domo, Kit said. He
could not take offence: they were drunk and this was Christmas
Eve, but he had not known that their friendship or alliance had
brought two worlds together. You are Aristotle to his Alexander.
Or Seneca to his Nero.

— You will not call him Nero, Frizer said with sudden

sharpness. I know of the emperors, you think I do not, and Nero was cruel but my master is not. Save to them deserving of it. Things are changed and changed mightily. There is to be no more beastliness.

— What beastliness do you mean? And on whose part?

— It is Christmas, I say no more. Think on the pretty child in the stable with beasts all about him. Though no geese either of Winchester or Jerusalem. It is the season of cleanly love.

Robert Greene, staggering in, took that as a stage cue. Love, he cried, and charity, which may be accounted the same thing. Of your charity a pot of Malmsey. I will pay on the feast of Stephen, my credit is good. He saw Kit and raised a finger as in menace. I forgive my enemies. My salvation is in my Saviour who saveth me hence the redundancy and pleonasm of my asseveration. Cutting cutteth and Em emmeth and Master Greene of arts a master is alone. Malmsey.

— Are all drunk this night save myself? said Kit rising and seeking to push his way out. Skeres pushed him back to sitting. He said:

— All friends here. I take it thou wilt spend Yule with a dog in the manger.

— I am not thou.

— Friends, Kit, thou art thou and I to thee am thou. With Ingram here the case may well be different.

— I will not thee and thou him, Frizer said with lofty humility. It is not deference but difference.

— I will thou thee, Greene cried, thou famous gracer of tragedians that hast said with the fool in his heart that there is no God. Yet all must meet him that will mete out condign punishment. Be warned. A pot of Malmsey.

— Oh, for God's good sake, Kit said, again seeking his way out.

— God, Greene said, he useth in manner of an expletive lacking a signification of ontological import. He will not buy me a pot. So let him proceed out into the darkness.

Kit was let leave, but old Shilliber called him to pay. Kit threw silver on to the table for what he had consumed and what

not. Greene bowed him officiously to the street and followed him.
He bawled:

— Ball, Ball. Butter-cutter. And there was Ball with his dagger
out. Come, Greene said, it is Christmas and we must love our
enemies. Ball did not clearly understand. Cutter, Greene said,
do to him what he did to you. The wrist he writeth his tragedies
withal, nick only. Kit had no sword (*sine die*) to draw. He put up
fists. This to Ball was a convenience. He struck with his dagger
and drew blood from the right wrist. The blood pumped. Kit
remembered a lesson from Warner. Not the vein, not. He ran
pumping blood. All of his body would be out through that one
grinning mouth. The candles from within had shown it. He ran
to another candle, one within a doorway. Tom Kyd was at the
door. Help me, Kit cried. I lose blood, I will lose it all.

— You are bleeding over everything, Kyd protested within.
It was, as I know too well, a very mean dwelling. Kyd had
decked it with a little holly for his Saviour.

— That kerchief there. Knot it tight.

The knotted kerchief was deeply embloodied. Tighter tighter.
Kit lay on what had been my bed, fancying he might soon meet
the God of whose existence he was unsure. Weak, he was weak.
Another, cleaner, bandage. Kyd rummaged and found an old
shirt of mine, torn, abandoned. The bleeding eased, thanks be
to God or someone, something. The wound was tightly bound.

— I had thought, Kyd said, to spend my Christmas alone.
I bought some boned beef, it may be enough for two. Mistress
Heywood made me a pudding that will go in the pot. I was on
my way out to buy pottle ale. It seems you have an enemy. This
season should be all forgiveness. I forgive you.

— For what you forgive me?

— For overbearingness and unlawful pride.

— Oh my God.

— Your God, aye, and the God of all. That blood is staunched
but not Christ's that floweth over all the world.

— Greene feigned to forgive me too but I was slashed just
the same. See, the blood starts once more but not so much. I
am thirsty. Get your pottle ale, I have money.

— I forgive without feigning.

— Forgive for success. I do not like jealousy.

— I am not jealous. I am he that wrote *The Spanish Tragedy.* You may stay a day or so and help me with the new work.

— Help the great Thomas Kyd? The honour is extreme.

— Only God is great. All honour to his Son that is born this night.

— Amen. Kyd nodded and left the little jail of a bedroom. He seemed to forget totally Kit's wound. Kit left the bed where I had slept and which had been untouched since my leaving to see with mild curiosity the chamber where Kyd had made his one masterwork for the playhouse. This had its pallet with a stained pillow and a mound of rags of sackcloth for blankets. The two candles had no sconces but were affixed by their own wax to the few bare portions of the table which was mostly deep in paper. There were plays abandoned – *Alexander and Roxana, Have at You Mad Knave, The Tragedy of Vitellius, Moses and Pharaoh, The Comedy of Perkin Warbeck.* Kyd, seeing Kit enter, was eager to lift towards him hands filled with manuscript as with flowers carelessly yet lavishly uprooted, saying:

— This is a great poem on St Paul.

— Who will buy it?

— All who love God.

— And all who love poetry?

— The poetry is in the fervency of belief. Read.

Kit read the sheet proffered.

> *Saul then smote hard all those of Hebrew bloode*
> *That saw in Christ arisen their sole goode,*
> *Enchaining them and striking with a rodde*
> *Them that acknowledged not the hidden Godde*
> *That never woulde affront His maiestie*
> *By in raw flesh descending from the skie.*

— You want my help in what capacity, poetic or theological?

— That is but a draft. I have worked long at it, I need a fresh eye and ear. Your bleeding has stopped.

— Saul did not smite the Christian Hebrews. He smote only

the Greeks who had turned to Christ. Of these St Stephanos was the first.

— I am no master of arts in divinity.

— And I am no lover of the turncoat Saul or Paul. A juggler only. Raleigh's man Hariot could give him lessons. Why not call your poem *Fast and Loose*? Fast-bound in devotion, loose in form. And he that was fast or speedy to persecute was loosed from his obligations by a fit of the falling sickness. The title could have manifold meanings.

— That is blasphemy but I am not shocked. I am not shocked by a dog's yapping or an owl's hooting. I will write *Greekish blood*. I thank you for your help. I will eat my boned beef and pudding alone.

Kit felt shame and pity. He said:

— That was foolish. I am somewhat lightheaded with the loss of blood. How do you live these days?

— Botching and collaborating. It is not easy. I am back to the noverint's work for the odd shilling. I cannot seem to conceive a play entire. Give me the plotting scene by scene and I can manage the verse. Can you lend that help?

— Alas. But Sir Walter will pay well for your Italian hand.

— That atheist?

— Not so. All his work at present is confuting the Arians. He needs the chief Arian arguments copied out the better to refute them. I have them in a book. I can bring the book. I can show what must be copied. Can you do that?

— Perhaps. I will see. Is it in reality some atheist trick?

— Devout as you would wish. A humble search for truth. The slashing of the Arians, the logical confirming of Christ's divinity. Will you do it? Your admirable Italian hand.

— I will see.

That was unwisdom on Kit's part, as time would show. And where was I that Christmas? I had found Tom Kyd very wearisome with his moans at what he termed the hell of dramaturgy and indeed also his envy at the acclaim Kit's work had earned. I had abandoned the Lord Admiral's Men through dislike of Alleyn's imperiousness and had discovered the talent of

song with Lord Strange's Men, as also the skill of comic gallantry
in what young noblemen's parts I was granted. And I was lodged
now with the new player and playmaker (botcher, collaborator)
from Warwickshire, a mild man but ambitious, who sucked me
dry, but ever with a mild smile, of all I knew of the craft. He
moaned this Christmas, indeed wept, because he was absent from
his three children that had ever loved the games of the season and
the gifts. He moaned less that he was absent from his wife.

LENT came and the playhouses were closed, but Henslowe
and Alleyn, in their money-loving cunning, found that they
might, without censure, play *The Rich Jew of Malta* at the
Cross Keys in Gracechurch Street. This was but an inn with a
fair-sized yard, the stage no more than a set of creaking boards
resting on empty barrels not well roped together, so that when
Barabas was told that he had committed and he proceeded to
complete the accusation with fornication, but that was in another
country and besides the wench is dead, he began to roll off as
towards that other country. But all was secured and all rolled
well to its end with Barabas falling from the upper gallery into
the seething cauldron with

> *Had I but escap'd this stratagem*
> *I woulde have broughte confusion on you all,*
> *Damn'd Christian dogges and Turkish infidels.*
> *But now begins the extremitie of heate*
> *To pinche me with intolerable pangs.*
> *Die lyfe, flie soule, tongue curse thy fille and die.*

Tom Watson was with Kit in the yard; both wished to be among
the groundlings. Tom had been found to have killed Bradley in
self-defence and recommended for the Queen's pardon, which
he graciously got before Shrove Tuesday. He had written some
of *The Rich Jew* in Newgate, cheering his heavy heart with most
bitter comedy.

— So the Admiral's and Pembroke's are joined together here?

— Aye, lofty men that are friends and became so when they presided over the murder of Mary of Scots.

— Say not murder so loud.

There seemed to be no informers here. Kit let his eye in panorama roll over the cram of chewers of sausages and nuts, drinkers too of ale, the Cross Keys being about its primal function, and wondered to himself what message they were receiving from the bawlings of Ned Alleyn whose great nose of pulped and painted paper was, like the barrels, insecure and had at times to be held fast by hand. They knew no Jews, an alien race of myth that had killed Christ and made money through usury. They were in leather and broadcloth, holding in their unwashed odour like precious incense, though it escaped in whiffs and slamming underarm blasts. Some held wormy cheese in one hand and a knot of garlic in the other, teeth champing and eyes on stage, a sort of divided animals. Were they then to be taught naught but gross comic murder, language mere noise (but was it more in the endless Sunday sermons they were whipped to attending?), history a gallimaufrey of rivalry and blood? They wished diversion, no more. Diversion filled no empty heads, save with ride in triumph through Persepolis and avaunt avoid Mephistophilis and (so it would be now) master I'll worship thy nose for this. The Countess of Pembroke had, so the Wizard Earl had told him, urged the need to use the playhouse to refine and instruct, following Garnier and such. History, she had said, was at least knowledge.

There was a prayer for the Queen at the end, might she be protected from filthy bugaboos and foul atheistical papishes and puritanicals, and then all rushed to leave, clumsy clogs clattering, keep thine elbow to thyself, what sayest thou bully, chill deal thee one, out on it, thy nose is like his though it will not come apart if I tweak it, and so forth. Then Kit, turning himself to leave with Tom Watson, saw Baines and another. Baines said:

— Well, there you have it, the diseases of money of which I spoke that time, the dire sin of amassing wealth contrary to Gresham. I am glad to see you both out of Newgate, that was no good spell. I was away after, as you may know. This is Mr Chomley, a Richard like myself.

— Chomley?

— Chumley or Cholmondeley, there be many spellings and soundings. I am happy to see you, Mr Marlin or Morley.

— Marlowe will do. There be many soundings and spellings.

— I have long admired, Cholmondeley said. He was an intense dark young man in dark doublet well cut and unstained. Kit felt he could not greatly like the maroon eyes that seemed to melt in admiration most factitious. The eyes seemed greatly under the control of him who had them. Admired you for poesy and for boldness also.

— Boldness?

— Come, if I do not presume, and let me buy you some potion apt for one I admire. They have wine at the Black Bull and we may broach a bottle. And your friend.

— Watson. Kit, I must go to my wife.

— And you no wife, Mr Marlowe, a free man. Shall we then?

So at the Black Bull on Gracechurch Street on an afternoon of Lent, a fine season for the fishmongers, they sat, Baines and Cholmondeley facing Kit, and a bottle was broached. The wine was not good, it had a flavour of nose-dropping when the throat catches it, but Kit drank and listened. Cholmondeley said:

— Boldness I said. There has been a man hanged for boldness each hour of the London day. You have been courageous in your boldness and remain, as I said, a free man.

— Bold in my boldness, so?

— If more were so bold then the world might grow less fearsome. That courage encourages. I would be bold too.

— Then be bold.

— Bold to say that there is no God, that all comes from an accidental seed, that sin is a fabrication of such men as would have others tremble in fear, that religion is a lie.

— You believe that?

— These are ideas that pass through the brain of the bold man. I think you hold such and speak them. I do not yet have the boldness.

197

— And where have I spoken such heresies?

— Oh, around and about. I would not say heresies.

— What are you? Kit asked. Where do you come from, where were you educated, in whose employ are you?

— A Cheshire man with a brother a knight, brought up in private tutelage, as for my employ I have been in the service of many but am too hot in nature to stay long. Last year I was apprehended in the Strand for rioting after the Portingal adventure. I was spoken well of by my lord Essex that lost most through the expedition.

— You are in the employ of my lord Essex?

— Well, Baines said, we must all go where we can. With Mr Secretary near to death the Service is like to fall apart.

— I take it, Kit said, that you would have me talk of Sir Walter's imputed atheism so that you may pass this on to my lord Essex. I am not so simple but you I think are, both. When I reach the street I will spew up your wine.

— You are wrong, Cholmondeley said very mildly. You have too much fire, it is the poetic faculty. I have fire too but it is held well in check. I thought there might be friendship.

— The friendship of fellow atheists?

— Fellow enquirers into the truth. Well, you are in some agitation it is no wonder, you found fault in the acting of your new play I do not doubt.

— *You* are bold enough in your talk, Kit said to Baines. You were quick to tell Poley of my failure in duty at Flushing. That is the way of the puling schoolboy. It was not manly.

— Nor is your speaking friendly.

— Here is a curse for your tablets, Kit said in glee and anger. May the hosts of Beelzebub bite off your pricks and then spit them out as unsavoury, may Belial juggle with your ballocks, may the great Lucifer himself pedicate and irrumate you in fine Catullan fashion. Hell's a fable, though not for you, in hell is a special stinking zone for spies.

— That is far from friendly, Baines said.

— Of which you are one, Cholmondeley said. So the hell is for you too.

— Like God, if he exists, I am what I am.

And Kit left, tipping the bottle of wine before departing, so that a quantity dripped into Baines's lap. He would not find that friendly either.

KIT rode on Jack Cade, Perkin was unwell in the fetlock, rode with reluctance (how free was he?) through Chislehurst, Mottingham, Eltham. The news of Sir Francis Walsingham's death had come to him and the Lord of the Manor at the manor house in Scadbury. I have not seen but have heard of this building, being told it was a fine one though somewhat neglected for lack of money, the great disease of our time, half-timbered with a long gallery some seventy feet by thirteen, a ceiling of curved braces and panels of devices with some meaning for the Walsingham family though not for others. There were carved corner posts and gables and surfaces of the style termed magpie because, I take it, of the black and white. There was wainscoting not hangings and there were touches of the Flemish, or so I was told. The building was said to be by Athelwold Smythson, of the family of the Robert Smythson who was to erect in Derbyshire Hardwick Hall more glass than wall.

Here after supper Tom Walsingham and Kit had been enacting part of the tragedy of Edward II, near-finished, with much frolicking and embracing. Tom, being Lord of the Manor, must enact the King with

> *What, Gaveston, welcome, kisse not my hande,*
> *Embrace me, Gaveston, as I do thee.*
> *Why shouldst thou kneel? Knowst thou not who I am?*
> *Thy friende, thyselfe, another Gaveston.*
> *Not Hylas was more mourn'd of Hercules*
> *Than thou hast beene of me since thy exile.*

And here is Kit in reply:

199

And since I went from hence, no soule in helle
Hath felt more torment than

Here Ingram Frizer came in to the supper room, still in his
riding gear, anxious to speak, but Kit cried:
— This is for you.

You shall not neede to give instructions.
'Tis not the first time I have kill'd a man.
I learn'd in Naples how to poison floures,
To strangle with a lawne thrust through the throate,
To pierce the windpipe with a needle's poynte –

— Here is grave news, master.
— Wait.

Or whilst one is asleepe to take a quille
And blowe a little poudre in his eares
Or ope his mouthe and pour quicksilver downe,
But yet I have a braver one than these.

— It has happened. Sir Francis died in the most frightful odour,
noxious urine pouring and spurting from mouth, nose and ears
and all holes else, the stench so great that they must bind the
body with bandages about their noses. And there be creditors
ready to seize his body but they have been foiled through hiding
of it.
— Well, Tom said, we have been awaiting this. He filled
himself a beaker of red and drank to his kinsman's safe passage
to the fields of everlasting protestant bliss, saying: A great man
for the safety of the realm and in the most profound debt because
of it. We mourn and now I must puff myself up as the last of the
Walsinghams until I wed and beget an heir that shall beget heirs
and so to the end of time.
He strode, drinking and thinking, along the eighteen paintings
of Virginia Indians by Captain White and then back again. These
he had bought on Kit's recommending, there was money now
though never enough. His eyes looked on inner visions of rich
heiresses. Kit pinched himself for twinges of jealousy but found

none. Let him then. The hiring of boys who would yield their
flesh for a penny when Frizer was not about might or might not
cease. Marriage was not for pleasure. It was right he marry and
beget. Dire punishments for those that abused God's instrument
of increase. They kept him down and withal put into his funda-
ment a horn and through the same they thrust up into his body
a hot spit, the which passing up into his entrails and being rolled
to and fro burnt the same. That was in Holinshed, the end of
the king that loved Gaveston's arse better than his own realm,
but how much of that might be shown in the playhouse was a
matter to be thought on. It could be regarded as most instructive.

— That, Kit had said, is the end of my commitment to
the Service, for there will be no more Service.

— You reckon without Poley and others.

— Mr Poley, Frizer had said, it was that gave me the news.
Skeres and I were together on the business and –

— What is this business? Kit had asked.

— None of yours, Tom had replied.

— I stand, or sit, rebuked.

— Oh, it is a matter of lending out at interest, Tom had
carelessly said.

— High interest?

— Tolerably high. Money must be put out at interest, that
is in the scriptures. The unjust steward that buried his talent
in the earth was consigned to the outer darkness, was he not?
Weeping and gnashing of teeth and so forth.

— And Skeres, Frizer had said, must report to Mr Poley
and I was with him, though discreet in the rear. He came out
into the garden very agitated with the news. And he would see
Mr Marlin.

So seeing Mr Marlin he was.

— It is Sir Thomas Heneage now, that was Sir Francis's
friend and there be none firmer in the faith. But that is as
it were a stopgap till a lasting appointment can be made.

— Sir Robert Poley?

Poley squirmed in a mockery of modesty, seated in his
fine chair beside his table loaded with papers. He had on

his lap a black cat that looked on Kit as in recognition. Ovid's metempsychosis? Were the eyes the eyes of one he had helped to the scaffold? Poley said:

— We will not talk of deserts but rather of duty. No, it may be that Lord Burleigh and his humpback son will add a new burden to their existing fardels of state. No efficacy, I fear, they know little of the special agonies. There is one other, and we know who that is.

— If it is my lord of Essex everything will be diminished to civil war.

— Meaning?

— The destruction of Sir Walter Raleigh in the interest of Essex alone, and what you term the papist and puritan menace to be granted very short shrift.

— The Spanish menace, remember that, that only are we engaged in.

— Not I, not any longer.

Poley's stroking hand tightened and the cat squealed, though soon mollified with a gentle scratching beneath its chin. Poley said:

— You are in the Service, you are bound to it.

— My allegiance was to a man now dead.

— Your allegiance is to your faith and your country. Sir Francis was nothing, a mere flagpole.

— An odd metaphor. True, he was thin enough. My indenture was to him.

— Papers are nothing, papers can be forged.

— But not with the old Philips or Phelips skill. I went to him to ask for money, but he has become an Essex man. Like others. The fool Baines for one.

— They go, they shift, others come. You are to go to Scotland with Matt Royden who promises well. And you are to go soon.

— I cannot take that as an order. I may do things for you as the granting of a favour, but I have other work. My trade is the poet's trade.

— You mean the ridiculous playhouse.

— Ridiculous or not, I am coming to the end of a play, and there is a clamour for it among the players.

— Lord Strong's players? I told you Strong must be watched.

— The Earl of Pembroke's. Must he be watched too?

— I told you the danger is only with the northern earls. The danger with those is great. That is what your mission to Scotland is about.

— I do not accept the mission. You look hurt and your cat views me with dislike, but no matter. Another mission I may yet take, but not now. The play must be finished and put into rehearsal.

— These fripperies and frapperies of plays. If you will not you will not but you must be warned.

— Warned of what?

— You have been privy to much that is most secret and you are not to be let loose to blather among playmen and others. Oh, Kit, Kit, are we not friends? And with the change of tone the cat began purring.

— Of a kind, yes. But not of the playman kind.

— Let that pass, there are friends and friends. You fear that I am to become a man under Essex? That would be a fair fear were it to happen. In confidence I tell you that Essex will not last. He married the daughter of our late master, God knows why, he seems not to love her, without permission of the Queen. God knows why the men of the court must apply for permission to marry, it is, may we say, the jealousy of a virgin desiccated but fierce in her demands for a devotion she knows to be a fiction and a fairy tale. To marry is to divorce her majesty. Essex mayhap had some fantasy of inheriting the Sidney virtues along with the Sidney widow. Well, it is done, and all was kept quiet and secret, but now she is *enceinte* and the Queen knows and she has slapped his face at the court and he has slapped back and much else. Raleigh, I believe, made sure that the Queen knew. Essex, you may be convinced, though he take Sir Francis's daughter (may he rest in some sort of peace) will not take Sir Francis's place. You may take it that little may change, that your friend Robin Poley will be steadfast in the old

203

policies and have power enough, and that Kit Merlin will do his old work when he can. Go to your play but be ready for duty after. That a man did his duty is all he would desire to be writ on his tombstone. But we will not talk of tombstones yet or ever.

— Still, you have talked of tombstones. And it is all dealing in death, is it not?

— The death of evil, Kit, the pounding into dust of the enemies of a fair realm.

— I THINK it may well be our end here, the Earl of Northumberland said, busily smoking. The smoke-filled chamber was a comfort. All puffed, and the smoke caressed the maps and the *mappamundi*, the tokens of a great world without.

— Do not, Hariot said, be suffused with Sir Wat's gloom.

— He has his glooms and his consolations, Adrian Gilbert said. These latter, though, will not last. He was ever a bold man. All of forty thousand pound, he says, and what to show?

— Tobacco and the *solanum tuberosum*, said Hariot, also an Indian chief. Though why he must be baptised into the Christian faith his own gods know.

— The Queen's insistence, said the Earl, relighting. Well, here he is at court to demonstrate to the sceptical that Virginia existeth. He must be prodded to prove palpable reality. He rightly hit back at the palpaters.

— He was brought to the Rose, Kit said. He wished to join in the fighting on the stage. He has a fine head, they appear to be a fine people. He counted for me: *akafa, tuklo, tukcina*. He pronounced Alleyn a *hatak kallo* and Henslowe a *hatak ikhallo*. A man strong, a man unstrong. You have discovered, he said to Hariot, a strange people and so have they.

— Well, I am done with navigating. Sir Wat hands all over to the stock companies and to them no poem such as You brave heroic minds will be written. And he goes back to privateering and plundering of Spanish gold, the Queen pretending ignorance. It is a hard life. And so we lose the head of our being.

— Here is Adrian to confer familial authority on our last sessions, said the Earl. Durham House no longer the sole eyrie of profitless speculation.

— Profitless, you say profitless? Adrian Gilbert spoke, that was Sir 'Walter's half-brother. He had none of Sir Walter's ruddiness and bulk, none of the Devonian burr, though much of the sharp eye of enquiry. And how are we to measure profit?

— He means, Hariot said, that the inspissation of a bigoted and superstitious nation with the new knowledge and the new scepticism is slow to accomplish.

— You will never instruct the bulk of the nation, the Earl said. And the heads of a nation do not cry out to know that their power is built on most flimsy foundations. They are quick – I think of the bishops mostly – to instruct the lower sort through the spoken word, since the unwashed are also the unreading, and will even, as with the Marprelate flimflammery, use the playhouse for damning what they wish damned. What has our Merlin here done to flush a clean wind through the brains of the sausage-chewers? *Faustus* could as well have come from the bishops themselves with its flouting of the virtue of knowledge.

— What is spoken on the stage, Kit said low and with some despondency, is pored over by the jailers of our souls. Only history is unassailable. Here is the truth of those that lived and it is nobody's office to praise or condemn.

— Her ladyship of Pembroke, Adrian Gilbert said, is always saying that the people whose forebears made the past, and she means the common sort, should know that past. Show that beliefs and manners do change, that all things are subject to change, that there is no stasis.

— You sound like Warner, Hariot said. Where is Warner?

— We were together in our alchemic enquiries at Wilton. He stayed, I am here at a near-brother's summons. He helps the Countess to make filthy her most delicate hands.

— *Honoris tui studiosissimus*, Kit murmured. All looked askance and he said: Pardon me. The letter she sent me stank of assafoetida or devil's dung. I was charmed. *Laurigera stirpe prognata Delia, Sidnaei vatis Apollinei genuina soror* I had written. This was the dedication to Tom Watson's *Amintae Gaudia*, writ for her but yet to be printed, my Latin is better than Tom's but not better than hers. She disliked my play for Pembroke's Men. Too much sodomy, she said, and not enough history. I cut out the buggering of King Edward with a branding iron. Well, she shall have history without sodomy, if it can be found.

Sir Walter's man came to the door to announce that Sir Walter and his lady were arisen and about, all might go down to the hall to partake of somewhat, an it please my lord and gentlemen. They rose and wondered if they should abandon their pipes. Lady Raleigh was a most delicate lady.

— Lady Raleigh, the Earl stoutly said, would not be Lady Raleigh if she abhorred tobacco. It is in the weft of her husband's skin. But we will descend pipeless.

— Below, there was a table with decanted wine white and red, cold small fowls, a sallet of cold boiled tubers diced with parsley, and a careless throw of kickshawses. Then Sir Walter, jewelled like the sun in his glory, entered with his lady. This was Bess (it was a kind of deference to her royal mistress to rustify her given name thus) of the Throckmortons, and, seeing her for the first time, Kit felt that the disposition of his inner juices might well undergo a kind of Pauline conversion, as in Kyd's wretched poem:

> *God in his glorie burnt his sightlesse eies*
> *And forc'd allegiance to another wise,*
> *For he was now not what he was before*
> *And in a flash old enmitie forswore.*

Though never enmity, indifference rather, all women being his mother and sisters and odd oyster wenches. She was termed one of the Queen's Glories, and so, by God, she was, or rather one of, by God, God's. Glory was in her eyes, and the sun in his glory debased through the mullioned window was caught and reglorified in her hair. Straight as a tree in farthingale of cloth of gold with scarlet petticoat, with a waist that a man might span with two hands, nay to be truthful three, her bosom demurely covered to show she had yielded her knot, she radiated qualities above virtue, the eyes grey and merry, a smile as of kindly mockery on her lips, and her scent not of the mixers of aromatic drops but of spring fields and the bruised fruits of the fall. Kit near went down on his knees. *O dea certa.*

— You said? she said, smiling.

— This is our poet Merlin, sweetheart. The rest you know. Well, my lord and gentlemen, here is Raleigh the married man, and we may expect the worst from her majesty, since the Earl of Essex is back in favour. A man must go his own way and a maid hers, in ecstasy we court disaster, but there will be time. *Amor vincit omnia*, though the royal displeasure may be said to be an exception. Tomorrow we ride to Devon, whence no doubt we shall be haled out and back. Now we eat together as friends.

And so they did, standing about the table with no stiff formality. Bess, Lady Raleigh, chewed a pheasant leg with exquisite greasy lips, a dancing beaker of white in an exquisite hand, and said to Kit:

— There was your *Dr Faustus* at court for the Shrovetide revels. Her majesty was much agitated by your parade of the Seven Deadly Sins.

— She may have known it was a tribute to dead Tarleton, my lady, who travelled the country with a play of the same name. And that doubtless took her back to the Earl of Leicester. She liked the rest?

— These days she likes nothing. And what Wat and I have done she will like least.

— An end, this Wat was saying, to our honest endeavours. But do not think there will be an end to enquiry less honest. There is some murmur of having Tom Hariot here up before the Privy Council.

— Oh no, not that, oh my God not that.

— Love and reason, it seems, are booted out of the door. Well, we expected this. Did we not expect it, Kit Merlin?

— I know not what to expect.

— Always expect the worst. *Exspecta pessima*. I think I shall change the family motto.

— *Exspectamus*, amended Kit the Latinist.

I MUST now with reluctance bring in the man I lodged withal and who was to be my associate for many years with the Lord Chamberlain's Men, a company not formed in Kit's brief lifetime. His name, like all names, suffered a multiplicity of deformation, from Shagspaw to Shogspere, from Choxper to Jacquespere, which was the ingenious etymologising of a drunken Huguenot, of whom London had many. He and Kit were at work on *The Contention Between the Two Famous Houses of York and Lancaster*, a most incommodious title which later would be changed to *Henry VI Part One*. The play of Edward II, though a brutalisation of historic truth, had pleased with its nobles and bishops and violence, and there was a need now for further theatricalising of old Holinshed. Kit had invited his collaborator to Scadbury, with Tom Walsingham's approval, and as they sat in the summer saloon Kit asked what he should be called, and he replied that Will was enough. Then he said:

— *Aio te, AEacida, Romanos vincere posse*. This will not do.

— You do not pronounce it aright. Are you an Oxford man?

— No, they whipped Latin into me at the grammar school, very little and no Greek. Perhaps I in my ignorance am the better fitted to say it will not do. It is learned and will not be understood.

— It will be by those that have read their Ennius. It is what the oracle at Delphi told Pyrrhus. It means both that he will conquer the Romans and that the Romans will conquer him. It is a pregnant ambiguity.

— Its pregnancy, like that of a wife two months gone, will not be easily apparent. But this I know. *Di faciant laudis summa sit ista tuae*. I have read a sufficiency of Ovid. But would York's son cry that to his murderer? It seems to me that you seek the praise of

208

PART TWO

my lord Pembroke and his lady rather than the comprehension of the multitude.

— The multitude oft likes to be mystified. It flatters them to think they are thought to know the classical authors.

— If you will have it, though I remain doubtful. I wrote this while you were wandering the woods with your Lord of the Manor.

> She-wolfe of Fraunce, but worse than wolves of Fraunce
> Whose tongue's more poisonous than the adder's tooth.

— So the adder Tom killed bit your fancy.

— We have enough adders in Warwickshire. Listen.

> How ill-becoming is it in thy sexe
> To triumph like an Amazonian trull
> Upon theyr woes whom fortune captivates.
> How couldst thou draine the life bloud of the childe
> To bidde the father wipe his eies withal
> And yette be seene to beare a woman's face?

— You have learned, you have been learning.

— You find yourself there?

— It lacks a shout. Hyena's heart, no, lion's, no, tiger's heart dressed in, no, wrapped in a female skin, woman's hide. Why did you come to this gear, as they say?

— To stop breeding. Three children were too many to keep on the wage of a lawyer's clerk. When the Queen's Men came I showed them part of a play and they had me because one of them had been beaten to death in the churchyard. I had been trying to translate Plautus but it seemed easier to pen my own lines. So I am here, though first as an actor. They will not have it that grammar-school boys can write plays. Botch and help when speed is needful, yes, but not sit to write a *Tamburlaine*.

— Well, I must leave much to you with this, and I am not sorry. The Lord of the Manor requires a poem so I must write a poem, he will lock me up with bread and water if not. Besides, I need to.

— What theme?

209

— Zero and Menander or some such thing.

— You mock yourself.

— It is all a great mockery. What is there for us who have no land nor goods to trade in? I think my lines from Ennius and Ovid are to comfort myself with the illusion that my learning has a use. Why, sir, you are a gentleman with your Latin tags, I had thought you to be a hedge-dragged sturdy beggar.

— You sang of profitable labour that time.

— When?

— In that tavern. I heard you. You nodded to me.

— I was abstracted. And now am abstracted in the other sense. Will you stay here while I am gone?

— I like not too much the man Frizer. He looks down his nose.

— He may mean harm but he lacks the skill to do it.

— And I am not used to the life of great houses. I will ride my hired nag back with you. O tiger's heart wrapped in a woman's hide. That is your touch, the learnable line. But I will learn. Where do you go?

— To a foreign country. Do not ask.

Tom Walsingham was away with Frizer on, Kit thought he knew, the dragging of high overdue interest on a loan out of some squire's son overspent in London. They led their horses from the stable and then took the London road. It was chill weather and they trotted under a sky that had no hope in it. Kit asked:

— You saw what happened at Holborn?

— It was indecent. I kept away. Tyburn surely is enough for their bloody shows without raising a special gallows in Holborn. Why?

— To fright the lawyers in the Inns of Court that are turning to papistry. Well, it was to do with your patron.

— Not mine, not yet, if ever, but I hope. I must steel my heart to comfort my hopes. I did not think John Florio was a spy, a harmless Italian protestant I thought, bowing to my lord, a good secretary. Nor did I know that the Southampton tutor was a papist and kept a tame jackdaw of a jesuit. You believe the story that this Fr Gennings

210

called on St Gregory when his heart was in the hangman's hand?

— It was I take it a gargling kind of scream sounding grrrgrrry. I come to believe little. I want peace, peace and again peace.

— There is only the one place where that is. Do not pray for it yet.

They cantered in silence and reached a dark London enlivened by fires whereon Spanish effigies were burnt. Would this never end? Kit found Poley in nightshirt and nightgown, groaning with rheum. His black cat played with a ball of wool that dangled from the table top. Poley offered a hot decoction of blackberries, saying: Peace? We are on the way to having it. It is a matter of giving the Spaniards a sufficient fright. If the Scotch Catholic earls can be seduced to come to Berwick they will be arrested, and all over.

— All over with their murder. You have had experience of murdering Scotch Catholics and one higher than an earl.

— You are morose, you are sullen. Your eyes are feverish in this candlelight. Are you sickening?

— Nothing your physician could cure. On what charge arrested?

— You need to ask? An act of war, the enemy on our soil. Then a trial at which they will dissemble nothing, this Philip of Spain may at leisure digest, then execution.

— And then a great march of all Scots skirling across the border. What am I to do?

— Deliver this letter to young Fowler in Edinburgh. It is to summon the papist nobility to a meeting in Berwick. The letter is signed by one they know.

— A forgery, of course. This is monstrous. Any *mezzo* will serve your *fine*. That is Machiavelli. Bruno thought differently. And if I say I will not do it?

— You break trust, and that is a kind of treason. You go alone, taking ship from Deptford tomorrow.

— Money.

— You shall have money. And you will sleep here tonight.

— Under lock.

— Kit, Kit, we are friends.

I know from what he said that he eased a grey trip up that eastern flank with fancied immersion in a kinder sea.

The god put Helle's bracelet on his arme
And swore the sea should never do him harme.
He clapp'd his plump cheekes, with his tresses play'd,
And smiling wantonly his love bewray'd.
He watch'd his armes and as they open'd wide
At everie stroake betwixt them would he slide
And steale a kisse, and then runne out and daunce
And as he turn'd cast manie a lustfull glaunce
And throwe him gaudie toies to please his eie
And dive into the water and there prye
Upon his breste, his thighes and everie limbe
And up againe and close beside him swimme
And talke of love. Leander made replie,
You are deceiv'd, I am no woman I.

Yet that kinder sea would drown the hero that swam to Hero's arms. The ship rolled and with pain he dipped into the ink of his writing case, alone and huddled in the lee. And once he had the mad thought that he would cast the sealed forged letter into the bitter waters, leave the ship at Scarborough and hide in York where the first Christian emperor had been crowned, so in a manner to be protected by old Rome and its legions. Or make the pretence that the letter had been delivered and young Fowler on his denial of this might be branded the liar. No, he would do what was called his duty. He had seen enough of his own blood shed but had by proxy shed quarts of other blood and would shed more. The pricked blood bladders of the playhouse sickened with their mockery. All wanted blood, blood was a beggar and screamed to be shed. He wished, as sickness struck him in the ship's bouncing by the Scotch coast, that he could live in the dead Greek dream he was in rhymed verses recounting. Free under a redder sun among fauns and myrtle and the treading of the grapes while on the hill smoke rose in some gentle sacrifice to gods crushed now by the monotheist heresy. What was he, what was he to be?

There was a foundering in him, the impaction of a weakness, a desire to be done with the living world and yet not yet in death. The stink of the playhouse rose feebly above the salt spray and he would have done soon with its feigning. You haled from the grave figures of old history who would be gladder to rest, the turmoil done, and there they were, Braile and Johnson and Robinson and Foyle and Rice and the great thundering Alleyn enacting them, suffering again that the rabble might with glee be spattered by swine's blood. He would wrap himself in an older past, and yet he smelt bad breath on Socrates and in the mouth of Alcibiades saw the decay of a tooth. Hero had lost a toe and Leander's laugh was inane.

While I leave Kit to his Scotch venture which there is no need for me to report I turn again to my chamberfellow and aspiring playman. I said, did I not, that I brought him in with reluctance, since his is another story and its nudging and shouldering into this of Kit's harms wholeness and bids break the frame. But *Natura abhorret vacuum*, and the same is true of what is against nature, nothing more against nature than our mad playhouse, and with Kit's return to England and Scadbury he left a vacuum in playmaking which had to be filled, and there was our Warwickshire man to fill it. *The Contention Between the Two Famous Houses* was finished by one pen only and that with a kind of speed of insolence. The play could hardly fail, nor its two successors, what with Talbot the terror of France at a time when a protestant French king was yielding to the Catholic League and France was once more a proclaimed enemy. And Will of Warwickshire, that had ever been mild, now became boastful. Boastful most in the presence of the sick and sneering Greene, in his cups at the Mermaid where Tom Nashe of his goodness had bought him a fish dinner.

— Well, it is as I said, there be two poles in the *mappamundi* of the writer's craft, ever opposed, and the scholarly and the mere crowd-pleasing cannot meet.

— There was enough of the scholarly in this chronicle, though that I left to my partner who defected. But I do not see how university study fits a man for filling a playhouse. It is better he go out in the world and observe manners.

— Meaning the world of butchers and glovers.

— Clothing five fingers need not be incompatible with clothing the five feet of a blank verse. And the whole world eats flesh.

— So we leave the nobility of the art to be traduced by grammar-school boys that strut on the stage and mouth country vowels.

— Envy, envy.

— The scholarly are above envy. Wipe off that false disdain.

— I could be angry. But you are not worth anger. I will pour out on the stage rhetoric that will not require justifying out of Cicero or Quintilian or whoever. There is no substitute for talent.

— Spit out your fishbones and go back to your mouthing.

— By God, I have had enough.

— Earned enough and more. The joybells of coin in your purse and you no more than a country upstart, what be this Hodge why it be a whole shillen and that chav not seen afore. Off ere I vomit.

— You have vomited often enough in fair company. Chief of the scholarly pigs without talent. We will beat you all yet.

— Cutting Ball will get you on my orders.

— I may have country vowels but I have also country muscles. I have butchered and will butcher.

But only once to my knowledge were there blows, and those on Gracechurch Street on a dark night. Greene was drunk and feeble and the country muscles prevailed all too easily. Yet there was shame and a quick desisting, for Greene's sickness was pitiable. And with the plague approaching and the impending closure of our playhouses Will of Warwickshire had set himself to shutting himself off from the world and starting an heroic poem to one that he hoped would be his patron.

It was at a performance of *Harry the Sixth* at the Rose that a black-clad fanatic burst on to the stage to denounce all plays with

The cause of plagues is sin and the cause of sin is plays therefore the cause of plagues is plays, a syllogism that did not please and he was bundled off crying to the heavens. Yet at Scadbury there was no intimation of coming troubles. Kit was able to say:

— I have not finished but I see a hope of finishing. Listen.

So Hero's ruddie cheeke Hero betray'd
And her all naked to his sight display'd
Whence his admiring eies more pleasure tooke
Than Dis on heapes of gold fixing his looke.
By this Apollo's golden harpe began
To sound forth musick to the ocean,
Which watchful Hesperus no sooner hearde
But he the day-bright-bearing carre prepar'd,
And ranne before, as harbinger of lighte
And with his flaring beames mock'd uglie nighte,
Till she o'ercome with anguish, shame and rage
Dang'd down to hell her loathsome carriage.

— A good time to pause, Tom Walsingham said. Have you a mind to riding to Canterbury? It is good weather for riding.

— Together? What business have you there?

— We are in Kent and Canterbury is the fair rose of Kent and I am become a magistrate of Kent. The business is to do with the great press of Huguenots and others pouring in and the native people becoming poor. That would include your own people.

— Huguenots buy Huguenot shoes but the native people have feet. My father holds his own, I have heard no cry of distress.

— The magistrates of the county are to meet, I being one, and talk of making your river navigable for boats and lighters, whatever those are, so increasing trade, how I do not know but shall doubtless be told.

— You must grey your beard and look grave, Kit said, leaning back in his chair, rubbing his wearied writing hand. Indeed Tom was much still the ephebe, sharing boys with his friend though talking of the gravity of marriage, hair hyacinthine, eyes bright and empty. You a magistrate.

215

— We start tomorrow. I shall wear sober black and a great black hat.

And so with the vermilion of the June dawn on their right hand they started, sleepily but merrily, in murmurations of starlings and exaltations of larks, unmocked by cuckoos, bachelors and friends, not properly now in the carnal sense lovers, chewing shives of beef and hunks of a loaf as they rode their first stage, passing from right hand to left left to right a cold flask of wine and water as they rode. On the narrow way out of Bexley they met a carriage with gold cherubim on its corners and a ducal blazon on its doors, driver and two footmen in their scarlet best, two fine Arabs drawing. They took left and right of it with the speed of youthful insolence, causing the ducal steeds to misfoot and whinny, the portly driver to raise his whip and the great man within, a mere youth of long nose, nodding feathers and a poncet box, to cry feebly: *Canaglia*. What vermin are these, belabour the swine. So that Kit fired back, very merry, with: *Sacco di merda, vostro disonore*. At Swanscombe was a cattle fair, all dung and lowing, slapping of haunches and chaffering, and they took ale in a tavern where a paunched farmer counted gold for the sale of a bull named Terror, pouching it with obscene love and spit and a snort for the poor who begged a penny for a cooling pot. Outside Frindsbury a man was beating his ass with hate, ferocity and a gnarled club because, overladen with a whole tree trunk about its own trunk tightly bound, already galled and with open sores, it could not engage the hill. He cried: Damned beast you shall go a third day without fodder. Kit and Tom alighted to grasp the club and beat the man in his turn, slashing off the burden with a knife and bidding the ass go free to the fields but it would not. At an inn in Gillingham they fed on cheese and the morning's bread and watched in near disbelief a contest of boys eating, each urged on by bet-placers and a father, the provender provided being a stale simnel cake, two date tarts, an apple pie in a deep dish, a dozen or so custards. At Sittingbourne an acid twisted man of great age, some sixty years, pawed and admired their clothes and horses, lamenting that after all his life as a town clerk he had nothing to show, Why should you be young and

merry and I not, there is no justice in the world. In a meadow
outside Faversham they saw a shepherd snoring in the sun, with
the bolder of his flock breaking through the hawthorn hedge and,
unnoticed, unchidden. And, dismounted for leg-stretching and a
roadside piss, not far beyond they heard human moaning under
birdsong, and, approaching the sound as it were tipatoe, they
saw from behind an elm, looking down into the grassy hollow, a
boy and girl busy in the act of love. Smock was up and breeches
were down, and he thrust hard moaning until he gave a weak cry
of joy to the empty heavens. And she beneath that was country
buxom seemed glad it was over.

— Seed shot in, Tom said, as they resumed riding. Nature
the brutal mother of all demanding more mothers. But these
rural folk have ways of cheating her, I know not what. Our
cheating is of a profounder and more metaphysical order.

Kit thought the words not well chosen. Soon on their horizon
the stained glass of Canterbury cathedral caught the late sun afar,
and Tom said:

— You recall Rheims? The cathedral there was indifferent to
our metaphysical cavorting in a field with the benodorous cows
looking on.

— No meta. Better than meta. But now we are past it.

— Not so. I refuse to be all magistrate. Let us roll naked in
that meadow. Thus you may bite both thumbs at old constric-
tions. Soon I think we meet your family. The great cathedral
frowns down. I hear the whistle of whips in your old school.
We are free men.

They tethered their horses in the meadow itself on the low
branches of an oak and, their clothes thrown off, heard the contented munching of deep June grass as they rolled. This sweet
air cleanses your skin of its tobacco smell, we are as we were,
there is this, aaaaaah. Well, yes, Eden recovered, God would not
come peering in the evening cool, he was locked up, puzzled at
reforms that had remade him, in the great sacring house of the
chief archepiscopate. It was Tom that took all the dominant part,
Kit yielding. Their reversal of roles was forbidden by the Lord of
the Manor and Kent magistrate, who shot his seed into a barren

place as of the right of some ancient *jus*. Kit clothed a swollen
rod and Tom laughed at it. Their feet beat the juicy meadow as
they led their horses to the road. The two gentlemen clopped into
the city by the North Gate, the King's School (whistle of whips,
smell of Ovid) to their left hand, seeking a lowly shoemaker's
shop.

— My friend, Lord of the Manor of Scadbury, a magistrate
of the county. I trust you have room for him.

The father and mother were older but still vigorous. Margaret
had at last married her tailor, nay more, their boy John had just
been baptised, he came early and folk talked. And poor Dorothy?
A woman now but little changed, she hath ten words, she hugs
all her old dolls. Poor Dorothy. I hope his lordship can take
our fare – a roast giggot as the Huguenots do call it. He is not
his lordship, he is plain master like me. Tom, you may call me
that. Thomas is of greater dignity, said Kit's father. Come back
when all is ready, Kit will show you the town.

This did not signify the cathedral. Tom did not wish to
see where another Tom had been butchered by four knights,
his sanctity, so swiftly bestowed, denied by a butcher king that
could unmake saints as readily as wives. They went to a tavern,
the Mule's Head, to ease thirst and found it full of French protestants. *Dew vang*, the tavern-keeper mocked Kit's order. There
was a drunken Gallic guest of the nation, nay no longer guest,
a tradesman here prosperously rooted and lavish host to toper
friends of his blood and faith. *Je pisse sur ces beaux citoyens de
Canterbourg*, he seemed to be saying as he circled, *qui possèdent
des mœurs ridicules et dont les femmes puent d'une réligiosité hypo-
crite. Car aux ténèbres elles acceptent volontiers une bitte française.*
And, to laughter and cock-crows and finger-horns to brows, all
watched him mime deep rutting and heard him squeal high *Oh
yu urt mon sewer thu art tu heeeeg.*

— No, Tom warned, hand on Kit's hand on pommel, no
swordplay here. The Scotch say *foo* and the French say *fou* and
he is both.

But when the man left to most cordial valedictions Kit was
(No, Tom said, again no) quick to follow. He was back in five

minutes with skinned fists, saying: He is able to totter home,
though blindly, no trouble. And then: home, I say, this town
is theirs and many of ours are homeless. Unity of faith permits
all, the granting of air, land and water and the right to scoff.

— You have no love of Canterbury. Why then so hot for
its protection?

— They do not respect our women.

— Nor you, though you do not choose that manner.

— You have not yet met my sister Dorothy.

— The idiot girl? You fear her ravishment by rollicking
frogmen?

— Something of that.

Indeed, as they saw at supper, Dorothy was now much
the woman in size and shape, with great breasts and haunches,
though in a stained frock fit for a child, and ever scratching
openly her privities. She did not recognise her brother, but she
bade Tom Walsingham kiss doll after doll after doll and then kiss
her. Throughout the eating of the giggot and parsnips she kissed
Tom slobberingly and sought to play with his long locks. It is
the way she is, we beg pardon, but what can be done we know
not, sir. Tom, Thomas. Speak thy words, Dorothy. *Hung, gyre,
grayne, fowre.* What is that that shineth in the sky in the night,
Dorothy? *Hoon. Harg.*

— This, Kit said, is, alas, my sole gift from the great city.
A problem of money. No, I am no longer a worker for the
State. A poet merely. And he handed to his father a copy of
Tamburlaine by Ch. M., printed by Richard Jones at the sign
of the Rose and Crown near Holborn Bridge. His father saw
blank verse and nodded blankly, then passed it to the mother
who blankly passed it back. Dorothy cried bitterly for it and,
having slavered and snotted thereon, sought to tear off the cover,
screaming when her brother snatched it. When Tom told her that
her tearing and wetting were a most direct manner of judgement
of a book's worth, she calmed and grasped a hank of his hair,
drooling. But Tom seemed much beguiled by the candlelit scene
of the poet and his idiot sister, the solid and flustered parents,
torn Tamburlaine.

219

— Tomorrow in the Guild Hall is I gather the time and place. It will be a long colloquy on raising of money to effect what will benefit the – do I say Canterburians?

— It is them that will get all, the father said in gloom, it is always the outlanders first. So, you had best sleep now. You have your chamber ready, it was once that of the elder girls, both now married. My wife has aired linen and garnished the bed with fresh lavender.

— Good and thanks. The giggot or *gigot* as it should properly be was of an exceeding savouriness. These Kent pippins are good.

— You have surely Kent pippins where you are.

— None like these.

But, Kit observed, Tom had cored one but left most of it. Nor did he greatly like the correction to *gigot*, the great travelled man of the manor raised so far above the hammerer whose leather smell had vied with the tang of herbs. So Tom was candled to bed and Kit talked awhile with his parents, still about the table and Tom's browning uneaten apple, while Dorothy crawled, pissed on the bare boards, and soon snored where she was, a court of dolls about her.

— She will not sleep in a bed. She wanders the house at night but does little harm except to clatter the skillets down. It is better thus. We have thrown away overmuch soaked bedding. Thus Kit's mother, and his father:

— What is it then that you now are or do? You make plays in the playhouse but you are in the country in Kent. You are with him and yet he is not your master.

— Friendship. He gives me the peace to write a poem.

— It is not what we foresaw, his mother said. The Church with a fair living and a wife and children. You are twenty-eight and that is not young.

— I am in the midst of things with lords and knights. All will be well. I am known as a poet.

— A poet, his father said, tasting the word, his bald head aglow in candleshine. We did not think to have a poet in the family.

— There is more truth in poesy than in the droning of sermons.

— We have had trouble about religion and we shall have more. These men that nose out Catholics and atheists have been around. They say the Spaniards will try a new landing at Dover.

— They will not. Do not fear the Spaniards. If there is to be trouble it will be with Huguenots and Flemings. There is a smell of it already in London.

— Why cannot we all be left alone? his mother cried in some distress. There were some saying that Dorothy is a witch because she babbled to the black cat next door. Well, to sleep, it is a blessing. All we must fear there is our dreams. And so, Kit, to yours. And, when Kit stood, she hugged him and the candlelight showed tears.

Kit lay in the small bedchamber next to Tom's. A full moon looked in, not long arisen. He could not sleep, since here he was, though this was not the house of his boyhood, put upon by ghosts of a younger self who plucked at him and said: You might have gone this way or else that. He fell into a slumber when the night watchman had called it was two of the clock and all was well or as well as it might be, the fine weather was menaced by a north wind newly sprung. He was drawn from that by a scrabbling at the door, that would be poor Dorothy, then the door's opening and it was not Dorothy but Tom. He could not sleep either, he could sleep well only at Scadbury in his great bed. And now you may allay your sunset engorgement. Here in my parents' house? Smear it with your manhood, you are no longer a boy. The rich drops of a manner of exorcism. His parents' chamber was across the stairwell; they would not hear. So Kit flooded the belled town in his fancy with a kind of defiant manhood, and they sank together to sleep, naked, entwined, uncovered like the drunken Noah.

At dawn the door was open wide and the Noah story was in reversal, for there stood the father in his nightshirt looking in on the son, Dorothy clinging to the father's hand and pointing drooling. Not so poor Dorothy wandering the house at night. The father showed great grey shock in the grey dawn while the cocks crowed.

221

— Oh God. Oh my dear God. Oh no. It is not possible. The poet. The filth of it all.

And then the mother, whom the father tried to thrust away from the entwined sleepy nakedness. Heard of these things, in their innocence not truly believed. Oh God, no.

KIT rode back alone against an insolent thrusting wind and through squalls. Shame shame shame rustled in the leaves. Tom, unashamed, would lodge in the inn in the cathedral's shadow, with brutal bells hammering at him when he rose betimes. The conference of magistrates would take long, he said when they met for their midday cheese and ale at a tavern where there were no French, and he was already sick of it. Kit had best return to Scadbury and, now that they were in their former intimacy, warm the great bed. Ingram Frizer would not be much around, having, with the aid of the daggerman Nicholas Skeres, much drubbing of debtors to do in London. Sixty pounds, as an example, lent out to a squire's son at centum per centum, the fear of some dying of the plague that was sharpening its teeth and the relicts unwilling or unable to meet obligations under law. But this usury was surely not lawful, it was pure Barabas. They be willing, their immediate need is so great, they will sign anything and must be held to it. I do not like it. You do not have to like it, my tenants' rents are slow to come in and meagre, you bade me buy the Smith pictures, I was cheated in a matter of tree-felling. Keep to your poem.

He returned not to Scadbury but to his London hovel. He had his own money to collect from Henslowe, an unpaid moiety on the Guise play which they said it was safe now to do. He entered London in a bad time. Tom Nashe told him, on London Bridge, of Sir Walter and his lady and their committal to the Tower. The Queen had been slow in discovery of their marriage. Lady Bess had made excuses of family sickness for her absences from court, the excuses now proved to be lies, and

the Queen had stormed and hurled small objects. Now both were
lodged apart in the stinking Tower, said Nashe, and he cited one
who had said that Sir W.R. had been too inward with one of Her
Majesty's maids and another that had spoken of all being alarm
and confusion at this discovery of the discoverer and not indeed
of a new continent but of a new incontinent. It was all Essex
stuff; the Earl was prancing and dancing and preening. A man
picked out by fortune, one said, for fortune to use as her tennis
ball, for she tossed him up and out of nothing and to and fro to
greatness. Kit's soul sank. And, Nashe said, Tom Watson was
sick. God, Tom Watson sick, oh no.

Kit visited him afraid, the *epidemia* as they termed it was
manifested, as they put it, in a most pernicious and contagious
fever. How was it contagious? Did it hover invisible in air and
invisibly bite? Tom was no longer in the great house where he
had tutored the stupid boy smelling of cinnamon. He was at his
old home in bed, his wife fluttering about. The buboes were
clear in his naked armpits; he lay sweating in a soaked bed.
Should they then be cut? They say not, they say they will go
down. But the cack, Tom Watson moaned, and the vomiting.
They say, said his wife, that vomiting is to be provoked with
walnut and celandine juice and powdered radish. There is no
need, I vomit enough. And he puked foully into the cracked
swilling pot by the bed. And, his wife sobbed, I am to carry
a red wand of three foot in length when I go out to buy so as
to show there is one sick here, and there is a notice outside I
have writ on wood, it is an order or command, saying Lord
have mercy on us.

— I will be back, Kit said. Vomit out the poison, the sweating
will go, take nourishment.

— All comes back and out. I am to die.

— Do not say that, Kit cried in distress. Dear Tom. We
have had this before, most recover. I will be back.

But he would not. Out on the street fearful citizens were, on
orders, sluicing the gutters with their twenty buckets from the
pumps, fearful old grandams sitting and counting. Afar there
were shots of guns and howlings of agony. It would be the

men of the Common Huntsman at their work of dog-shooting. A dog's bite would do it if it had been bit by a rat.

Some said rats, others said foreigners that had brought it in on their ships. I was playing at the Theatre in *Have At You Pretty Rogue*, a comedy that did not please knocked swiftly together by Nashe, Dekker and Munday, when the apprentices rioted. They heard what they thought was Dutch or Flemish spoken by a huge-bellied man who laughed aloud and drank pottle ale, this was during the prayer for the Queen after the jig, and they set upon him. He was in fact from the north of the kingdom on a London visit and his speech sounded outlandish. Outside the playhouse they had stripped him bare and were like to hang him from a sycamore until they saw on the street the man's wife who cried out that he was English enough and desisted, having also seen a known Flemish master weaver slinking by, and him they got. Then three mounted troopers of the Lord Mayor rode into this territory rightly beyond the City's jurisdiction and hit out with staves, though one with a sword that sliced through the belly of an apprentice who screeched in great pain till he died. Then there was fighting without cause for fighting's own dear sake until a cart loaded with five or six corpses came by, a bellman tolling in front, and there was running away in horror, though where to run, since the plague was within and everywhere, and the time had come for our players to run to the country and perform in air uninfected. Criers at all corners read what the magistracy put out: A strong and substantial watch sufficient to suppress any tumult is to be kept. Moreover for the avoiding of unlawful assemblies no plays may be used at the Theatre, the Curtain, the Rose or other usual places until the Feast of St Michael.

Will of Warwickshire would stay. He sat calmly at his work while I put my garments together in a basket and a leathern bag.

> *Ev'n as an emptie eagle sharp by faste*
> *Tires with her beake on feathers, flesh and bone,*
> *Shakinge her winges, devouring all in haste*
> *Till either gorge be stuff'd or prey be gone —*

— Well, I said, peering, the empty eagle, not a good phrase, is pecking all around, you had best keep yourself aloof.

— One cannot be aloof of an eagle. The Muse will look after her own. And he looked on me with a kind of smug fatness as I prepared to flee with the others. Then he quoted something not his: Croyden doth mourn, Lambeth is quite forlorn, The want of term is town and city's harm. What does Nashe mean by that?

— Best ask him. For I was in haste.

In truth it was only in late summer that he met Tom Nashe, leaner than ever but untouched by contagion as was he himself, in the beer garden of the Dansker, where a sweet breeze sighed from the south and the plague howled some way off. Nashe said:

— You know Robin Greene is dead? No, not of the plague neither. A cracked heart and a burst liver, somewhat like poor Tarleton. Indeed, this pestilential Harvey, Gabriel not the other, has said something of the king of the paper stage playing his last part and is gone to Tarleton, a filthy man. I blame myself a little. I fed him on pickled herrings and Rhenish, he drank thirstily and gorged greedily, then he collapsed in the street and was taken in by a kind cordwainer. His wife crowned him with bays or perhaps parsley, he rambled much about his greatness while dying. Well, he spits venom as well as that boast from the grave. You have seen the book?

Will took and opened it, having first wiped its cover on the grass. He read: For there is an upstarte Crowe beautified with oure feathers that with his *Tygers harte wrapt in a player's hide* supposes he is as well able to bombast out a blank verse as the beste of you; and being an absolute *Johannes fac totum* is in his own conceite the onlie Shakescene in a countrie. He said:

— Spite. And he thinks that line to be mine.

— He gets at Kit another way. Read back and aloud.

— Wonder notte, thou famous gracer of tragedians that Greene, who hath saide with thee like the fool in his hearte There is no God should nowe give glorie to his greatnesse; for penetrating is His powre, His hande lyes heavie upon me, He hath spoken unto me with a voyce of thunder – There is danger there, I would say, an imputation of atheism in print. For me, nothing. For him –

— He will ride over it, safe with Tom Walsingham in leafy Kent. He rides over much, there is protection there. Have you noted that the whole town is suffused with poetry? Lord have mercy on us makes a good last line. It is everywhere, but now it is my own. Dust hath closed Helen's eye, I am sick I must die, Lord have mercy on us.

— The present number?

— Something over fifteen thousand, they say. The whole city a charnel-house.

NAY, for the end of that year we have an exact figure of sixteen thousand five hundred and three. And it was a warm Christmas, very green, and the deep pits were dug and the carts trundled. The Queen, safe as she believed from contagion at Greenwich, had her plays of the grim festal season performed, and it was a mingling of all the companies that had returned to town that gathered in her great hall to enact Kit's *Rich Jew of Malta*. She was not against the Jews as so many were and I, who took the part of Pilia-Borza, observed her so closely that I near missed a cue, noting that she laughed little though munched much from a silver dish of candied figs. It was not, to speak the truth, an audience all that easy to please, no groundlings here content with a cracked sconce and pig's blood and leering quips, all ladies and gentlemen finely dressed though many discreetly drunk, Essex stroking the Queen's hand but often thrust irritably away, candles candles and again candles, and at one point a damask curtain enflared but swiftly doused out. It seemed to me that the epilogue that Alleyn, great nose plucked off, spoke to the court sneered at absent Kit:

It is oure feare, dreade sovereign, we have bin
Too tedious; neither can't be lesse than sinne
To wronge your princely patience. If we have,
Thus lowe dejected, we youre pardon crave,
And if aught here offend your eare or sighte
We onlie acte and speake what others write.

— My princely patience, she cried out while Alleyn was bowing low, is not over-wronged. But do not put blame on your betters, who make what you oft mar. In the beginning was the word.

This seemed to be a kind of blasphemy, but none of the black bishops there that had fidgeted during the play were like to arraign her with it. She spoke, like poor dead Greene, for the makers not the puppets. Then she left, bowed and curtsied at, with a great rustling of skirts and clink of necklaces and winking of jewels. As she left to resume, for all I knew, crafty statecraft and raving and striking at ministers, there was a sigh of relief like a gale and they that had been covertly drunk were more openly so. There was a gap among the Queen's simpering and tittering Glories and no silver armour flashed at the head of the Queen's Guard. We players were given by disdainful footmen but scant fodder as befitted our beastly status – spiced ale let cool and tarts of mince rank and salty – but chewing Alleyn was high with his performance and in exultation said:

— Tomorrow we see Henslowe. He may open up the Rose.

— Without permission?

— This was a manner of permission. The Queen desired a play and by God she has had it, her subjects may too, the law is for all.

But it was not until January 26 of 1593 (I must from now till the end be most exact of dating) that Henslowe dared frowns and the frost to blare the trumpet for the play of Guise and the Paris massacre. At last Kit, plump from a Scadbury Christmas, had the triumph of witnessing a work long boxed and locked, and the afternoon's gather was £3 14s, but 3s 4d lower than *Harry Sixt*, which was in the nature of a whisper as to the future rule of the stage. And to Kit's joy and that of many

others Sir Walter signalled his new freedom by showing himself
to the lower world, gorgeous in his raiment, striding alone into
the Rose, planting himself very visibly on a stage stool, and most
vigorously making some of the players cough with draughts and
puffings of ample tobacco. And after he was glad to take drink
with the players before a fire in the tiring room.

— And your admirable lady?

— Out, thin, defiant, eating hearty at Durham House.
You must not think I am just come from the Tower. I was
sent under guard to Dartmouth to quiet rioting and ravaging
sailors who were not pleased at Sir Wat's incarceration. The
Queen cannot have it all her own way. The sailors were busy
looting the *Madre de Dios*, my take, my prize. Mace, nutmegs,
satin, amber, ebony, pearls, gold. The Queen's officers could
not control them, but I did. Fourscore thousand pound for her
ungracious majesty and for me nothing but what is my right as a
man. Free, at least. And if I cannot speak freely at court without
termagant rebukes, then I shall speak freely in parliament as one
of the people's tribunes.

— Speak freely on what?

— I will find something.

Parliament opened on February 19, with the knights and
burgesses coming up but timidly from their country estates, for
they rightly feared contagion. The Queen feared nothing, and
glared from her throne in the Upper House while she exhorted
all not to lose good hours in idle speeches full of verbosity and
vain ostentation. She said bluntly that she required the voting
of money to meet the imminent invasion of the Spanish from
the north and the passing of laws to put down Catholic and
puritan alike with brisk severity. There was also the matter of
the stranger in our midst, it was in the nature of this realm and
its tolerance to welcome all such as were sorely misgoverned in
their own lands, and such as, preferring life in a free country,
frisked up trade and helped goods to flow, whatever that
meant. Still, the bill that was presented was against Alien
Strangers selling by Retail any Foreign Commodities, but it
was meant for a stuffed figure to be pierced or burnt by the

speeches of the liberally given. But Sir Walter was loud in its defence:

— You argue that it is against Charity, against Honour and against Profit to expel these Strangers. In my opinion it is not true Charity to relieve them for those who flee hither have forsaken their own king, and religion is only a pretext for them. As for Honour, it is indeed honourable to use Strangers as we are used among Strangers, but it is baseness in a nation to give liberty to another nation which they refuse to grant to us. In Antwerp we are not allowed to have a single tailor or shoemaker living there; at Milan we cannot have so much as a barber. And as for Profit, they are discharged of subsidies, they pay nothing, yet they eat our profits and supplant our own nation.

Some disagreed, many did not and, when the speech leaked out to the lowlier world, it was seen as an incitement on a high level to the continuance of rioting against the outlander. But on February 2, the feast of Candlemas or the Virgin Mother's churching, the playhouse that had against the law opened was by the law shut, and there were few places for apprentices to gather with clubs and daggers and shards of broken glass.

— We have had all this afore, said the squire Sir Richard Bradbrooke in parliament. My father did speak much of the day he was not speedily to forget, videlicet May Day of 1517, when there was great apprentice rioting against insolent foreigners. It cannot be put down, as it is the people's voice, though in the tongue of the young. The Sheriff of London of those days, who was Sir Thomas More, he could not well do it.

— He, said one with no pertinence, was a Catholic traitor.

— They were all Catholics then and he had not betrayed at that time. What I say is let them do what they will, it is sport that breaks but few pates, and it showeth to these overbearing Dutch and Flemings and French that flaunt their money that they be but guests of the commonweal and no more.

229

— It is known, cried a voice, that you are indebted to a Fleming I will not out of decency name, and here is a fine way of cancelling an obligation, kill all Flemings and while your hand is in all other outlanders.

— I protest. This is monstrous slander, I will not have it, I will have his words put to the arbitrament of steel.

— Order order.

It may be that this mention of Sir Thomas More, whom as a Catholic martyr Lord Strange was known privily to admire, put into the heads of some, perhaps his lordship himself as protector of his players, the notion of a play on the man that some thought blessed and others cursed, and it is certain that Sir Thomas Tilney, that was Master of the Revels, received such a play for his approval and he rejected it instanter as foully seditious, though not returning the fee of seven shillings that had accompanied the submission. It was known that Tom Kyd had the chief hand in writing it, and this was to do him little good.

Indeed, it was the writers rather than the brawlers who now became most under suspicion during the time of the troubles. I come to the month of May, a most perilous period, and in particular to May 5, when the verse libel was set up in several copies on the walls of the Dutch Church and there was great howling in the Dutch embassy. It began

> *You strangers that do inhabit in this lande,*
> *Note this same writing, do it understande.*
> *Conceive it well for safeguard of youre lives,*
> *Youre goodes, your children & youre dearest wives.*

And it went on

> *Cutthroat-like in sellinge, you undo*
> *Us all & with our store continually you feast.*
> *Our poor artificers do starve and die.*

And then it attacked not the Dutch but those high English that protected them and doubtless were paid in foreign gold to do so.

With Spanish gold you are all infected
And with that gold our nobles winke at feats.
Nobles, saie I? Nay, men to be rejected,
Upstartes that enjoie the noblest seates,
That wounde their countrie's breaste for lucre's sake,
And wronge our gracious Queene and subjects goode
By letting straungers make oure heartes to ache.

It was clear that the poor but vicious poetaster had read or seen Kit's plays, for not only did he invoke Kit's last play in

Wele cutte your throates in your temples praying,
Not Paris massacre so much bloode did spille

but he signed with the pseudonym of Tamburlaine.

Kit knew little of this, being at Scadbury. News of Tom Watson's death and burial, brought to the manor house by Frizer, hurt him sorely, but he would not go to London to throw flowers of the season on his deep grave. Talk in the town of what Greene had writ on his atheism was also, by the same messenger, brought, with, Kit thought, a certain glee unconcealed. Of the libel nailed to the Dutch Church he as yet knew nothing, nor the one in prose that followed, ending with these words: Be it known to all Flemings and Frenchmen that it is best for them to depart out of the realm before the ninth of July next. If not then to take what follows. For there shall be many a sore stripe. Apprentices will rise to the number of 2336. And all prentices and journeymen will down with Flemings and Strangers.

And it was now that the Privy Council instructed the Lord Mayor and aldermen to search out the writers of libels, examine such as were quick with the pen, rake them for admission of seditious scribbling, and, for the speedier execution of a confession, put them to the torture in Bridewell. So it was, on May 12, the very day after the Council put out its order, that two officers appeared at Tom Kyd's lodging to arrest him.

— On what warrant?

231

— We will have no talk of warrants. You are under suspicion of expeditious writings and must come your ways.

— Not expeditious, said the other officer, seditious is the word.

— All one. Here is the basket and here are the papers, there are a many. It is unnatural that there be so many. And both officers proceeded to thrust in, with fists that had never handled book, papers they crumpled, all and every paper, bills and notes and plays unfinished, the poem on St Paul, documents well copied beginning *Noverint*, all. And one led Kyd manacled to the Bridewell while the other grumbled at his basketload. May rain fell, though not heavily. The Bridewell stank of its freight of misery, but the room to which Kyd was pushed, with a jovial tripping or two on the way, had large May light coming in from the window and there were May flowers on the table of the man who was to examine him. He was a well-fleshed gentleman of some thirty years, who had ale and rolls by him and kind eyes. He said:

— Sit, sit. He of the *Spanish Tragedy*? Well, I have seen it, blood and the biting out of a tongue, difficult to do. It will save time for us all if you state at once what here in this over-filled basket is pertinent to our enquiry. For I take it you admit guilt.

— Guilt of what?

— Of dangerous writing.

— Never, never. I write for the theatre and you will find there an heroic poem on the blessed St Paul. I court no danger.

— I have a note here sent from high up on your writing a play on Sir Thomas More. Do you admit this?

— I admit it.

— He was a notable scoundrel that denied the lawfulness of our gracious Queen's father his rule of the Church, and he was tortured and lopped for it. And you writ a play on him.

— A play on him only in his time as Sheriff of London.

— But he ended on the scaffold rightly and it was perilous to write on him.

— The play was not permitted to be performed. Nor was the

play my notion, it came from my lord Strange in the manner of a commandment and I could not well disobey.

— Well, that is one thing but there are others. We will not throw away time which is a most precious commodity. I will read and you will proceed to the torture. Nick Gardner, he called.

— Why is this? Why torture? I hold nothing back. I beg, no torture, I claim the clerk's exemption by law.

— On that you can read and write? That will save you only from Tyburn. Yours is not a Tyburn matter. Or I think not. Ah, here.

The Nick Gardner he had called entered, a gross man in a leathern apron, chewing a bever and cheery enough. He led Kyd somewhat kindly to his chamber of terror, where an assistant or prentice was cheery too, though with few teeth and those black. Gardner shewed Kyd with some pride the machines of his profession – a rack well bloodied, a thumb and finger screw, the ceiling manacles for hanging, the oil lamp for skin-singeing, the wire whips of fine steel for whipping.

— What is to be, master? You are to be put to it till you scream you are ripe to confess of infamy, that being the manner of it. Will you come to this gear?

— I will confess now. And Kyd shook as in a dance that the assistant greatly admired. There is no need of this.

— Ah nay, master, you know not the game of it. Well, there are others to be done, this is a fretful morning, so we will break fingers only. See, Jack, this is how it is done. Aaaaargh.

Kyd's writing hand was a mess of throbbing and swollen flesh, a nail or two had been pincered out before the cracking of bone in the little render as it was termed, and he howled and groaned as he was led back to his interrogator who had been steady in his reading.

— Well, all this is enough and more, it shall be taped in red and sent up to the Council. And writ with so fine a hand, what, man, were you thinking on, what were you then about? And he showed Kyd what he had written in a crude hand on the verso of the outer folded leaf. 12 May 1593: Vile Heretical Conceits denying the Deity of Jesus Christ our Saviour found among the papers of Thomas Kyd prisoner.

— Aaargh. Not mine.

— You deny this to be your scrivener's fist?

— No. Writ under constraint. Dagger at back. Mr Marlin, Marley, Marlowe. Kyd swooned but was face-flapped back to attention.

— Marlowe of *Tamburlaine* and *The Jew*? His words but your copy?

— That.

— It is not always good to interrogate directly after the torture, I have said that often. A man does not speak clear. Well, you shall have a day and night in the cells, you may bind up your wounds in rags of your own shirt and tomorrow we may resume.

AND, of course, at Scadbury Kit knew nothing of this. He was being honoured by a visit from Robert Poley, who had ridden express from the Garden. He greeted Tom Walsingham friendlily and with a superior affability slapped Frizer on the back, a known confederate in lowly tasks in the past. Great swollen left ballock of St Athanasius, was the whole world then in it?

— To talk, Kit. We will take a turn among the trees this fine May morning. Such fine leafy canopies that bid the sun be gentle, but in this blessed uninvaded island always gentle. The Spanish are fiery because they have a fiery luminary in the heavens burning their souls to furious madness. They will come, Kit, if they can.

— I am to do something?

— You are not longer sporting with the flummeries of the playhouse, that is a good thing. What do you do?

— I finish my heroic poem. I translate a little Ovid, a little Lucan.

— Like a gentleman, good. Well, here is the story. The

234

Catholic earls of Scotland did not arrive in Berwick. Who forewarned them? We do not know. Do *you* know?

— How could I know? Unless you suggest –

— Suggest nothing. Your loyalty is unassailable. I have my suspicions of our little man in Edinburgh, the world is full of turners about and twisters, a foul world. To my story. The Scottish Catholic earls will not appear on English soil at all, not yet. All seems to be in the hands of Sir William Stanley. I told you of him?

— The cousin of Lord Strange.

— Even so. He has this papist army in the Low Countries, English scoundrels and Irish kerns. He is to come over to meet his noble cousin and confirm that he is to be the centre of Scottish Catholic hopes. And, of course, Spanish. There is to be a London meeting – when it is to be I must find out in Flanders. It seems that we are go back to the old days, Kit – Babington and the rest of them. Will Lord Strange be able to accept your feigned conversion?

— Lord Strange will no doubt have heard of my supposed atheism. I have not met him. But atheism and Catholicism are easily wrapped in the one blanket.

— We shall know better what to do when I return from Flanders. Two weeks only of absence, I cannot afford more. I sail out from Deptford and sail back thither. Let us meet there on May the thirtieth. You know the house, Tom Walsingham tells me. Mistress Bull is now the Widow Bull. Come early in the day to be on the safest side.

— I am unsure of this. Unsure of my power to perform the old feigning.

— That is why we shall have to talk. Deptford is cool, the garden is leafy. The plague has not struck there, it seems unwilling to swim the Thames.

— No harm in our meeting.

★

TOM Kyd was dragged from his cell in the early May morning, haggard and in pulsing pain. With his left hand he could raise the cup of water he was surlily given, but he could eat no bread, having small stock of saliva. He was taken, not pushed, to the room of his yesterday's interrogation. Here there were now two men, the one he knew who, in acknowledgment of the formality bestowed by the other, now gave his name as Cooper. The new man was of a higher order, a servant of the Privy Council who called himself Stephen Wheelwright. Kyd's spinning world of great agony caught a bond of ancestral craft between the two names, what he could not say, something to do with axeing, cutting and sawing. Mr Wheelwright was in black very neat and smelling at the new flowers of the morning. He said somewhat grimly to Kyd:

> *Did I not give you gowns and goodly things,*
> *Bought you a whistle and a whipstalk too*
> *To be avenged of their villainies?*

I dislike not these verses. Odd lines of your tragedy adhere to the memory. You are not to be dealt with as any common scribbler of subversion. That is why you are not to be put further to the torture. I take it you are dextrous not sinstrous. Your writing will be somewhat hampered. This now must be explained. And he gave Kyd's face a cooling draught from the waved papers marked Vile Heretical Conceits.

— I have already. Marlowe.

— Or Marley or Morley or Merlin. Copied under duress saith Mr Cooper here. How then?

— He is of extremest violence. The copying of heresies from a book he brought. A commission. From Sir Walter Raleigh. He said. I would not but there was vile and foul importunacy.

— For Sir Walter Raleigh you say. Yet they remain among your papers. That argueth *contra*.

— They were never collected. The commission was forgot.

— You were paid for an act of scrivening?

— I am owed still. Those papers not truly mine were shuffled among papers mine truly. I am in pain.

— A man of violence, you say, this Marlowe. Also of violent and atheistical speech, as is much reported. His atheism has gone into recent print. Or the imputation thereof. You confirm this from your knowledge?

— Ever mocking God and our blessed Saviour. He mocked at my great poem of St Paul. He said that St Paul was but a juggler. That Hariot that is a Raleigh man could perform better.

— Back ever to Sir Walter Raleigh. Did he speak of a nest of atheism?

— He spoke of no nest. The heretical speech was all his own.

— Do you swear to all you have said?

— Bring me the blessed Bible and I will swear on it. Bring me the communion cup to drain. So fervent am I in abhorrence. I swear as I hope to be saved.

— You will see the virtue of torture, Mr Kyd. It bringeth a man to a manner of humility in which the truth is the sole garment. He cannot say like your Hieronimo *Why then I'll fit you*. All is not over but you may go. You will be called when wanted. And then we shall have done with the matter.

So Kyd left in great agony to abide the subsidence of the gross swelling and the mending of his fingers to strange and useless shapes, like twigs of a dead tree. And the interrogation was reported to the Privy Council and the Heretical Conceits delivered up to the same. And on May 18 one of the Messengers of Her Majesty's Chamber, a Mr Henry Maunder, was directed, in the words of his commission, to repair to the house of Mr Thomas Walsingham or to any other place where he shall understand Christopher Marlowe to be staying and to apprehend him and bring him to court.

PART THREE

KIT had long to wait, in that afternoon of May 20, in the gallery outside the chamber where he was to be examined. It was in Westminster and he wondered why not in the cooler salt air of Greenwich, away from the stench and howls and moans and bells of the ever-present plague, though that, they said, was abating. It had all something to do with Tom Kyd, and he did not properly understand. Mr Maunder, who had ridden with him from Scadbury, spoke in a manner saturnine of Kyd's not writing much any more since he was dextrous of fist, and this he did not understand either. So he patrolled on soft shoes the corridor, murky with dusty mullioned windows against which leafy summer struck silently like ghosts of old time in vain demand of entrance. There were in a corner between the great doorway of the chamber and the windowed wall dried-up flies, muscal mummies, in abandoned webs and, as a good poet, he forbore to convert them into figures of a possible future state for himself. He was not under arrest, merely here for examination in some matter pertinent to no longer dextrous Kyd, whatever that signified. A liveried man, bald though young, was near-deferential when he came out of the examining chamber, nodding that Kit might now enter and holding open the door.

— Sit, sir, sit. So he sat. The Archbishop of Canterbury had spoken, for this session not garbed for ceremony but in the plain gown and square cap of his quotidian business. That lined and acid face was of Sir Thomas Heneage, appointed head of the Service: him Poley had once pointed out at a distance. There was Sir Robert Cecil, of the great family, whom fate, unmindful of familial greatness, had endowed with a hump on his back. His eyes were affable, he even nodded. Of course, they were of a year at Cambridge, what now had been his college? And the peevish boy's face over a snowy ruff and gold and scarlet beneath was

241

of my lord of Essex. Kit had not thought him to have joined the Privy Council; this was exceptional honour for one so young and must be of most recent date. His Grace of Canterbury held up a taped bundle, saying:

— To be brief, there are heresies written here duly noted, found in the chambers of a Mr Thomas Kyd, yeoman not gentleman, admitted by him to be in his own hand, imputed by him to have provenience in your request or, as he puts it, impetuous importunacy that they be copied from your dictation. The heresies are foul and blasphemous. What do you say?

— I deny the impetuous importunacy, as your grace or Mr Kyd has it. I admit that this work was done. As a noverint by trade turned playwright Mr Kyd was willing for a fee to do it.

— These are not Kyd's opinions?

— Far from it. I know him for a man of somewhat whining piety.

If he had expected then a smile he did not get it. His lordship of Essex said:

— Are these then your opinions?

— No, my lord – if, as I take it, that is how you are to be addressed, I have not had the honour of an introduction – no, they are Arian arguments taken from an old book. They were copied that they might be discussed and refuted. My lord of Canterbury will doubtless know the book. It came my way in my studies of theology. It was printed in the reign of Queen Mary of inglorious memory. *The Fall of the Late Arian* is the title. Its author I have forgot.

— Let me say now, the Earl said, that you had best not teeter in the direction of insolence. These be grave matters and modesty and deference are on your part in order.

— I modestly defer, my lord. The Archbishop said:

— I do not see what this is about. The book, as you say, I know or knew. Arianism is finally confuted and there is no further need of argument. Did you consider you could do better?

— Not I, your grace. I was fully satisfied. But some whose

learning I respect thought there were gaping holes in the arguments that might lead some to consider there was a possible truth in the heresy that Jesus Christ was not the Son of God.

— Who are these paragons of learning? Sir Robert Cecil gently asked.

Kit now hesitated. He smelt danger. He said:

— Mr Thomas Hariot, for one. The Earl of Northumberland for another. There are several men of learning most warm to give to the truths of our faith the structuring of what must appeal to reason.

— Reason and faith, the Archbishop said, do not of necessity cohere. Reason saith that water will not be transformed to wine. Faith has a contrary answer.

— We were warned at Cambridge, your grace, of the dangers of what is termed fideism. The *Summa* of Aquinas makes an appeal to reason.

— Was this Kyd one of these reasonable enquirers? Sir Thomas Heneage asked.

— Never, sir, never.

— And you? the Earl of Essex asked.

— I was admitted to the company, my lord.

— A company that held up the truths of religion to the examination of reason?

— Yes, my lord.

— A company that met at Durham House under the shield of the man Raleigh?

— Sir Walter, if I am to be absolute in matters of title and address. This company enquired in full legitimacy of the nature of the stars and the planets, and of divers matters of cosmogony.

— And, the Archbishop asked, of the nature of Almighty God and His Blessed Son?

— The presence of the outlines of Arian heresy in those papers you hold, your grace, doth indicate that that most deep and awful matter was never raised. The company deferred to the teachings of the Church over which your grace presides.

— It is the monarch that presides, the Archbishop harshly

said. Be mindful of that. One of her titles is *Fidei Defensor*.

— A papal bestowal, Kit unwisely said. Be mindful of that.

— How dare you, sir, the Archbishop cried. How dare he, the others seemed to mutter.

— I beg pardon, your grace. I should have said be mindful of that, your grace. I do not however beg pardon for the truths of history, your grace, my lord, gentlemen. The late King Henry was granted the title for his defence of the seven sacraments, of which his reformed Church appears to have lost two or three. I say no more on the matter. I am here not to question but to be questioned.

— Questioned, that, the Earl said. Questioned on your association with one that teacheth atheism. I mean the man Raleigh.

— Sir Walter, yes, my lord. He has never taught atheism.

— In the House of Commons he has been preaching it.

— I do not think that can be so, my lord.

— Confute your Arians, whatever they be, but not me, puppy. He speaks against the strangers in our midst and advocates riot, he follows with loud pleading for freedom of belief.

— That is not atheism, my lord, and I will not be called puppy. We are both grown to reasonable doghood.

— This, Sir Thomas said most reasonably, is neither time nor place for spleen and insult. If my lord of Essex would fire guns against Sir Walter, there are occasions and *loci* where we others would not wish to be implicated. With all due and most humilous deference, good my dear lord. This Mr Marlowe has been one of the faithful hounds that smell out treason and dissidence. He is a master of arts. He is known to be a most mellifluous poet. There are occasions for deference which are unconcerned with mere rank.

— Mere? *Mere?*

— Enough, the Archbishop said. Mr Marley, I am unhappy about the condition of your Christian faith. I fear a contagion unrelated to the present, though thank God dying, pestilence. I think you may well have been touched by heterodoxy. I think we require from you a deposition in writing concerning what you know of what has been diffused in a certain company.

— You mean, your grace, that I am to write down Sir Walter Raleigh as an atheist and all his companions, myself included, as such?

— That is most raw and brutal, Sir Robert Cecil said. We are all concerned solely with the safety of the realm.

— The craft of the playwright, Kit said, which alone I may be said to understand, though I have much to learn, must deal, alas, with the rawness and brutishness of the life of men. The safety of the realm, as you term it, is not best served by the terror of its subjects.

— What terror is this? the Archbishop asked.

— The terror of punishment at opening what has been too long hid, at voicing doubt which is man's natural state in a world that is God's enigma, at tearing off a mask of high-mindedness to disclose the nakedness of rivalry and hate.

— Tell us, the Earl said somewhat mildly, of this rivalry and hate.

— You will know more of it than I, my lord. Of Sir Walter I will say this, that I admire and honour him. He more than any has consulted the safety of this realm, and not that only but also its wealth and the expansion of its territories.

— First to his own profit, the Earl said. Only traitors are sent to the Tower.

— So treachery is to be sought out in the making of a fair marriage with a most fair and estimable lady?

— You tread on very perilous ground, Sir Robert Cecil said. This is unseemly.

— This word *doubt*, the Archbishop said.

— You require a definition, your grace? Kit said, again unwisely.

— I must ask you, Mr Marlin, Sir Robert Cecil said, to consult your own situation as regards this present enquiry. You are being questioned on grave matters and you respond with reprehensible pertness and flippancy.

— I again beg pardon. I am not well schooled in the manner of comportment before Her Majesty's Privy Council.

— Doubt, you say, the Archbishop continued. The company

you spoke of was concerned with the free resolution of doubt in matters of faith?

— I think this may be said.

— So doubt about the teachings of our divines was voiced so that it might be resolved through rational enquiry?

— I would not go so far.

— Very well, the Archbishop said. You admire Sir Walter Raleigh. In consequence you may not be relied upon to render a frank and candid disclosure as is required.

— I have told lies, your grace, to the Queen's enemies, but that was a matter of policy imposed by circumstance. You have no need to put me to any torture to impel true speaking.

— You are not as yet under arrest, the Earl said.

— But I will be, and then I will be tortured? What will the charge be, my lord?

— No talk of that, the Archbishop said. I think we may for the moment end. What must he now do, Sir Robert? You have the formula.

— Yes. Give daily attendance to their lordships until he shall be licensed to the contrary, thus remaining within close distance of this Palace of Westminster until the case under review is decided. So you may leave.

Kit bowed to all in the manner of a single wave of obeisance and left the chamber in some anger and disquiet. Outside the door he saw Baines waiting for entrance. Kit spat and said: No buboes yet? The devils of the plague know their own. Baines said:

— That is not friendly.

We may not yet accompany back to Scadbury fuming Kit, orphaned, with one friend in the world but of him he was unsure. We must, behind his bowed back, return to the chamber where the Privy Council deliberated on this Mr Marley or Merlin. The Earl of Essex said:

— This is my Mr Baines. Baines, read out your note.

— Baines read: A note containing the opinion of one Christopher Marley concerning his damnable judgment of religion and scorn of God's world. He affirmeth that Moses was but a juggler and that one Heriots being Sir Walter Raleigh's man can do more than he. That Christ was a bastard and his mother dishonest. That he was the son of a carpenter and that if the Jews among whom he was born did crucify him they best knew him and whence he came. That Christ deserved better to die than Barabbas and that the Jews made a good choice, though Barabbas were both a thief and a murderer. That all protestants are hypocritical asses. That if he were put to write a new religion, he would undertake both a more excellent and admirable method and that all the New Testament is filthily written. That the Angel Gabriel was bawd to the Holy Ghost, because he brought the salutation to Mary.

— Is there much more? the Archbishop asked, his mouth tasting a kind of spiritual vinegar.

— Yes, your grace. Much more. But I would ask you to note that Mr Richard Chomley or Chumley or Cholmondeley, that is also in his lordship's service, has confessed that he was persuaded by Marlowe's reasons to become an atheist but only in pretence that he might be the more persuaded, and he is now ready to testify to this and much in my note and other things besides.

— Fair copies of your notes are required, the Earl said. We will have a deeper perusal.

— Apart from the heresies, your grace, my lord, sirs, Baines said, there is other treasonable matter. I read from here. That he had as good right to coin as the Queen, and that he was acquainted with one Poole, a prisoner in Newgate who hath great skill in mixture of metals, and having learned some things of him he meant through help of a cunning stampmaker to coin French crowns and English shillings. And he said that all that love not tobacco and boys are fools. And that the holy communion would be best administered in a tobacco pipe. And much more.

— Very well, Baines, enough. Do as I say, we will peruse. You have done good work and may go.

— And so, the Archbishop said when Baines had left.

— And so, the Earl of Essex agreed.

*

KIT, much troubled, rode back to Scadbury. He had heard from Tom Nashe that the knives were being sharpened for the puritanical or Brownist persuasion. There was to be a trial before the King's Bench the next day, Nashe was unsure of whom, something to do with a book printed in Amsterdam or some such outlandish place entitled *Reformation No Enemy*. The author? He knew not. It was full of the scourging of the bishops and even of the Queen as one that had turned against Jesus Christ. The London air had seemed thick to Kit's lungs; he smelt burning entrails and tasted the blood of a wrenched-out liver. He rode back to the sweet country, greeted by thrushes and larks and the bellowing of rams. The shepherd swains shall dance and sing for thy delight each May morning. A smeared May, a May defiled. The maypole gone for that it did resemble a man's prick, and Jack in the green a foul idol, and the hobbyhorse forgot.

Sitting with Tom Walsingham after supper, he spoke his troubles.

— I fear that next time it will be an arrest.

— The charge?

— They are digging out heresy and treason. I am no true target. I am the salty herring before the great roast of Raleigh. I saw this Baines go in with a paper. There is talk of the arraignment of Tom Hariot.

— So, Tom Walsingham said, chewing a piece of marchpane and showing a tooth in decay, they will be coming here to drag you off. And then to the torture chamber and your screaming that it was all the fault of Sir Walt the tobacco man. Well, we have tortured each other over the years, though to the end of pleasure. And you torture my nose and gullet with your damnable pipes.

— You have not said this before.

— You have not listened or, listening, taken notice. Much may be pardoned in a poet. I shall not be stifled with the reek of it again. At least not here.

— You smile, smirk or leer at the prospect. So I am to leave?

— I did not think this would be the manner of your going. I shall marry soon, I think you have guessed that, I need the dowry. You would have to go, but I did not think your departure would be enforced by the Privy Council. Nor did I think your new and final home would be a tree. No, no, I but jest. Poley is your best protection.

— Poley takes orders from Heneage and Cecil, both of the Privy Council.

— He can plead with them, though not, I think, with the Earl of Essex. Poley can defend your great shouts of atheism and disaffection as the mere cloak of a deeply loyal purpose. You were provoking the true dissidents. And if Poley fails you, well, there is always a ship to board. He fails you at Deptford, you sail from Deptford.

— Sail whither?

— You are expert in theology. You can lecture on divinity abroad. Catholic divinity at Rheims or Douai. Calvinist divinity in Scotland. Or perhaps both there. And you can write your plays and send them on hot horseback to Alleyn or Henslowe.

— I am done with plays.

— You are done with a lot of things. You knew this would happen. There has been a deal of jealousy around.

— So. We are to part. One should always pay attention to the future. My sole future so far has been the writing of *Finis* to a play or poem. When do you think they will come for me?

— Dirty men rattling their manacles here in the unpolluted manor house of Scadbury. It brings me low. I know not. I think not before you meet Poley. Poley will have discussed a possible mission for you with his masters. Fear not yet. All will be well. We shall eat together in Southwark the day before. There is something to show you.

— What?

— A small secret. You would not begrudge your dear friend a small triumph? Ask no more for the present.

And so on May 29 they rode into London, with, to Kit's dislike, Ingram Frizer on his nag at the rear. They ate their noon dinner at the New Tabard – soup of boned beef, roasted veal, and a medlar tansy. Frizer was served apart in the kitchen. Tom, made merry by red wine from Bordeaux, said:

— It may then be Scotland for you. You recall our visit together? I had to see his dribbling majesty with a small request from the Queen and the Archbishop. He was much taken by me. He toyed and pawed and mauled, it was not pleasant. He moaned in his pleasure and then leered in the little death, his silken breeches were soaked. Aye, laddie, ye see that a king is mickle like monie anither mon. Well, the request was fulfilled, though very late.

— What request?

— You hear the bell of St George's? That is not for a plague burial. It is for the passage of a prisoner of the Bench prison to his condign end on the gallows. You know St Thomas à Watering?

— A place to drench horses for the Canterbury pilgrims. Who are, of course, no more. What happens there?

— You will see all. Come. Frizer shall come too.

— I may speak boldly about Frizer now. If there is any pleasure in leaving Scadbury it is that I shall see Frizer no more.

— A wonderfully necessary man. So devoted. He has been my perambulating moneybag. Of course, he ever disapproved of what you and I did together. You, he always said, seduced me into evil ways. But then he came to believe that it was in the nature of a poet to court perversion. Poesy, he argued, is a perverting of words, and one thing must come after the other. Come.

The gallows at St Thomas à Watering was new erected, and two boys apprenticed to Harley the hangman were completing the hammering, nails in their mouths. There were but a few onlookers, idle artisans, a legless soldier, some small urchins. Why here? It has not been well announced, here is not usual, he has a gift of words and might inflame a Tyburn assembly. Who? Then Kit saw. Penry, that had eaten herring with him at Edinburgh, that had begged him to look to his soul, that desired a

lover's embrace from his blessed Lord, was dragged to the ladder
on a hurdle of wattles. He did not look at the lookers; his eyes
were on an inward vision. Tom said smiling:

— Penry has evaded capture for long. Over the border and
back. The Scotch slobberer has been true to his word. He has
caught him and faithfully delivered. A proof of amity.

— You call this a triumph?

— I gave my body that it might be done. Or so I wish to
believe. Here is evidence that Scotland's king is no menace.
Look, Kit, you see here what will not happen to you, whatever
you may fear. The poet of *Tamburlaine* will not have his guts
wrenched out. Such things do not happen to poets.

Penry on the ladder spoke:

— I address your Queen, may my words carry. You are turned
rather against Jesus Christ and his gospel than to the maintenance
of the same. Your bishops are no more than a troop of bloody
murderers of souls and sacrilegious robbers of churches. And I
would – But here he was swung from the ladder. The hangman
Harley was not skilful with his cutting off of privities and the
tearing out of heart, for Penry saw nothing, dead swiftly with
the cracking of his neckbone. The small crowd had been foolish
enough to expect a Tyburn performance, and it turned away
soon enough from the mesh of bloody entrails exhibited. Tom
grinned, though little, but Frizer cried displeasure at the lack of
art. *He saw nothing, it was ill done.* Kit thought he would deliver a
damned clout but contented himself with a damned kick with his
heavy riding boot on Frizer's shin. Things may be better done,
he almost said, when they deal with me at Tyburn, you may be
pleased then. He turned his back on Tom while Frizer whined.
He did not want the horse that was not his. He took from the
saddle the leathern bag in which his few possessions lay. He
walked away, very sick: have us all up there on the scaffold, all
except Archbishop Whitgift and perhaps the Queen, we are all
schismatics and heretics whose inner light contradicts the outer.
They would certainly have Jesus Christ up there, had they not
done so already?

The lodging of Tom Nashe was in Southwark. Kit found

him there, dashed down his leathern bag, sat heavily on the tousled bed. He said:

— Brightness falls from the air. Does that have a meaning?

— It was meant to be *hair*, not *air*. To most there is no difference. The less a meaning can be ascribed the better the poetry.

— Yes, yes. Shadowing more beauty in their airy brows Than have the white breasts of the queen of love. Meaning above meaning. So meaning means little.

— Where do you come from?

— A hanging and drawing. I did not stay for the quartering.

— Martin Marprelate, yes, I heard it was to be today. Well, I did no more than vilify him in those plays already forgotten. Do we all bear blame for the poor wretches that are given a lesson in anatomy before dying?

— Penry missed his lesson. He is now embracing the Lord Jesus in a kind of spiritual physicality. What have you to drink?

— Sour wine. Have you money?

Kit counted what was in his purse. £1 11s 5d. It would not take him far. He asked: May I stay here the night? I must be at Deptford tomorrow.

— You are welcome to the floor and a blanket. And a bundle of books for a pillow. You travel?

— That is to be seen. We can afford a bottle of something. But I must be sober in the morning.

Cheese and bread and some shallots in aliger. And some Rhenish.

— I taste Robin Greene's death when I drink Rhenish, Tom Nashe said. Is he too embracing Jesus Christ? The stink of his breath must be a handicap. But of course he is now purified.

— And so the less Robin Greene. Is there truly anything after?

— You are the divinity scholar.

— To be dissolved in elements. To lose all that is or was Christopher Marlowe. I have a great name, though not many call me by it. I bear Christ on my back. And who or what is Christ?

— A fine poem, though burdened with too much meaning. The only true meaning is syntax.

252

— There is a fine heresy.

— Heresy pushes us forward. Church and State drag us back. Now you may report me to the Privy Council.

— So we hang together.

— Brightness falls from the air. That could be Lucifer or Icarus. Or both in one. But it is also greying tresses.

— Grey hair is a privilege. The badge of him who survives.

— Pretty countryfolk survive. And grave senators with influence. I know of no greyheaded poets.

— The dissolution will be a relief.

— You are gloomy, Kit. Drink, Christopher.

MORNING Deptford and the shipbuilders early awork. The chandlers' shops busy. Hounds from the Queen's kennels howled bitterly. A faint stink from the Queen's slaughterhouse. But was not the whole land her slaughterhouse? A firmer stink from the tanneries. Inland gulls wove over the waters and crarked. Sails, sails, a wilderness of them. Ships – the *Peppercorn*, the *Great Venture*, the *Majesty*, the *God Shield Us*, the *Neptune* (a safer god) – would leave with the morning river tide. And there the *Golden Hind* lay, to be chipped of its timber by the new pilgrims. Kit walked in the clean air to the house of Mrs, Widow rather, Eleanor Bull. She greeted him at the door in her plain black. Doubtless, unmolested, she visited the Brownist houses to worship a plain God. She said:

— They are already come. They wait on you.

— They?

— You have this chamber and the garden for your meeting. They have ordered dinner at noon. Fish in a pastry coffin. I have wine.

They? Kit went where told, bearing his leathern bag. It was the room he knew, he had dined there with Tom before they embarked for Scotland. Frizer and Skeres sat together at the table, counting money. Skeres had endued his dirty self. Frizer whined at once:

— Nothing. I bear no grudge. Your anger was in order. My shin hurts but it is a reminder that I was wrong. It is enough that a man die without our sneering.

— You did not sneer. You exclaimed on the hangman's bad art. Well, so I am forgiven. I am to meet Mr Poley here. I was not told of my meeting you too.

— Friends, friends, again and again friends, Skeres said. May we thou and thee? May you be called Kit?

— Christopher.

— Formal, aye, but a holy name. Shall I explain? Ingram and I are in Deptford to collect a debt. We have collected it and now count.

— A hundred per centum?

— A hundred and twenty. A difficult young man, dead of the plague, alas, but his father very hearty. He too was difficult but we prevailed.

Kit sat. Frizer and Skeres were already on wine. There were four cups. Without invitation Kit poured for himself. Money was neither clean nor filthy, it was merely needful. He said:

— Are you in the lending spirit now?

Both looked up from their coins in some surprise. Frizer said:

— What in the way of pledge?

— I understood you loaned without security.

— Never, Skeres said. There is always something – a messuage, a fine wardrobe, a stable of horses. You need money?

— Somewhat desperately. Else I would not ask.

— Else you would not lower yourself, Frizer said. Well, your good life at Scadbury was assured by lending on what you would call usury. But you praised usury in your play of the rich Jew.

— Hardly praised. He died in a hot cauldron.

— And dies again soon with the opening of the playhouses, Skeres said. Dies and is reborn. Plays preach of the resurrection.

— Profound, Kit said. Most deep.

— You repeat yourself. The words mean the same. How much do you require?

— Five pound only.

— At one hundred and fifty per centum, Skeres said. Do you agree?

— I must.

— As a pledge we will have your sword and belt, Frizer said. A mere token. A manner of a receipt or quittance.

— So, Kit said, unfastening, I am disarmed.

— You are with friends, Mr Christopher, Skeres said. And you shall be with another friend at noon. Ingram's master will be along to eat with us.

— He was most distraught at your manner of parting, Frizer said. What he called his triumph was, he saw, very hollow and unworthy. He will not have it that dead Penry was arrested in England. Young men will have their dreams and boasts.

— And the money?

— Fear not, Skeres said. It will be placed down for you when we play at the tables.

— I am not here to play backgammon.

— You are here to eat and drink and make merry, and what better merriment than a clinking of dice over the tables?

— Much depends on the dice.

Skeres laughed, showing teeth that appeared paint-blackened. Have no fear of the dice. I am no man of the barred catertreys. Nor is our Ingram, no cleaner or fairer man ever walked. You are among friends.

— As you are warm to remind me.

— Good, good and again good. Skeres stood, stretched, and walked to the wall where a lute hung. An instrument of music among people who detest pagan twanging, he said. Ah well, they are in barber-shops too. This is damnably mistuned, dirty thumb on the strings.

— There is a softness in you then, Kit said.

— You know how soft and sugared and dulcet. I am most pliable. I will do anything for peace. And gain, of course, I must live. What shall I sing? Ah, I know. Listen. It appeared that he

255

knew but one triad of the mode major. He sang, and the voice was high and sweet, nay over-sweet:

> *Come live with me and be my love*
> *And we shall all the pleasures prove*
> *That*

I forget the words. Their author must remind me.

— No matter, Kit said. I have forgot them myself. The writing down of verses is a means of cleansing the mind of them.

— Cleanse? Frizer said. You say cleanse as if the verses were filth. They are surely not so. A shepherd sings to his love, what could be prettier or more wholesome? But writing them did you have a shepherdess in your mind? Did you see some young and pretty lass ready to be wooed to lift her kirtle and say *now Roger?*

— A boy rather in a shepherdess guise, Frizer said, twanging. There is a sour note, let me screw. It is the way of the stage, is it not? Now thrust in to the sticking place. There, better. I have wondered oft what a man and a boy will do together. It is against nature.

— It is called the sin of Sodom, Kit said. The God of the Hebrews warned his people of the need to fill the land with little Hebrews. Those who took their love otherwise must be punished with fire and brimstone. We inherit the law of the Hebrews.

— But even in Aristotle, Frizer said, it is laid down that love is for engendering.

— You have read Aristotle?

— I have little Greek, alas. But it is logic, is it not, that entwining is for engendering?

— Do you entwine and engender, Mr Frizer?

— Oh, I have had moments in hayfields but not in indentured beds. Nick Skeres here too. Couple but not beget, not knowingly. We are like you, not men for marriage. But why should a boy's body excite lust?

— Because of smoothness and pliability, much like a woman you will say. But love is raised above the animal, for animals are

256

driven only to beget. So was it prized by the Greeks. Including
Aristotle.

— But it is against nature, Frizer said again.

— Many things are. This for an example. And Kit took out
his pipe and tobacco. Skeres was eager, over-eager, to look for
a flint and kindling on the window ledge. On the mantelpiece
a candle waited in its sconce. Skeres inflamed. Kit lighted from
the candle and drew in, drew out. Frizer feigned suffocation,
saying:

— Well, that is a stink that Scadbury will no longer know.
Though it seems to me embedded in the walls and hangings.

— Novelty, Kit said, puffing, oft entails suffering.

— Like the sodomitical act, Skeres said, sitting. It must be
most painful to have a hard rod thrust into the nether orifice.
That was a most painful punishment you had for the King in
your play. Painful but fitting.

— There are emollients, Kit said, oil, butter and the like.
The pleasure is considerable.

— For the giver or the taker?

— For both.

— Ah, both Skeres and Frizer went. For the serving girl the
Widow Bull employed had entered with knives, trenchers, and
a fine salt cellar. Kit said:

— The Lord of the Manor is to come when?

— Oh, Frizer said, we may eat without him. This is a feast
for us three. As for the reckoning, there is time enough. You are
a good girl, my dear? he said to the wench who placed knives and
trenchers. He stroked her arm. You go not with naughty men?
Which of us three would you say was the naughtiest?

— I know not, sir. And she left to collect the fish baked
in its coffin.

— He may come early or late, Frizer said. He rides about
London on marriage business, lawyers and the like. And there
is Mr Poley to come. Well, we shall sup together. What shall
we sup on?

— Flesh, Skeres said. The Widow Bull oft visits the royal
slaughterhouse. There is good flesh there. Flesh, he said again.

In his mouth it seemed not savoury. Then the steaming coffin was brought in. Frizer served, cracking the brown crust, letting odours arise. Dates, mace, nutmeg, cloves, rosemary, thyme, dace, trout, pike.

— You recall Dover, Mr Christopher? Skeres asked. There is nothing like a sole of Dover, but this is good. And he piled spiced fish on pastry and hungrily and smokily ate. He said, through smoke: We eat the fishes of the seas and the rivers. We do not speak of hunting or killing but of catching. They are caught and napped on the head. Or, with crabs and lobsters, they are not napped but boiled alive. Do we feel pity or compassion? No, they belong to a world not ours. Now, to slaughter a calf or a bullock or a lamb is to feel a certain remorse, for they seem close to us. Is that not so? A man is a kind of brute but he is not a kind of fish. But to kill a calf is to wish to eat it, to kill a man is what? Whatever it is, it is, like your manner of love, against nature. But if your manner of love is good, why is not the killing of a man?

— There is little connection, Kit said, eating with small appetite. Except that the loving and the killing are acts gratuitous that proclaim the nature of humanity. But to kill a man or indeed woman or child is to offend against a principle of cognition. For we know the world to exist only by our seeing it. You shut eyes in a man's death and in a sense you kill the universe.

— At Cambridge you learned this? Frizer asked, the palm of his hand a mess of broken crust and fish.

— At Cambridge I thought on these things.

— He is a man of thought, Skeres said to Frizer, not like us, who are more lowly. But thought will have a man killed sooner than following his round of work and rest and devotion and begetting. Thought is a dagger, he said, and looked for applause. Frizer nodded many times and, feigning a greater pain than he could properly have felt in his kicked shin, picked up the emptied wine jug and went with it to the kitchen to be filled. Skeres in small irritation spat into his hand a multitude of pike bones, saying: Why have they so many? A man's bones are few and sturdy. I know them all.

— You have broken them all?

— Mr Christopher, I break no bones. You mind the time you puked at the Babington executions? I puked too, inwardly. The tearing and cracking. An end should be quick and sharp without malice.

— For whom do you work now?

— For myself. For one and another. Not much now for Robin Poley. Sometimes for him. But not now much. The ship from Flushing is in late today. It is the *Good Hope*.

— I sailed thither on the *Peppercorn*.

— Aye, the *Peppercorn* now doth the coastal waters. It leaks and needs caulking. Ah, here is Ingram with a brimming crock. We are having a good day together. Shall we play the tables now?

— I cannot bend my mind to it. Later. When Robin Poley has come and we have talked.

— You seem much agitated. You have brought your bag. You need money. Are you to be sent on a voyage?

— Why do you so swing between filth and cleanliness?

— Is that meant unkindly? I think not. It depends on the part I must play. This morning it was a foul part, a villainous part. You are a man of the playhouse, you know of playing parts. Great God in heaven, he is here.

And indeed Poley was there, in travelling gear of leather, great cloak eased off his left shoulder, surprised at the sight of Frizer, who stood in deference, not so surprised at Skeres's presence, smiling with a certain weariness at Kit. He said:

— Gusts when we did not expect them. A calm sea churned without warning. A little sickness. Take that wreck of a dish away. I munched bread, my stomach is a basket of it. I will, by your leave, taste wine. And so he did, sitting. He sniffed and rotated upper lip and nose. Fie, what a stink. There is a Raleigh smell about. Ah, yes, Kit. Out into the garden with us. I fancy landward air.

In the garden, among the pinks and primroses and violets, under a beech and the mild sun, they took seats on a gnarled bench. Poley said he must take breath after the voyage. He was becoming weary of it all. To live in retired ease, plant

259

the bergamot, watch walnuts fatten. Had Kit heard ever of one Jane Dormer? No, she had been near friend to Queen Mary that we now term bloody, had wed the Count of Feria that had been near friend to King Philip. And now as a duchess she is appointed governess of Flanders. This strengthens the Catholic cause. The danger hath a stronger smell than it had hitherto.

— So now Lord Strange must have a watch set on him?

— His cousin is coming. He is no fool, very wary. We must arrange a Catholic welcome, have intimate meetings, gain evidence in good black ink, strike. It will be Babington over again. I rely on your play-acting. Practise the *signum crucis*.

— I have my own troubles.

— I know of your troubles. I know of your one trouble. Your trouble is not with the Privy Council but with one sole member thereof.

— Absent in Flushing as you were you know of these things?

— It has been in preparation, the destruction of Raleigh. The outer works are first attacked. You should never have let yourself be befriended by him.

— He is one of the men in England who look forward. Must I fawn on the spoilt brat Essex?

— Cut out Raleigh's heart and present it to Essex on a gold plate and you will be raised, knighted, ennobled. I see what is turning in your brain. You think I have influence.

— You have. With Heneage, Cecil.

— They are my masters. The question is whether they have influence over his lordship. Only her majesty has influence, but he is still, as you say, a spoilt brat. He will do for himself yet, you will see. Or perhaps you will not see. What I can do is to cry out the weightiness of your part in what must be done.

— Is it so weighty?

— It could be done by any man of wit and skill loyal to the Service. But there is the matter of experience. You helped send the Babington plotters to the gallows.

— I saw them go to the gallows. I think you did not.

— It is best not to see these things, as I have said before.

— I saw Penry hanged and drawn.

— Aye, the other face of the seditious coin. Atheism is in comparison a friend to the established Church. The Raleigh atheism, which even the exiled Catholics now scream at, harms none. But by definition it is foul subversion. Essex plays on that. It is madness that a private though most virulent quarrel should film and obscure the true struggle. As a servant of the Service you must play your part and hope that you be not too strongly drawn into the other contention.

— The poet was in ancient times considered a *vates* or prophet. It is in some measure true. I cannot prophesy of the future of this realm but I see in terrible clarity a future for myself. The arrest, the charge, the dungeon, the rack.

— You will never go to the gallows, Kit. As for arrest and the rack, it is the common expectation of us all. You think myself to be unaffected? I feigned papistry so well that the mask was taken for the true visage. Even Walsingham had his doubts of me. I spent, to my thinking, too long in the Tower. These are gloomy thoughts for a May day. See the bees and butterflies, blessed creatures. Hear that blackbird, or perhaps it is a thrush. We take what life we can.

— I think I must be done with the Service. It was unseemly to think on a bargain.

— There is no bargaining, there never is. We do our duty, and there are no reservations, also few rewards. You must not say you are done with the Service. Ponder the consequences of that. You know too much.

— Meaning enough to wreck a plot through treasonous exposure? I may be many things, but I am a loyal subject.

— Aye, like the stout patriots who sought England's redemption through a Spanish invasion. Loyalty is a wide word.

— Now I am made to see Lord Strange hanged and hacked, screaming to heaven of a long occluded faith.

— His lordship would have a cleaner death, the privilege of his rank. A clean lopping on Tower Hill. His supporters would, true, not fare so well. But it is the price they know must be paid. Do not talk of leaving the Service. Think on what you said. I must take now what the Spanish call the *siesta*. That means the

261

sixth hour, noon. The sun is past its zenith. The rolling and
tossing have made me sleepy as well as queasy. Do not add to
my queasiness. Think. We will meet at supper. I must ask the
Widow Bull for a bed.

And he rose, nodding also yawning. Kit sat on among the nodding flowers, the green bushes that gleamed as with a varnishing,
under the great tree that breathed through the multiple mouths
of its leaves. Butterflies, yes, bees. He had lost family, country
must be next. He did not propose pain or death for himself;
though lined and losing hair he was still young. The power of
the poet pulsed blood through his body. The truth of life lay in
the vatic messages words sent, meanings beyond what the world
called meaning. The old gods lived; Apollo blazed in the sun. He
must serve what must be served. He pondered, and the answers
to questions of immediate import made little sense. Kill that you
be not killed. Bring to birth rather, one whose forfeiture of the
right of fatherhood granted an unfleshly manner of begetting. He
stood, somewhat sick with too much wine, the wine over-heavy,
a slight crown of pain about his temples, then he walked to a
patch of grass, somewhat over a grave's length, with daisies on
it, under the arching branches of an elm that was rooted not in
this garden but in the neighbour garden. There he laid out his
length. He would think no more, he would sleep.

He dreamed in fragments, sudden flashes of light (could
light inhere then in the brain?), scenes with a mild sun, with a
burning sun that seared the eyeballs of the figure in the dream
that was the dreamer, with a moon gibbous or dying. He was
in a Hellas he did not know except from books, a warm Hellas
conjured by a northern scholar. All was absurd – fauns, cen-
taurs, the fruits of an imagined lawful coupling. There was the
Minotaur too, bred out of the cursed Pasiphae lying waiting for
the bull's impossible pounce on the wooden cow, made on orders
by Daedalus in distraction, obsessed as he was by the mastery of
the mystery of flight. These, like the words of a poem, were all
signs of a deep reality not with ease to be fathomed. Then Helen
approached him from the Trojan battlements. She should not do
this, she should know his nature, she should not be naked, bore

his eyes with her breasts, oppose to his flaccid rod the mouth of the cave whose interior was the labyrinth where the rending Minotaur bellowed. No, no, he would not. And then blissful darkness, real daylight not intruding, resting on his eyelids.

He woke stiff, yawning and unrefreshed. The sun had sloped down the sky. He must deliver his message of one word, cheat the lenders, put money in his purse and take the river that would take him to the sea. Through the window he saw Skeres and Frizer playing at tables. He went round to the side of the house and entered that room. Skeres said:

— Take Ingram's place. He is on a losing streak, though it is but for a penny, discountable enough.

— I will lie down, Frizer said. It is the pain in my leg. I bear no ill feeling, but there is the pain. And wincing he lay on the daybed.

— The loan, Kit said.

— Shall I put it as your stakes by the board? You may be in luck. Shall we play high?

— Low, very low.

— As you will. Sit. Take the dice. Start.

Kit tossed the pair. He moved his discs but his finger-ends were clumsy. Skeres had a monkey quickness with his dirty paws. He was easily first to move his store to the inner table. Frizer on the bed groaned. Kit dropped three of his coloured pieces. Enough, in no mood for play. You fear the catertreys? Fear not. Again? Kit rose, saying he must go. The loan. You already have your pledge. I do not see it.

— Stored for safety, along with your baggage. Urchins in and out, quick of the finger. Come, you mar the merriment of the day. It will be suppertime soon. What is it to be, Ingram?

— A beef pie in a deep dish. With onions and pounded peppercorns.

— You hear? The *Peppercorn* sails tomorrow at dawn. Some that come from afar for it sleep on board. It saves the cost of an inn.

— And so?

— To exhibit my knowledge of the traffic of the river I

263

grant such breadcrumbs of information. And so nothing. Ah, the awakened Robin.

Robin Poley was down, washed, combed, neat, a marvellous proper man, yawning and smiling.

— Sleep is like hard labour. It promotes powerful appetite. I smell good news from the kitchen.

— Sleep is strange, Skeres said. Some die in it. Dreams are strange. A man can wake sweating in terror. What is that dark country of the mind through which we wander in sleep?

— A forest, Poley said, in whose depths the soul lieth hidden like a golden egg.

— Pretty, Skeres said. You are something of a poet. Is he not so, Mr Christopher, oh I will say Kit, we are all friends.

— As you please.

— May I too say Kit? Frizer asked from the daybed.

— As you please. I have small dignity to maintain.

— I will ask you three riddles, Poley said to Kit, comfortably sitting at the table now cleared of its backgammon board and counters. Your answer must be in one word only. You are ready? Good.

Ready, yes. The riddles and their solutions were to no purpose at all. The answer was to something else and must be in the manner of a triple amen.

— Is the Queen a virgin?

— No.

— Is God in his heaven?

— No.

— Have you ever bedded a woman?

— No.

All except Kit sighed out as it were with a kind of reverence. Poley said:

— War, you will remember, depended that time on a straight yes or no in a message from Flushing. Well, we know by that no. The stout smell of beef and onions marches towards us. The wine danceth.

And so it did. The Widow Bull herself brought in the crusted mound, her girl the trenchers and horn spoons not knives. It was, said the widow, stewed very soft for them without teeth. But all had teeth and strong ones. They ate smokily, Frizer left his daybed limping but limped not in his steady devouring. Good, he said, excellent good. Thou eatest but little, he said daringly to Kit. Thou drinkest overmuch of the wine. Eating and drinking should be nicely in equipoise.

— *Supper*, Poley said, is a word of strange finality. Perhaps that derives from the scriptures. Revenge is a good supper but a bad breakfast, they say. Do I have that right?

It was indeed a deep dish, they could not eat all. There was a sighing and a loosening of belts after. The scullions would be glad of the leavings, the fragments, the orts. Kit had not loosened his belt. Skeres called somewhat roughly that the table be cleared, though let the wine and the cups stay. And he called too for the reckoning. He said to Kit, while the others faintly smiled:

— We thank thee for the kindness of the bestowal of this merry day. Good wine, food, company. That one who should have come did not come we must account a small disappointment. Ah, here is the reckoning.

He took it from the hands of the Widow Bull (Pasiphae, Kit thought for a moment madly) and said:

— It amounts near enough to the amount you asked to borrow. Dear, true, but she keeps a dear house. Thus – *item*, one fish in a coffin 11s 5d; *item*, two quarts of Bordeaux wine 15s 0d; *item* –

— You jest, Kit said, and it is sour. I was invited. The reckoning is not mine.

— Not altogether jest, Skeres said. There is a reckoning to be made. Let me play a manner of president of a council. I sit here, and you two gentlemen sit either side of the carrier of Christ.

Kit started at hearing his name's true meaning in that mouth. There was no pretence of merriment now. Robin Poley, smiling, moved his chair to Kit's right. The limping and wincing Frizer skirred his chair along the floor to the left. So now all three faced Skeres for what Kit did not know. But these others seemed to know.

265

— What dost thou do, Skeres asked, with a quill pen that is past sharpening?

— Do you really require an answer?

— Good, thou knowest.

— I am not thou.

— Very well, you. *You* are not anything. You need not sword, money nor goods. Not even nutriment, though you have eaten little enough. The wine will assist your passage.

— I understand nothing. I will be off. And he rose, but Frizer's arm, surprisingly strong, pulled him down. I will not be pawed, I will not be hindered, let me pass.

— Listen, Skeres said, and he looked to Poley for approval. Poley nodded. You are in the situation of one that is no proper criminal, unmeet for trial or hanging. Of one, rather, that had best be voided. We heard your threefold *no*, we speak not of treachery but of its possibility. There is one reason for your being voided. There are two others, and you will never know whether it is a knight or an earl who wishes the voiding. The wise man takes his money where he can, like the judge that takes bribes from both sides. One deletes you from life's book as a warning to others, or because he fears your tongue, or for dislike and no more, or as payment for insolence. The other is afraid of a speaking out under duress that will light the powder of his own ruin. Whatever it is, you had best go, though not out of that door. This is by no means an execution. We three here seek only to defend ourselves against a wild man. For you are wild to leave, are you not?

Skeres took out a dagger and slid it across the table so that it lay under Kit's hand. Kit hesitated and then grasped it. He was permitted to rise.

— Go on, strike, you passionate shepherd.

Kit struck at Frizer's head but grazed his brow. Frizer spoke foully. He reached over for Kit's striking hand but the reach was too far. It was Poley that seized the right hand while Frizer seized the left. Poley wrested out the weapon and threw it to Skeres. Skeres, on his feet, came round. He said:

— I will hold. Thou, dear Ingram, shalt have the privilege

266

of the strike. You have been broody long and may now lay the egg. The eye will serve, the right one.

He was round to take Kit's left arm from Frizer. Frizer and Poley wheeled Kit so that he faced the light from the garden. Frizer stood before him with the dagger.

— It is, Skeres said, a target permitted in fencing, though the sword's length doth not always allow the accurate thrust. Ugly hell, gape not, come not, Lucifer.

— There is nothing in truth, Poley said. The blowing out of a candle. They tell me he was a good poet.

Kit's mind rose above all, observing, noting. The fear belonged all to his body. The dagger-point was too close to his eye for his eye to see it. Frizer spoke very foully:

— Filthy sodomite. Filthy buggering seducer of men and boys. Nasty Godless sneering fleering bastard. Aye, I will lay the egg.

So he thrust. The eye's smoothness deflected the blade to what lay above under the bone. Kit felt at first nothing. Then dissolution, the swooning of the brain, great agony. He heard the scream in his throat and saw with his left eye Poley, recoiling from him, making the *signum crucis*. Dying, he knew the scream would not die with him, not yet. It lived for a time its own life. He even knew, marvelling, looking down on it, that his body had fallen, thudding. Then he knew nothing more.

So I suppose it happened, but I suppose only. The finding of the coroner, endited in good black lasting ink, was that on Wednesday the thirtieth of May in the year of our Lord 1593 Messrs Marlowe, Poley, Frizer, Skeres (now come his words) about the tenth hour before noon met together in a room in the house of a certain Eleanor Bull, widow, and there passed the time together and then dined and after dinner were in quiet sort together there and walked in the garden until the sixth hour after noon and then together and in company supped; and after supper

Ingram Frizer and Christopher Marlowe uttered one to the other divers malicious words for the reason that they could not agree about the payment of the sum of pence, that is *le recknynge*, there. Christopher Marlowe then lying upon a bed in the room where they supped and moved with anger against Ingram Frizer and Ingram, sitting with his back towards the bed where Christopher Marlowe was lying and with the front part of his body towards the table and with Nicholas Skeres and Robert Poley sitting on either side of him so that he could in no wise take flight, it so befell that Christopher Marlowe on a sudden and of his malice against Ingram maliciously drew the dagger of the said Ingram, which was at his back, and with the same dagger gave him two wounds on his head; whereupon Ingram, in fear of being slain and sitting between Nicholas Skeres and Robert Poley so that he could not in any wise get away, in his own defence and for the saving of his life then and there struggled with Christopher Marlowe to get away from his dagger, in which affray Ingram could not get away from Marlowe; and it so befell that in that affray Ingram in defence of his life, with the dagger aforesaid to the value of 12d, gave Christopher a mortal wound over his right eye of which wound Christopher Marlowe then and there instantly died.

And so the Jurors say upon their oath that the said Ingram Frizer killed and slew Christopher Marlowe aforesaid on the thirtieth day of May in the thirty-fifth year of the reign of our Sovereign Lady Queen Elizabeth at Deptford Strand within the verge in the room aforesaid, in the manner and form aforesaid, in the defence and saving of his own life. In witness of which thing the Coroner as well as the Jurors have interchangeably set their seals.

Le recknynge? What Frenchified madness is this? It is a lie of language, unpurposed maybe, that is a badge or brooch of the lie of the whole. Even the covering of the body with its ravaged eyesocket, that the delicate stomachs of the jurors might not be turned, this too was a kind of lie. And there is the lie of anonymity, since, as the plague growled still, that body was, straight after the lying verdict, interred in a grave unmarked in the churchyard of St Nicholas in Deptford.

I have lived long. I have seen both the Earl of Essex and Sir Walter Raleigh, in that order, go to the block on Tower Hill: treason, like loyalty, is a wide word; at length the two concepts become one. I saw Thomas Walsingham knighted and married to a wife who grew much in favour with the Queen of the Scotch slobberer that was less of a man than the irritable harridan he replaced. I even, as a player with the King's Men at Valladolid, saw the sealing of perpetual peace between Spain and the new Britain that contained England as one of its provinces. Most names in this brief chronicle faded from sight, so we may envisage their owners dying in peaceful beds perfumed with lavender. My own name you will find, if you care to look, in the folio of Black Will's plays, put out by his friends Heming and Condell in 1623. In the comedy of *Much Ado About Nothing*, by some inadvertency, I enter with Leonato and others under my own identity and not, as it should be, the guise of Balthasar to sing to ladies that they sigh no more. So a useless truth obtrudes on to a most ravishing lie. I would say finally that, as the earth turns and the truth of summer and the lie of winter interchange (interchangeably set their seals), so the bulky ball of history revolves, and what a man dies for may become the thing that dies for him. The England that killed Kit Marlowe or Marley or Merlin will define itself in one of its facets by what he wrote before he died swearing. And there, you see, we have another lie. Let me lie down and, fair or foul reader, say farewell.

Not quite. Your true author speaks now, I that die these deaths, that feed this flame. I put off the ill-made disguise and, four hundred years after that death at Deptford, mourn as if it all happened yesterday. The disguise is ill-made not out of incompetence but of necessity, since the earnestness of the past becomes the joke of the present, a once living language is turned into the stiff archaism of puppets. Only the continuity of a name rides above a grumbling compromise. But, as the dagger pierces the optic nerve, blinding light is seen not to be the monopoly of the sun. That dagger continues to pierce, and it will never be blunted.

Author's Note

ＩN 1940, months before the Battle of Britain began, the *Luftwaffe* trundled over Moss Side, Manchester, on its way to the attempted destruction of Trafford Park. In Moss Side, in the small hours, I sat, my induction into the British Army deferred, typing my university thesis on Christopher Marlowe. The visions of hell in *Dr Faustus* seemed not too irrelevant. "I'll burn my books – ah, Mephistophilis." The *Luftwaffe* was to burn my books and even my thesis. Mephistophilis, as Thomas Mann was to show in his own *Doktor Faustus*, was no mere playhouse bogeyman.

I determined some day to write a novel on Marlowe. The year 1964, which was his natal quatercentenary, was also that of William Shakespeare, and the lesser had to yield to the greater. In that year I published the novel *Nothing Like the Sun*, a fantastic speculation on Shakespeare's love-life. Now, with the commemoration of Marlowe's murder in 1593, I am able to pay such homage as is possible to an ageing writer.

I make a certain claim here to secondary scholarship. All the historical facts are verifiable. One of the known Elizabethan thugs was named George Orwell, which is embarrassing, but truth must not yield too much to discretion or delicacy: after all, that expungeable bravo had a better claim to the name than Eric Blair. I acknowledge the help I have received from the major biographies by John Bakeless and F.S. Boas as well as the extremely useful "informal" life by H.R. Williamson. The most recent study of Marlowe as a spy is *The Reckoning* by Charles Nicholl. The scholarly delving will go on, and other novels will be written, but the true truth – the *verità verissima* of the Neapolitans – can never be known. The virtue of a

271

historical novel is its vice – the flatfooted affirmation of possibility as fact. As for the man Marlowe, he smiles, somewhat ironically, and is still, not exactly out-topping knowledge but continuing to disturb and, sometimes, exalt. Ben Jonson knew what he was talking about when he referred to the mighty line. Shakespeare may have outshone him but he did not contain or supersede him. That inimitable voice sings on.

A.B.